THE RAILWAY KING

by Margaret Mayhew

THE MASTER OF AYSGARTH
THE CRY OF THE OWL
THE RAILWAY KING

THE
RAILWAY
KING

By

Margaret Mayhew

DOUBLEDAY & COMPANY, INC.
GARDEN CITY, NEW YORK
1979

ACKNOWLEDGMENTS

I should like to thank the following people, who have so kindly helped me with research for this book. I am very grateful for the time and trouble they took on my behalf.

The librarians at the North Yorkshire County Library, York, at the Railway Museum, York, at the National Coal Board, London, and at Lewes Library in Sussex. Also Mr. Quine, Manager of the Theatre Royal, York; the Lord Mayor's Personal Assistant at the Mansion House in York; Mr. Tony Botting of Garbutt & Elliott, Chartered Accountants at 44 Monkgate, York; Mr. Toms of the National Coal Board, who arranged for me to visit Betteshanger Colliery; the Kent and East Sussex Railway at Tenterden and the Bluebell Railway of Sussex, both of whom let me ride on the footplate. And, finally, Pat Norman, of the Society of Friends Meeting House in Brighton, who gave me so much information about the Quakers, and Editha Jackson, who lent me her great-grandmother's Quaker bonnet.

Library of Congress Cataloging in Publication Data

Mayhew, Margaret, 1936–
The railway king.

I. Title.
PZ4.M4716Rai 1979 [PR6063.A887]   823′.9′14
ISBN: 0-385-14603-5
Library of Congress Catalog Card Number 78-18553

FOR SHAUN AND FERGUS,
WITH LOVE

AUTHOR'S NOTE

The idea for this book was suggested to me by the story of the real-life Railway King, George Hudson of York.

Although many of the events are imaginary, the basic story is his. A common draper, of character similar to my hero, did rise in such a fashion in the nineteenth century to become Lord Mayor of York and a millionaire railway tycoon, only to die in poverty and disgrace.

All other characters are fictitious, with the obvious exception of George Stephenson and other well-known figures of the day who are mentioned. But the names of the railway companies are accurate and the story of their building and development is true.

FOREWORD

If you take the Hull road from York and turn off somewhere before a small town called Market Weighton, you may, if you look out carefully as you go along the narrow, winding lane, notice the remains of an old railway station. If you wish you can, without much difficulty, climb through a broken-down fence, wade through a patch of nettles and walk up the slope onto the platform.

The red brick station house is derelict now; its windows are boarded over, its guttering hangs broken, and telephone wires trail unconnected to anywhere. The station clock still stares from the wall—glass missing, rim rusted and black hands motionless for many years. Look up and you will see three curious chimneys shaped like railway arches on the slate roof.

The platform is spongy and slippery with green moss, and brambles have crept across the cracked stones as far as the edge. The iron rails have been taken away, and the track below is traversed instead by lines of cow parsley, tall thistles and dandelions. But its path still runs straight and true, as far as you can see in each direction—away across the wide, flat Yorkshire fields, where black and white bullocks graze and summer swallows swoop.

Turn northwards and you will see a long line of elm trees bordering an overgrown avenue that led from the little station to a castle. The castle exists no more, and rabbits and squirrels run where fine carriages drove.

Before you leave, look about you again. There is the deserted station house, the silent clock, the empty track . . . You are seeing all that is left of one man's dreams and ambitions—the door to his vanished kingdom. And if you close your eyes and listen to the sound of the wind in the trees, you may fancy you hear, as I did, the ghostly echo of a locomotive steam engine coming from far away across the fields as it once did, long ago.

THE RAILWAY KING

CHAPTER I

No speed with this can fleetest horse compare,
No weight like this canal or vessel bear;
As this will commerce every way promote,
To this let sons of commerce grant their vote.

Thomas Gray—
Observations on a General Iron Rail-Way

On December 30, 1833, a carriage was traveling south at break-neck speed on its way from Sunderland to York. The single occupant of the smart brown and black britska sat slouched in a corner, his coat collar turned up about his ears, his black hat tipped forward over his eyes. He was a big man, broad-shouldered and heavily built, and the little that showed of his face put him at about thirty years of age. He seemed to be half asleep and to be viewing the passing snow-covered Yorkshire landscape with complete indifference, until something caught his attention and caused him to sit up and rap sharply with his cane to signal his coachman to stop. The driver pulled the horses to a slithering halt, cursing under his breath.

The big man descended from the carriage, crossed the lonely road and stood staring intently down into the valley below. His coachman rubbed his frozen hands together and, following the direction of his master's gaze, tried to see what on earth had merited leaving a comfortable carriage for the snow-laden wind that swept the ridge. He blinked his watering eyes and peered downwards. There was nothing out of the ordinary to be seen except a smudge of smoke, a thin trail of white that hung on the cold air in the valley. Perhaps something was on fire? And then he saw that the smoke was moving steadily across the wooded valley, vanishing now and again behind trees to emerge triumphantly again like some playful will-o'-the-wisp. The coachman blinked harder. This time he saw that the smoke was rising from the tall black chimney of a curious wheeled engine that ran along a track, drawing a line of loaded wagons behind it. He snorted in disgust. He'd heard about the newfangled railway that had been built hereabouts but this was the first he'd seen of it. He'd also heard men say that these new steam engines would mean the end of coaches and horses—not that he believed that for a minute. Anyone with half an eye and a pinch of common sense could see that the clumsy, ugly-looking machine down in the valley would never take the place of the coaches and horses that were the pride of the country.

He steadied the restless grays with the skill of long years on the box, and wished Mr. England would be quick about it. It wouldn't do the horses any good to be kept waiting much longer —nor himself either, come to that. He felt the cold more these days. He coughed loudly, hoping to attract attention, but there was no response. He had no way of knowing that his master was seeing a vision and had not even heard him. It was not the kind of vision the coachman might have supposed if he had known— the kind which consists of angels and heavenly choirs and ghostly voices. Instead, it was an image in the mind's eye of the future. As his master stared downwards, he was seeing not one engine moving through the valley, but hundreds of them steaming across the country from city to city, from town to town, from north to south and from east to west, and in that image was himself bestriding those railways like Colossus, as high above them as he was standing on this ridge now.

But the coachman knew nothing of this, nor would he have understood. He waited, not daring to show his impatience, but the Stockton and Darlington Railway engine had long disappeared from sight before, at last, Mr. England turned back towards his carriage. The coachman took up the reins with relief and they moved off again.

2

About three miles from York they turned in through a gateway leading to a large and beautiful mansion. The coachman had driven fast, on instructions, and he now pulled the grays up outside the front door, where they rested for a few moments, blowing hard. The owner of Murton Hall came out, head bent against the wind and snow, and entered the carriage. Without delay, the coachman drove on towards the city.

The two passengers were jolted this way and that as the britska bounced and swayed over the rough frozen surface. Henry Latham pulled his cloak closer about him and shivered; after the warmth of his fireside the carriage felt as cold as a tomb.

"Good of you to invite me along this evening, Kirby," he said.

The big man grunted. "Bloody rubbish, lad! There's nowt good of me about it. I'm taking you because you'll be useful to me . . . I hope."

Henry smiled at this blunt speech, delivered in broad Yorkshire tones. It was one of the things he liked about Kirby England. There was no pretense or disguise about him—just forthright talk and action. He knew many thought him rough and crude, but he, personally, found it reassuring and refreshing to know exactly where he stood with a man. And Kirby England was known to keep his word, once given. The same could not be said of many.

"This meeting," he said tentatively. "You wrote that it was important. What precisely is it about?"

The other smiled in the dimness of the carriage. "About a railway—that's what."

"A *railway!*" Henry could not conceal his disappointment. He had expected some kind of political affair—a discreet gathering of influential Tory citizens who might be instrumental in progressing his election as Member of Parliament for York. He knew nothing about railways and cared less.

"I thought that'd surprise you. But just you listen to me, lad. If you're to be our representative at Westminster, it'll concern you all right. A group of us York tradesmen are meeting to discuss building a railway from York to Leeds. I don't need to tell you that the city's in the doldrums, do I? Trade's bad, and while others have had the sense to move with the times, we've been

3

looking back over our shoulders at past glories and nowt's been done. York was once ranked second city in the kingdom and capital of the North. Look at us now. We're no more than a bloody market town. We need to expand our trade, and to do *that* we need a *railway*. Cheap carriage of goods, Henry, and, most important of all, cheap coal. We've seen what it's done for Liverpool and Manchester, and we want the same for ourselves."

The lights of the city shone ahead in the growing darkness and the massive shadow of the Minster rose above the encircling walls. As the carriage went in through the gate, Henry watched his companion's face in the lamplight.

"You love York, don't you, Kirby? I've never met a man who cared more about the place, even among those born here."

"Aye—I do that. You may have that grand estate of yours, Henry, but I've got my city . . ."

The two men could not have made a greater contrast. Henry Latham was the younger by five years and was obviously a gentleman born and bred. He was quietly dressed and pleasantly featured, with frank blue eyes. Kirby England was clearly no gentleman. His features were in no way refined, but rugged almost to the point of coarseness. He had curly black hair and wore long and luxuriant side-whiskers. His eyes were dark brown and his hands were large and square, with thick, strong fingers—hands made for the plow or scythe, but not for the idle existence of a gentleman. The upward tilt to the corners of his mouth gave him a good-humored look, but to have taken him for an easygoing man would have been a mistake—as many had discovered to their cost. He was not only physically powerful but also powerful in personality. Everything about him was flamboyant, from the showy clothes he wore to the large diamond cravat pin that shone with unashamed ostentation on his breast.

The carriage slowed to go down the narrow cobbled street of Goodramgate. Kirby pointed to a shop on the corner. Its bow-fronted windows were prettily laced with snow which sparkled in the lamplight.

"Have you ever visited my draper's shop over there, Henry? No, I don't suppose you have. You've no wife yet and no need for silks and ribbons and furbelows. I'm proud of that place. And you know what's said of me now, don't you? They say I've jumped over the counter and got too big for my boots. Happen it's true enough that I've come round t'other side. I don't stand about in that shop there anymore with a yard measure in my hand. No need to. Since I've come to York and taken over that business I've worked like a dog and turned it into twenty-five-percent profit."

"I wish I had half your head for business," Henry said.

"Aye . . . well. It's time now to move on to bigger and better things. I've got plans, lad. You want to be elected Member of Parliament for York—right? Well, keep close by me and you'll find I can help you there. I know the way things work in this city —how to get things done, and so on—and most of it's not at all what you've been brought up to in that milksop nursery of yours."

"I already have to thank you for seconding my nomination with the Selection Committee."

Kirby waved his hand impatiently. "'Twas nowt. Support this railway at the meeting and I'll make damn sure you get to Westminster at the next election. I promise you that."

"I should be most grateful—"

"Don't fool yourself it's you I'm thinking of. I told you, I need your support this evening—as a landowner—and, if things go the way I intend, I'm going to need your help in Parliament before long."

Before Henry could say anything further, the carriage drew up outside Tomlinson's Hotel in Petergate. It was a small, shabby place, and Henry looked at it doubtfully. It did not seem to him to promise well.

The meeting had already begun when they entered a dingy back room of the hotel. A small group of men were gathered round a table, and the room was poorly lit by a green-shaded oil lamp that hung low from the center of the ceiling. It was cold enough for the breath of those assembled to cloud the air, and several kept blowing on their fingers and rubbing their hands together. Among those present were two lawyers, a number of shopkeepers and some proprietors of small businesses. A currier named Mr. Queeg was in the chair and had opened the meeting a few minutes before.

Thomas Chadwick, a coal merchant, was speaking as Kirby and Henry took their places. He repeatedly cleared his throat, and it was apparent to his listeners that only the strength of his convictions and the weight of his grievances had given him the courage to address the gathering at all.

"Fact of the matter is, as most of us knows, gentlemen, the canals are a sight too slow and costly. What's more, we never know where we are with 'em. In summer when water's down the boats can only go half loaded and in winter they can be frozen up for weeks on end. Aire and Calder Navigation can charge us what they like, never mind how slow or late the goods, and we've to put up with it because we've no choice. That's why we need this railway."

"What about the turnpikes?" somebody asked him.

The coal merchant shrugged his shoulders. "So far as coal is concerned, nearest pits to York are beyond Garford—fifteen miles or more away." He leaned forward a little, his face red and eager. "But if we were to build a railroad from here to Leeds and make it go through Garford, why, *then* we'd get our cheap coal all right. And we could tell Aire and Calder Navigation to go and jump in the Ouse!"

He sat down abruptly, mopping his face with a handkerchief. There were rumblings of accord, mingled with a few sharper sounds of dissent. The chairman unrolled a map across the table and chairs scraped the wooden floor as everyone moved to get a better view.

"Now then, gentlemen," the currier said, prodding the document before him. "You've heard the views of one amongst us. Mr. Chadwick tells us we should build a railway to go by the Garford collieries and then on to Leeds." He traced a rough route with his finger. "Let's hear what others have to say to that notion."

The next to stand up was the proprietor of a large glassworks, Joseph Meek. He could treble his output at least, he told them, if only he could get coal cheaper and quicker. An alternative to the canals must be found, and one that could accomplish the regular and punctual conveyance of goods at all seasons. It was no good looking to the turnpikes—he had tried having coal delivered by horse and cart, but the round journey from the pits entailed close on forty miles of turnpike road and the price of coal was nearly doubled. Their only hope of progress lay in building a railway.

He sat down and several men thumped the table with the palms of their hands in support. There were others, however, who could see no real advantage in building a railway at all, who mistrusted the whole concept and had come only to voice doubts and fears. The meeting wore on as men spoke for and against the project. An alternative route was proposed—east to Selby instead of west to Leeds. Ideas poured forth, arguments became heated.

A sharp-featured man got to his feet. He was olive-skinned and so dark as to look foreign. His eyes were set close in a long face and the tips of his thin fingers were spread delicately on the table before him as though he were playing the pianoforte. His dress was elegant, his manner superior to most of those present and there was no trace of Yorkshire in his accent.

"Mr. Snell," the chairman said wearily, "we'd value your opinion as a legal man."

"Thank you, Mr. Queeg." The lawyer's speech was cold and precise. His gaze went slowly round the table, passing from one man to the next.

"I must confess to you, gentlemen, that I find myself somewhat at a loss for words. I have, this evening, heard it calmly proposed by intelligent persons that we should build a *railway*, as though it were no more difficult than building a poorhouse or a tannery." He turned to the coal merchant, who, now that the room had become warmer with the heat of so many bodies, was once again mopping his brow with his handkerchief. "We have only to build a railway, you tell us, Mr. Chadwick, and all our problems will resolve themselves, as if by magic. But answer me this. How will conveying tons of coal, however cheap, in through the gates of this city rid us of the disgraceful conditions in which our poor live? How will it clean up Jubbergate, Nunnery Lane, the Bedern and the Water Lanes? Last year there were over two hundred deaths from cholera and typhus. If there

7

is any money being raised, it should be spent on putting our house in order and not on ludicrous schemes and dreams of easy wealth for a few. And not only that." The thin fingers lifted and pointed. "Just a few yards up the street stands our Minster, the finest cathedral in the land. This is an archiepiscopal city, a place of ancient tradition and dignity. We are not, and I pray God never will be, an industrial city like Liverpool and Manchester, who have been held up tonight as such shining examples. Do we want the din and clatter of mills and factories to disturb our peace, black smoke from their chimneys to pollute the air we breath? Those of you who propose a railway are proposing just such a fate for York."

Joseph Meek interrupted him. "My glassworks give work to the men of this city, I'd remind you, Mr. Snell. And with cheaper coal there'd be more work for more men and more bread in the mouths of the poor you spoke of."

The lawyer said smoothly: "More money in your pocket, you mean, Mr. Meek."

The glassworks proprietor was on his feet, pale with outrage and shaking his fist. In the ensuing uproar the chairman had to pound repeatedly on the table before order was finally restored. The lawyer seemed quite unruffled and continued speaking.

"Before I was interrupted, I was about to ask you, gentlemen, if any one of you has the slightest idea how much a railway would cost. I will tell you. I am reliably informed that the cost is more than seven thousand pounds a mile. Imagine it for yourselves. Excavations, embankments, tunnels—let alone the iron rails themselves. Nor have I taken into account the long list of other expensive contingencies—surveyors' and engineers' fees, lawyers, the conveyancing of the necessary Bill through Parliament—not to mention the price of purchasing the land needed and the compensation that would have to be paid to landowners and anyone else who could claim to be inconvenienced by the railway. The Stockton and Darlington and the Liverpool and Manchester Railway companies had years of opposition and litigation in the courts. I put it to you, gentlemen, that we are not in any position to consider such an enterprise."

"I agree with you, Mr. Snell," a shopkeeper called out.

8

"Where's the need for rush? Let others show first if there's brass in rail. Canals and roads are good enough for most. Besides, them that owns the land between here and Garford aren't likely to let an iron road be built right across their deer parks in sight of their fine mansions!"

"As to that point, sir, I think I may speak with some authority."

Henry Latham, receiving a dig in the ribs from Kirby and a nod from the chairman, stood up. "Some of you may know me, but others not. I am the prospective Tory candidate for Parliament for York and one of the landowners that the gentleman has just referred to. My estate lies directly between York and Garford, and if the railway were to follow the approximate route proposed it would certainly cross a large portion of my land. I should like to make it clear to this meeting that I am in favor of any such scheme and intend to give it my wholehearted support, both here in this city and, if I am elected by you, in Parliament. Furthermore, I shall do all in my power to encourage neighboring landowners to think likewise."

This speech was rewarded by warm applause, and the chairman smiled at him approvingly. "We're indebted to you for those brave words, Mr. Latham, we are indeed. However, we're no nearer deciding one way or t'other, it seems to me. There's some for and some still dead-against." He peered into the gloom beyond the lamplight. "Mr. England, I've not known you to keep silent so long before when there's owt to be decided of importance to this city. What do you say?"

Kirby England had been sitting beside Henry with his chair tilted back on its legs so that his face was in shadow. All that had been visible to the meeting had been a broad expanse of black velvet waistcoat adorned with large pearl buttons and a heavy gold watch chain that glinted richly. By way of reply he let the chair fall forward with a crash and got slowly to his feet. He stuck the thumb of his right hand through the lapel buttonhole of his coat, a habitual gesture of his.

"I've not said owt till now, friends, because I've been content to let others argue themselves silly. For a man who tells us he's at a loss for words, I reckon Mr. Snell had plenty to say. According to him, we can't *afford* to build this railway. We should spend any money we have on worthier and better things—like making this city more sanitary and cleaning up our slums. Worthy thoughts, indeed! And, of course, you must realize how important it is to Mr. Snell to be seen and heard to be properly concerned for such things. How else is he ever going to regain the Monk Ward seat on the Council that I took from him at the last election?"

There was a ripple of laughter at this remark. Elias Snell's lips tightened, but he said nothing. Kirby went on softly.

"I'm as concerned as any man to improve living conditions in York, but the only way we're going to be able to do that is to make a lot more brass—to expand our trade beyond a few little shops and market stalls. We've got to fight for a place in the whole new growth of the country. The truth is, fellow citizens, that we can't afford *not* to build this railway. Are we such a group of timid little tradesmen that we're going to turn down the chance of sharing in the big profits to be made? This year the Liverpool and Manchester company paid a ten-percent dividend to their shareholders. How can we turn our backs while others with more guts and vision reap such benefits? The South Yorkshire coal owners are going to build a line from Leeds to Selby, and they'll leave us high and dry unless we build one for ourselves."

He smacked the palm of his hand down on the center of the map. "Take a look for yourselves. There's no medals given for seeing that a railway to Leeds through Garford makes sense since we want cheap coal. But look closer still. Why do you think the Romans made York the headquarters for the whole of northern Britain? And the Saxons after them, and the Danes? Why did the Normans burn it to the ground? Because it was the very *center* of resistance in the North. Why did York flourish in the Middle Ages, trading in wool, leather, tin, lead, and so on? Why were so many famous battles fought round and about here—Towton, Fulford, Stamford Bridge? Why is York the center today for stagecoaches passing the length and breadth of the country? The answer to those questions is plain for any of us with eyes to see." He pointed. "Our city lies at the junction of the main routes—

north–south, east–west. We may lack the aces but we hold the trump card." He paused and there was silence in the room. "I promise you all," he went on in quieter tones, "that if we build this railway it'll be only the first of many. There's plans for them to be built all across the land—nothing but talk of them wherever you go. And they won't just transport merchandise but people as well, people paying good money to travel hundreds of miles from one end of the country to the other. If we play our cards right, from the beginning of it all, we could restore Old Ebor to her former glory—make her a railway center and once more the capital of the North!"

He sat down, and the small hotel room reverberated with cheers and clapping. The lawyer, Elias Snell, alone, remained still, arms folded across his chest. When silence had returned he said:

"You have the dreams of an eternal optimist, Mr. England. I am afraid that you have allowed the silks and satins in your draper's shop to color your imagination and the ribbons that you sell to weave themselves into a frivolous fantasy."

He had spoken disdainfully, but the object of his contempt appeared unmoved. He merely smiled and replied:

"I spoke of the future, I grant you, Mr. Snell, rather than the present. But my dreams, as you see fit to call them, will come true enough one day. I wonder which of us will look the fool in ten years' time."

Mr. Queeg consulted his watch; he was tired and losing patience. "Mr. England, your prognostications are interesting, but we've not met to discuss a whole lot of railways—just the one, a small one from here to Leeds. Now, I propose we put the matter to the vote directly without more ado. Do we form ourselves into an official Railway Committee and take things a step further or do we not? Those in favor of doing so, please raise your hands."

It was snowing outside, and bitterly cold. The vote taken and the meeting closed, the men had disbanded slowly, drifting away from Tomlinson's Hotel in ones and twos. Henry Latham and Kirby England walked down Petergate together, their feet crunching over the fresh powdery white snow that covered the cobbles. Overhead the pointed gables of half-timbered houses leaned towards each other; chinks of yellow light showed from behind shutters and curtains. Henry bent his head against a sudden flurry of icy flakes that stung his face, and increased his stride to keep up with the vigorous pace of his companion. He glanced sideways at the tall figure in the caped greatcoat and top hat. They passed a gas lamp, and its light showed a grim and angry expression on Kirby England's face.

"The meeting ended well, after all, Kirby. But you don't look too pleased about it."

"There's nowt to be pleased about, that's why."

"But surely a vote passed in favor of forming a Railway Committee, with yourself nominated as treasurer, and a company to be set up . . . *And* you've taken up most of the few hundred shares to be offered."

"Aye, and that's because few others had the stomach to follow suit. For all their talk, they're most of 'em croakers—dead-scared of a risk or a gamble. I called 'em timid tradesmen, and that's what they are. Oh, they'd like a railway, they know they *need* one, but mark my words, at the first difficult fence they'll shy away like silly frightened horses and give up the whole idea. I could see it in their faces. I watched them as they sat round that table, yattering away like old women at a tea party."

He kicked disgustedly at the snow in his path.

"Aren't you being unfair, Kirby? They seemed perfectly serious about it to me. They've even chosen the engineer to survey the route. That must prove something."

The other snorted and flicked with his cane at a drift of snow on a window ledge, scattering it as he passed. "It proves only, Henry lad, that they know nowt about engineers! Tannahill's no good. He couldn't build a footpath, let alone a railway."

"I've always heard that he has a very sound reputation."

"Oh aye, he makes few mistakes, but that's because he hasn't the gumption to stick his neck out! If there's no difficulty he'll soon invent one just to show what a solid, cautious sort of fellow he is. We should have gone for a man like Stephenson. Nothing less than the best!"

"Mr. George Stephenson?"

"Who else? He built both the Stockton and Darlington line and the Liverpool and Manchester. I've not met him yet myself, but any man who can build an iron railroad across five and a half miles of peat bog, as he did at Chat Moss, has my vote."

"They said only a fool or madman would attempt it," Henry said dryly. "I remember all the tales in the newspapers at the time: hundreds of men and horses sunk, an engineer swallowed alive!"

"All rubbish and exaggeration, put about by drivers of stage-coaches trying to frighten people and put them off railways. I can't blame them though. Their future's threatened, same as the canals, and they don't realize just how much of a threat the railways are yet."

"It's hard to believe they could ever supersede canals and coaches."

"Of course they will, Henry. And the quicker, the better. Now, if we could get a man like George Stephenson to build *our* railway for us—*and* to build us one of his steam engines—a *locomotive* one, we'd be getting somewhere. I saw one working on the Stockton and Darlington line today on my way back from Sunderland."

Henry stared at him. "I say, aren't you going a bit fast, Kirby? Infernal machines roaring through our peaceful countryside? They're known to be dangerous and unreliable, as well as harmful to crops and animals, to say nothing of the game. No one round here will want them. I thought the idea was to use horse-drawn wagons, or stationary engines at the most."

"I daresay that will be Mr. Tannahill's idea, but I can tell you it's not mine. It'd be no use to us. It must be steam locomotives or it's not worth the building. A glorified bloody tramway's not what I've in mind."

Henry was silent for a moment, digesting this. He said slowly: "If that's what you're planning, you're going to come up against a great deal of opposition. Mr. Snell, for one. Why does he dislike you so much?"

Kirby chuckled. "Like I said at the meeting, I beat him in the Council election for Monk Ward—and that's one thing he'll never forgive me for. An educated Whig lawyer being ousted by an

upstart Tory draper! And there's another thing he can't forgive me for either—having the cheek to move into the same street as him, polluting the rarified, gentlemanly air of Monkgate, *and* in a much bigger and better house than his own!"

Henry laughed. The Minster clock struck faintly in the distance, its chimes muffled by the snow. Henry held out his hand.

"I'd almost forgotten that I meant to call at the Theatre Royal this evening. If I don't hurry I'll miss the performance. There's a new singer engaged, and it's rumored that she's quite ravishing and sings like a nightingale. Why don't you come and hear her, Kirby? I know you appreciate beautiful women."

"Nay, thanks all the same. I've had a bellyful of warbling already this evening. Good night to you, lad."

He was gone, striding away down the long curve of Goodramgate towards the city walls and Monkgate, and was soon lost to view in the white flakes and darkness.

Henry stood for a moment, looking thoughtfully after him. He had met Kirby England only a few weeks ago through the local Tory Party, but already the man had made more impression on him than anyone else he knew. Thinking over the meeting at the hotel, Henry realized that while the other tradesmen had thought only of their own particular, petty transport problems, Kirby, alone, had seen the railway as part of a much larger scheme of things. Henry sighed. There was going to be a lot of trouble over this railway and he might well become deeply involved himself. There would be violent opposition from every quarter—fierce prejudice, irate landowners, indignant citizens. Despite his bold words at the meeting his heart sank. And as for Kirby's proposal to insist on steam locomotive power, it would make matters far worse. Most people he knew considered locomotives to be nothing more than a passing prodigy that would soon fizzle out to nothing. He hoped very much that Kirby would change his mind and direct his energies in more realistic paths.

Henry had an uneasy feeling that Kirby England might bring him a lot of trouble. However, he had every intention of staying close by him. Kirby was on the City Council and had fingers in a great many pies besides his profitable draper's shop. He knew

that Kirby could get him to Westminster, and beneath Henry's quiet, gentlemanly air lay a hard determination to become a Member of Parliament. He might have idled his life away pleasantly on his estate, but he had decided that he wanted more than that. Both his parents were dead, and he had no brothers and sisters. His life had become pointlessly centered round himself. Election to Parliament would change all that and give him the chance to do something for his fellowmen.

The snow had settled thickly round the brim of his top hat. He took the hat off and brushed it clean before replacing it carefully at a slight tilt. Conscious that he was not alone, he turned and saw a small ragged child watching him from a dark alleyway. It was a girl, thin and barefoot, wearing a ragged dress far too big for her, one of the hundreds of starving urchins in the city. He drew a coin from his pocket and threw it to her. She caught it skilfully and scuttled away like an animal. Henry shook his head sadly and turned back along the street in the direction of the Theatre Royal.

The house at 44 Monkgate was just outside the city walls. It had been built in the reign of King Charles II, in a wide street lined with similarly elegant residences. It fronted directly onto the pavement and had a handsome paneled door painted black, with a fanlight over the top. Long symmetrical windows graced its brick façade.

Inside, the hall was large and impressive. An immense gasolier was suspended from the molded ceiling, a dazzling affair of pink glass globes and crystal pendants, all winking and sparkling in the light from half a dozen burners. A magnificent Turkish carpet covered the floor, and the staircase, descending grandly from the upper stories in a wide sweep, had a fine balustrade of ornamental white cast iron.

Kirby England paused only long enough to toss his greatcoat and hat to a waiting manservant, and then went straight upstairs to the drawing room on the first floor. This room extended the whole width of the house and its windows looked out onto Monkgate. The curtains were drawn and a coal fire burned in the grate of a marble fireplace. The latest kind of goose-necked gas brackets burned on the walls and the furniture was of heavily carved mahogany, with upholstery in rich velvet and tapestry. Nonetheless, there was a cold and uninviting look about it all: everything was too unused, too neatly in its place, as though it were part of a museum rather than a home.

There was a woman sitting in a chair near the fire, and she lifted her head sharply as the door opened. She was ugly and angular, with gray hair arranged with elaborate stiffness around her cap. Her appearance had all the overdecorated vulgarity of the gasolier in the hall below. Her gown of a violent magenta satin was frilled and beribboned in a fussy style that did not suit her stern looks, and the jet beads that festooned her neck, as well as the multitude of rings that covered her bony hands, only added to the unfortunate gaudery.

"Good evening, Mother."

Kirby bent to kiss her cheek before moving to warm his hands before the fire. Mrs. England watched him proudly. What a fine figure of a man her son was, she thought smugly. He was so tall and strong, and so very striking with his black hair, dark eyes and firm features. None of the pale, watery looks of some of the gentry she had come across in York who thought themselves so well bred; they could never achieve in a lifetime half of all that her son had done for her so far. At the age of fifteen, after his father's death, he had come on his own to York with scarcely a penny in his pocket and, from a humble apprenticeship at a draper's shop, he had worked his way up until he was taken on as a partner and, finally, bought the whole business. He had sent for her and his sister to live there with him in premises over the shop. It had been simple enough accommodation, but after the bleak loneliness and discomfort of their old farm cottage in the Wolds it seemed so civilized and pleasant to be living in a city. She had always hated the mud, the wind, the miserable cold. How she had loathed looking after demanding, dirty animals and slaving away at all the endless drudgery that had been her life, with nothing else to look forward to! Sometimes she dreamed at night that she was back in the poky, damp little cottage, and it was an inexpressible relief to wake and realize that it was only a dream. She was living the life of a lady now, with smart clothes, servants at her beck and call, good food to eat and everything she wanted. There would be no hardship for them anymore.

"You're cold, son. I'll ring for some port wine to warm you."

She tugged at the bell rope by the side of the mantelpiece. Unlike her son, she had tried very hard to conceal her poor origins, and usually attempted to hide her native accent and speech. The result was often odd and affected. Only with Kirby did she sometimes, momentarily, abandon the laborious struggle to speak like a lady.

"Where's Adelaide?"

Mrs. England shrugged her shoulders. "Still crying upstairs in her room, I expect. She was upset today. Some of the girls at the school made fun of her. You know what they can be like. They tease her now and then about her raising, though what some of them have to be so hoity-toity about I don't know. We've more money than most of them."

"She's too sensitive," Kirby grunted. "She'll have to learn to grow a tougher skin. What does it matter what they say or think? We're as good as anybody here in York."

Mrs. England was silent for a moment; her fingers twisted the strings of jet beads back and forth. She knew that for all their newfound wealth she was mocked among the gentry she tried to emulate. And she was aware of the torment that her shy daughter suffered at the select academy for young ladies that Kirby had insisted his sister attend. Whether her son was also mocked she did not know. Not to his face, certainly; she was sure of that. Kirby was not the kind of man that any dared ridicule openly. But there were bound to be some who whispered and sniggered behind their hands, deriding his way of speech, his dress, his want of polished, practiced manners . . .

A servant appeared at the door and Kirby asked for a decanter of brandy to be brought. Mrs. England opened her mouth to say that port would be better for him and then shut it again. She had a vague idea that port was a healthier drink than brandy but she had the sense to say nothing. Kirby had never permitted her to interfere in his life; his father had been a weak man and easily bullied, but her son was a different matter. She had great respect

17

for him, as well as gratitude, and was sometimes even a little afraid of him. She looked at him as he stood with his head bent, hands gripping the edge of the mantelshelf, as he stared down at the fire. It was no surprise to her that women found him fascinating. Since he was a small lad in the village, girls had always eyed him, fancying his dark looks and bold manner; now that he was so rich and successful, she knew that he had had a long succession of mistresses. None had seemed able to keep his interest for long; she did not know who was his current favorite.

"We had a meeting tonight." He had spoken suddenly, still half absorbed in watching the flickering flames.

Mrs. England was gratified; he rarely spoke of business to her. "What about?"

The servant returned with a silver tray, decanter and a glass, and Kirby told him curtly to leave it on the table. He poured himself a large measure of brandy and sat down in the chair opposite his mother. Leaning back, he raised the glass before him, as though offering a silent toast, and drank deeply.

"We're going to build a railway."

She looked at him, bewildered.

"Or rather," he corrected himself, "they've voted in favor of *trying* to build one and I'm going to see that it's done."

"A railway! Whatever for?"

He would not normally have tried to explain any matter of business to her, but tonight, for some reason, he had a compulsion to talk. There was an excitement and an exhilaration stirring within him that he had never felt about any other undertaking in his life. The draper's shop had meant long years of grinding, humdrum work, necessary to climb the ladder; his other interests and enterprises had since been satisfyingly profitable or carefully calculated to raise him yet another rung in the city hierarchy. But this was different. He cared very much about this railway. It was bound to make money—he knew that—but money, for once, had little to do with his preoccupation. Contrary to his native down-to-earth way of thinking, he had found himself dreaming of the little York railway as his first step towards a kind of destiny. At the meeting he had spoken of the city with a genuine emotion: he had come to love the place as though he had been born within its ancient walls and not in an insignificant village ten miles or more away, and he had come to identify himself with her fate and her future.

Mrs. England listened doubtfully as her son told her about the gathering at Tomlinson's Hotel. She could see that there was some sense in building a road of iron rails if it meant that a horse could then pull a line of heavy wagons, one behind the other, along it; exactly why this should be so escaped her, but she was prepared to accept it as a fact. But when Kirby began to speak of using moving steam engines to draw the wagons she became seriously alarmed. She remembered seeing a picture of one of those strange machines in the *Yorkshire Gazette,* and she had not forgotten some of the tales she had heard of the terror and disaster they caused as they roared through the fields like dragons, breathing flames and smoke. Crops were burned, land was made barren, cows would not give milk, hens refused to lay, lambs were born dead and women miscarried. And yet here was her son talking of them as though he really believed they would take the place of horses, and, worse, he was going to invest a tidy sum in this railway company.

She said anxiously, the specter of poverty at her shoulder: "You'll lose a pile of brass, son. Why not let others take the risk?"

He smiled and drank again from his glass. "I've put money here, there and everywhere in Yorkshire—in a merchant bank, land, a newspaper, a sawmill, a glassworks, the gas light company—and none of 'em was any sort of real gamble. This time I'm backing something that's a big risk, but in the end it'll pay ten times more than anything else. Mind you, that's not my only reason. I want a hand in what's going to revolutionize this country as well as put York back on t'map. After I'm dead I want people to remember me as the man who built railways across the length and breadth of the land."

One of the gaslights hissed and spluttered in the silence that followed. Mrs. England's fingers were clenched so tightly round her jet beads that the thread was in danger of snapping. He must have a fever, she thought, or he was losing his senses. There was an odd look about him. She was torn between fear for his health and sanity and fear that all his money would be squandered on this mad idea of railways. Visions of having to return to the old way of life rose up and seemed to choke her so that she could say nothing.

Kirby had got up to pour himself more brandy. He lit a cigar with a taper at the fire and puffed at it thoughtfully. He understood something of his mother's dismay; in many ways they were alike, but prolonged deprivation had left its mark on her for life and turned her into a bitter, insecure person.

He said quietly: "How would you like to move one day, Mother? From the fortune I'm going to make from railways I promise you that you'll be able to take your pick of any mansion in the county. We'll have a proper country gentleman's seat, with acres of parkland and a big lake—whatever you want."

Her gaunt face relaxed a little; he seemed so confident that some of her anxiety began to recede.

"This place is grand enough, Kirby. Happen when you marry I'll have to move somewhere else. I shouldn't like to play second fiddle to another woman."

He was amused. "I've no other woman in mind."

"You won't stay single forever," she said sourly.

"Mebbe not. But I'll not settle for anything less than the best, and the kind of woman I want for a wife, and to bear my children, wouldn't look at me—yet. When I wed it's going to be to a lass with a blue-blooded pedigree as long as her arm. And I'm going to make so much brass I'll have half the gentry in the county down on their knees begging me to marry their thoroughbred daughters to get the bailiffs off their backs. I'll wait till then."

He wandered restlessly over to the window and pulled aside the heavy velvet curtain. It was still snowing hard, and the gas lamp on the wall across the street shone on glistening white drifts. He watched a carriage go by, the horses' hooves soundless, the big wheels leaving deep, dark tracks behind them.

"At this rate the river'll freeze over solid, let alone the canals. There'll be no deliveries by water carrier for weeks, I reckon." He drew on the cigar and spoke softly to himself as he stared out into the night. "Jumped over the counter, have I? Just wait till they see which way this cat's going to jump now."

CHAPTER II

*"I consider," said Mr. Weller, "that the rail
is unconstitootional and an inwaser o' privileges."*

Charles Dickens

Benbow Hall lay about fifteen miles southwest of York and seven
miles east of Leeds. Its main gates, of imposing and elaborate
wrought iron, were just north of the main street of Garford, a
small market town which straddled the Great North Road. A
long carriageway led through rolling parkland up to the house.

Kirby England, seeing the Hall for the first time from his carriage window, was disappointed. The entrance and approach
had caused him to expect something magnificent, but the house
was a gloomy graystone hotchpotch of differing styles of archi-
tecture with no grace or beauty about it at all. The roof was of
dreary slate, and chimneys sprouted over it in all shapes and
sizes like mushrooms in a field. Small mullioned windows would
not make, he guessed, for light and airiness inside.

On the journey out from York he had thought about the man
he had come to meet—Amos Gurney, owner of Benbow Hall and
Benbow Colliery, a profitable coal mine. He knew two other
facts about him: he was a rich man, and he was a Quaker. Kirby
had met a number of Quakers in the course of his business
affairs. In York, as elsewhere, they were highly respected for
their integrity, honesty and for their philanthropy; they were
also thought to be excessively quaint and distinctly odd, and
were frequently the object of mockery. Kirby himself found their
curious speech and dress irritating, and their strict and sober

piety was often ironically at odds, to his mind, with a single-minded pursuit of wealth. They were very shrewd businessmen—pronounced sly by envious enemies, but admired by all for their judgment and foresight in their dealings—and this was something that Kirby found entirely estimable.

Amos Gurney would be the third landowner that he had called on that day. Like the previous two, the Quaker's estate lay on the railway route proposed by the engineer. Mr. Tannahill, the engineer, had done no more, so far, than make an approximate plan for the York Railway Committee; the proper survey had yet to be undertaken, and for that they needed the consent and cooperation of the landowners concerned. The committee was agreed to avoid, at all costs, the violent scenes that had ensued over the building of other railways in other parts of the country, where such enmity had been engendered that surveys had had to be carried out at night by stealth in order to circumvent the fury of bitterly opposed landlords.

As treasurer, it would be Kirby's responsibility to negotiate the compensation paid to landowners for any land taken for the railway, and he intended to call on them all himself. He also had every intention of accompanying the surveyors everywhere, when the time came, prepared to smooth away objections and trouble, and to walk every inch of the route himself.

The other two landowners had been difficult. The first had flatly refused to discuss the possibility of a railway being built anywhere near his land, let alone across it, and had threatened summonses against anyone who trespassed. Kirby would have doubted his ability to persuade him at all had he not known that the gentleman was up to his ears in debt and that the substantial compensation he had hinted at was certain to win the day in the end—once outrage had abated. The second had been even more difficult: his objection had been no less fierce, but he was concerned principally for his fox covers and the effect on his game. Kirby was counting on Henry Latham's gentle persuasion to convince his lordship that neither pheasants nor foxes would come to harm and that his sport would not suffer in consequence.

Kirby stared out of the window, deep in thought. The Act of Parliament would compel landowners to sell eventually, but resorting to law meant delay, disputes and haggling, and was to be avoided if possible. Unfortunately, most big landowners had influential friends at Westminster who would certainly do all they could, if asked, to prevent their Bill's safe passage. Many snares and pitfalls lay ahead.

The carriage jerked to a halt outside the house and Kirby descended slowly, looking about him before he climbed a flight of steps to the front door. He lifted the iron knocker and brought it down sharply. It was some time before he was answered, and he waited impatiently; a north wind was blowing across the parkland, and there was a look of snow to come in the heavy yellow clouds; in the distance he could make out the dark shadows of deer, huddled together beneath the trees. He had raised his hand to knock again when the door was opened by an elderly servant, gray-headed, stooping and melancholy.

The interior of Benbow Hall was as cold and depressing as Kirby had anticipated. He was surrounded by heavily paneled walls, bare stone-flagged floors and sepulchral gloom. There were a few pieces of good, solid furniture, but all of it was simple and functional and without embellishment. An oak staircase leading up from the hallway was uncarpeted; he could see no paintings, looking glasses or ornamental fripperies of any kind. The servant had gone away to inform his master and returned to lead the way down a long passage and into a room at the far end.

Kirby found himself in a library. It was high-ceilinged and surprisingly agreeable after the starkness he had seen. This was partly due to the decorative effect of the rows of leather-bound volumes lining the walls and partly to the fact that there was a rather fine Turkish carpet on the floor. There were also two or three armchairs, and a log fire was crackling pleasantly on the hearth. Two men were standing before the fireplace, and the elder came forward at once, holding out both hands in a friendly greeting.

"I am Amos Gurney. Thou art welcome to my house, Kirby England. Wilt thou come and warm thyself, Friend?"

Kirby studied the Quaker carefully. He was a frail-looking man of above fifty with a pale, thin face marred by the shadows and deep lines of poor health. He was bearded, and wore the distinctive Quaker garb of a collarless, straight-cut black coat, plain white shirt and neckcloth and dark trousers. He seemed a gentle, mild man, but Kirby, noticing the sharp intelligence in the gray eyes that looked him over, guessed him to be nobody's fool.

Amos Gurney ushered him politely towards the fire. The other man who stood there was similarly dressed in Quaker clothing, but he was much younger, of about the same age as Kirby. He was fair-haired and strikingly handsome, with well-molded features and very blue eyes.

"My cousin, William Gurney."

The cousin bowed civilly but coolly.

"William is also my lawyer," Amos Gurney explained. "He is here today at my special request to be present at our discussion. Please be seated."

He indicated the most comfortable chair nearest the fire and seated himself close by. William Gurney sat opposite, his fingers drumming lightly against the arm of his chair.

"I know the purpose of thy visit from thy letter," Amos Gurney continued. "The York Railway Committee is investigating the building of a railway from York to Leeds by way of Garford. And thou wishes to carry out a survey on my land?"

"Aye, that's it, Mr. Gurney. The purpose of this railway is to provide better transport for all merchandise and cheaper coal for the city. Garford coal is high quality, so to bring the railway near the collieries makes good sense for all concerned. Unfortunately, Mr. Tannahill, our engineer, has recommended that the most satisfactory route would be one crossing the southernmost tip of your deer park."

"Which would bring it within half a mile of this house, closer than I'd expected."

"I can understand your objection to that," Kirby said quickly. "But as a colliery owner you'll no doubt appreciate the advantages such a railway would mean for you. I'm told that you yourself have had the foresight to build a small railway to take horse-drawn coal wagons down from Benbow Colliery to Garford.

Now, if this railway of ours can be built, connecting Garford to both York and Leeds—"

The Quaker interrupted him, raising his hand. "My dear Friend, thou misunderstands me. I am not in any manner *against* thy railway. I wish it did not have to pass so close to my house, but that is all." He was about to go on when a sudden fit of coughing took hold of him. He pressed his hand against his chest and his thin body shook helplessly until the paroxysm had subsided. When he could speak again, he went on quietly: "On the contrary, it has been one of the ambitions of my life to build just such a railway as thou proposes—and thereby to link our coal staithes with York and Leeds. And were it not for my indifferent health in recent years, I might have achieved it. But, to my regret, I no longer have the strength to undertake the task that confronts thee now. I envy thee, believe me. Thou hast no need to explain to me the advantages a railway will bring us: it will benefit every man, woman and child in Garford, and I wish it had been in my power to confer such a blessing on the people of this town years ago. As thou knows, the Great North Road goes through Garford, but even so our collieries cannot compete with other mines further south and nearer to the canals and the rivers; nor can we compete with those to the west and nearer to Leeds. We have to contend with turnpike costs and slow wagons for transporting our coal."

He smiled gently. "So I shan't oppose thy railway, Kirby England, thou may be assured of that. Indeed, I welcome it with open arms, and if it crosses a small part of my parkland . . . well, that is surely a low price to pay for seeing a dream come true. I have only one thing to ask of thee: that provision may be made for our colliery railway to connect with thine. That is our chief concern, is it not, William?"

The lawyer had been listening attentively. "Our condition of agreement, in fact, Cousin Amos, as we discussed," he said with a cold preciseness, his eyes on Kirby. "And providing, of course, that adequate and proper compensation is paid to thee by the railway company for land purchased—which naturally must take full and fair account of loss of trees, quarrying that may be necessary for embankments, dumping of spoil and any form of nuisance whatsoever to thyself or thy estate."

Amos Gurney said dryly: "As thou can see, my cousin is a conscientious and astute legal adviser."

"I see no reason why your condition should not be met," Kirby replied. "And the company will not try to cheat any landowner, you have my word on that. Fair compensation will be paid to all concerned." He spoke to the elder man, ignoring the other. The lawyer, he had known at once, would be nothing but trouble, whereas this man was on his side.

"I don't doubt thy word," Amos Gurney said. "And thou wilt find me a reasonable man. I have all the wealth I need. My wife has been dead for many years now, and with her died much of my enjoyment of life. I no longer care much about the things of this world. However, I have a daughter, Hester, who is my sole heir; William would be guilty of neglecting his duty if he did not see that *her* interests are protected, since the colliery and the whole estate will be hers when she is twenty-one."

"Compensation will be properly negotiated and paid," Kirby repeated. "And your condition met."

"Then thou hast my full permission to conduct a survey."

"Thank you."

The Quaker rose. "We understand each other, and there is no need to say more at this moment. I have confidence in thee. Tell me, thou hast heard of my colliery railway, but hast thou ever seen it?"

"Nay, I've not set eyes on't."

"Then thou must. And I shall show it to thee myself, for I am very proud of it. I built it four years ago to replace our old coal road down to Garford. The carts were too slow and the road was so bad in winter that an iron rail road seemed our only hope. I had already seen how well they worked at another colliery in Northumberland: one horse can pull ten tons' weight behind him on rails, as thou must be aware. Hast thou the time to come and see it now?"

"Aye—I'd be glad to."

"Thou wilt come with us, William?"

The lawyer declined. "I have seen it many times before,

Cousin. I shall wait here for Cousin Hester. I should like to see her before I have to return to York."

"Thou may have some time to wait; I don't expect her back until late."

"Nevertheless, I shall stay—if I may."

Amos Gurney gave a small shrug. "Very well, William. As thou pleases."

They left him in the library. Kirby wondered idly whether the Quaker's daughter would be as anxious to see her cousin as he evidently was to see her. The father, he judged, did not encourage William Gurney's interest in his heir. The lawyer was more than welcome to the Quakeress, Kirby thought to himself with some amusement. He had seen Quaker women on their way to their Friargate Meeting House in York, all dressed alike in their dreary grays and browns: plain bonnets, plain dresses and, so far as he had ever troubled to notice, plain faces. He found their demure and prim air boring. He liked women who dressed flamboyantly and who behaved with gaiety and style and who had the courage to display their charms, not hide them away in a tiresome, affected fashion.

A carriage was brought round to take them the mile or so down into Garford. The market town was hardly more than a village, its shops and houses running in two long, straggling lines each side of the Great North Road. At the north end of the street lived a motley assortment of inhabitants: wheelwrights, pigeon fanciers, dog breeders and poachers, and further south were found quarrymen, the saddler, the cobbler and the miners. At that end also was the ale shop, where the miners' wives queued for jugs of beer for their men coming from work at the colliery. At Tallow Yard, opposite the Swan Inn, there was a kiln fired with slack coal from the depot, to which farmers brought their corn for drying after a wet harvest; at the far end of the yard there was a candle factory which supplied green tallow candles to the pits.

As their carriage progressed down the street, an overloaded stagecoach, bound for the North, rumbled past them, passengers and luggage piled high on the roof. The coachman, with astonishing speed and skill, swung the whole top-heavy and cumbersome equipage in through the narrow entrance to the inn's courtyard with a timing and judgment that a Roman charioteer would have envied.

Amos Gurney followed Kirby's gaze. "How much longer will coaches like that survive, I wonder."

Kirby turned his head. "No longer than it takes to build the railways."

"I hope thou art right. If railways become accepted and understood by all as the wonderful revolution in transport that they are, then stagecoaches will no longer be seen passing through Garford."

They stopped for a moment to allow a herd of cattle to pass each side of the carriage. The beasts were wild-eyed, lowing and frightened, their drover's black and white dog weaving from side to side at their heels.

"Scots cattle on their way south," Amos Gurney explained. "In spite of its small population, there is a good deal going on in Garford, as thou canst see today. We have five fairs a year and a Wednesday market, as well as hirings at Berwick Lane corner. And every day a mail coach takes on letters and packets for London and Scotland outside the Swan Inn. Even so, there are only three carriers a week and no other transport for the people."

"When our railway is built all that will change," Kirby said. "They'll be able to go daily to York or Leeds."

"So I am hoping, Friend. And I am hoping that thou wilt bring us not only better and cheaper transport for our coal, but better transport for our people too. With thy help this town should prosper and we shall be able to build more homes, a new school for the children and almshouses for the old and poor."

Their carriage pitched and swayed as they turned into the depot yard over rough ground. The two men stepped down and Kirby looked around. He saw the coal staithes where a cart was being loaded, the horse drooping patiently between the shafts. Two other carts waited their turn. It was a grimy, cheerless place, and coal dust lay thick everywhere. Beyond the staithes ran an embankment of earth about twelve feet high, and along its top Kirby saw a line of empty chaldrons, linked together one behind the other. At their head was a closed wooden wagon with three small windows on each side; at their tail, a dandy cart to carry the horse when freewheeling. A large dappled gray stood at the front of the whole assembly, harnessed to the leading wagon.

"This is the end of our railway," Amos Gurney said. "From here the coal must go by these horses and carts all the way to its destination—Wetherby, Tadcaster, Knaresborough . . . Hast thou the time to ride up to the colliery?"

Kirby looked up at the sky; small flakes of snow were drifting in the air like loose feathers and there were clearly plenty more to come. He hesitated. To delay his departure back to York might mean becoming snowbound; on the other hand, the Quaker's railway interested him despite the fact that it was small and horse-powered. He decided to risk the weather—a railway was a railway, whatever its size, and must concern him. He followed Amos Gurney up a steep flight of steps set in the embankment. They boarded the closed wagon and sat on hard wooden benches. The six tiny windows gave only a dim light; it was chill, and there was a pungent smell of coal. Seeing that they were ready, the brakesman climbed onto the wagon's platform and clanged a warning bell. They began to roll forward, pulled by the dappled gray, who plodded along between the parallel iron rails set in stone sleeper blocks.

For Kirby the slow haul upwards to the moors where Benbow Colliery lay was a mixture of pleasure and impatience. Much as he had grown to love city streets, there was some pleasure at seeing the open Yorkshire fields, glimpsed through the little windows, and in a wintry wood of majestic dark beeches. As they progressed through the woods the bare branches tapped, ghostlike, at the glass of the windows and rattled against the wagon's sides. But there was also impatience at the pace of their journey: the horse could manage no more than five miles an hour or so. He thought of Mr. Stephenson's locomotive engines, which could achieve thirty miles an hour at least, and with five times the pulling power.

The line entered a shallow cutting where the ground on each side was covered by long, deep puddles.

"This stretch is constantly flooded by a spring," the Quaker told Kirby. "It keeps undermining the track, and so far we have never succeeded in solving the problem. In wet weather this section sometimes looks more like a canal, but in the spring it is covered with bluebells and can look as innocent as a newborn babe. I hope thy engineer will not encounter similar troubles."

He sat very proud and very upright on the bench, his pale, emaciated features composed and dignified beneath his black broad-brimmed Quaker hat. Occasionally he gave a cough, quickly suppressed.

They rolled on across a bridge over a stream and then plunged suddenly into a tunnel. Light from each end, as well as faint shafts of light filtering down from ventilation holes overhead, showed Kirby a grottolike scene. Water had dripped from the roof to form miniature stalactites and the walls were green and spongy with lichen. It was an eerie place, and the rumbling of the wagon and chaldrons echoed loudly like thunder about them.

The brakesman clanged the bell as they emerged again into daylight. Kirby saw that the track was now running high towards the moors. Benbow Hall had been left far below on their right. From now on the gradient increased noticeably and the horse progressed slower and slower as it strained to drag its burden over ground already covered with a slippery carpet of snow. It was very cold, and the wind whistled in through every crack and cranny in the wagon. Kirby was not a man to care much about the temperature, but his fingers were feeling numb inside his leather gloves and his feet were frozen. He drew the collar of his greatcoat closer round his neck and wondered about the effect this journey might have on his companion, who was beginning to cough more and more frequently. He was obviously a dying man and this intense cold could only hasten him into his grave. The heiress daughter would come into her fortune even quicker than her lawyer cousin anticipated, he thought cynically.

There had been no room for sentiment in his own life, but Kirby found himself regretting that the Quaker had not more time left to him in this world. He had nothing in common with the pious man—except a belief in railways—but he felt an odd accord with him. It seemed a pity that Amos Gurney was unlikely to survive long enough to see the railway come to Garford; and it seemed even more of a pity, Kirby thought practically, if he died before he had been able to give the Railway Committee all the support it needed. The daughter was an unknown quantity and might not share her father's foresight.

He shifted uncomfortably on the bench and rubbed his hands together to try to warm them.

Amos Gurney said apologetically: "I'm afraid our passenger accommodation compares very unfavorably with the first-class carriages I have seen on the Liverpool to Manchester railway. They are extraordinarily luxurious."

"I can do without footwarmers and rugs," Kirby replied.

"Nonetheless, they would be very welcome on this journey," the Quaker said. His face looked gray and pinched. "I suppose," he continued between coughs, "that we might be said to be traveling second-class. I believe most of those carriages are very similar to this one."

"Aye—about the same, from what I've seen. Lucky we're not going third-class or we'd have no seats or roof at all!"

Amos Gurney smiled. "I sometimes wonder why the Duke of Wellington worries about railways encouraging the lower classes to move about too much if they are expected to do so in such conditions."

"It'll change," Kirby said. "They'll have their seats and roofs in the end, but it'll take time."

A cluster of grim-looking buildings came into view; the black silhouette of turning wheels stood out against the leaden sky. Kirby saw tall chimneys and ugly spoil heaps.

"This is Hester Pit, sunk only two years ago and named after my daughter," Amos Gurney said. "Elizabeth Pit, named after my wife, is higher up, and the two are connected by air shafts." They stopped, and he added in explanation: "The gradient becomes too steep for the horse now so we use the winding engine up at Elizabeth to pull us the rest of the way. The horse is being unharnessed and will ride up with us in the cart at the back."

They waited. The wind blew hard round the stationary wagon, so that it swayed and creaked; snowflakes spattered against the windows. When they moved again it was with a sudden, sharp jerk, and Kirby, propelled backwards against the wall behind him, felt, in his whole body, the strength of the force that was now drawing them rapidly upwards. He leaned forward and looked down to see the ground slipping away quickly beneath them. This was better than their plodding pace behind the dappled gray.

Amos Gurney, watching him, smiled. "Thou appreciates the difference between the two sources of power: this incline is one in seventeen, but the engine makes easy work of it. We have three steam engines up at Elizabeth—one for pumping, one for winding and a smaller winding engine that is drawing us now. All told, they cost more than three thousand pounds, but it was money well spent, I can assure thee. Before that we had only a horse gin."

At the summit of the slope they came to a halt and stepped out onto the wild wastes of Benbow Moor. A flurry of snow obscured the pithead momentarily from Kirby's sight, and then as it cleared he saw the familiar group of buildings against the skyline and the massive iron wheels spinning. A tall engine house towered aloft, breathing two vapory columns, one of black smoke and one of white steam, that slanted together in the wind resembling some black demon escaped from the underworld with a white spirit in his keeping whom he was compelling to endless labors. From the upper part of the engine house a huge wooden beam protruded like a giant's arm, alternately lifting itself up and falling again. Kirby watched, fascinated by the thought that the arm was attached to the rod and bucket of a pump which must be lifting water from deep down in the ground, enabling men to work where they would have drowned in subterranean floods. Not far from the buildings there was a vast mountain of spoil, and to its left he saw a line of chaldrons loaded with coal and ready to go down to Garford.

They walked across to the pithead, where the colliery viewer, a big red-faced man, greeted them. Kirby forgot about the bitter cold at the sight and sound of the great beam engine powered by the effects of atmospheric pressure and steam. The apparatus was screened from the winding side of the mine's shaft by wooden bratticing, leaving no more than six feet in diameter clear for the passage of the wooden coal corves, and the men themselves, to be lowered and raised to and from the dark depths of the mine.

"The miners call the engine Old Bess," Amos Gurney said. "She does eight pumping strokes a minute and brings up more than five hundred gallons of water in the same time. She needs to: we have to fight night and day to keep the mine from flooding. The shaft is lined with cast-iron tubbing and we've driven a new drainage sough up from Kippax Beck, but unfortunately, it has made no real improvement."

A shaft frame supported pulleys which overhung the pit, and over these wheels ropes passed by which men and corves descended and ascended. They watched the banksman handling the full corves of glistening coal as they swung to the surface, heaving them away onto small hurdles on which they were drawn to the screens to be separated into large and small coal and thence to the chaldrons.

Some of the miners had finished their eight-hour shift and were being hauled to the top of the shaft, sitting astride empty corves and clinging like monkeys to the rope. They appeared, blinking in the sudden daylight, their eyes red-rimmed with weariness, faces black with coal dust. Their clothes were drenched—checked flannel jackets, waistcoats and trousers all sodden with water and caked with dirt, and their heavy boots were thick with mud. Others were lowered to begin their stint, precipitating themselves casually into the black and bottomless-seeming crater, a canteen slung across their backs, and with no more than a wooden corf and a hemp rope for protection as they plunged down into the depths of the earth.

But whatever hardship they endured, it was apparent that these miners took pride in their work and in themselves and they bore themselves with dignity. They were renowned for hard drinking, swearing and fighting among themselves, but there was a curious courtliness about them. And to see them made Kirby think, with a nostalgia he had not experienced before, of his own upbringing among the tough village lads, where plain speech and a useful pair of fists counted for more than anything else.

He asked the Quaker questions about the pits and was told

that they were both four hundred feet deep. The winning was of two thousand acres at that time, and the tramplates laid to carry the corves underground would mean that the workings could now be extended further and more easily.

"Your men look contented workers," Kirby said.

"I see to it that they are," Amos Gurney replied gravely. "Thou wilt hear no ill spoken of conditions in this colliery. I cannot deny that the work is hard and unpleasant, but wages are twenty-five shillings a week and each man is given six corves of coal a month for his own use. They work regular hours—never more than eight hours at a time in the pit. We have some lads as hurriers but none under the age of twelve, and I will not permit women or girls in my mines." He coughed again. "As for their safety, we have never had an explosion or accident yet, beyond a man falling and breaking a leg. I do all I can to see that no unnecessary risks are taken; next to flooding, a firedamp explosion is the greatest danger, but naked lights are forbidden in the pit and we have used Mr. Stephenson's safety lamp for some time now." He smiled tiredly. "The one thing they do lack, perhaps, compared with other collieries, is excessive quantities of ale. I will not tolerate intemperance in any man and a man who is a friend of publicans will not remain long in my employ. The first time he is seen intoxicated he is dismissed and the sum due to him as wages forfeited."

Kirby made no immediate reply to this. He was in entire agreement with dismissing drunken miners; he would have done exactly the same himself, although not from any moral conviction. Miners' lives presumably depended daily on the clearheaded actions of their fellows, and an inebriated man—or one suffering from the aftereffects of too much ale—was a bad risk. No doubt, Amos Gurney's severe ruling included that consideration too, but it must spring mainly from his puritanical faith. *A sedate, sober, silent, serious, sad-colored sect* . . . Kirby remembered hearing the Quakers described thus, and it seemed to him a good description. They had some absurd beliefs that he called to mind: they refused to take oaths, to doff their hats to any man, lady or even to the King himself. They shunned music, dancing, singing, gambling, the theatre. All in all, he thought, it must make for a very dreary life.

He said with a touch of irony: "Aye, well, it's lucky for the country's trading that Quakers don't seem to consider it a mortal sin to make money, as well as to drink—seeing they're not bad businessmen."

"We have nothing against making money, so long as there is the intention of doing some good with it, and that it was not made by doing bad. And provided, of course, that there is always moderation in personal and domestic expenses."

"I doubt if anyone could accuse you of extravagance, Mr. Gurney," Kirby remarked, thinking of the sparsely furnished Benbow Hall.

"We do not believe in needless expense in the furniture of our homes. Our Saviour was lowly in heart and lived a simple life. We follow His example."

Kirby did not reply.

It was still snowing when they left the colliery but had not settled thickly enough to cause alarm. Kirby turned to look back once more at the pithead behind them.

"You say that your daughter will inherit the colliery as well as the rest of your estate. That's a heavy burden for one lass to bear."

"Hester is fitted for it. She has courage and spirit, as well as a fitting sense of responsibility to her fellowmen. She has started a school in Garford for the miners' children and teaches them to read and write herself."

"How old is she?" Kirby asked. He thought: Not only a Quakeress but a bloody schoolmarm too!

"Sixteen. She will be seventeen in June."

They were standing with the full force of the north wind in their faces. The Quaker began to cough violently again.

"Best get back to the wagon," Kirby said, "before either of us gets pneumonia."

The chaldrons had been loaded high with coal and the dappled gray horse was standing, comically, in the dandy cart at the rear, looking like a wooden horse out of a child's nursery.

The journey down was much faster. With the brakesman ringing his warning bell loudly and the horse riding in the cart behind the chaldrons, they freewheeled merrily down the steep gradient and on past Hester Pit, descending almost to the mouth of the grottolike tunnel before they came to a gentle halt. The horse was led round to the front and harnessed there once more to pull them the rest of the way to the staithes at Garford.

They returned to Benbow Hall in the gathering gloom of the winter's afternoon; black rooks flew overhead, cawing discordantly as they made their way home to roost.

Amos Gurney courteously offered shelter for the night, but Kirby, thanking him, refused. He was impatient to be back in York, and if he stayed he might find himself snowbound for several days by morning. Furthermore, the frugal aspect of the Quaker's household did not attract him. They shook hands.

"I wish thee well, Kirby England. I shall pray for the success of thy railway."

Kirby looked back once as his carriage drew away from the house. Amos Gurney was still standing at the foot of the steps, an upright, postlike figure in his somber black against the white snow.

As Kirby's carriage neared the gates, another conveyance, drawn by a pair of bays, drew aside after entering to let his pass. He caught a brief glimpse of a small gray bonnet and one graygloved hand before they were gone. The Quaker schoolmarm returning home, he thought, and, leaning back against the cushioning, shut his eyes.

On the whole, he was satisfied with the day's work. Amos Gurney's agreement and support would undoubtedly help a great deal: he was a respected man and must have some influence in and around Garford. The colliery railway had been an interesting demonstration of the advantage of iron rails over road, even with horsepower. As for the superiority of a steam engine over a horse, that had been shown clearly. Now, if it had been not a stationary engine but a *locomotive* one, then they would have journeyed up to that bleak moorland and back not at a paltry, labored five miles an hour, but at twenty or even thirty. He fell deep in thought and the darkening landscape passed unnoticed as his carriage bowled fast along the road towards York.

The other carriage had reached the steps of Benbow Hall. A young girl got out and was embraced by her father. She was small and dark and wore a plain dove-gray dress and fringed shawl. Her bonnet was of gray silk, unadorned except for the cream-colored ribbons tied in a bow under her chin, and it framed a face that, while not beautiful, would never pass unnoticed if only on account of her very fine gray eyes.

Amos Gurney held his daughter at arm's length. "I have two things that I am proud of in my life," he said. "One is my railway and the other my beloved Hester."

She smiled at him and scolded him gently. "Thou shouldst not be standing out here in the cold like this, Papa. Thou knows very well that it makes thy cough worse. Come indoors."

She took his arm and they walked together up the steps and into the house; he leaned a little upon her.

"Who was thy visitor, Papa? I passed a carriage as I came in."

"A man thou dost not know, called Kirby England."

"And who is he?"

"Treasurer of the York Railway Committee."

"What does that have to do with thee?"

"He wants a survey to be conducted on my land. The committee are proposing to build a railway from York to Leeds by way of Garford."

Hester frowned. "Surely not across Benbow land?"

"Only a small part, child—just the southern tip of parkland."

"Dost thou want such a thing to happen? Canst thou not stop it? It would be dreadful to have a railway so close to the house."

He patted her arm. "Think carefully, my dear. It's not the peace of our deer park that should be thy concern but the good of our people of Garford. This railway, if it comes, will bring great benefits for them. Nor should thou forget the advantage it will bring us in transporting our coal cheaper and quicker than we could manage in any other way."

She looked doubtful and anxious. "But this man who came to see thee—is he honest? I have read of landowners being cheated over railway building and forced to sell against their will. Thou art so straight thyself, Papa, thou imagines every other man must be the same."

"I liked him," her father replied simply. "He is no more and no less honest than most men, I daresay. But he has great faith in railways and, more than that, he has the resolve and strength he will need to fight for them. My dear, thou must understand that no revolution of any kind can be achieved by a scrupulous, sensitive or unselfish man—and the railways will mean revolution." He sighed. "My one regret is that I am not strong enough to take any part in it."

They had reached the library door, and as they did so, William Gurney came out.

"I did not know thou wast here, William." Hester accepted her cousin's kiss on her cheek, then pulled off her gloves and removed her bonnet. Her dark hair was parted in the center and coiled in two plaits over her ears, a style which suited her very well, emphasizing the beauty of her gray eyes and the straightness of her small nose. She had a high forehead and a determined chin.

William was watching her. "I stayed especially to see thee, Cousin," he said softly.

He turned to her father. "I also wanted to speak further with thee, Amos. As thy lawyer I am deeply concerned that thou consented to a survey being done. Surely we agreed before the meeting that no concessions should be made to the Railway Committee until we had proper evidence of their intention to meet our conditions."

"I asked only for thy counsel, William. Thou wilt forgive me if I remind thee that I always make my own decisions."

"Thou art making a mistake. Kirby England is not to be trusted. He came from some village in the Wolds and worked as a common draper's assistant in York. Since then he has managed to make a fortune by all manner of devious and dishonest dealings."

"Harsh words, cousin."

"But true ones, Amos. His reputation amongst Friends in York is very low; he does not understand the meaning of a gentleman's word. Thou wilt live to regret any business done with him. I advise thee most strongly against it."

Amos said sharply: "I have listened already to thy advice,

Cousin, and I thank thee for it. But, I repeat, I have made up my mind and there is no more to be said."

He refused to discuss the matter further and went into the library. Hester saw her cousin to the door. She knew that he was angry and his concern alarmed her: with Papa in such poor health, she wanted nothing to happen that might distress him.

"I think I shall write and ask Aunt Kitty about this railway man," she said to William. "Gossip is food and drink to her, so she may have something to tell of him."

"Undoubtedly. There is hardly anyone in York who has not some story to tell of Kirby England. He is an instrument of evil, debauchery and wickedness. I pray thee not to inquire of Aunt Kitty. Thou shouldst not try to learn anything of such people, Hester, if thou wishes to keep a mind that is pure within thee to guide thee to God. Instead, thou must do all thou canst to persuade thy father of his folly."

He took his leave of her, and she stood at the open doorway. She had known William since her earliest childhood and could not quite, even now that she was grown-up, rid herself of a feeling of awe towards him. Her senior by more than ten years, he was a successful lawyer, brilliantly clever and cultured, and he was a zealous Quaker. He never missed meeting for worship and, according to Aunt Kitty, who also went to the Friargate Meeting House in York, he was frequently inspired to break the silence to speak, pray or read a passage from the Bible. He was a very fine-looking man who carried himself well. As she watched his carriage leave, Hester contrasted her cousin with the slouched figure she had glimpsed in the passing carriage on her return. She had not seen Kirby England's face, but his demeanor then, coupled with William's information, was enough to convince her that he must be a coarse creature.

A gust of wind caught at the hem of her gray dress and flapped it against her ankles. She drew her shawl closer round her shoulders and, shivering, went inside.

It was dark by the time Kirby England's carriage reached York. He came into the city through Micklegate, the horses' hooves clattering loudly as they passed beneath the ancient stone archway.

The streets were slushy with melting snow, but all the eight-month lamps were lit and shone welcomingly. The carriage rattled on downhill towards the Ouse Bridge. Kirby watched the rows of small shops as they went by them, their signs projecting high over the pavements: John Rex, Assam Tea Dealers with an outsize tea caddy overhead; Peter Pickering, the apothecary and druggist with his glass bottles and stoneware leech jars in the window; Thomas Bell, the tobacconist and snuff dealer, who had a snuff-taking figure of Napoleon above his shop door and a small metal horse's head on the left-hand lintel, a gas jet flaring from the animal's nostrils to provide a light for passing smokers. They passed a confectioner's, a clock- and watchmaker, a cordwainer's, a toyman and haberdasher, T. Cooke, optician with a pair of giant spectacle frames attached to the wall and Seale's brush and mat warehouse, where an immense broomhead swung high over the entrance. Kirby knew every one of them. He had lived half his life in this city, and he thought he must know every inch of its maze of narrow cobbled streets, its beautiful old timbered buildings, its hospitable inns, its wide river with the stately barges, the bridges and ferrymen carrying its citizens to and fro. He loved the noisy market in Parliament Street, the quiet churches, the peaceful courtyards, as well as the dark and stinking alleys. And, rising over it all, there was the majestic beauty of the Minster. To see the city unfolding before him moved him as little else could.

The carriage had crossed the Ouse Bridge and swung left down Coney Street. In a few moments he would be back at the house in Monkgate. The prospect of spending the evening there suddenly did not suit his mood. He rapped with his cane and directed his coachman to set him down at the George Inn a few yards ahead and to go on without him; he would walk home later.

The George Inn was only one of nearly two hundred hostelries in York, but in Kirby's opinion, it was the best. And since it was not his practice to settle for anything less, he seldom visited any of the others—except occasionally the Black Swan, further along the street. The front of the George was decorated with some handsome and intricate plasterwork: friezes of flowers entwined with whorls and scrolls, and patterns and figures and curious fantasies beautified its old timber walls.

Inside, the inn was equally appealing to the weary traveler's eye and senses. The rooms were kept very warm, the floor was always well swept, the seating restful, the copper and brass well polished, the ale unwatered and the food excellent. In addition, the innkeeper was a genial and courteous host.

The Leeds mail coach had just come in, and the main parlor was crowded with people, all still dressed in heavy, damp-smelling traveling clothes, with pinched, cold faces. As many as could get in front of the big log fire were busy thawing out their frozen hands and feet. Kirby pushed his way past them and ordered some wine and a dish of mutton to be brought to one of the smaller parlors. He found the room empty and pleasantly quiet after the other; there was a fire burning in the grate and a comfortable, well-worn oak settle beside it. The meal was brought to him promptly by the innkeeper himself, with the appropriate deference due to an important patron. As he had expected, the boiled mutton was very appetizing and the red wine good.

He ate steadily and was on the point of finishing when Henry Latham appeared in the doorway.

"Kirby! This is a piece of good fortune to find you here. I called at your house this morning to be told you were out of York; they didn't know when to expect you back."

Kirby waved one hand towards the empty seat on the other side of the fire. "Sit down, Henry."

"I'm not disturbing you?"

"Nay, I've finished. And I'm all ears. What did you want to see me about?"

Henry sat down and stretched out his long legs. He hesitated for a moment and then said carefully: "I've been thinking about this vote buying."

"Aye? What about it?"

Henry cleared his throat. "Is it really necessary, Kirby? I know it's common practice, but I can't help feeling that I'd prefer to be elected because men *want* to vote for me, not because they've been bribed to do so."

Kirby was looking down at the glass in his hand; there was a tiny speck of ash in the wine and he removed it deftly with one finger. When he raised his head his eyes were hard.

"I hope this is only a temporary fit of moral rectitude, Henry, or I'll begin to fancy I've backed the wrong horse. I thought you'd more gumption."

Henry said stiffly: "I'm sorry. You're entitled to be angry. You've done a lot to help me."

"You're mistaken, lad; I'm not angry—just disappointed. I've spent a lot of time and trouble on you because I thought you were worth it. I thought you'd a strong enough stomach for the fight. You'd best get one thing straight and clear in your mind now: if you want to get to Westminster you're going to have to *pay* for the privilege, like everybody else. If we don't buy votes for you, then the Whigs'll get 'em instead and you won't stand a cat's chance of being elected." He raised his glass and drank from it slowly, staring across at Henry. "Oh aye, I can see that it doesn't really match up to your idea of gentlemanly behavior. I daresay they don't act quite like that on the hunting field—or mebbe they do, I wouldn't know—but if you've been treasuring an innocent's notion that you can afford to act like a sporting gentleman in politics then now's the time to disillusion yourself."

Henry opened his mouth to reply but Kirby silenced him, wagging a forefinger. "Do you imagine that the Whigs don't do just the same as us? Of course they do, and worse. They use gangs of rowdies to intimidate electors at the booths. We don't threaten any man, but we pay the market price for his vote— three pounds for a plumper—else we'd be bloody fools. The Tory Party'll be spending nigh on two thousand pounds for this next election and a thousand pounds or more for rewards after it, and every penny spent will count towards your winning. If you can't accept that then stand down now and go back to that fine country estate of yours."

He had spoken with a brutal and calculated contempt.

Henry Latham flushed deeply and looked troubled. "I suppose I have no choice but to condone bribery."

"Not if you want to be Member of Parliament for York." Kirby set down his empty wineglass and said more kindly: "Put away that gentleman's conscience of yours, Henry, or it'll lose you your seat. Listen to me. The Poor Laws have cost the Whigs too dear, and at the next election they'll be out of power—mark my words. And just to help you on the way even more, they're fast losing their popularity in York. The present Lord Mayor has obliged us by making sure he doesn't get himself reelected, and do you know why? He conveniently forgot to pay all those who voted him into office. No one's forgotten *that*. So, next time round, we'll have a Tory Lord Mayor instead and a Tory Council." He eyed Henry speculatively. "Let's have no more of your lily-white scruples, lad. I want you at Westminster to support our Railway Bill."

"How have things progressed with the Railway Committee?"

"Well, I've spent today with three landowners on the route Tannahill is proposing. The first two of 'em will oppose it for a while, but I fancy adequate compensation and a seat on the railway company board will win them over in the end, as well as some persuasive and soothing words from you, if you'll oblige us."

"Give me their names and I'll do all I can. What about the third?"

"He can't wait to see it built."

"That's a surprise! Who's he?"

"A Quaker by the name of Amos Gurney who has an estate and colliery at Garford."

"Amos Gurney! But I know him well. His late wife and my mother were very close friends. We used to visit Benbow Hall often when I was a child. Mind you, I haven't seen anything of him since Elizabeth Gurney died. Her death was a terrible loss to him, and he lives almost a recluse's life."

"Aye, and he's a dying man himself now, I'd say by the look of him."

Henry frowned. "Are you sure? I'm sad to hear that. Poor Hester. If her father dies she'll be alone at Benbow."

"Ah yes, the schoolteacher daughter. I didn't meet her. She'll be a rich lass when her father goes." He grinned. "You'll be doing me a favor, Henry, if you wed her before anyone else does, seeing that you know her so well. Otherwise we may have to deal with a much less obliging husband if her father dies before the railway is built."

"Oh, Hester and I are like brother and sister to each other," Henry replied, laughing at the idea. "Besides, she's only a child, not a schoolteacher."

"She's nearly seventeen and she runs a school for miners' children."

"Good lord! Is she really—and does she? I'd forgotten that she must have left the nursery. Quakers only marry Quakers, don't you know, otherwise they're disowned."

"In that case the lawyer cousin will probably get his heiress in the end."

"You must mean William. Was he there too? I knew him as a child. He was at Benbow sometimes, but I see little of him now. He's a highly successful lawyer in York, of course, as you probably know. But I'm delighted to hear that Amos is so much in favor of the railway."

"With his colliery so close, it's unlikely he'd've been against it," Kirby said dryly. "Even so, I'll admit I was still surprised by such enthusiasm. I thought he'd object to it crossing his parkland at least."

"You're too cynical, Kirby. Amos is a good man. His colliery would have been only part of his reason for accepting it. The benefit it will do for Garford would have been his principle consideration."

Kirby looked skeptical. "Maybe, maybe. He was better than most Quakers I've ever met, I'll grant you. They're so moral and upright, they bore me stiff. They're a tedious lot."

"I'm sorry you think them so. I think them just the reverse—fascinating and worthy people, and nothing like as dull as they first appear. I can assure you, Kirby, that some of the very best performers of my acquaintance in the hunting fields, in the ballroom and at the card tables are gentlemen to be found every Sunday sitting solemnly and silently under their black hats at the Meeting House, waiting for divine illumination."

Kirby laughed loudly. He got to his feet. "Well, I'm off,

Henry. You'll find me in York for the next day or two if you get any more wild notions."

Henry rose too and followed him out into the street.

"You remember that new singer I told you about, Kirby? You really should come and see her. She's at the Theatre Royal this evening, and I've reserved a box. Come and hear her. I guarantee that you won't regret it."

Kirby was tired and feeling rather sleepy after the good food and wine, but he was still not in the mood to return to Monkgate. He agreed and the two men walked the short distance down Coney Street to the theatre's entrance in Lop Lane.

A playbill on the wall outside the doors informed the passing public that this present Thursday Evening would be performed the *Musical Play of Clari*, or, *The Maid of Milan*, composed by Henry Bishop. Underneath was a complete list of characters and performers, as well as mention of some of the songs to be rendered. Henry jabbed his finger against one name.

"There you are. Miss Love is taking the part of Clari. You'll see how splendid she is."

Kirby grunted and yawned. The theatre was a shabby-looking place with peeling paint and litter accumulated like flotsam round its entrance. There was no separate entrance to the boxes, which prejudiced the attendance of the better-class patrons, who were accustomed to some degree of privacy from their inferiors. Kirby had been once before, and the play he had seen had been so atrociously performed that he had never bothered to repeat the experience.

Henry was continuing to read from the bill: there were some additional attractions offered.

"*A Fancy Wreath Dance by Miss Beckwith and Miss Hatton; A Grotesque Dance by Mr. J. Green*. Great heavens! I hope we've missed those."

They went in through a dim and dreadfully dingy saloon. When they found their box and sat down the evening's entertainment had already begun. The auditorium was in darkness and the box stage brightly illuminated by gas lighting. The large unwashed pit audience below them was restless and noisy, and there was an overpowering stench rising with the heat. Onstage, two oversized ladies, coyly dressed in frilly white muslin and pink satin ribboning, were tripping about the boards, trailing long wreaths of paper flowers while they rotated in time to soulful music from the orchestra.

"As graceful as a pair of elephants," Henry said, appalled.

The patrons of the pit evidently shared his opinion, for very soon the musicians' tuneless scraping was drowned by their hisses and boos. Miss Beckwith and Miss Hatton danced on grimly to the end and retired into the wings as hurriedly as their pride would allow.

The second turn fared no better. Mr. J. Green's Grotesque Dance was greeted by a fresh outburst of derision from the pit, and rotten tomatoes and bad eggs sailed through the air to rain on the unfortunate man. Like his predecessors, he carried on courageously and finally backed off the stage, nodding and bowing and smiling as though he had been rapturously received.

Kirby stood up. "Well, I've seen enough bloody rubbish for one evening."

Henry caught at his sleeve. "They're performing Clari next. Wait and see this. You mustn't miss her."

Reluctantly Kirby sat down and waited impatiently for the tattered red curtain to be cranked up again. At last it rose with much jerking and stopping, and the musical play began. For once the management appeared to have spent some money on the scenery, which had been freshly painted, and some of the costumes looked promisingly good. The audience, still boisterous and objectionable from the previous attempts, grew quieter and good-naturedly bided their time and their verdict. Kirby folded his arms across his chest and shut his eyes; he began to doze off.

He was awakened by Henry digging his elbow into his side.

"That's Miss Love. *Now* what do you say?"

Kirby stared down at the exquisite beauty who stood at the center of the stage. She was dressed in cornflower blue and was very slender, with a tiny waist. Her blond hair was curled in shining ringlets that bobbed charmingly about her face. He could not tell the exact color of her eyes from such a distance: he saw only that they were brilliant and sparkling.

The singer stepped forward a little towards her audience and stood alone, perfectly poised, with both arms lightly extended, the palms of her hands turned upward in supplication as though entreating a fair hearing from the darkened ranks below her. The incessant shuffling and muttering ceased as though by some magic spell; the orchestra struck up and, for the first time that evening, played in tuneful unison. Miss Love began to sing, and her voice was amazingly pure and clear; it filled the run-down, stuffy little theatre with a rare sweetness and quality.

> "'Mid pleasures and palaces though one may roam,
> Be it ever so humble there's no place like home!
> A charm from the skies seems to hallow us there,
> Which seek through the world, is ne'er met with elsewhere.
>
> Home! Home, Sweet, Sweet Home!
> There's no place like Home! There's no place like Home!
>
> An exile from Home, splendour dazzles in vain!
> Oh! Give me my lowly thatch'd cottage again!
> The birds singing gaily that came at my call,
> Give me them with the peace of mind dearer than all!
>
> Home! Home, Sweet, Sweet Home!
> There's no place like Home! There's no place like Home!"

Applause, like thunder, rolled round the walls. The audience would not let the singer go or the play continue until she had repeated the song twice more. And when the curtain came down for the last time at the end, Miss Love took many calls, curtsying with a dancer's grace and laughing and waving her hand with unaffected delight at her reception, while generously including her aging leading man and fellow performers although they had done regrettably little to deserve a share in the acclaim.

With the illumination of the gas brackets along the front of the boxes all illusion was instantly shattered. Flaking plaster, faded paint and threadbare draperies of tawdry green and gold met the eye. Ten years previously the theatre's interior had been remodeled into a semicircular form with two tiers of boxes, a gallery and a large pit. Since then lack of profits had prevented a long succession of managers from any refurbishing, despite ingenious efforts to attract more customers with burlettas, melodramas, harlequinades, rope dances, performing animals, jugglers, fire-eaters and extravaganzas with trapdoors and elaborate stage machinery.

"I know what you are asking yourself, Kirby," Henry said as they made their way out of their box. "You are wondering how it is possible to find such a jewel as Miss Love in a place like this. She should be in London—at Covent Garden or Drury Lane. How would you like to meet her? I have already made her acquaintance to offer her my congratulations. Shall I inquire if she will see us?"

"Aye, do that."

Kirby was no longer feeling tired. The singer had appealed to him very much: she had all the vitality and style that he liked in women, as well as outstanding beauty.

They walked round to the stage door, a poky little entrance where several people were already gathered. Henry handed his card to the doorkeeper.

"Give my compliments to Miss Love, please, and ask if she will receive me for a few minutes to present a good friend of mine."

The man, recognizing both Henry and Kirby, beckoned them inside. They waited in a narrow, brick-walled passageway, and after the stifling heat of the auditorium it felt cold and draughty. The doorkeeper returned to conduct them up a bare wooden stairway and along another passage. He knocked at a door and then opened it to let them go inside.

It was a small, square-shaped room with one high window covered by red curtains. There was a velvet chair of the same color, missing one front castor, and two other plain chairs; a screen concealed the far corner of the room beneath the window. A dressing table stood against one wall, lit by two gas brackets and littered untidily with boxes and pots of powder and grease-paints. The singer was sitting at this and turned at their entrance.

"Mr. Latham—*another* visit! What a compliment you are paying me!"

With unaccustomed extravagance, Henry bowed over her

hand. "Allow me to say, Miss Love, that your singing this evening was magic itself."

She thanked him and turned her eyes to Kirby; they widened. "And is *this* your friend?"

Henry hastened to make the introduction. Miss Love smiled up at Kirby.

"Oh, I have heard of *you*, Mr. England. You are *very* well known in York. I am highly honored that you should want to meet me."

It was said with a pretty provocativeness, and another man would have responded with a gallant and flowery phrase; Kirby said nothing. The singer had risen from her chair, and he looked her over slowly and with great interest.

Close to, she was everything he had hoped she would be. She was taller than he had expected, but her looks were as breathtaking offstage as on. She still wore the blue gown, and he saw that her eyes matched it in color and were fringed with long curving lashes. Her complexion—unlike those of most actresses he had ever met—was flawless, and her speaking voice as melodious as her singing one. The blond ringlets were no false addition but a natural part of her hair, which was quite as lustrous as it had looked from afar.

Henry looked from one to the other and waited expectantly for Kirby to speak, but when his companion merely continued to stare at Miss Love he felt it necessary to cover the omission with more compliments of his own, particularly about the song, "Home Sweet Home," that she had sung so well.

"Oh, did you like it?" she said, turning to smile at him. "I've sung it so many times now I think I shall *scream* if I ever have to do so again. But it's very popular with the patrons, so I mustn't disappoint them." She glanced once more at Kirby. "Next week we are performing Auber's opera, *Fra Diavolo,* with *entirely* new scenery. You must come and see it, Mr. England. I have two important songs, 'On Yonder Rock Reclining' and 'O Joy of Hour,' and I don't know which I dislike the more!"

She was laughing at—or with—him, and he smiled slowly in return. Her frankness and lack of conceit amused him. He also recognized in her a fellow traveler, one who, like himself, had started from humble beginnings and who would permit nothing to deter her from her progress to success. She was a woman after his own heart.

Henry looked at his watch and gave a sudden exclamation of dismay: "I'd forgotten I'd promised to call on the Derbys this evening! They'll think me the most ill-mannered brute for being so late, and he'd pledged me his support in my campaign."

"Then you'd best hurry," Kirby said. "Though Alfred Derby won't make any difference to your election. For all his huffing and puffing he's not worth a brass farthing of influence to anyone."

"Nonetheless, I'd better go."

"Please yourself then, lad."

Henry took a polite farewell of the singer and hurried from the room. There was a short silence.

"Well, Mr. England . . ."

"Well, Miss Love . . ." he responded.

They looked at each other.

"I'll escort you home," he said, making it a statement, not a question.

Rosa Love turned away to her looking glass and pretended to busy herself combing her hair. She watched him surreptitiously, thinking hard. She saw that he was a domineering man who would not easily take no for an answer. Even so, she was not in the least nervous of him. Some of the admirers who called at her dressing room, or who waited for her at the stage door, were a nuisance and could sometimes be alarming. They were usually either painfully shy and clumsy or else crude and boorish in the extreme, assuming that because she was an actress they were under no obligation to treat her as a lady. But this man was none of those things, and far from overloading her with fulsome compliments, he had not so far paid her a single one, yet his eyes told her clearly that he found her pleasing. He was not a born gentleman—that was obvious at once from his voice and manner. She was accustomed to contending with wealthy young rakes and could assess a man's income to within a few pounds from his style and dress. Mr. England's clothes were far from high fashion, but she recognized excellent cut and quality when she saw it.

She peered more closely into the looking glass, fiddling with a ringlet; he was leaning against the wall behind her, arms folded across his chest. She considered him carefully. She liked his dark, rather coarse, good looks, the powerful breadth of his shoulders, his thick black hair and curling side-whiskers; and, most of all, she liked the aura of strength and self-confidence about him. He was rich and successful and, from what she had heard, likely to be much richer and even more successful. So far her own life had been one bitter struggle against poverty; her profession was too precarious and ill paid for her not to appreciate a piece of good fortune when it came her way.

Rosa Love reached her decision. She changed out of the blue gown behind the screen in the corner and reappeared in one of a similar shade, simpler but just as flattering. Then she put on a little blue bonnet lavishly decorated with flowers and ribbons and allowed Kirby to drape her mantle about her shoulders. She looked up at him candidly.

"I'm grateful for your protection, Mr. England. The streets can be unpleasant at this time of night. I have rented lodgings only a few minutes' walk away in Stonestreet."

He offered her his arm. "It's on my way."

A few people still waited outside the theatre, and one man, the worse for drink, pushed his way forward and seized hold of Rosa's arm, leering at her. Unhurriedly Kirby reached out and sent him sprawling into the gutter. They walked on down Lop Lane. Rosa rubbed at her arm.

"Thank you for that. They can be very persistent."

"No trouble, lass. I used to wrestle a lot years ago. Never lost the knack, and it comes in useful now 'n' again."

She smiled a little to herself in the darkness of the street. It was pleasant to walk along beside this big man and, for once, to feel perfectly safe. So long as he was with her she would come to no harm.

They waited to let a carriage go by, stepping back out of reach of the spray of slush that spurted from behind its churning wheels, and then crossed in front of the Minster. The great cathedral loomed above them, dark and silent in the winter night; the gas lamps standing round its base were dwarfed into little glowworm lights. They turned down Petergate and then right into Stonestreet. Rosa stopped at a house halfway down the cobbled lane.

"This is where I lodge."

He glanced up at the brick building; it was modest but cared for.

"I've rooms on the first floor," she said, following his look. "It's not a palace, but it's better than most of the places I've been in." She hesitated, trying to judge his mood. "Will you come in? I've some good port wine if you'd like a glass."

He shifted his gaze from the house down to her face. She thought, in panic, that he was going to mock at her or, worse still, just walk away. But he said quietly:

"Aye—that'd be nice."

Without another word she unlocked the door and led the way up a steep flight of stairs that rose directly from inside the entrance.

He was surprised by the place: it was altogether better appointed than he had expected. She showed him into a room where one gas wall bracket was already burning low; she turned it up and lit the other two, and the yellow light flickered and spread, revealing some plain but comfortable furniture, a patterned carpet on the floor and red flocked paper on the walls. A coal fire glimmered in the grate and above the mantelpiece there was a handsome mahogany-framed looking glass.

Rosa went to remove her bonnet and mantle and returned to find him prodding the fire into life with the brass poker. His back was to her and she watched him for a moment before moving. He was the first man she had invited to her lodgings for many weeks; not the first ever by a long way—nobody could live in the world of the theatre and remain chaste. She had learned young that the more obliging the actress, the better the parts. However, she had been as discriminating as possible even when it had been almost a matter of survival. The greater her success, the more she had found she could pick and choose as she pleased; it was no longer so much a question of having enough food to eat and a roof over her head but whether a certain gentleman might, or might not, help her further along her road to fame and fortune. She had been careful never to indulge in any sentimental attachment that might cloud her judgment.

She fetched the port decanter and glasses from the sideboard, chatting gaily to him as she did so. Gentlemen, she knew, liked and expected her to sparkle and amuse. It came naturally to her to be vivacious, but tonight, as luck would have it, she had a headache, and when he failed to respond she began to think that she had badly misjudged him. To her surprise, he told her to sit down.

"No need for all that talk with me, lass. I'm not a great one for idle chatter."

Gratefully, she sank down into a chair beside the fire; he remained standing, leaning against the mantelpiece with one arm resting along its edge.

"Tell me about yourself. Where d'you come from? How've you got here to York?"

This was not the sort of exchange she had expected: few people were interested in her past life. She said wryly:

"Scarborough. I was born there and lived there all my life until two years ago."

"A Yorkshire lass!" He was surprised. "I'd taken you for a southerner."

"My mother came from the South; she only came north when she married my father, and she never learned to like Scarborough—or Yorkshire."

"It's a fine place."

She wrinkled her nose at him. "I'm afraid I agreed with her; I don't like the North either—it's too cold, too gray and too wet."

He let that pass. "What about your father?"

"His work meant so much to him I don't think he would have cared where he lived. He was a Methodist minister."

"A Methodist minister with an actress daughter!"

"Oh, I didn't go into the theatre until after his death. Satan's synagogue, he used to call it. But my mother paid for me to have singing lessons secretly—she saved up the money somehow and he never knew. I should never have managed it without her."

53

"And after the singing lessons?"

She shrugged her shoulders a little. "There's not much to tell. Both my parents died in a fever epidemic when I was eighteen. There was a little money left, just enough to keep me alive until I found work at a theatre in Hull. The York Theatre Royal Company came there on tour last autumn, and when they left I persuaded them to let me go with them as a singer in the chorus. We went to Doncaster, Wakefield and Leeds and, finally, came back here. By that time they'd decided I was good enough to take bigger parts."

"And where next? London, I suppose?"

Her blue eyes shone brilliantly in the gaslight. "Yes . . . London . . . and Covent Garden, if it'll ever have me. Or Drury Lane. I won't stay a *day* longer in the North than I can help. Oh, I like York well enough, but the Theatre Royal is a dreadful place to work in. Do you know that the stage is so old we have to step round the rotten boards in case we fall through them? And the scenery is horribly bad; there are hardly any props worth speaking of. The same moth-eaten grove scene drop and the same old rustic bridge has been used in every presentation, and I am heartily sick of the sight of the triumphal arch and castle gates!"

He laughed, and she went on, smiling: "As for the manager, he is always drunk, and Mr. Webster, the leading man, is not a minute less than forty-five and quite bald under his wig!"

"And yet you go on."

"I go on, Mr. England, because I love the theatre. So long as I can go onto a stage and sing to an audience I'm happy. You don't know how wonderful it is to hear all the applause and to see rows and rows of people all smiling at me—to know that I have sung well and pleased them."

"And if it should go wrong and they throw bad eggs and fruit instead?"

"They've never done that to me yet and I don't intend that they should ever have cause to. Do you think that I sing that badly, Mr. England?"

"I think you sing like an angel," he replied.

"Do you realize," she said with mock solemnity, "that that's the first compliment you've paid me?"

"The first, mebbe—but not the last."

The gas lamp on the wall above her head began to hiss and pop. She got up and struggled to adjust it, but it continued to splutter and flicker wildly. She grimaced.

"I hate this new lighting—it terrifies me. With candles I knew where I was, but with these lamps I'm frightened they will explode."

He reached across in front of her and regulated the offending light so that it burned steadily once more. The movement had brought him very close to her; he stood looking down at her, one hand still against the wall beside the bracket. "The iron pipes get rusted and clogged," he said. "And the burners silt up. That's the trouble."

Rosa was quite tall, but he seemed to tower over her; she noticed that his lashes were as black as his hair and as thick and long as any woman's.

"You haven't drunk any of your port wine, Mr. England."

"I hate the stuff, Miss Love. Brandy's my drink."

"Next time I'll see that there's some for you."

They looked at each other in silence. He took his hand away from the wall and lifted her chin with one finger.

"You'll find me a good lover," he said.

She made no reply. His touch had made her tremble. She did not move. At last he bent his head to kiss her lips, and when he drew her into his arms she leaned for a moment against him and closed her eyes, savoring the sheltering strength of him. When he began to kiss her again, much less gently, she made no protest but lifted her arms to his neck. In a little while she led him to the other room.

CHAPTER III

Her parents held the Quaker rule,
Which doth the human feeling cool;
But she was train'd in Nature's school;
Nature had blest her.

A waking eye, a prying mind;
A heart that stirs, is hard to bind;
A hawk's keen sight ye cannot blind;
Ye could not Hester.

Charles Lamb

Aunt Kitty's house was at No. 1 Precentor's Court, a quiet little cul-de-sac near the Minster where the sound of the cathedral clock striking passed the leisurely hours with mellow chimes.

The house was small and simple in exterior; it had a plain brick façade, white-painted sash windows and four spotless stone steps with an iron handrail which led up to the front door.

But inside simplicity gave way to a bewildering array of furniture and decoration. Despite her strict Quaker upbringing which frowned on all frivolous furniture, unnecessary ornament and ostentation, Aunt Kitty had a great weakness for all three. Her small house was crammed from top to bottom with all kinds of knickknacks. She justified everything by explaining that it was all entirely functional or essential, for one reason or another.

Her front parlor, a room which contained scarcely an empty square inch, must have plenty of comfortable chairs for visitors

to sit on, and it was only sensible that they should be uphol-
stered in the very best quality materials since these lasted so
much longer than their cheaper counterparts, which made it an
economy, not an extravagance, and therefore, in Aunt Kitty's
view, perfectly in accord with Quaker principles. The same was
argued for the sumptuous red velvet curtains, the large quantity
of silk cushions and for the thick-piled carpet on the floor. The
magnificent gilded looking glass over the fireplace helped to
lighten the room and therefore saved on gas and candles. The
French porcelain clock on the mantelpiece was required to tell
her the correct time in case, with increasing deafness, she failed
to hear the Minster's chimes. As for the exquisite little escritoire in
the corner, it was used for working at all her correspondence and
could not be considered other than strictly functional, while the
several colorful footstools scattered about the room like exotic
toadstools, and all beautifully embroidered, helped relieve the
rheumatic pains in her legs. Her nerve had failed her over the
ivory inlaid surface of the table and she had covered it with a
chenille cloth, but the splendor of a four-branched gas chandelier was impossible to conceal, and at night the golden arms
glowed richly in the light from the white opalescent globes suspended like four moons above the table. All ornaments and pictures could be excused on the grounds that many of them had
been given as gifts, and as she could not now remember who
had given which or what, it was impossible to get rid of a single
one without the possibility of giving someone offense.

Hester Gurney was very fond of both Aunt Kitty and her
house. Respecting her father's insistence on simple living at Benbow Hall, she nevertheless found the riotous contrast at No. 1
Precentor's Court enthralling. Her favorite room was the parlor,
and on a sunny morning during her visit to her aunt in York in
this spring of 1834, she sat down in one of the armchairs and
looked about her with pleasure.

Nothing had changed since her last visit many months ago; indeed, the nicest thing about the house was its constant, unalter-
ing familiarity. She knew every item in the room intimately since
the days when she used to visit with her mother as a child, sitting then on the same chair as she sat on now, her feet in their

black buttoned boots sticking straight out before her, too short to reach the sinking softness of the red patterned carpet. Everything was still the same: carpet, curtains, chairs, pictures, ornaments . . . She touched the arm of the chair: the brown velvet was a little faded here and there but that was all, bearing out Aunt Kitty's theory that the most expensive was the cheapest in the end. She picked up the bobbin holder from the table beside her; she had played with it often as a child, and now she spun it again so that the reels of colored silks blurred and blended before her eyes.

"To see thee sitting there and doing that reminds me of when thou wast a solemn, round-faced little girl. Thou used to play with that holder for hours."

Aunt Kitty had come into the room. She smiled at Hester over the rims of her spectacles. She was a plump woman, as comfortable-looking as her parlor, and though she was dressed in a plain Quaker gown of drab with a white shawl collar and a white day bonnet, it was nonetheless obvious to a discerning eye that the drab was of the best grade and that both bonnet and collar were of the finest workmanship.

"I was thinking to myself, Aunt Kitty, that one reason why I love to visit thee is that I know that everything will be exactly as it has always been."

"Thou makes me sound very dull, child."

"That thou couldst *never* be!"

Her aunt looked relieved. "I'm glad thou thinks so. I know I am a foolish old woman, but I shouldn't care one bit to be thought of as dull. Almost anything seems better than that."

She came to sit near her niece and spread out on the table some cloth patterns that she had been carrying .

"Now, my dear child, I want thee to help me choose for my new spring dress."

The materials lay discreetly against the chenille cloth; all were in sober colors of gray, drab and brown of varying shades and all were silks of beautiful quality. Aunt Kitty fingered each one in turn, and no gay society dame could have been more eager or more anxious in making her choice.

"I think this dove gray would be best. What dost thou say, Hester dear?"

"I think it's lovely."

Aunt Kitty put her head on one side. "But perhaps the dark brown might be more *serviceable*. What dost thou think?"

The discussion lasted for some time before she finally decided on the dove gray that she had selected in the first place.

"As to the style, of course, it must be quite plain." She sighed wistfully. "I should dearly love to have some ribbons."

"Then why not?"

Aunt Kitty shook her head. "With ribbons I know I should be nervous. Thou hast no idea how extravagant I am already considered among Friends. At Meeting for Worship only last First Day, Minister Caleb Williams—usually such a kind and gentle man—cautioned us *most* severely against frivolous extravagance, especially in our homes. It is a weakness, he said, which bespeaks a mind engaged in trifles and a fondness for show which is inconsistent with the Christian character. And all the while he was speaking he was looking straight at *me*. I hardly knew which way to turn!"

Hester laughed. "Thou imagined it, Aunt."

"No, no, my dear. I assure thee it was so. His eye was on me all the time." She looked depressed. "I try my best, but sometimes my inadequacy stands between me and the Light."

"Then thou art not alone. I grieve Papa greatly by speaking so seldom at Meeting for Worship, but my natural disposition somehow has a great aversion to becoming a mouthpiece for the Almighty. I find nothing to say."

Her aunt's face cleared a little. "Ours is not an easy faith, is it, my dear? Thy dear father, of course, is blessed with a most godly spirit. I'm sure he has never had a minute's doubt in his life—or not that I can remember. When we were children together he was always reproaching me for my frothiness of behavior, and with good reason, for I was a very silly and vain little girl. When thy mama died, God rest her soul, I was so afraid that he would not allow thee to visit me here; he disapproves of this house, as thou must know, and thinks me a poor example."

"He knows how fond I am of thee, Aunt Kitty. Of course he would not stop me coming to see thee."

"As I am fond of thee, child. Thou art my only niece, and having no children of my own, I should be very sad to lose thy company on these little visits."

"Thou needst have no fear of that."

Aunt Kitty smiled at her niece with affection. "I am so thankful to know that thy papa's health is better."

"It was so last week or I should not have left him." Hester put down the bobbin holder carefully. "I have been so worried, Aunt, for fear that he was getting worse. All this long, cold winter his cough has been dreadful. With the spring it seems to have improved, but now there is all this trouble over the railway—"

"Railway? What railway?"

Hester explained. "The odd thing is that from the day that this man came to see Papa he has seemed to improve and has been more cheerful than I have seen him for a long time. He is so much in favor of this railway being built—it has been a dream of his for years."

"*I* should not care for such a thing to come anywhere near *my* home," Aunt Kitty said in dismay. "It will quite ruin the deer park at Benbow."

"But as Papa constantly reminds me, it will also benefit the people of Garford, as well as our colliery. It's not the railway itself that I am so anxious about, Aunt; it's the man who has to do with its building, Kirby England. I am so afraid that he may not be as honest as Papa believes him to be. William has warned me against him, but Papa will not listen. Tell me, what dost *thou* know of Kirby England?"

Aunt Kitty cleared her throat and fiddled with the patterns. "My dear, what an awkward question. I hear so many tales told in York. I'm sure half are quite untrue and few would have much to do with *business* affairs—more likely affairs of the heart, if thou understands me. All that I know of Kirby England is that he is a draper who has made a fortune, whether by honest means or not, I really couldn't say. I *do* know that he has a beautiful house in Monkgate with a deer park, that he entertains most lavishly and has all the trappings of considerable wealth—fine

clothes, carriages, horses, servants . . . I have never met him myself, but I'm told he's very rough in speech and manners. His
mother is certainly a very vulgar woman. I met her once—a very
strange creature, loudmouthed and pushing, and with no taste at
all and the most peculiar clothes. I couldn't help feeling sorry for
her though: everyone was laughing at her behind her back. I believe she has a daughter too, but she is much younger than the
son. Of course, the Englands are not asked in the very *best* circles." She lowered her voice and her cheeks colored pink. "His
mistresses are the talk of York, my dear; he changes them like
hats! The latest, I hear, is a singer from the Theatre Royal; a
pretty little thing, so they say, but thou dost not need me to
remind thee what *dreadful* sinfulness abounds in the theatre.
Thy papa would certainly never let thee come here again if he
knew I was even speaking to thee of such things."

"I don't care in the least how many mistresses this man has
but only that he does not cheat Papa or do anything that might
harm him."

"Thy father is a wise man, child. I don't believe he would be
fooled by anyone."

"He is also a sick one, and William surely knows better in this
case, since he lives in York. Yet Papa *will* not listen to him."

Aunt Kitty snorted. "As to that, my sympathy lies with thy father. I'm sure that if Cousin William were to tell me to do one
thing I should do another out of sheer vexation. Clever he may
be, but I do not care for his superior ways; he is always at great
pains to make me feel foolish and at fault. It is a constant mys-
tery to me how the Almighty can bring Himself to speak through
William Gurney so often at Meeting for Worship. Scarcely a First
Day goes by without him being inspired to open his mouth at
length."

"Thou art being unfair, Aunt. Thou art unreasonably prejudiced against him."

"Where William is concerned thou hast a blind spot, my dear.
Thou art too used to thinking of him as older and wiser than
thyself. And he has a great regard for thee, as thou must realize."
She touched Hester's arm. "I hope thou wilt never be so mista-

ken as to consider marriage with him. I know thou wouldst not be happy."

"He has not asked me, Aunt."

"Nor will he do so, I think, while thy father is alive and thou art still not twenty-one years old. Thy papa does not wish thee to marry thy cousin. But William will bide his time; he is the kind of man who will wait a long while to gain what he wants."

"Don't let's argue about William, Aunt Kitty. Tell me instead how I can contrive to meet Kirby England. Much as I love to come here, I must admit that the ulterior motive for this visit to York was to see him and confront him. I want to judge for myself what manner of man he is."

"I don't see how such a thing could easily be arranged," Aunt Kitty said, looking alarmed. "It sounds most unsuitable."

"Then I shall simply go round to this fine house of his in Monkgate, knock loudly on the door and ask to see him!"

"I beg thou wilt do no such thing! Give me time and I may think of some way it can be done."

Aunt Kitty thought hard, knowing her niece to be perfectly capable of doing exactly as she had said.

"There is one way perhaps; Henry Latham knows him well. When he called on me a little while ago he spoke of Kirby England helping him with his election campaign. It might be arranged—" She stopped suddenly and shook her head. "Oh no, my dear, the more I think about it, the less advisable it seems."

"I am determined, Aunt," Hester said, her chin up and wearing a look that told Aunt Kitty that she was fighting a hopeless battle.

"Very well, I will do what I can. Henry may help us, but I promise nothing. He must be very busy now. I can hardly believe that he is our Member for Parliament. It seems such a short time ago that he used to call here with his mother as a child; he was a shy boy who hardly uttered a word and was very fond of chocolate cake. Dost thou remember?"

"I haven't seen him for years. After Mama died he didn't come to Benbow anymore. Nobody did. Papa has not wanted visitors."

"Thou wilt find him changed; he is no longer shy and has become very handsome-looking." Aunt Kitty looked at her niece

63

thoughtfully. "Of course, he is one of the most eligible young men in York, if not in the whole county."

Hester seemed uninterested. She persisted: "Thou said that Kirby England helped Henry with his campaign, didst thou not? That must mean that he was responsible for all the bribery and corruption that won the day—"

"Hester! How canst thou say such a thing! I'm sure that Henry was fairly elected. Why, I should certainly have voted for him myself if I were a man."

"But it's perfectly true, Aunt. I read about it in the *York Courant* this morning." She picked up the newspaper from the table. "Listen to this if thou dost not believe me. *This election has been discreditable to the city. Where is the morality, the common decency of those brawlers for the altar and throne? They brought up their hired voter, reeling from the dram shop, to hiccup forth the bribery oath and perjure themselves in the face of their neighbors! Where is the morality of bringing to the poll, men—we almost repudiated the term, when applied to such in a state of beastly intoxication—to exercise one of the most solemn and important rights of freemen? Carriages, too, which bring up the halt and the sick, have now been kept in constant requisition, to carry the healthy and the strong, except they might be incapacitated by inebriation, some two or three hundred yards from their reveling rendezvous to the poll.*"

Aunt Kitty looked very upset and shocked; her chins wobbled in distress. "It grieves me to think of dear Henry implicated in such things. *Hired* voters, drunkenness, brawling, perjury—it sounds quite wicked to me."

"I don't think it's Henry's fault, Aunt. I daresay the candidate is made to dance like a puppet on strings. The blame must lie with those who work for the Party and pull those strings, men such as Kirby England. How can we trust a man who connives at such dishonesty?"

"I'm sure the Whigs are no better," Aunt Kitty said, comforting herself.

Before they could discuss the matter further, a maidservant knocked at the door and announced that Mr. Henry Latham had called and was waiting in the hall.

Aunt Kitty gave a squeak. "Now that *is* good news. And he will be delighted to find thee here, Hester."

Henry came into the room, looking tired but in good spirits, and his surprise and pleasure at seeing his childhood friend once again was equaled by hers. His eyes lit up and he seized her hands in his and held them tightly. He was amazed at the fact that she had grown into a young woman while he could remember her only as a little girl playing with her dolls. He studied her and admired the look of her. The demure gray Quaker dress with its white collar and cuffs suited her well; she was not a beauty and was only small, but her dark hair was coiled most becomingly over her ears and the wide gray eyes that had always impressed him in the child had now become unusually beautiful in the woman's face, as well as being intelligently aware.

At last he let go of her and turned to kiss Aunt Kitty's cheek, dropping a packet into her hands. "I've brought you some of your favorite mint lozenges."

"My dear boy, thou art most thoughtful. And we are so pleased to see thee. We congratulate thee, don't we, Hester, on thy success yesterday. How fortunate we are to have thee for our representative at Westminster!"

She smiled warmly at him and patted the chair beside her. "Sit down. It's most providential that thou called. Hester has a favor to ask of thee."

"If it's in my power, it shall be done."

Hester said directly: "Thou knowest a man called Kirby England, I believe."

"Heavens, yes! He seconded my nomination and has helped me ever since. But for him I should never have been elected yesterday."

Aunt Kitty coughed warningly, but Hester made no comment on this remark.

She said: "I want to meet him. Canst thou arrange it for me?"

Henry stared. "Meet Kirby? Whatever for? I doubt if you would care for him at all, Hester. He comes from a very different world from yours."

She gave him her reason and Henry was amused, as well as intrigued. He looked at her sitting small and straight on the brown velvet chair and smiled.

"The idea of you face to face with Kirby England conjures up a picture of David and Goliath in my mind," he said. "But seriously, Kirby may not act like a gentleman, but his word is as good as one's. You need have no fears, Hester. Whatever William may say, he will not cheat your father over the railway land."

She continued to look totally unconvinced, so he added obligingly: "If you really must see for yourself that he is not some wicked ogre, then nothing could be easier. The Tory Party is holding a reception at the Assembly Rooms on Thursday evening. Kirby has just left for Whitby to inspect some property he owns there, but he is expected back in time for the reception. If you and Aunt Kitty would care to come as my guests I can present him to you."

Aunt Kitty demurred. "A reception? Will there be music? And dancing?"

"There will be no music and no dancing," Henry assured her gravely. "It will be a very dull and proper affair, I promise you."

"In that case we may attend. Amos can have no objection to my taking Hester to something as respectable as that."

Henry teased her gently. "You know very well, Aunt Kitty, that nothing would keep you away from such an excellent opportunity for gossip."

She pretended to be offended. "That is not so, Henry. However, I admit that the prospect of an evening out is quite agreeable. What a pity that my new dress may not be ready in time."

"Then it's all settled," Henry told them. "I shall call for you both with my carriage at six o'clock on Thursday."

The Assembly Rooms were in Blake Street. The building was fronted by a magnificent portico with wide steps and had been a fashionable meeting place in York for four reigns. The principal room was no less than ninety feet long: a vast hall decorated in the Egyptian style with marble columns marching down each side and glass chandeliers suspended in a long line from the ornate ceiling.

By the time that Aunt Kitty and Hester arrived with Henry Latham, the rooms were already overcrowded and it was with some difficulty that they forced their way through to the Egyptian Hall.

Aunt Kitty was in fine fettle. She had bullied her dressmaker unmercifully into making up the dove-gray silk in time for her to wear her new dress. Looking this way and that and standing on tiptoe, she spotted at once several acquaintances and engaged herself happily in pointing out to Hester all those of note and distinction who were present. They gained a small oasis of space near the wall and Aunt Kitty, with a clearer view of the proceedings, quickly snapped her fan shut, turned it upside down using the closed ivory sticks as a handle and raising it to her eye to peer through the tiny spyglass joining the sticks in place of a rivet.

"I don't think that Minister Caleb Williams would approve of thy lorgnette fan," Hester said in mock reproach as she watched her aunt scanning the crowd.

"Nonsense, my dear. I find it indispensable to be able to see properly at these sorts of occasions or I might give grave offense by passing someone by. My eyesight is not what it used to be." She reversed the fan and unfurled it again in all its glory of gold sequins and brightly painted flowers on black silk, waving it vigorously in front of her face. "Also the heat can be stifling with so many people; without its aid I might easily faint and therefore be a great nuisance and inconvenience to others."

"Then thou art perfectly justified," Hester said solemnly.

Henry had vanished, dragged almost at once from their side by well-wishers, and the two Quakeresses stood together, surrounded by glitteringly gowned and bejeweled ladies, and resembling two small sparrows in a pen of tropical birds.

Henry returned with the news that he had been unable to find Kirby England anywhere. "He may have been delayed at Whitby; no one has any news of him. I hope your time won't be wasted."

Aunt Kitty assured him that it would not. "Don't fret thyself, dear boy. We are enjoying the spectacle, and I have seen many acquaintances with whom it will be a pleasure to pass the time."

"I shall have to leave you again for a while. There are several people who insist on talking politics with me and who would bore you both. I'll come back as soon as I can."

"Poor Henry," Aunt Kitty said as they watched him being accosted by a gross and hearty man who clapped him so hard across the shoulders that he winced. "Success brings penalties in its wake." She clutched suddenly at Hester's arm. "Look! There is Martha England, Kirby England's mother—over there beside the pillar. And that must be her daughter with her."

She shut her fan and fixed her eye to the little spyglass. "Yes, it is. My dear Hester, didn't thou ever see such a hideous shade of green? Poor creature, she must be color-blind."

Hester followed the direction of the spyglass and saw a tall and angular woman standing with her back to one of the marble columns. She was plain, with sharp features and a beaky nose, and her gown was far too fussy for such a severe-looking wearer. It was an elaborate concoction of bilious green with huge, stiffened and ballooning sleeves, and a profusion of ruffs and ruches festooned her from neck to ankle. A necklace of precious stones encircled her throat and heavy bracelets hung from bony wrists.

Near her stood a pale-faced girl dressed in white muslin. She was young, pretty and very shy in manner, sheltering a pace or two behind her mother and looking as though she wished to be anywhere else than where she was.

Despite Mrs. England's aggressive stance and stare, there was an air of vulnerability about the pair and they were completely alone.

"If mother and daughter are here then the son must be also," Hester said.

"Not necessarily, my dear. Martha England has certainly the nerve to come without him, even if nobody addresses a civil word to her all evening. If *he* is here they will take notice of her; we must assume, I think, that he is probably not coming." She lowered the lorgnette fan. "Poor woman, I feel sorry for her. I think I should go and speak to her—much as I should prefer to talk to someone else."

She was diverted from this good intention by the strains of an orchestra tuning up somewhere at the far end of the hall. She gave a horrified gasp.

"Music! I distinctly hear music! And Henry promised me that there would be no frivolity. What would thy papa say?"

"Nothing since he is not here to know of it," Hester reassured her aunt.

"That's very true."

"Besides, it is only a very *small* orchestra and the tune they are playing is of a most serious kind."

The musicians had launched into a stately gavotte; Aunt Kitty listened hard for a few moments. "Well, it is certainly not one of those fast waltzes. I think we may safely stay. Oh, look, Martha England and her daughter have disappeared. What a relief! Now I may go and talk to Lucy Faraday with a clear conscience. She is just over there."

"Then thou must go to her at once before she vanishes too," Hester said. "I shall stay here, Aunt. Henry will be back soon, I'm sure, and he may bring Kirby England with him."

Aunt Kitty wavered and then, seeing her old friend already moving off into the crowd, agreed. "Very well, child. Stay here. I shall just exchange a few words with Lucy and then come back myself."

She hurried off and Hester stood watching the comings and goings before her. The noise of conversation was so great that she could barely hear the orchestra above it. What exactly were they playing? She wished she knew; it sounded very pleasant. It was a pity that no music was ever heard at Benbow, but as Papa had explained many times, it was not that Friends disapproved of or disliked music, any more than they disapproved of great art, but rather that they believed that all life should be sacramental and that everyday lives of ordinary people should reveal the presence of God. But couldn't God perhaps reveal Himself also through the sound of music? She debated this while she listened.

The press was worsening every minute, and Hester, buffeted by a group of laughing and chattering people, stepped backwards to avoid them. As she did so, she blundered into someone behind her. She lost her balance and nearly fell, to be saved by a hand grasping her elbow firmly and setting her right. She turned to see a dark-haired man standing there.

"I'm exceedingly sorry," Hester said, dismayed at her own clumsiness. "I'm afraid I trod on thy foot."

He glanced down at her small black satin slippers, then at his own considerably larger feet, and said, with some amusement, that he hadn't felt a thing.

"You look lost," he said. "Are you trying to find someone?"

"No—not really."

"But you must be. You can't have come alone. I'll help you find them. I know most people here."

"I'm quite all right. I thank thee all the same."

"Nonsense," he said brusquely. "If you're trying to find someone just tell me the name and I'll do what I can. You could search for hours in this crowd."

She hesitated. He was a Yorkshireman—that much was clear from his speech—and he was probably of York. He might know Kirby England and could point him out to her without any fuss. On the other hand, he was a complete stranger and to continue talking with him like this might give an unfortunate impression. Aunt Kitty would have fifty thousand fits if she knew, but fortunately, there was no sign of her aunt. She weighed the various considerations and prudence lost the day.

"As a matter of fact, I'm looking for a man named Kirby England. Dost thou know him?"

"Oh, I know him well."

"Hast thou seen him here this evening? Couldst thou point him out to me?"

He said curiously: "What are you so anxious to see him for?"

Again Hester hesitated. She did not want to discuss private matters with a stranger; at the same time, she was afraid he might not help her if she refused to say more. Nor was it in her nature to lie easily.

"I have heard . . . certain things said of him and want to judge for myself if they are likely to be true."

"Just by looking at him?"

"I shall be able to tell a great deal of him from his appear-

70

ance," she said seriously. "A man's character is written on his face and in his manner."

"Is that so? But you'll need to talk to him as well if you want to make a proper assessment."

"Possibly."

She frowned. There was an uncomfortable suspicion now that he was mocking her.

He folded his arms and said: "Tell me, what have you heard of Kirby England that makes you so cautious of him?"

She remained silent, not wanting to reply to this.

"I'm interested," he pursued. "Do tell me what kind of a man you imagine him to be. You can do no harm by telling me that."

"Well, if thou insists—"

"I do."

"From what I have heard, he must be very boorish and vulgar."

"Aye, that's often remarked, I believe."

"And I imagine him fat, ugly and *very* conceited."

He lifted his eyebrows. "Is that so? Everything sounds against him in your eyes. Haven't you heard anything in his favor?"

"Only that he is very clever at making a lot of money, a talent which is not necessarily an asset, especially if it is not used honestly," she said. "Thou hast not said what *thou* thinks of him, knowing him well, as thou dost."

He considered the question a moment, rubbing his chin with one hand. "Now that's a hard thing to answer. What do *I* think of Kirby England . . ."

"Well, is he honest?"

"As honest as any other man I know."

"Thou art sure of that?"

"Why does it matter so much to you whether he is or not?"

"He has business dealings with my father."

"Indeed."

"Papa is very ill. I don't want anything to happen that might make him worse. Thou canst understand my difficulty?"

He looked at her in silence for a moment without speaking, then said: "Is your father's name Amos Gurney?"

"How didst thou know?" she asked, astonished.

"You have his eyes." He nodded his head to her briefly. "Excuse me, Miss Gurney. I can't help you further. I've some urgent business to see to."

He walked away and then stopped to call back over his shoulder, as an afterthought: "All the same, I'd be careful of Kirby England when you do find him if I were you. I've heard he sometimes eats Quakers for breakfast!"

She stared indignantly after him as he threaded his way through the crowd, head and shoulders above many of the guests. He had simply been making fun of her all the time. She wished very much that she had not been so indiscreet or outspoken. Aunt Kitty was always telling her that she allowed her tongue to run away with her. Supposing the stranger was a close friend of Kirby England; the conversation, repeated, might make an enemy of a man who, from all accounts, would be a powerful and unpleasant adversary.

Aunt Kitty bobbed up beside her, puffing and panting from the effort it had cost her to fight her way through the assembly. She leaned against the wall and fanned herself weakly.

"Well, my dear. So, tell me what thou thought of him."

"Of whom, Aunt?"

"Of Kirby England, of course. I saw thee talking to him a few minutes ago. Lucy Faraday told me who it was."

"*That* was Kirby England?" Hester had gone white and then red.

Aunt Kitty goggled. "But didst thou not realize? How couldst thou talk to him so long and not know who he was?" She let the fan fall slowly away from her face and peered more closely at her niece. "Thou art looking very strange, child. What didst thou say to him? I hope thou said nothing unguarded to give offense?"

"I'm afraid I did."

Aunt Kitty shut her eyes and moaned. "How often have I warned thee to guard thy tongue at all times?"

"Thou dost not understand, Aunt." Anger had begun to replace Hester's shock. "He deliberately concealed his identity from me. He should have said who he was."

"Thou canst not blame *him* for thy indiscretion." A thought came to Aunt Kitty. "But did he know who thou wast?"

"Yes—or he guessed."

"Oh dear, oh dear! Amos will say that this is all my fault for bringing thee here in the first place. If thou hast offended him badly, then thy papa's precious railway may perhaps be in jeopardy. Not being a gentleman, there is no knowing how this draper may react to insult. The lowbred can turn *very* nasty, I believe. Thou must apologize to him."

Hester looked very stubborn. "I refuse to do so, Aunt. He was quite as much to blame as I."

Aunt Kitty was prone to panic in adversity. She dragged her unwilling niece into the shade of a large potted palm tree. "If thou wilt not apologize, then we cannot allow matters to be made worse by Henry bringing him here to be introduced. We must conceal ourselves for the moment and then leave as soon as possible."

"Mrs. England, this is a great pleasure to see you here this evening."

Henry Latham bowed politely and turned to the girl, who shrank even further behind her mother, as though she hoped to remain unnoticed.

"Is this your daughter? I have not yet had the honor of an introduction. If you would present me . . ."

Mrs. England grunted and pushed Adelaide forward. "She's shy, Mr. Latham. Not used to big assemblies like this."

Henry took the hand that was timidly outstretched; it lay in his only for a second before being snatched back again. Adelaide retreated once more.

He tried to see her face properly, but her head remained bent low and she would not look at him.

"I am delighted to make your acquaintance at last, Miss England. I know your brother well. I wish I had had the privilege of meeting you before this."

He waited hopefully for a response, but she mumbled something he could not hear and kept her eyes fixed upon the floor.

Mrs. England dug her daughter in the side with a sharp elbow. "Speak up, Adelaide, or Mr. Latham will think you've no tongue in your head."

73

She lifted her gaze reluctantly. "I said that I was pleased to meet you, Mr. Latham."

He looked at her with curiosity, seeing her clearly for the first time. She was very young and extremely pretty, much fairer in coloring than her brother, and although her eyes were as dark brown as Kirby's, they were gentle and sensitive instead of bold and direct.

"Have you seen Kirby, Mr. Latham?" Mrs. England asked him impatiently. "We've been waiting some time for him. I hope he's not been kept at Whitby."

Beneath her forbidding tone he sensed that she was willing her son to appear and rescue them from the cold-shouldering they were receiving from the other guests. Henry, whose manners were both kind and impeccable, had already noticed the two standing so much alone and had gone out of his way to speak to them. If only Kirby would arrive the embarrassment would instantly be remedied. He stopped admiring Adelaide England and searched the huge hall for her brother.

"If you would like to wait here, Mrs. England, I shall go and see if I can find him and send him to you."

"I doubt if anyone could 'send' my son anywhere," she said dryly. "But if you see him, Mr. Latham, tell him we'd be obliged by his company."

He left them and, with difficulty, pursued an uninterrupted course across the hall, past many who tried hard to engage him in conversation. He had begun to despair of finding Kirby when suddenly he caught sight of his broad back, half concealed by one of the pillars. He was talking to someone but turned at that moment, and seeing Henry signaling frantically to him, came across.

"Well then, Henry, how does it feel to be hailed as our Member for Parliament wherever you go?"

Henry grinned. "Unbelievable! I shall become used to it one day, I suppose."

"Make sure you do. Those that voted you in will be watching you all the time like hyenas waiting to kill."

"I've already had a foretaste of that." Henry drew him a little

74

aside, away from a man who stood near, trying to catch their attention.

"Kirby, your mother and sister are at the other end of the hall. I have an idea that they have been standing on their own for a long time."

Kirby said grimly: "I can imagine. I've come straight from Whitby. I'd no idea they were here." He took Henry's arm. "I'll go and find them in a moment, but first I want a word with you in peace. Let's go into one of the other rooms."

They discovered a small anteroom that was empty and shut the door firmly behind them against the din of orchestra and conversation in competition. The sudden quiet was welcome. Both men were tired and sank into comfortable leather chairs. Kirby leaned back and shut his eyes. After a minute or two he opened them and Henry saw that he was in a remarkably good humor.

"We had Tannahill's survey report on the York to Leeds railway before the committee," he said. "I haven't told you about it, have I?"

"No. What did it say?"

"Just what I'd expected from him. I tramped every inch of that route with him and a more fainthearted thickwit I've yet to meet." He leaned forward in his chair. "He recommends that we use *horses*, not locomotive engines, as motive power."

"I can't say I'm surprised to hear it," Henry said cautiously. Nothing had yet convinced him of either the advantage or safety of steam. "What reasons did he give?"

"I quote him: for reasons of *economy*. In short, he's proposing that we build nothing more than a bloody little tramway."

"Then what on earth are you looking so pleased about?"

"Am I?"

"Like a dog that's caught a rabbit."

"Nay, not a rabbit, Henry, but the world's finest engineer, that's what I've caught."

"You're talking in riddles, Kirby."

"Aye. Well, guess who I met in Whitby. Just by chance he and I were there together."

75

"From what you've said, I'd say it must have been Mr. George Stephenson."

"Who else would I call the world's finest engineer? He happened to be at Whitby supervising a local railway that's being built to Pickering. Some Whitby tradesmen friends of mine introduced us and we found we'd plenty to talk about. We've something in common, after all: both of us come from poor homes in the North and both of us believe in building railways and in steam engines. That was a good basis for discussion, you might say. The only difference between us is that I've learned to read and write a damn sight better than him and he knows a damn sight more about engines than I'll ever do."

He paused to offer Henry a cigar and to light one himself. The aromatic smoke curled above their heads.

"I don't suppose you've the least notion of how much the man's had to overcome," Kirby continued. "He's put up with all kinds of ridicule and stupid ignorance; at Westminster they had an inquiry on the Liverpool–Manchester Railway before it was built and they made a complete fool of him. Clever counsel tied him in knots and got him to damn himself out of his own mouth. They thought him a maniac fit only for Bedlam because he spoke of his engines reaching twenty miles an hour! But he kept on working and building them and listened to no one. Now there's a man worth his salt—not like lily-livered Tannahill! I was that impressed. Do you know, Henry, that since 1813 he's built more than fifty steam engines, and sixteen of them locomotive? But it wasn't until the Rocket won the Rainhill trial that folks took notice of what he'd been trying to tell 'em all along. In my opinion, he's a great man."

"What can he do for you?"

"He's agreed to speak to the York Railway for me and persuade them that Mr. Tannahill's wrong. His name alone's enough to guarantee a good hearing. *And* he's offered to survey a new line himself."

"A *new* line!"

"Aye, I've a different and much better plan in mind since I've met up with George Stephenson. He told me that he's completed his own plans for building two new lines right through the Midlands: one line from Derby to Leeds and t'other from Rugby to Derby—both joined together to be called the Midland Counties Railway. And he's already got the firm backing of some capitalists from Liverpool, as well as the Derby and Nottingham coal owners."

"How does that affect us?"

"Use your head, lad!" Kirby drew deep on his cigar and flicked the ash away. "I tried to persuade Mr. Stephenson to make *York*, not Leeds, his terminus, but he won't be budged on that; he's very fixed notions about maximum gradients and suchlike. So . . . if the mountain won't come to Mahomet, what's there to prevent Mahomet going to the mountain? Don't you see it, lad? It's as plain as the nose on your face. We don't build ourselves a little local line out to Leeds; instead we go south and make ourselves a railway that'll link up with George Stephenson's Midlands line."

He drew an imaginary map on the leather chair arm, marking each city with a jab of his forefinger as he spoke.

"We link York to Derby and to Rugby, with the aid of the Midland Counties line. After that it's only a matter of time before there's a railway all the way down south to London. So tell me why we should waste our time anymore on some bloody little horse-drawn tramway, like Tannahill recommends, when we've this chance of joining York to the Midlands and, after that, to the capital."

He prodded once more with his finger at the center of the chair arm. "Not only that, like I said at that meeting at Tomlinson's, York's geographically at a crossroads; it can become the pivot of the whole system of railways that will spring up in the country. And remember, it's a direct line north from us up to Newcastle and so on up the eastern seaboard to Scotland. I tell you, Henry, I'm going to see to it that all t'railways come t'York!"

Henry blinked. Kirby seemed to be aiming for the moon. Not so much as one iron rail had yet been laid for any York railway, in whatever direction, and yet the man was talking of routes through to *London*, not to mention northwards to Scotland! He began to wonder if Mr. Stephenson might not indeed be a candidate for Bedlam and if Kirby might not shortly be joining him there: he seemed obsessed by the whole idea of railways.

"Do you think you can make the committee change their minds about the route, let alone the motive power? It strikes me that it will be a hard job."

Kirby appeared to have no doubts. "Yes—with George Stephenson's help. Consider the facts, Henry. *I* know how to raise money, while *he* knows how to build both railways and engines. Doesn't that say owt to you?"

Henry had to admit that it made some sense. Then he thought of the powerful canal owner who had demanded his support against the proposed York to Leeds railway that very evening. His position, as Member of Parliament, was going to be delicate, to say the least.

He sought refuge for the moment in a change of subject. He slapped his forehead.

"I'd almost forgotten! An old friend of mine is here with Amos Gurney's daughter. They would like to meet you."

Kirby grinned and stubbed out his cigar. "Then we mustn't keep them waiting a moment longer. I'd like very much to meet them myself."

Henry glanced at him, surprised. Such gallant interest was quite unlike Kirby, especially in people who would be neither important to him nor reputedly beautiful.

They left the peace of the anteroom and rejoined the crowds in the Egyptian Hall.

The palm leaves shook in agitation as Aunt Kitty spied the two men approaching. She caught at Hester's sleeve.

"My dear, we are observed. I told thee thou shouldst stay well back. Henry has certainly seen us and is bringing Kirby England with him. Of course it would not do to look as though we were hiding; we shall pretend instead that we were admiring this very fine palm tree."

She was deeply engrossed in examining one of the leaves as Henry reached them. Hester, meanwhile, stood alone with her hands clasped calmly in front of her at her waist. With a puzzled

78

look at Aunt Kitty, who still affected not to notice him, Henry said:

"Aunt Kitty, may I present Mr. Kirby England?" He spoke so clearly that she was forced to abandon her pretense and to feign astonishment and pleasure.

Kirby bowed gravely to both women. He behaved charmingly to Aunt Kitty, as he could when he wished. To Hester he said: "I met your father at Benbow Hall some months ago, Miss Gurney. What a pity we missed meeting then!"

She saw at once that he intended to act as though they had never met, and responded similarly. Aunt Kitty, looking apprehensively from one to the other, was bewildered but relieved.

Kirby looked at the young Quakeress. He had been much amused by his encounter with her, and part of the entertainment had stemmed from the thought of her discomfiture when she discovered to whom she had been talking so frankly and freely. He was rather disappointed to see that she did not seem in the least put out or embarrassed by seeing him again; on the contrary, she was meeting his eye with complete calm and composure. He decided that he had somewhat misjudged her and, without appearing to do so, studied her more closely. No, she was definitely not the meek and blushing maiden he imagined most Quakeresses to be; in fact, she had an exceedingly determined and unsubmissive air about her, and her gray eyes, so like her father's, were intelligent and appraising. He did not altogether care for the deep disapprobation they contained when turned in his direction.

He was about to make some remark to her, designed to tease her out of her self-possession, when Mrs. England arrived on the scene with a faltering Adelaide in her train. She descended on them like a swooping eagle alighting on its prey and placed herself firmly at her son's side, fixing both Aunt Kitty and Hester with a suspicious and resentful glare. Introductions were made.

"We've met before, as I recall," Mrs. England acknowledged Aunt Kitty's friendly greeting with a curt nod and careful enunciation. "Your niece and I are not acquainted, I believe."

She inspected both Quakeresses as though they were unusual insects, her sharp eyes lingering critically over the plain gray

79

dresses which contrasted so completely with her own creation.

Hester thought her as overbearing and ill mannered as her son. The daughter, on the other hand, was a sweet-faced girl and obviously of a very different nature. Henry had succeeded in coaxing Adelaide from her mother's side and in engaging her in some conversation. With his natural kindness, he had managed to elicit some shy responses from the girl, who had even found the courage to raise her eyes from gazing at the floor.

Aunt Kitty, meanwhile, floundered in an unsatisfactory exchange with Martha England. And Hester, to her dismay, found herself left with Kirby England for a conversation partner. After a moment of pretending to adjust the button on her cuff, there was no alternative but to pay attention to his inquiry after her father's health.

"He is much improved," she replied shortly.

"I'm glad to hear it."

"Art thou? Dost thou depend on him so much to support thy railway?"

"It's nowt to do with railways. I respect your father. I wish him well."

"He thinks well of thee," she said accusingly.

"Oh aye."

He met her hostile look with equanimity; he saw that she mistrusted him profoundly, and it occurred to him that she was perfectly right to do so. If he got his way with the York Railway Committee, and he was certain that he would, then Amos Gurney would never see the realization of his dream. No railway would be built at Garford, at least not for several years to come; the coalfields of Derbyshire would supply York instead. He wondered how such news would affect the sick Quaker. There was nothing to be done about it: the hopes of one man could not be allowed to influence him. All the same, he would have preferred it to be otherwise.

He asked a few commonplace questions about her stay in York which she answered in monosyllables, and she did not conceal her relief when they were joined by some other guests.

Soon after, they left the Assembly Rooms. Aunt Kitty, who was feeling hot and exhausted and had had more than enough for one evening, insisted that it was high time they went home. Henry was obliged by duty to remain longer, and so Aunt Kitty and Hester went home in his carriage without him.

"I do wish that I could find it in myself to like Martha England," Aunt Kitty said dispiritedly as they drove down Blake Street. "I try hard to feel Christian-spirited towards her, but I'm afraid I fail after a few moments of her company. She makes me very nervous." She settled her shawl more comfortably round her shoulders. "As for her son, I was very relieved to see that, after all, he behaved as though nothing had happened and pretended that he had never met thee before."

"Oh, he considered it all a *great* joke—I could see that. He is the kind of person who finds entertainment in another's discomfiture," Hester said bitterly.

"I think thou art mistaken in him, Hester. He was merely trying to spare thy feelings."

"I know I am not mistaken, Aunt. He is quite as unprincipled as William warned me; I don't trust him at all."

Aunt Kitty sighed. "Well, I found him a very striking sort of person, and handsome in a rustic way. He was surprisingly charming, I thought, and rather intriguing; perhaps not being a *gentleman* has something to do with it."

On that muddled conclusion she fell silent and remained so until the carriage arrived back at Precentor's Court.

Mrs. England, sitting bolt upright in her carriage, was discussing the encounter in less kindly terms than Aunt Kitty.

"What odd women those two were! I remember meeting the aunt before somewhere and thinking how peculiar she was. Fancy coming to the Assembly Rooms dressed like that!"

"They're Quakers, Mother." Her son spoke absently from the opposite corner of the carriage. "They don't believe in wearing a lot of frippery."

"I could see *that!* And all that thee-ing and thou-ing is stupidly old-fashioned, not to say overfamiliar. I heard them call you Kirby England, with no *mister* to it at all."

"They don't use titles of any kind."

"Whyever not?"

He shrugged. "I suppose because it makes a distinction between one person and the next: they don't think that's right."

She sniffed, unimpressed. "Anyway, I was that surprised to find you and Mr. Latham talking so much to them; they can't be of any importance."

"They're not."

Mrs. England peered into the darkness, trying to see her son's face better. Despite his words, she had an uneasy feeling that he had taken more account of the Quaker women than she cared for.

"I thought Miss Gurney was right plain and dumpy-looking," she said after a moment or two of silence. "And what a haughty air she had about her! As for the aunt, she never stopped talking, though what she had to say wasn't worth the breath."

"Oh, but I liked them both," Adelaide said unexpectedly and with uncustomary staunchness. "Everybody else was horrible. I could see them all whispering about us behind their hands. And no one came to talk to us at all—except Mr. Latham."

"We don't care what they think of us," Mrs. England told her sharply. "Don't *you* let them see that you mind about the way they treat us, my girl. Keep your head up high! When your brother is richer and more important than any of them, they'll suffer for their arrogance. They'll learn we're not to be despised and ignored so easily. They'll be sorry."

She went on to grumble about the evening—the poor refreshments that had been served, the inaudible music, the heat, the crush . . .

Kirby was no longer listening. He was brooding about Hester Gurney. His amusement had evaporated and the memory of her cool disapproval irked him. *She*, after all, had been in the wrong, and yet she had looked at him down that pious, straight Quaker nose of hers as though *he* were at fault. His village days were close enough still for him to be incensed by any hint of condescension. God save him from prissy, well-bred women! He switched his thoughts more pleasantly and profitably to Rosa Love and leaned forward suddenly to rap on the carriage roof with his cane.

Mrs. England paused in her catalogue of criticism to demand

to know why they were stopping. Her son merely told the coach-man to drive on and, banging the carriage door shut behind him, strode away down the street. She rubbed at the misty window with her gloved hand, trying vainly to see which direction he had taken.

Rosa was waiting for him in the little upstairs room in Stone-street. The curtains were drawn and the gas lamps burned low. Kirby liked the room; within its walls the world was far away. He enjoyed the world well enough and his zest for life was unquenchable, but it did no harm, he thought, to turn one's back now and again.

He took Rosa into his arms, stirred instantly by her warmth and beauty. His passion for her showed no signs of diminishing even after months. She was the first mistress he had not tired of quickly. He sat down and pulled her onto his lap; she curled her arms round his neck and she touched his forehead lightly with her lips.

"Call that a kiss?" he asked her in mock indignation.

She smiled down at him. "I've caught a cold—can't you hear it? I don't want to give it to you."

"To hell with your cold! I've not seen you for a week!"

He drew her against him and kissed her long and soundly, his hands sliding down under the bodice of her low-cut gown. He was both rough and gentle—gentle in skill but rough in mastery. He was easily the best lover she had ever known.

After a while she drew away from him and fetched him some brandy. She drank nothing herself, but sat on a low stool at his feet.

He drank from his glass and surveyed her.

"You're looking pale, love."

"It's this cold." Her voice croaked slightly. "I'll be better to-morrow. I sang so badly this evening at the theatre; I could hardly reach some of the top notes. I was afraid the pit might start throwing rotten tomatoes at me."

"Not likely! They'll never bloody do that!"

She smiled at him again, but her blue eyes lacked their usual sparkle.

"How was your trip to Whitby?"

He told her, describing his encounter with George Stephenson, making it all come to life for her benefit. She had a lively interest in everything.

"I'd love to meet him myself."

"You shall. He's coming to York soon."

She clasped her hands round her knees and rocked to and fro a little. "And those moving steam engines that he builds—shall I see one of those?"

"You'll do better than that. I'll see that you ride on one of 'em one day—if you'd like to."

"Could you really, Kirby? That would be dreadfully exciting! I can't imagine what it would be like to be carried along so fast by a huge iron horse with wheels."

"It doesn't look like a horse, you know," he told her, amused by her naïveté.

"I know," she said seriously. "But that's what it is in a way, isn't it? Only instead of a real live flesh-and-blood animal it's made from iron with steam for breath and wheels for hooves and coals to feed on instead of oats!"

He laughed at the picture she had painted and tweaked a ringlet which had fallen forward across her cheek.

"You're a lovely lass, Rosa," he said. "I'm glad we met, you and I."

He fished around in his coat pocket. "That reminds me I've a present for you." He tossed a small leather box into her lap. "Open it."

The little box contained an exquisite sapphire necklace; the blue gems winked up at her from their bed of crimson velvet.

"I chose them to match your eyes," he told her, and was surprised to find that when she looked up at him they were full of tears.

"They're beautiful."

"Well, try it on then."

She did so, setting the necklace carefully round her neck and twisting and turning in front of the looking glass so that the stones caught the light from the gas brackets.

"I've never had anything so lovely! It must be worth a fortune!" She looked at him, bemused. "You've already given me so much, Kirby. I've never known a man so generous. And look what you've done for the theatre. Thanks to you, we've a new manager, new scenery, a new stage . . . This week they repainted the proscenium and we've a lovely new red velvet curtain. There's going to be chandeliers hung in front of the boxes and in the saloon, and glass lanterns on the stairways, and they're even talking about some kind of hot-water apparatus to heat the place."

"The corporation could do no less as landlords," he said dryly, "if they wanted anyone to take up the expiring lease. It was a simple matter of making them see the good business sense of keeping their property in order. By the way, I've seen some architect's plans for building a whole new front to the theatre, to face onto St. Leonard's Street instead of Lop Lane, with a separate entrance for the boxes. Eight hundred pounds is to be spent."

"But that's wonderful!"

"Of course," he said, "by the time the theatre is a fit place for you to sing in you'll be at another Theatre Royal—in London."

"It's my ambition."

"If I've owt to do with it, it'll come true."

"I'd miss you if I went to London."

"Bloody rubbish!" he told her. "You know as well as I do that we're two of a kind, you and I—both interested only in getting what we want out of life. In any case, I'll be in London a lot myself."

"The railways?"

"Aye. The railways."

She thought, as Henry Latham had done, that he seemed almost possessed by the railways. For her part, she could see them as nothing more than a diverting novelty. She began to undo the clasp of the sapphire necklace.

"Keep it on," he ordered her brusquely. "Keep it on but take the rest off."

She did as he asked, carefully undoing the buttons down the front of her dress and letting it slither to her feet in a billowing ring of silk. One by one she removed each undergarment—petticoats, stockings, corset . . . He watched her unmoving. Her golden hair gleamed as brightly as the necklace she still wore about her throat. He stretched out one hand and drew her towards him slowly.

CHAPTER IV

Here's to the dear little damsels within,
Here's to the swells on the top, sir;
Here's to the music in three feet of tin;
Here's to the tapering crop, sir.

Let the steam pot
Hiss till it's hot
Give me the speed
Of the Tantivy trot.

Old coaching song

"You are telling us then, Mr. Stephenson, that you do not agree with Mr. Tannahill's recommendation to us that horsepower be employed instead of stationary or locomotive engines?"

The Lord Mayor of York was presiding over a public meeting of the Railway Committee at the ancient Guildhall in the city. He put the question to the engineer politely but with a note of skepticism in his tone.

"I am, sir."

Mr. Stephenson stood facing the committee in a quiet and dignified manner. He was a gray-haired, rather careworn man of about fifty with dark brows; he spoke with a strong North Country accent.

He went on patiently: "I have already explained to the committee that one horse can pull ten tons behind it on a railway line but a locomotive engine can pull at least *five times* that load

87

and can travel at speeds as great as thirty-five miles per hour and more. These are proven facts that I can substantiate, if you wish. In my opinion, no company building a railway today can afford to consider seriously the use of horsepower any longer, if they want to compete profitably with others. Last year the Liverpool to Manchester railway, using my locomotive engines, carried more than half a million passengers, let alone livestock, merchandise and produce, with consequent profits for their shareholders. Nothing approaching that could have been achieved using horses."

The Lord Mayor cleared his throat; he was beginning to feel somewhat out of his depth.

"Mr. Stephenson, you have also heard Mr. England, our treasurer, put forward the proposal that, even at this late stage, we completely alter the proposed route of our railway line to go *south* instead of building west to Leeds, the object apparently being to connect our line with your own proposed Midland Counties Railway somewhere about Normanton. I'm bound to say that this would take some very careful consideration. What do you say?"

"I agree with Mr. England. The Midland Counties line is already under construction; to connect with it would give your city a ready-made link to Rugby and Derby. I have already told Mr. England that I would be prepared to survey such an alternative route for the York Railway Committee."

"There has also been a further proposal advanced at this meeting, namely that we should build a direct line ourselves south through the eastern counties to London. What do you think of that?"

"In my opinion, a bird in the hand is usually worth two in a bush. At this stage I would recommend that you build a line to Normanton, or thereabouts."

"Thank you, Mr. Stephenson."

The engineer sat down; whisperings and murmurings rippled through the crowded Guildhall.

Elias Snell, the saturnine lawyer who had opposed the railway from the very first committee meeting at Tomlinson's Hotel, was the next to speak.

88

"Mr. Stephenson," he said in clear, dry tones, "you are recommending in fact that we totally ignore the advice of a reputable engineer and surveyor—a gentleman of considerable experience—to blindly follow some new folly concocted jointly by Mr. Kirby England and yourself, namely that we build a completely different railway in another direction simply in order to connect with a further railway that is not even yet built." He looked round the hall. I ask the ladies and gentlemen present at this meeting to consider whether this sounds a wise course of action. I am not, myself, by any means convinced that *any* railway is necessary for the benefit of this city, whether it goes north, south, east or west; and I am most certainly not prepared to accept Mr. Stephenson's statement that it would be necessary—nay, *vital*—to employ locomotive steam engines. He tells us that these engines will travel more than twice as fast as horses, but where is the good in that if it means that our land is to be taken over and terrorized by these dangerous and infernal machines? Do we want our countryside to be ravaged by these iron monsters, threatening life and limb—to say nothing of property? The tragic and hideous death of Mr. Huskisson at the opening of the Liverpool to Manchester railway should be a dreadful warning to us all. We should remember his sacrifice and not speak of the profits to be gained by greedy speculators."

He raised his voice a little. "These locomotives carry the *devil* as postilion. They will destroy our beautiful and peaceful country, bringing death, injury and misery in their wake. They are known to terrify all animals, to set fire to crops, to turn both land and livestock barren. And what is to become of those whose livelihoods depend on horses if these machines are permitted to take their place? What will happen to the coachmen, the coachmakers, the innkeepers, the horse dealers, the farriers, the harness makers? Many of these gentlemen are present here today. Must the bread be taken from your children's mouths? And what will happen to the turnpikes—the pride of our land—if these abominable machines are allowed to breed and multiply like Satan's spawn? It is the right and duty of every man and woman present at this meeting today to see that they are crushed now, at birth, forever!"

His speech received prolonged applause and shouts of approval from all parts of the hall.

"Mr. England, you wish to speak again?"

Kirby England had risen slowly to his feet. He stuck his thumb through the buttonhole of his right lapel and surveyed the watching and listening citizens.

"My Lord Mayor, ladies and gentlemen. First of all, I think every one of us owes a vote of thanks to Mr. Stephenson for giving his time to the citizens of York today. He consented to attend this meeting—at my special request—despite the huge load of work he has undertaken in other parts of the country, in places where no doubt whatsoever is cast on his genius and where full recognition is given of his achievements by farseeing and intelligent men." He paused to let this sink into his audience.

"Friends, you have heard Mr. Snell remind us of some old wives' tales concerning locomotive engines and railways. None of them has any basis in fact. The simple truth is that animals quickly accustom themselves to the sight and sound of passing locomotives; crops are not affected, nor is game or hunting. Mr. Stephenson has proved in the most practical terms to the whole world the vast superiority of his locomotive power over that of horses. Those who still doubt his word should make the journey to watch his engines at work on the Stockton and Darlington Railway or between Liverpool and Manchester. Ask anyone who has seen them! The point at issue today is how many of us here present understand the full meaning and significance of Mr. Stephenson's marvelous invention. What *I'm* asking you, my friends, is to consider the certainty that these engines—if only we've the nous to use 'em—are going to transform the lives of all of us."

Kirby was speaking quietly, but his voice carried to the far corners of the Guildhall and they listened to him closely.

"I'll tell you what, men and women of York: railways and steam engines are going to change *everything* for us. We're going to eat better, work better and live better! Fish, meat and vegetables will be able to be carried hundreds of miles across the land without rotting. People will no longer have to live right beside where they work when they can travel to and fro quickly and cheaply on the railway each day; and they'll be able to visit family and friends, to go to London, to see the seaside for the first time. Folks'll journey safe and sound for a few pence where before it cost pounds, and all thanks to the same infernal machines that Mr. Snell and others would have us stamp out!"

He tugged at his buttonhole. "So—what's to be decided among us all today is whether we're to go *forward* or to stay *back* with the old life, where no man can travel faster than the pace of a horse or transport a load greater than that horse can bear. Aye, I've no doubt there are some faint hearts among the lot of you who'll listen to Mr. Snell and his womanish wailings. But there'll be plenty of others to see the light. As I recall from the long history of this ancient city, we've never lacked the courage for the bold venture nor the stomach for a good fight. Let's fight together for this. Let's fight for progress! For the railways! And for Mr. Stephenson's steam locomotives!"

The gardens at 44 Monkgate were among the most beautiful in York. Lying beyond the confines of the city walls, they were large enough to include a deer park with some very fine trees. The library windows overlooked the park at the back of the house, and it was in this room, some time after the Guildhall meeting, that Kirby England received an unexpected visitor.

Amos Gurney's appearance interrupted Kirby at work at his desk. He barely recognized the Quaker at first. The man had lost a great deal of weight and had become so thin that his cheeks were sunk inwards in cavernous hollows, and his eyes were deep gray pools of exhaustion and pain. His beard drooped lifelessly and his skin had the transparent pallor of a corpse. After the exertion of mounting the stairway, it was a while before he could regain enough breath and strength to speak. Kirby, who had pulled a chair forward for him, waited for a bout of coughing to subside. The two men looked at each other.

"I received thy letter."

"Aye." Kirby, leaning against the front edge of the desk, cigar in hand, waited.

"I've come to persuade thee to change thy mind."

"Impossible. I told you in my letter that the committee have decided against building a railway through Garford. There's nowt to be done about it." He stared at the Quaker. "You should never've made this journey—you're not fit for it."

Amos Gurney smiled, lips drawn back tightly across his teeth; in his emaciated state it was like the grin of a dead man's skull.

"My dear Friend," he said hoarsely, "thou knowest well how much the railway meant to me. Was I to give it up meekly and without another word or effort to save it?"

Kirby could admire such sentiments, but said:

"It's too late, Mr. Gurney. We're going to build a railway to South Milford or Normanton that'll join up with the Midland Counties line going from Derby to Leeds. We'll get our coal just the same from other pits."

He looked straight at the Quaker. "At the beginning I wanted to build that Garford line as much as you, but this turned out to be a far better proposition. You're a business man yourself—you can see the sense. But, if it's any comfort to you, I reckon there'll be a railway at Garford within ten years anyhow."

"Not in my lifetime."

"Mebbe not. *You* may not see it, but it'll come, never fear."

Amos Gurney folded his hands over the silver knob of the stick he held. He said quietly, but with intense conviction in his voice: "A while ago, Friend, when I was lying feverish in my bed, I had this dream of railways. They covered this kingdom from north to south, from east to west. I saw steam engines pulling long lines of carriages at high speed, conveying thousands of people across the land, and wagons loaded with hundreds of thousands of tons of goods. There were no more coaches or coachmen, and the canals were choked with weeds. It was clear to me that I had seen some kind of vision."

His voice had faltered and he began coughing. After a moment he said firmly: "God has spoken to me, Kirby England, and showed me that the railways are good and shall come to bring benefit to His people; and those that build them will have His blessing."

Kirby chewed at his cigar.

"Aye, well, I've had that very same dream myself, Mr. Gurney, but I can't speak for God like you. I wouldn't know what He thinks about it. But I know what *I* think."

"There will be immense fortunes to be made," Amos said shrewdly, watching him.

"I'll not deny that I intend making all the brass I can."

"I don't blame thee for that. But remember, Friend, that money can only bring true contentment of spirit when used for the well-being of others."

"I've seen plenty of very contented rich men who never part with a farthing if they can help it," Kirby said dryly. "But I'll bear it in mind. Would you like a glass of brandy?"

"I never touch liquor."

"I'd forgotten. That's a pity; it would do you good now."

The Quaker lifted one thin hand mutely, repeating his refusal. "Tell me then about this railway that is to be built instead."

"The survey has been done as far as South Milford by Mr. Stephenson himself and the Bill has already been drafted for introduction into Parliament. We've formed a Provisional Committee with myself as treasurer, a Mr. Thoman Richardson as solicitor and one of Mr. Stephenson's best assistants, Mr. John Caley, as our engineer."

"And the name of the company will be?"

"The York and North Midland Railway Company."

"The necessary capital has been raised?"

"In part. It's been fixed at three hundred thousand pounds, and the shares at fifty pounds. We've had poor support from Yorkshire landowners, so we've had to approach some London capitalists to add their weight."

"Well, here is one Yorkshire landowner who will support thee. I'll buy shares in thy railway company, Kirby England, even though thou wilt not build me the railway I want." He fingered his beard thoughtfully. "I heard a rumor that might interest thee. The other day a Friend came from Newcastle to see me. He talked of a meeting that the Quaker capitalists of the Stockton and Darlington line held there; they're proposing to build a line between Newcastle and York—if I remember his words right. Hast thou heard of that?"

"Not a word. I'm grateful to you for the information. The two companies might collaborate, with advantages to both camps."

Kirby tapped the ash from his cigar. "I'm sorry your journey's been wasted. You shouldn't have come all this way."

"My time has not been wasted, I assure thee. And since thou hast refused my first request, I have another to ask of thee which thou must surely grant."

"I will—if I can."

The Quaker said: "When I die my daughter, Hester, will be left alone except for her aunt, a well-meaning but scatterbrained woman. As I told thee, all my estate will be left to her; she will have need of good advice and protection."

"I imagine your cousin, William Gurney, will provide that."

Amos Gurney frowned. "There lies my difficulty. Let me explain. William is a clever and successful lawyer, but I do not want him as a husband for my daughter."

"It's what he's in mind, unless I'm mistaken."

"Thou art very observant, Kirby England. Yes, William has wanted to marry Hester for a long time. He asked my permission a few months ago, but I refused it. I shall never give my consent. When she is twenty-one my daughter must do as she wishes, but until then, at least, she can be kept safe from him."

"So where is the difficulty?"

"As thou canst plainly see, I have not much longer left in this world. It's unlikely that I shall see Hester come of age. If I die while she is still so young, she may accept her cousin: William is very persuasive."

"It's none of my affair," Kirby said. "But I don't see it as such a bad match—same faith, same family, even same name. Better the devil you know."

"I do not like to speak ill of any man, but I will tell thee that I have no regard for William Gurney—other than as a lawyer. I know that he would not make my daughter happy. I cannot say more than that."

"You could be wrong."

"Perhaps, but I don't think so. I must act for her as I believe to be right, and I can protect her from an unwise choice of husband—even from beyond the grave. This concerns the favor I ask of thee."

"Aye?"

94

"Wilt thou agree to become my daughter's guardian until she comes of age?"

There was dead silence in the library. Kirby had not known what to expect, but it had certainly not been this. He suspected that the Quaker's illness must have muddled his wits. It might have been amusing, if it were not also pitiful.

"Mr. Gurney—is this a joke?"

Amos Gurney looked shocked. "How canst thou think that I would joke about such a thing? I have given the matter the deepest thought."

"You want *me* to be your daughter's guardian?"

"I realize that it is a great deal to ask of a man who already bears great responsibilities and has much on his mind; but in my experience of life, such a man is always the best choice to ask for help."

"Why not ask another Quaker?"

"William is very well regarded by many Friends, particularly in York. I do not want a guardian for Hester who will be easily influenced by her cousin. I want a man who dislikes him quite as much as I."

Kirby stared at his visitor. Amos Gurney met his eyes with an ironical expression in his own.

"I could see thou didst not care much for him thyself when thou met him at Benbow. And William certainly does not like thee. Thou art admirably suited to the task of keeping him away from my daughter. I know thou wouldst never give thy consent to his marrying her."

Kirby laughed. He walked over to one of the long windows and looked down at the gardens below; the trees were in summer green and the deer grazed quietly beneath their shade. It was a pleasant and gratifying scene. He drew on his cigar unhurriedly.

He could not yet take Amos Gurney's request seriously. The idea was preposterous: for him to take on a Quaker miss as a ward would make every eyebrow in York rise to its owner's hairline. Not that he cared two hoots for that, but it was not his style exactly to have some prim and proper ward hung about his neck. He turned back to the father.

95

"Your daughter would hate the idea—you know that?"

"Why shouldst thou say that?"

"She finds me a boorish oaf and she distrusts me."

"But she has never met thee."

"We met at a reception at the Assembly Rooms in York when she was staying with her aunt in the spring."

"I told thee that her aunt was a frivolous woman," the Quaker said, vexed.

Kirby had sat down behind his desk. "So you see, Mr. Gurney, it would be much better for you to find someone else. There must be other men more suitable to the role than I."

His visitor shook his head stubbornly. "Thou art the man I want as her guardian. Dear Friend, it is not only the matter of her cousin, William, I know very well also that thou art likely to become an exceedingly powerful man, with great influence in York. Thou understands the value and use of money, thou canst protect her inheritance—advise her, guide her."

"I might also cheat her."

"If I believed that of thee I should never have asked thee this favor."

Kirby drummed his fingers impatiently on the desk. "I am not a moral man, Mr. Gurney. I don't even believe in God, and I certainly don't hold with your faith. My reputation, both with business and women, is the subject of a lot of gossip and censure."

"So I have heard."

"And yet you still want me to be your daughter's guardian?"

"I know what will best protect her."

There was a long silence while Kirby considered his decision. He had not reached where he was now by going out of his way for people unless it suited him to do so. In this case there was no advantage to himself whatever—unless he counted the possible satisfaction to be gained from thwarting William Gurney's suit for the heiress—and from seeing Hester Gurney's outrage. He grinned to himself: there was a certain appeal in the prospect of her indignation. Fancy having an uncouth, sinful, jumped-up draper in charge of her life! He reviewed the potential entertainment.

"All right. I'll do as you ask."

The Quaker gave a small sigh. He got to his feet with the aid of his stick and held out his right hand.

"Our business is therefore concluded, Kirby England. I bid thee a final farewell. We shall not meet again."

"Happen we may."

"Not in this world. I do not fear death. Were it not for my daughter I should welcome its release. I shall be going to my God and be reunited with my beloved wife. My only other regret is that I have not been given more time on this earth: at the age of fifty, Friend, we discover that not much is done in one lifetime. I shall pray for thee and thy success and, most of all, that thou may bring great advantage to mankind with thy railways. Let no man deter thee from thy course."

"I'm not in the habit of letting people stand in my way."

Amos Gurney smiled gently. "But be warned against my cousin, William Gurney. He will resent what I have done today."

"I've plenty of enemies. I know how to deal with 'em."

"That is why I chose thee." Amos walked slowly towards the door, leaning on his stick. He turned once again.

"I thank thee for giving me peace of mind. Good-bye, Kirby England."

After the Quaker had gone, Kirby returned to the papers on his desk. He took up his quill pen and tried to resume his work, but the image of Amos Gurney, sitting black-hatted, proud and exhausted in his carriage as he traveled homewards through the summer fields of Yorkshire, kept coming into his mind. He wondered which need had really driven him to make the sacrifice of the journey: daughter or railway? He had spoken first of the railway, but Kirby thought that the true and only reason for coming to York had been for the daughter's sake. He frowned and cursed himself for a fool; he had other things to do than play guardian to a seventeen-year-old girl. Even so, to have refused would have been to deny a dying man his wish: there were a few ethics that Kirby did not care to sidestep.

The library door opened and Mrs. England stood there. "Who was that man I saw in the hall just now?"

"A Quaker named Amos Gurney."

"Not related to that girl and her aunt at the Assembly Rooms?"

He was surprised that she had remembered the meeting. "He is Miss Gurney's father, brother to the aunt."

"What did he want with you?"

"My business affairs are my own, Mother, but in this case I may as well tell you that he has asked me to be guardian to his daughter."

She went pale. "Why should she need a guardian?"

"The father is dying."

"But why *you?* What have you to do with them?"

"Nothing. He had his reasons."

There were two red spots of color in her cheeks. "There must be some trick about it! The man didn't look as though he had two halfpennies in his pocket. He's lost all his money—gambled it away, no doubt—and wants to make you responsible for her!"

"Amos Gurney is a rich man. And Quakers don't usually gamble, Mother."

"But that girl— How could you have agreed to such a thing! You know how much I disliked her. She looks down on you, and all of us; it was as plain as anything."

He threw down his pen and got to his feet. "Very possibly. But I don't intend discussing the matter further. I've agreed and that's an end to it. I must go. Henry Latham is leaving for London tomorrow and I want to see him before he goes."

She stopped him at the door, her hand clutching at his arm. "Mr. Latham called twice last week while you were away."

"Aye?"

"To see Adelaide."

"He has my full permission to do so, Mother. Henry is a wealthy aristocrat, as well as a Member of Parliament. What better husband could you wish for your daughter? If he can persuade my sister to marry him, then he has my blessing."

He disengaged his arm firmly and left her. Mrs. England went to sit alone in the chill magnificence of the drawing room. The old fear of being deserted by her children had returned to haunt her; she did not want to lose Adelaide yet, and the thought of her son with a ward, even one as dowdy as the Quakeress, filled her with uncontrollable jealousy. She wanted no other woman in his life at all; she had come to terms with his mistresses because she knew that they seldom held his interest for long and they did not threaten her own position in his household. A ward would be a greater danger: she would have to receive her, to pretend welcome . . . She shut her eyes in despair—the idea was intolerable. She had taken an instant aversion to Hester Gurney at the Assembly Rooms, but now she felt that she hated her.

She opened her eyes slowly, forcing herself to be calm. There was no cause for alarm, when she thought about it: the father might not die for a long while, and even if he did, it was unlikely that Kirby would take more than the most perfunctory account of his ward. The girl was neither aristocratic nor beautiful; he would certainly find her dull Quaker ways very tedious. Mrs. England breathed a long sigh of relief; there was really nothing to worry about after all.

CHAPTER V

You may seek it with thimbles—and seek it with care,
You may hunt it with forks and hope;
You may threaten its life with a railway share;
You may charm it with smiles and soap.

But oh! beamish nephew, beware of the day
If your Snark be a Boojum, for then
You will softly and suddenly vanish away,
And never be met with again!

Lewis Carroll

The following winter William Gurney rode in his carriage through the gates of Benbow Hall to pay a call on his cousin, Hester. He had not seen her for some time. Her father's death three months previously had been a great blow to Hester, and William had thought it prudent to give her time to recover from her grief. William's last visit had been after the funeral, which Hester, according to custom, had not attended. Only men had been present at the simple interment in a nearby Quaker burial ground. There had, of course, been no extravagant or expensive mourning: the coffin had been plain and unadorned; there had been no headstone and no words spoken. Amos Gurney had been buried as all Friends were buried and entirely as he would have wished.

William looked out of the carriage window. Everything he could see belonged to his young cousin now—and a great deal more besides. Benbow land stretched away into the far distance —parkland, farms, woods, as well as the colliery up on the moor. And when he married Hester it would all become his. William did not want for money and his house in York was more than respectable, but the idea of being a big landowner appealed to him very much.

The horses trotted on briskly up the final sweep of the long carriageway. William watched the house thoughtfully. With his cousin still in mourning he could do no more today than hint at his intentions for the future. He frowned. There was also the intolerable question of her wardship. It was not insurmountable— not in the long run—but it could be a problem. When Amos had told him of appointing Kirby England as guardian, William had been too angry at first to trust himself to speak. He could not understand how Amos could have chosen anyone so grossly, so *criminally* unsuitable. He had done everything possible to persuade his cousin to change his mind, but Amos had refused to alter his will and would give no reason for it. William had concluded, as other Friends had done, that his cousin had lost his senses in the last months of his life—that the wasting disease he had endured had finally eaten into his brain and affected his reason.

William had considered various courses of legal action against Kirby England, who he was certain had brought some kind of evil pressure to bear on Amos, but for want of any evidence, had decided in the end to bide his time.

Hester's dismay at discovering the identity of her guardian had equaled his own. She would be eighteen next summer. In little more than three years she would be of age and her guardian's powers would end. William adjusted his broad-brimmed black hat carefully and brushed a few spots of mud from his coat sleeve. Since being appointed an Elder it seemed to him that he heard the voice of the Almighty speaking to him more than ever. The Lord had given him patience, and the Lord would certainly see that the vile sinner, Kirby England, received punishment.

He thought of Hester's gray eyes, her smooth, dark hair, her small hands and feet . . . Her looks had always pleased him: there was a quality and purity about her that so many women with their overblown, vulgar prettiness lacked. Only her strong spirit offended: the self-willed, independent side to her character might prove useful where her guardian was concerned, but it would eventually have to be subdued. He would have to teach her the obedience and humility suitable in a wife.

He was admitted to the house by a manservant and shown into the library. The room was unchanged. It had been Amos's favorite room, and his possessions still remained undisturbed: his desk, his pen, his papers, his books, his chair and the footstool beside it—all were there as though the owner were still alive. For a moment William had an uneasy feeling that the shade of his cousin was present and watching him.

When Hester came into the library he was gratified to see that there was color in her cheeks and a spring in her step. It was a few moments before he realized that it was not due to his own arrival, but to the fact that she was furiously angry.

"William! I am very thankful to see thee. I was about to write to thee for thy advice."

He bent to kiss her cheek, letting his lips linger longer than usual, and replied that he only waited to be told how he might be of service.

"It's this letter," she said indignantly, holding it out to him. "I received it this morning from *that man!* Read it, I beg you, and tell me if thou dost not agree with me that it is the greatest piece of impertinence. How dare he interfere in my affairs!"

"Calm thyself, my dear cousin. I take it that thou art referring to thy guardian. Sit down and let me read it through."

She did so, tapping her foot while she waited for him to finish reading.

William looked up. "He advises thee to dismiss the viewer at the colliery, as well as all the pit lads! What does *he* know of the matter?"

She said bitterly: "Papa made particular arrangements, it seems, for him to have access to all estate accounts and those of the colliery. I cannot imagine why."

"Nor I, since I can give thee all the advice thou needest. Thy guardian apparently considers the viewer to be a dishonest drunkard. Dost thou know if there is any truth in this?"

"I'm sure there is not. I hired Mr. Atkins myself when our previous manager left Garford. He comes from Durham, and the men are always prejudiced against strangers from another part of the country." She hesitated. "It is true that there have been *some* complaints against him."

"What complaints?"

"The men say he is sometimes late with their wages."

"That should be easily rectified. *Is* he intemperate?"

"Not that I know of."

William looked down again at the letter.

"This maintains that colliery sales have fallen badly in the last six weeks; I see that he recommends the pit lads' going as a matter of economy."

"How could I dismiss them? Families depend on every penny that can be earned, and where else would they find work in Garford? And if anyone is to blame for bad sales it is Kirby England himself. It was *he* who stopped the railway being built at Garford; it would have given us better and cheaper transport. As it is, we must still rely on the wagons. Micklestone Colliery have sunk a new shaft near the Leeds and Collingham turnpike and the north coal leaders' route will be two miles less to their pit than it is to Garford. We have lost a lot of our trade to Micklestone."

He was surprised at her grasp of the situation; he had thought her interest in the mine extended only to the school she ran for the children. He was silent for a while, thinking. His first reaction had been of cold anger at Kirby England's high-handed meddling, and his hand was still shaking as he held the letter; his second, carefully controlled, had been that the advice given might possibly prove to be right. However, to agree with Kirby England was unthinkable; the man was a blackguard and an evil sinner and must be completely discredited in Hester's eyes.

"If thou art satisfied with Mr. Atkins as viewer, then there is no more to be said, Cousin. This letter may be taken as unwarranted interference, such as I would expect from a man of thy guardian's nature. I see no reason to dismiss any pit lads at this time; sales may improve over the next few months. Let us wait and see. I suggest thou replies to thy guardian, rejecting his advice."

She said gratefully: "I'm so glad to hear thee say that. To have done as *he* tells me would have gone much against the grain."

"Thou dislikes him that much?"

"I disliked him from our first and only meeting. I am thankful that he has not come to Benbow since Papa died for I don't know how I could be civil to him. I cannot forget that he hastened Papa's death."

"Indeed? How so?"

"There is no doubt of it in my mind; I have thought of it ever since. Papa was brokenhearted when he learned that the railway was not to come through Garford after all. It was all Kirby England's fault that it was abandoned, and Papa thought he might be able to persuade him to change his mind if he went to see him in York. I tried to stop him going, but he insisted on it. When he came home he took to his bed and never rose from it again. But for that journey he might still be alive."

"Then thy guardian has a great deal to answer for," William said. "Hast thou received other letters than this one from him?"

"Only one. He wrote some weeks ago to say that he had bought some more shares on my behalf in the York and North Midland Railway Company. Papa had already invested in the company. He has control of my inheritance, as thou knowest."

William tapped his fingertips together. "That is very unfortunate; the value of those shares has been falling steadily over past weeks. No doubt thy guardian neglected to tell thee of all the difficulties and delays that have arisen over the building of that railway, but since he has been elected chairman of the company perhaps he thought it more prudent to keep silent. I am told that the contractors have yet to set to work. There have been endless disputes with landowners, appeals from court to court, engineering problems, opposition of all kinds. Thy guardian has been in London trying to see the Bill through Parliament; the fact that it was not instantly thrown out has been due only to Henry Latham's efforts; he has shepherded it through at every stage."

"I cannot understand why Henry should be so concerned with it."

"Dear cousin, it is all a matter of returning favors. Kirby England helped Henry to be elected by buying votes for him and bribing voters; Henry is now obliged to return the compliment. He must have a long spoon that sups with the devil."

Hester said in sudden despair: "I shall never understand why Papa made such a man my guardian."

"His illness had unbalanced his judgment, my dear. There can be no other explanation. But do not distress thyself too much. I shall protect thee and thy interests. I shall be making some investigations into Kirby England's business affairs that may prove his downfall."

"Aunt Kitty wrote to me the other day saying that he has now been elected alderman and that there is a rumor that he may even become Lord Mayor of York. It seems impossible to believe."

"Unlikely, but not, unfortunately, impossible," her cousin answered. "He has a peculiar popularity with tradesmen and the like. Many in York see him, quite mistakenly, as their champion, and he is cunning enough to give them plenty of encouragement and inducement. Half the city is entertained at 44 Monkgate in a vulgarly lavish and profligate manner."

"Thou hast been to his house?" Hester inquired, curious despite herself.

"Certainly not! It is nothing but a sink of corruption and decadence, where people of the loosest morals congregate."

"Amongst them a singer from the Theatre Royal."

William was shocked. "How didst thou know of her?"

"Aunt Kitty told me."

"It is not surprising that thy father always considered thy aunt to be unreliable in the matter of thy guidance. She should not have spoken to thee of such things."

"But thou hast just done so thyself!"

"I spoke only to warn thee," William said quietly. "Thy welfare is important to me." His eyes were fixed intently on her face. "My dear Hester, thou knowest of my deep regard and affection for thee: it has grown over the many years we have known each other. We are cousins, but not so close in blood that it could be a bar between us, and we are of the same persuasion. Out of respect for thy recent bereavement I shall not speak yet to thee of the hopes I hold for our future. I shall wait instead, with patience, and shall pray daily for thee that thou may find grace in the sight of the Lord."

He took from the pocket of his black coat a small piece of paper; lines of verse were written on it in his hand. "I came across this memorial poem recently; it was written to a virtuous and godly Friend. Repeat it daily to thyself, Cousin. It will help guide thee to the Light." He read aloud:

> *"Oh for thy spirit, tried and true*
> *And constant in the hour of trial,*
> *Prepared to suffer or to do*
> *In meekness and in self-denial."*

He pressed the paper into her hand; his fingers were cold against her own.

He stayed awhile longer, reading aloud to her from Amos Gurney's Bible, which he had taken down from a shelf in the library. He sat in his dead cousin's chair beside the fireplace and Hester listened dutifully, sitting opposite him with her hands folded in her lap, just as she had listened to her father.

When William had left Benbow to return to York, she threw her guardian's letter onto the library fire. It was a childish gesture of defiance but it made her feel better. After a moment's thought she screwed up William's verse and threw that on too. She watched the scrap of paper with its thinly penned, neat writing curl up and fall into ashes. Her cousin would have been shocked at her action, and perhaps it was shocking to set fire to someone's prayerful words. She hoped the Lord would understand. It did not seem to her at all sensible to pray for meekness and self-denial just at the moment when determination and self-assertion were surely needed instead to defy her guardian. She wished sometimes that William would not always pray so assiduously for her. It made her painfully aware of her many short-comings.

She stared down at the flames and thought about her cousin's allusion to marriage between them. It was not unexpected—it was not the first time he had hinted at his intentions. And it was both flattering and worrying. Flattering because he was so hand-some and clever, and worrying because she still did not know the answer she would give him. Such a marriage—to a Quaker of her own family—should be ideal, except that she did not love him. She understood that love for a husband, or wife, could be acquired, or learned after marriage, in which case there was no reason to refuse William. He was her cousin, a man she had known since childhood, and one who would take the sometimes heavy burden of responsibility for the Benbow estate from her shoulders. At seventeen, she was still capable of feeling as much in need of comfort as a child.

Hester knew of one other person in the world who could give her comfort; she sat down at her father's desk and wrote directly to Aunt Kitty.

"It's a bloody marvel to see it happening at last, Mr. Caley, and no mistake!"

Kirby England stood on the ridge of a deep cutting, looking down at the railway line in process of construction far below him. The scene was of unceasing activity: metal clinked and rang on stone as an army of men worked away with picks and shovels, moving slowly across the raw earth like foraging ants. It was a cold day with a sharp wind, but the navvies sweated from their labors and worked with unbuttoned shirts, rolled-up sleeves and open waistcoats. The handkerchiefs they wore knotted round their necks made bright, flowerlike splashes of color against a muddy background. The gangers walking amongst them could be heard cajoling and reviling, and the answering curses from the men floated high on the wind to where Kirby and the young engineer watched from above.

John Caley said grimly: "They're a right tough lot down there, Mr. England. They only care for the present and they don't give a damn for past or future. They live to eat and drink, to fight and fornicate, and they rampage through every neighborhood as they go, like an invading army. They've the strength of oxes, but I've not met many old navvies: most of 'em are dead before they're forty, worked out and worn out." He pointed ahead towards the far end of the cutting. "Tunneling starts there. It's solid rock, so the contractors'll be blasting the way through for half a mile to the other side. It'll be dangerous; it always is. Gunpowder fumes and foul air make for accidental explosions. I'll be glad when we're through."

Kirby grunted in reply. He was watching some navvies making the running with loaded wheelbarrows up the steep sides of the cutting. Long runs of wooden planks stretched from the base to the summit of the incline, each with a horse and pulley at the top. Kirby paid close attention to one man taking hold of a barrow piled high with spoil at the bottom of the run. A rope was attached to the barrow and to a belt round the navvy's waist; the rope extended all the way up the slope, where it was fastened to the waiting horse at the top. With the heavy barrow balanced before him on the narrow plankway, the navvy tugged at the rope to signal the driver of the horse that he was ready. High above him the horse moved forward, pulling both man and barrow up the near-vertical incline. Kirby watched, greatly impressed by the strength and skill required to steer the load up such a narrow and precipitous path. When the navvy finally reached the top he tipped the spoil out and, without pause, plunged back down to the bottom of the cutting, drawing the empty barrow after him; all the while the horse kept the rope taut.

John Caley followed his companion's gaze.

"They make it look easy," he said. "But it's a hell've a job. If the horse stumbles or lets the rope go slack, or the man loses his balance, then the barrow will roll right back on top of him. I've seen navvies hurled down the cutting with their limbs crushed—unless they manage to throw the barrow to one side to get out of its way."

"I'll have a go."

The engineer turned his head, thinking he had misheard.

"I'll try that trick with the barrow," Kirby said equably. "Come on, lad, hold my coat for me while I go down and take a turn."

"You can't do that, Mr. England! You might be killed!" John Caley looked appalled.

But Kirby had already stripped off his coat and tossed it to the engineer. He rolled up his shirt sleeves. "Who's chairman of this bloody railway company, anyhow? This is *my* railway, and it'd give me a power of satisfaction to know that I've shifted even one barrow load of muck towards the building of it." He took the cigar that he held clenched between his teeth and handed it to the other man. "Hold this for me too will you, Mr. Caley. I'll be back before it's finished."

"Wait, Mr. England," the engineer called desperately after him. "You don't understand—"

His company chairman paused and shouted back over his shoulder. "What don't I understand, Mr. Caley? I grew up among lads like those down there. I know what I'm doing."

John Caley watched helplessly as he set off down the cutting, slithering and sliding in thick mud towards the bottom. It was of little comfort to tell himself that the chairman seemed to have the build and physical strength of a navvy. Brute force was not enough. A successful run, made without injury, required practice and skill, as well as a cool nerve and the agility of a mountain goat. And to make matters worse, it had begun to rain. The engineer lifted his face to the skies to feel the wet drops sploshing down; the conditions would worsen rapidly as the rain turned earth to liquid mud and the wooden planks of the run to a greasy slipperiness. He wished wholeheartedly that he had never brought Mr. England to see the work in progress on the railway. But the chairman had insisted on it, just as he had insisted on walking every yard of the survey route with him, long before a single spadeful of earth had been dug. At first John Caley had resented the man: he had been irked by his constant presence, by his endless questions and demands and by the way he refused to consider any form of compromise. However, as the weeks and months went by, the engineer had discovered good reason to be grateful for Mr. England's ubiquitousness. It was he who had overcome the many difficulties and obstacles that had beset them, who had overridden the fierce opposition and smoothed the ruffled feathers of landowners along the route, and who had pacified the local populace at every turn. And it had been the chairman who, by his timely and authoritative intervention, had averted a pitched battle one night between the surveying party, operating by stealth, and the servants of an angry landowner, armed with pistols and clubs. Without him it was doubtful if the railway could ever have been properly surveyed—let alone built.

Clutching the coat to his chest and holding the still smoking cigar gingerly between his fingers, John Caley edged forward to see better. Mr. England had reached the bottom of the cutting and was talking to one of the gangers. Even from that distance the engineer could sense and see the suspicion and hostility invariably displayed by the navvies to any outsider. He hoped the ganger would have the wit to stop the whole mad idea, but to his dismay, he saw the man nod and lift his arms from his sides in a wide shrug of capitulation. He watched as Mr. England walked across to a navvy busily shoveling earth into a near-full barrow. He was an enormous brute of a man with bright ginger hair and a red scarf tied round his neck. The engineer waited for him to turn and set upon the intruder for his meddling, but to his astonishment, he saw that the man stood docilely aside and, still more amazing, helped Mr. England to attach the leather belt with its rope to his waist, even showing him how to position himself well at the foot of the plankway and how to grasp the handles just so.

John Caley blinked away the rain from his eyes and, leaning forward, stared down at what was taking place far below him. Mr. England, ready now, jerked at the rope and the horse moved forward at the top of the ridge. Man and loaded barrow began to make the running. The engineer held his breath. Mr. England moved with surprising adroitness for a big man, and he was succeeding in keeping the barrow on a straight and even course.

John Caley crossed his fingers and watched. He drew in his breath in a hiss as he saw the chairman's foot slip on the wet planking and the barrow begin to wobble. As its propeller struggled to regain his balance and momentum, the engineer shut his eyes with a groan. He reopened them minutes later to see man and barrow continuing on upwards steadily towards the summit. Despite the cold, the engineer was sweating: he had once seen a navvy hideously mutilated by a falling barrow, and had no wish to take the blame for any such misfortune befalling the chairman of the York and North Midland Railway Company. His relief when he finally saw him reach the top was short-lived, for the chairman paused only to empty out the spoil before starting down again, drawing the barrow after him. Caley watched, fearing that he was going to try to make a second running. The man was completely mad! He then saw, thankfully, that Mr. England had merely decided to finish the job properly by returning the barrow to the ginger-haired navvy. In his distraction the engineer had not noticed that the lit end of the cigar he held was burning a large hole in the sleeve of the chairman's coat.

It took Kirby England a while to reappear on the ridge beside Caley, and when he did so he was a wild and disheveled sight: he needed only a colored kerchief round his neck to be taken for a navvy. His waistcoat and trousers were thickly plastered with mud and his white silk shirt was torn and streaked with blood from a cut on his arm; his curly black hair was dripping wet, and rain and sweat mingled together on his forehead. He stood there, both fists on hips, breathing in great, rasping lungfuls of air and grinning with triumph. After a moment he rolled down his shirt sleeves and held out his hand.

"I'll have my things back now, Mr. Caley."

The engineer held out the coat without a word; both men's gaze fell upon the burn mark.

"I'm that sorry—"

"Nay, not to worry, lad. Give us the cigar then."

The railway company chairman put on the burned coat, stuck the cigar back in his mouth and puffed out a thick cloud of smoke.

"Right, Mr. Caley—if you're ready. We'll go and take another look at that place where the embankment's to be made, further along the line. I've a few questions in mind to ask you about the costing . . ."

He strode off ahead; the engineer looked after him, shook his head resignedly and followed.

When Aunt Kitty received her niece's letter inviting her on a visit to Benbow Hall, she firmly put aside her deep dislike of the place and set out as soon as possible. She had been worried for a long while about Hester's solitary existence, but her repeated pressing that she should come on a prolonged, if not indefinite, stay at Precentor's Court had met with polite but consistent refusal. In the end, she had given up and decided to wait until an opportunity arose to renew her efforts at gentle persuasion. And the opportunity having presented itself at last, she was packed and ready to leave within the day and on the road to Garford.

The journey seemed long, cold and uncomfortable. She was getting too old, she decided, to be rattled about inside a carriage like a die in a box, and with only the prospect of a chill, gloomy destination at the end of it all. It seemed extraordinary to her that Hester could choose to stay at Benbow when there was an alternative as snug and agreeable as the little house at Precentor's Court to make her home.

She thought nostalgically for a moment of the pleasant house where she and her brother had been brought up outside York; strict Quaker parents had in no way diminished happy childhood memories of a place that had been modest and simple but infinitely preferable to the rambling, grim, gray house that her brother had bought as his married home when he had begun to make a fortune out of merchandising. For all its size and sweeping parkland, Benbow Hall was not to Aunt Kitty's taste at all: she favored softer, more mellow surroundings, and she missed the comfort and color of ornaments and pictures around her, the convenience of gas lighting, the warmth of carpets beneath her feet, cushions at her back, and screens to shield her from the terrible draughts that seemed to whistle through every room and down every passage at Benbow.

She was pleased, on arrival, to find her niece apparently much improved in spirits, and disappointed, looking round, to find that everything was just as it had always been. Hester had made no changes or improvements that she could see: it was quite as cold and cheerless, and the draught blowing through the cavernous hall was actually lifting her skirts about her feet. Aunt Kitty was more determined than ever to persuade Hester to return to York with her.

"Only consider, my dear," she said later, when they were sitting in one of the smaller parlors beside a very sulky-looking fire, "winter will soon be over and there is so much to see and do in York. I shall stay on here as long as thou wishes, of course, but I am quite resolved that thou shalt come back with me."

Hester shook her head. "It's good of thee, Aunt, but for the moment my place is here. Papa left it to me to look after the estate—he expected me to take his place."

"But surely, my love, it is not necessary for thee to be here? There is a viewer for the colliery, a steward for the estate, a housekeeper to run the household . . ."

"Papa always concerned himself with every tenant and with every man who worked for him. I intend to do the same. Besides, there has been some trouble at the colliery."

"Then let the viewer deal with it, as he should. And if he cannot, refer him to thy guardian."

"My guardian! Don't speak of him, Aunt! I prefer to forget that I have a guardian at all."

Aunt Kitty looked a little flustered. "Well, to be sure, my dear, I do admit that when I heard that thy Papa had appointed Kirby England to look after thee I thought it *very* strange at first. But since I have come to know him better—"

"Know him better? What dost thou mean, Aunt Kitty?"

"He quite frequently calls on me at Precentor's Court, and we have had the most pleasant conversations. He really is a charming person, and I have quite overcome my prejudice against him."

Hester was staring at her aunt as though she had just confessed to high treason.

"I don't know how thou canst speak any good of him, especially when he drove Papa to an early grave."

"An exaggeration, I think, my dear. Kirby England did not shorten thy father's life by so much as one day."

"In my opinion, he did. Papa never recovered from the journey he made to York to see that man!"

Aunt Kitty rearranged her shawl calmly. "Well, thou must think as thou wishes, child. We are all entitled to our own view."

There was a short silence in the parlor.

"Why should he call on thee?" Hester said at last, curiosity getting the better of her.

"My dear, he calls for news of thee. He is well aware of thy dislike for him. How could he not be after that unfortunate meeting at the Assembly Rooms? And such letters as thou hast written in reply to his contain no more than a few lines and give him no information whatever."

Hester stood up and paced about the room. "There is no need for him to concern himself with me. The very idea of him poking his nose into my affairs is perfectly obnoxious!"

"I daresay that he feels the same sort of duty as thou feels towards thy tenants," Aunt Kitty remarked innocently. "After all, thy papa left him in charge of thee just as he left thee in charge of this estate."

"I should have thought him incapable of any such feelings of duty—unless they were to his material advantage."

"What advantage could there be in this case—unless he were to marry thee?"

"Don't be absurd, Aunt Kitty."

"I agree that such an idea would be ridiculous, especially as he already must have a far greater fortune than thine own. Doubtless his sights are set on a duke's daughter at least. No, it is simply a matter, so far as thou art concerned, of keeping his word to thy father—however tiresome and tedious it might be for him."

"Did he say that? That he finds me tiresome and tedious?"

"Well, my dear, thou canst hardly expect him to find it very diverting to have to take up his time in looking after the interests of a seventeen-year-old minor as uncooperative as thyself. He is a very busy man. It must be a great nuisance for him. Do sit down, child; thou art making me feel quite dizzy with all that marching up and down."

But Hester was too agitated to sit still. Aunt Kitty's betrayal had upset her too much.

"Thou canst not really like him?"

"But I do. He is *very* charming, as I have told thee. And very handsome—if one overlooks the lack of breeding in his features. And I find his speech most refreshing. Of course, he is richer than ever now, and it is almost certain that he will become the next Lord Mayor of York."

"Stop, Aunt Kitty! Because he is rich and powerful thou art blind to everything else. Canst thou honestly tell me that thou wouldst ever have appointed him guardian thyself?"

"Perhaps not, my dear. But then I have not thy late and respected father's cleverness. He was always an excellent judge of character."

"Papa was very ill. In William's opinion, his mind was badly affected. He didn't know what he was doing."

"Stuff and nonsense!" Aunt Kitty declared with surprising fierceness. "Thy father knew exactly what he was doing and his mind was crystal-clear to the end. I saw him here two days before he died, as thou knows, and he told me just why he had asked Kirby England to be thy guardian. At the time I thought it odd; now I see how wise he was."

Hester stopped her pacing to stare at her aunt. "What reason did Papa give thee? I should like to hear it, for he never would give me one."

"In that case I must not say—"

"But thou must!"

"I'm sure I should not. Amos did not *precisely* bind me to any secrecy, but if he had wanted thee to know then he would have told thee himself."

"Aunt Kitty," Hester said in measured tones, "if thou wilt not give me the reason then I shall wait until I am next at Meeting for Worship at Friargate and I shall tell Edith Frohawk that thou hast had *twelve* new bonnets this year."

"Thou wouldst not!"

"I would!"

"But I have only had six."

"Edith Frohawk will much prefer to believe me, being the ill-natured, wicked old gossip that she is. *And* I shall tell her about the new painting thou hast bought."

"Hester! Thou art sometimes a great trial to me and far from the obedient and dutiful niece thou shouldst be." Aunt Kitty sighed. "Very well, I will tell thee, though I daresay it will do no good and thou wilt not be at all pleased."

Hester sat down, fixing her eyes on her aunt's face. She waited.

"There were two reasons, so far as I remember," Aunt Kitty said reluctantly. "The first was that thy father considered Kirby England to be the best man of his acquaintance to take care of thy fortune—to manage thy investments, to see that thou art not cheated."

"Set a thief to catch a thief," Hester murmured.

"Speak up, my dear. My hearing is no better."

"Nothing, Aunt."

"Well, thy guardian's own wealth is evidence enough that thy papa was right. And I daresay thine inheritance will have increased substantially by the time thou art of age. I have taken thy guardian's advice myself on several modest little investments and they have turned out *most* satisfactorily—"

"And the second reason?" Hester asked with gritted teeth.

"To stop thee marrying William."

Hester was so astonished that she sat, mouth open, without speaking. Aunt Kitty went on.

"I thought thou realized, my love, that thy papa did not care at all for thy cousin. He had his reasons, I presume, but he never spoke of them—any more than he spoke ill of anybody. He refused William permission to speak to thee not long before he died. He did not think that William would make thee happy—a view which I have always shared."

Hester had shut her mouth tightly. She was very white. "And what has all this to do with Kirby England? What business is it of his?"

"Surely it must be obvious to thee, my dear. The second reason for choosing Kirby England was because he and William were hardly the best of friends. It must have been a pleasure for him to agree to see that thou did not marry William—so long as he was thy guardian."

"I see," Hester said in a deceptively quiet tone.

"And now they are the bitterest of enemies," Aunt Kitty said happily. "William made a lot of trouble for him recently. He got together with a number of Friends in York and some of the Whigs and they petitioned Parliament about the electioneering methods of the York Tories. Remember what we read in the *York Courant*. Well, sixty Tories from York, including Kirby England, had to go to London to testify before the Commons Committee, and thy guardian was questioned for two days. It might have succeeded, but the Tories found witnesses to testify against the Whigs and accuse *them* of intimidation at the polling booths."

"Whom they bribed handsomely, no doubt."

"I don't know about that, my dear. All I know is that it made very entertaining reading in the newspapers for several weeks!"

Aunt Kitty turned her attention to the failing fire and rang the bell for the servant to bring more coals and attend to it.

Hester picked up her embroidery and wielded her needle fiercely. Aunt Kitty's revelation was quite enough to make her determined to marry William as soon as he asked her. Her mind seethed with indignation at the thought that Kirby England had the power to prevent it. If necessary she would elope with William. She would do anything to defy the authority of such a man as her guardian. How she hated him! She did not care that it was unchristian to do so—she hated him! She was more than ever convinced that William was right and that Papa's mind had been disturbed by his illness. He had never spoken of a dislike for William, and if he had done so to Aunt Kitty at the end, it had been because his mind had become confused. He had chosen Kirby England because of that confusion and Kirby England had accepted because, for some reason, it had amused him to do so. She felt no duty to respect the arrangement.

The school which Hester had opened for the miners' children was to be found in a small stonebuilt house not far from the coal staithes at Garford. Later she planned to move to a better place, but for the moment, the modest building with its one classroom would do. She had come home to Benbow from the Quaker school in York a well-educated young woman and for the first time she had become aware of the complete lack of schooling for the children she saw running wild about Benbow Moor and the colliery. None could read or write and none had any hope of improving themselves unless they learned.

With her father's encouragement, and with the aid of Miss Fowler, a spinster of Garford with a gift for teaching, she began a school for the colliery children. They had cleared out and cleaned the little stone house, painted the walls, mended the windows, bought desks, chairs, an easel, chalks, pens, ink, books and copybooks . . .

At first few had come. One or two, sent by their mothers, had appeared, giggling and apprehensive, or scornful and lordly at the school door. Most of these had not returned a second day. Undaunted, Hester and Miss Fowler had visited every miner's home, talking to the wives and mothers and persuading them to encourage their children to attend classes. In many cases they had met with refusal and incomprehension. Where neither parent could read or write they rarely saw any need for their son or daughter to learn. In their view, it would only lead to trouble and discontent. Besides, what use, they said, was fancy book-learning down the mine, or in the mill?

But some of them, who did want to learn, continued to come to the school. And, gradually, others joined them—out of curiosity, a grudging interest and respect for Hester and Miss Fowler. Before a year had passed they had a regular class of more than thirty children.

During Aunt Kitty's visit Hester continued her teaching as usual. It was tiring work: the children could be noisy and difficult, and the wilder ones could quickly cause havoc in the class if she relaxed her attention for a minute. However, they were making steady progress. Even Tom Bartlett, the slowest of them all, had read aloud a passage from the Bible, and she was proud of him. Hester returned to Benbow Hall on that day, feeling encouraged and hopeful. Her pleasure was short-lived: Aunt Kitty greeted her with the news that Kirby England had called and was waiting for her in the library.

"Thou must see him, my love. He has come all the way from York."

"I shall certainly see him," Hester said. "I am not afraid of him. But I cannot imagine what we shall find to say to each other. I have *nothing* to say to him."

She went into the library and Kirby England rose to his feet. She was annoyed to see that he had been sitting in her father's chair.

"I've been waiting some time to see you, Miss Gurney."

"I'm sorry. I had no idea thou wast here."

"You've been busy teaching at that school of yours, your aunt tells me."

"Yes."

"What do you teach them?"

"Reading . . . writing . . . simple sums."

"Don't you find it a waste of time sometimes? In my village half the children didn't want the bother of learning and refused to go to school. They thought it sissy."

"There is always the other half. We have more than thirty in our class."

He looked at her thoughtfully. "Aye—that's true. There'll always be some who'll want to learn. One or two out of your thirty may learn enough from you to pull themselves up by their bootstraps. I congratulate you on giving them the chance."

He seemed to be studying her hard. She moved away from him uneasily, and there was silence.

"Aren't you going to ask me to sit down?"

"Of course."

He sat down—again in her father's chair—and she took a seat opposite him. Time had not improved him, she thought. He looked more affluent, and coarser with it. She stared back at him.

He said bluntly: "I know what you're thinking, lass. You're no keener to have me for a guardian than I am to find myself with you for a ward. I'm a very busy man and there's only one reason I've come here today—to keep my promise to a dying man. It looks like we're stuck with each other for the next three years, so the sooner we both get used to the idea, the better."

Hester was silent, not knowing what to say. She turned her head away from him and looked out of the window; the skies were a sullen gray, and it had begun to rain.

"Well now, suppose we get down to brass tacks," he said. "I take it you've made no changes at the colliery as I advised?"

"I have not."

"You've not dismissed the viewer?"

"Certainly not."

"Nor cut down on the pit lads?"

"I have not," she repeated.

"Then you're a foolish lass. You've a drunken, no-good viewer in charge of your colliery, discontented miners because of it and, as a result, falling production and sales. And you're too proud and stubborn to do anything about it."

"Things will improve—"

"They won't. I know the signs. If you don't take steps to rectify matters you'll have real trouble on your hands before long."

"I can manage quite well, I thank thee."

He shrugged his shoulders impatiently and stood up to walk

over to the window, hands clasped behind his back; his heavyset figure blotted out light, making the room dim.

He said matter of factly: "I take it that you don't mind letting your father's work go to ruin . . . You're happy to see the colliery run down and the miners starve for lack of wages."

Hester bit her lip: put like that, it sounded terrible. She could no longer deceive herself that things were any better at the colliery—in fact, they were worse. And last week there had been an unpleasant accident in which a miner had broken his leg in a fall due to another man's carelessness. He had been injured so badly that it was doubtful if he would ever be able to work in the mine again. She had ordered him to be paid two weeks' allowance of seven shillings and sent him coal and candles, as well as food, and she would continue to do all she could for him and his family. But if one accident had occurred, so could another: she could remember her father saying once that unrest in the mine was the same as unsafe. There was the constant threat of a firedamp explosion or flooding from the water that poured without cease into the mine and was kept at bay by the great steam engine, pumping night and day. The responsibility for it all lay on her shoulders and she was finding it a hard burden; there had been whispers already that as a woman she was bringing them bad luck. At Christmas she had punctiliously continued her father's old custom of distributing a guinea to each miner and fourteen pounds for the colliers' annual treat. She had not neglected the three hundred corves of coal for the poor of Garford, nor the blankets for the needy and charity for the widows and orphans. But it was not enough: she longed for help, but could not bring herself to ask it of Kirby England.

Instead she said defiantly: "If sales have fallen it is thy fault."

He turned from the window, eyebrows raised. "That's a novel thought! How d'you reckon that?"

"If the railway had been built through Garford, then we would have been able to sell more coal than ever before. Papa had even planned to sink a new shaft above Elizabeth Pit. Didst thou not admit to Papa that the change of route was thy suggestion?"

"I did that."

"Well then."

"Well then nothing! If it hadn't been for me there'd've been no railway going anywhere at all. I'll build you a railway through Garford soon enough, just as your father wanted. Meantime, it so happens that I can help improve sales at the colliery."

"How? We can't compete with other collieries nearer the turnpikes."

"Listen to me, lass. The Leeds to Selby railway line has just opened. Don't use the turnpikes. Get your coal taken by railway from Newthorpe, south of Garford, as far as Selby; from there it can be shipped up the Ouse to York." He tapped at his coat pocket. "I've an order with me from a friend of mine, a Mr. Joseph Meek, who owns a big glassworks in York; he'd like you to supply him with a thousand tons annually. And there's plenty more like that, if you want them. I'm a director of the York Union Gas Light Company. I can see that Benbow Colliery supplies them. I'll see you get all the orders that you can fill—but only on one condition."

"Papa taught me never to accept conditions."

"He'd agree with this one. If you dismiss that intemperate, useless viewer of yours and get rid of half the pit lads to make an economic work force, *then* you'll have your York orders from me, but not otherwise. I'm not recommending Benbow to anyone unless I know it can produce the coal in enough quantity, on time and at a competitive price. At the moment it can't."

Hester knew she had no choice but to agree; it put her under an obligation to Kirby England and she resented the fact bitterly. When he took his leave she was unwise enough to attempt to even the score.

"Those York and North Midland Railway Company shares that thou bought on my behalf—"

"Oh, aye."

"I'd like them to be sold at once," she said firmly. "My cousin tells me that they have fallen steadily in value. He says that they are a very bad risk."

"Does he now!"

"I'm told that there have been long delays and difficulties in building thy wonderful new railway."

Much to her irritation, he only grinned. "Unfortunately, lass, your father left *me* and not your cousin in control of your investments. I've no intention of selling your railway shares, whatever you think about it. They'll make you a small fortune in the end."

"I have only thy word for that."

"Aye . . . just so." He looked down at her, unsmiling now. "And you're going to have to learn to trust my judgment. In any case, there's nowt you can do about it."

After that he left so abruptly that Aunt Kitty, who had been listening to every word from behind the door, had hardly enough time to retreat decently before he strode from the room. She found her niece fretting and fuming that her guardian was the most self-important, arrogant boor that she had ever had the misfortune to encounter. Aunt Kitty's gentle protests that her niece should be grateful to him fell on deaf ears.

Before returning to York, Kirby went up to Benbow Colliery. He rode up again in the closed, horse-drawn wagon that he had taken before with Amos Gurney. As they rumbled slowly up through the beech woods towards the moor, it seemed to him that the dead man's ghost sat beside him. When he turned his head he half expected to see the somberly clothed figure with its broad-brimmed black hat sitting proudly on the uncomfortable wooden bench. Kirby felt like cursing the shade of the man who had led him to waste his time like this on a stubborn, unappreciative chit of a Quaker girl with too sharp a tongue and only a pair of unusually beautiful gray eyes to commend her. God knows why he had bothered at all. Just the same, the colliery was worth helping if the daughter was not. He had been fascinated by the mine on his previous visit and impressed by the colliers themselves. He understood such men perfectly, and could not rid himself of the ridiculous notion that they had now become, in a sense, his responsibility. The Quaker girl was incapable of saving the situation: she was far too young and inexperienced, and since she would not listen to advice, there had been no alternative but to take matters into his own hands. If he did not intervene, the miners could soon be out of work, and Kirby knew all about the poverty that would follow for them and their families. He was very familiar with the gnawing pain of an empty stomach, the misery of constant cold, of damp and ragged clothes, of leaking boots stuffed with rags and paper . . . all the degradation and deprivation that slowly and surely destroyed both spirit and flesh.

He arrived up at Elizabeth Pit to find Mr. Atkins dead-drunk and asleep at his desk. Taking command, he sent for a bucket of cold water and emptied it over the man's head, reviving the viewer just sufficiently for him to hear and comprehend his own instant dismissal. With the willing assistance of a handful of the men, Kirby had him removed bodily and bundled into an empty coal wagon to be transported, still only half conscious, down to the Garford staithes. That done, he appointed another man, slow-witted but sober and honest, to take charge until he could find a proper replacement to put the colliery back on an even keel. He listened patiently to an unending stream of complaints from the miners and promised them improvements, wages paid on time, better conditions. The half-past-three shift was waiting its turn; he singled out one of the men as a guide and announced his intention of going down with them to inspect the mine.

It was an experience that Kirby never forgot. Nothing in his imagination had prepared him for the dizzy plunge down that narrow black hole into the depths of the earth. Balanced astride an empty corf and gripping onto the rope that lowered him, he found that without the miners' easy knack his arms and elbows were rubbed raw against the side of the shaft. The four-hundred-foot descent into darkness was endless; time and distance were measureless; the breath seemed knocked from his lungs, and a strong smell of coal dust and damp filled his nostrils.

The mine itself proved a hellish underworld of black tunnels where lamps glimmered feebly like distant stars, barely penetrating the dreadful darkness. The heat was intense and the lack of good, clean air stifling. Kirby was a hard-nerved man, but even he had to suppress the primitive fear of suffocation that took hold of him, and to reject from his mind the thought of the crushing weight overhead—the hundreds and thousands of tons of rock and earth that bore down on the fragile, man-made warren.

Instead, he concentrated on looking and listening as the function of the ventilation furnace at the foot of a shaft was explained to him. The heated air rose up the shaft, drawing more air from the lowest part of the mine to be heated in its turn and that air's place was taken by fresh air finding its way down another shaft. Thus a continuous current of air was made to circulate through the mine.

He examined the wooden pit props supporting the roof and watched the wooden corves carrying the hewn coal along iron tramplates. These tramplates, he discovered with interest, were broad flat rails with a flange while the wheels of the corves that ran on them were made without flanges. Self-acting inclined planes helped the movement of these lines of corves, and ropes connected both full and empty containers, passing round the drum of a jenny, with a brake and winding handle to slow or speed the corves as necessary on their journey through the mine. The sound of their rattling progress echoed loudly down the long tunnels, together with the ringing of metal tools, the clanking of chains and the muffled, menacing rushing of subterranean streams.

Kirby followed his guide down passages so low that he had to stoop to avoid hitting his head, and sometimes they were so small he could only crawl on hands and knees. And everywhere there was water: it drip-dripped from the roof, it trickled insidiously down the walls and formed black, sludgy puddles with the coal dust on the ground. Soon he was wet through. He had left his coat and waistcoat at the top and was thankful for it; the heat and the wet made clothing a liability.

The miners themselves were half naked, begrimed black beings, their faces and bodies streaked with running sweat. They moved about with the ease of long familiarity with the cramped blackness of their world. The mine was worked pillar and stall: headways were driven into the coal seam and along these headways, at intervals of several yards, stalls were cut as working places for each hewer. The hewer crouched or lay—there being no possible room to stand—in his stall, smiting at the hard wall with his pick and levering away great slabs of coal with a crow-bar. Kirby saw that many of these men had knobs and scars down their backs where their flesh had been torn and rubbed by the low roof. The putters worked behind the hewers, shoveling the coal into the empty corves. The hurriers, who were mere lads, then guided and pulled and pushed the loaded corves along the tramplates to the bottom of the shaft, aided by the ropes and jenny.

Kirby, used to hardship, was nonetheless appalled at the working conditions he saw, and his admiration for the miners increased tenfold. They seemed to take their unnatural, animal-like existence below ground for granted. And if they had any fear of the unpleasant death that might come upon them at any time, they did not show it. It was not difficult to picture the nightmare that would follow on any major accident—roof-fall, explosion or flood—where a sudden, quick death would be merciful compared with the alternative slow suffocation of being buried alive. For himself, he was glad to be hoisted back up to the normal world, to see the gray Yorkshire skies above him, the open moorland round him and to feel the cold wind on his face. He breathed deeply, savoring the simple freedom of it all. The visit had decided him: he would do all he could for the miners of Benbow Colliery. First, he would find a good man to replace the dismissed viewer; after that he would see what else might be done.

Kirby returned to York that evening. He changed his clothes and dined at home; from there he went on to the Theatre Royal. The evening's performance was nearing its close, and he entered by the stage door and walked up the draughty passageway that led him behind the scenes. The prompt man, perched on his high stool behind the curtain, gave him a quick nod. Kirby leaned against a wall, arms folded, and watched from the darkness of the wings. Rosa was on stage. The sharp contrast between the dazzling, make-believe world being enacted before the floats and the gray, unglamorous starkness of backstage struck him as never before. There was little magic about the theatre, he decided. It was all an illusion—a clever conjuring trick perpetrated on a willing audience who wanted nothing better than to forget their troubles for an hour or two in a fantasy of music and color. He thought again of the miners still working their eight-hour shift fathoms deep in the ground at Benbow. The gaudy glitter before him seemed as far removed from the dark and grim world of those men as the moon from the earth.

Rosa was singing. She held the center of the stage, wearing a gown of the same cornflower blue as when he had first seen her. If possible, she looked even more beautiful than then. There had been a time when she had grown so thin and pale that he had been alarmed for her health, but she had recovered slowly from whatever had ailed her and bloomed like a flower once more. He watched her, and another contrast came into his mind: the warmth and devotion of the lovely, feminine Rosa and the cold hostility of his ward. The first embodied everything he liked in women; the second everything he thoroughly disliked.

Kirby half shut his eyes and listened to Rosa singing.

> *"Cherry-ripe, cherry-ripe, ripe I cry,*
> *Full and fair ones; come and buy . . ."*

Her voice had a pure and bell-like tone that lifted the simple song into something of rare quality.

When she had finished she curtsied to the loud applause and came running offstage towards him. At first she did not see him standing in the shadows, and when he stepped forward she gave a cry of delight and flung herself into his arms.

He went with her up the flight of stairs that led directly from backstage to the principal dressing room; he sat down and waited while she changed out of her stage costume behind the corner screen.

"You look tired," she said, her voice muffled by the blue gown as she pulled it over her head. "That's not like you—you're as strong as an ox."

"I've been busy."

"You always are!"

He grunted.

"Well, tell me what you've been doing today then."

"Amongst other things, visiting my ward at Garford."

Rosa's face appeared round the side of the screen; she looked startled.

"The Quakeress?"

"She's the only one I have, so far as I know, thank God," he commented.

"Why did you have to visit her?"

"Business. Duty."

"What is she like?"

He shrugged his broad shoulders. "All in gray and dreariness, like Quakeresses usually are, except this one's a bloody sight less meek and mild than I thought they were supposed to be."

Rosa pouted. "Is she pretty?"

"No. And she's as sour as a quince."

"She must have something to commend her."

"Nowt that I can see."

"I'm glad to hear it. I shouldn't like you to fall in love with her."

"Pigs may fly!"

"She might fall in love with you."

Kirby laughed. "Even less likely. She doesn't fancy my rough ways—nor anything about me."

Rosa emerged from behind the screen, ravishingly beautiful in pink satin. "Then she must be blind and deaf."

Kirby held her against him and kissed her. "Let's talk about you, not her. I'm leaving for London the day after tomorrow; I'll be away a fortnight, probably longer. Come with me."

"You mean that?"

"I wouldn't say it if I didn't. I want you with me. And I'll get you that audition at Drury Lane. It's about time you finished with this third-rate theatre."

Rosa smiled up at him, arms round his neck. "I'll come to London with you Kirby, and not only for the chance of an audition—though I'd do anything for that—but because I want to. I told you—you're the best lover I've ever had."

He kissed her again with a roughness that she did not mind; she tightened her arms about him. She had come as near to loving this man as any she had known. But Rosa was a realist and love was something she could not afford as a struggling actress.

Kirby would not want her forever: one day he would tire of her, and on that day she must be established enough for it not to matter—except to her pride. It must never matter to her heart.

The small success she had had in York was all very well, but it was London that counted. London . . . and Drury Lane.

CHAPTER VI

Soon shall thy arm, unconquered steam! afar
Drag the slow barge, or drive the rapid car;
Or on wide waving wings expanded bear
The flying-chariot through the field of air.

Erasmus Darwin, 1731–1802

Elias Snell did not greatly care for William Gurney. It was not precisely a personal dislike, but rather that he found the company of all Quakers uncongenial. Perhaps their renowned philanthropy made him uneasily aware of his own shortcomings in that direction. He had been an eloquent member of the Public Health Committee and loud in his condemnation of the slums of York, but any citizen asked what exactly Mr. Snell had *done* for the poor would have been hard pressed for an answer. However, he had two things in common with William Gurney: both men were lawyers and both were united in their hatred of Kirby England.

Elias Snell paid an unexpected visit to William Gurney's chambers in Coney Street and slid smoothly into the chair he was offered. He was, as always, impeccably dressed, with hardly a speck of dust to mar the perfection of his attire despite walking some way from his own chambers through the streets of York.

"What can I do for thee?" William inquired politely. He watched his visitor with cool and speculative eyes.

Elias Snell crossed one leg carefully over the other and squinted down his long, sharp nose. "The matter is of some delicacy, Mr. Gurney."

"Yes?"

"You are, of course, acquainted with Mr. Kirby England. We have had, I recall, occasion to discuss both him and his business affairs."

"Yes?"

"And we share a mutual distrust of him, I believe."

William waited. He was too cautious a lawyer to show any cards before he knew the game to be played.

Elias Snell coughed and touched his lips with his olive-skinned fingers. "Certain rumors have reached me concerning the York and North Midland Railway Company which, as a shareholder, I find *most* disturbing . . ."

"I had understood that thou disapproved strongly of the building of the railway and yet thou hast bought shares in the company?"

Elias Snell looked pained. Quaker principles were beyond him. "I felt it expedient and desirable that I should place myself in a position to maintain a close watch on that company," he protested. "Where Mr. England is concerned I have come to regard myself as the citizens' watchdog . . . so to speak. Three days ago I attended a half-yearly meeting of the shareholders, and although many of them were lulled into a state of confidence by clever blandishments of Mr. England and his directors, I was not among them."

"I can readily believe that thou wast not."

"Quite so. I made a strong protest to the board about the continual delays in the construction of the railway line, which we were originally informed would be completed within a year. In fact, only one quarter of it has been built so far. Mr. England was compelled to admit to the meeting that the survey had been too hastily prepared and had had to be revised at several places where it was found to be faulty. We were told of all manner and variety of unforeseen engineering problems, accidents, setbacks . . . There was no end to the excuses trotted out. I suggested to the chairman and directors that the whole scheme had been nothing but a gambling speculation delayed to suit the share market."

William's eyes flickered with appreciation. "And what answer was given?"

132

"Naturally, it was denied. What else would you expect? Mr. England was at great pains to inform us that Mr. George Stephenson himself was prepared to guarantee the soundness of the enterprise."

"George Stephenson is their trump card," William said. "His name is produced to confound any opposition or silence any critics."

"So I am beginning to understand. We were also told that Mr. Stephenson himself has invested over twenty thousand pounds in the company and induced his friends to follow suit. Meanwhile, the facts are that precious little of the railway is constructed and the much-vaunted steam horses of Mr. Stephenson's have yet to emerge from their stables at his Newcastle factory."

"I am not clear exactly how this concerns me."

Elias Snell examined his polished fingernails carefully. "I have formed the definite conclusion that, as with most of Mr. England's dealings in this city, there is a strong odor of speculation and manipulation surrounding this railway company of his. I consider it nothing less than my duty as an officer of the law to protect innocent shareholders and honest citizens from him."

"How dost thou propose to do that?"

"By uncovering irrefutable proof of irregularities and illegalities that I am certain exist, and by leaving no stone unturned until he is completely discredited."

"The Lord God punishes sinners," William said. "No one is wicked without loss and punishment."

"Quite so," repeated Elias Snell, who had no intention of waiting for God to act in the matter. "But do I have your support? May I count on you to keep vigil for any evidence that might bring this sinner to justice before his fellowmen?"

"It will not be easy; many are deceived by him."

"Oh, he is popular with tradesmen and the like," acknowledged the other. "He is clever enough to be seen to be lavishly hospitable to all, as well as overtly generous; his name is to be found at the top of every charity subscription list."

"He also has great influence with the Council. I have even heard it rumored that he may be the next Lord Mayor."

Elias Snell smiled thinly. "There are so many facets to Mr.

Kirby England, are there not? Draper, banker, director, railway company chairman, newspaper proprietor . . . er, guardian. The list is a long one. If Lord Mayor is added to it we shall have to endure the unwelcome spectacle of him crowing like a cock on his own dunghill. It should not be beyond our capabilities either to bring him down from that height . . . or, better still, to see that he never attains it."

William Gurney said nothing; he seemed absorbed in straightening some papers on his desk. His visitor stood up.

"I fear I have taken up too much of your valuable time, Mr. Gurney."

The Quaker raised his head. "He must have fingers of iron that will flay the devil," he said softly. "Thou hast my support."

Elias Snell lowered his lids, well pleased. He had approached William Gurney because he knew that the York Quakers were deeply suspicious of Kirby England, and he could think of no better ally than the Society of Friends, where honesty and business integrity were at stake. There was another reason, which concerned the man in front of him personally. Elias Snell was gratified to see that his judgment had proved sound, for he had, at that moment, surprised an expression in the lawyer's eyes that had told him instantly that behind the pious façade lay a thirst for Kirby England's blood that was quite as vengeful as his own; the ironical fact that the upstart draper was guardian to the Quaker's heiress cousin added a flavor to the hunt that promised to make it altogether a most entertaining and satisfying affair.

It was the following autumn before Hester returned Aunt Kitty's visit. Affairs had improved so much at the colliery that she felt no anxiety about leaving Benbow. The new viewer had shown himself to be an excellent manager—his only flaw in Hester's eyes being that he had been put forward by her guardian. However, the consequent increase in the mine's production had been so impressive that she could only, in honesty, be thankful. And she was further in Kirby England's debt: considerable orders had begun to come in from companies in York, and in five months the colliery had transported nearly six thousand tons to the city by way of the new Leeds to Selby railway and the

River Ouse. To her delight, the railway company had proposed to consider building a short branch line out to Garford. The colliery had to provide its own wagons for use on the railway, but the higher sales were offsetting this cost, and the locomotive steam engines used to haul them had proved greatly superior to horses. The only disadvantage, so far as Hester could discover, was that the engine's wheels tended to slip very badly on the iron rails if the weather was wet, though this was rectified to some degree by the fireman strewing ashes. According to the newspapers, her guardian's York and North Midland Railway was still, by contrast, a long way from completion.

To Hester's relief, she had heard nothing from Kirby England since his unwelcome visit to Benbow Hall, beyond one letter commending the new viewer to her employ. And on arriving to stay with Aunt Kitty in York, she was pleased to find that he was safely away in London, where he apparently spent an increasing amount of his time.

No. 1 Precentor's Court was unchanged save for the addition of a new clock which Aunt Kitty had lately acquired.

"The old one kept such bad time," she complained. "What could I do but purchase a new one?"

Hester looked at the massive and very splendid timepiece with its black marble and ormolu case, smothered with golden cherubs, bunches of grapes and garlands of flowers.

"What does Minister Caleb Williams think of it?" she inquired innocently.

"I have no idea . . . and I do not see the need to ask him," Aunt Kitty replied defensively.

Time passed pleasantly. Aunt Kitty would not hear of her niece returning to Benbow. When Hester began to talk of leaving, her aunt declared that she felt very low-spirited and was in need of company and comfort.

"How canst thou think of deserting me, my dear; it would be quite heartless of thee! After all, thou art my only remaining relative."

"There is William."

"I don't count him."

So Hester stayed in York and the weeks turned into months; Christmas was only a short way off.

Life followed a peaceful and ordered pattern. The two women received visitors, paid calls, went shopping; on every First Day they went to worship at Friargate, where they sat on polished, pitch-pine benches in the Meeting House. The women assembled all on one side, resembling a flock of doves in their gray dresses, gray bonnets and China crepe shawls. The men sat on the other side—more ravenlike in their black garb. The Elders faced the gathering from their raised bench at the end of the room.

It was the only time that Hester knew Aunt Kitty to be silent. Her aunt sat, head bowed and apparently deep in thought, but Hester noticed that it was quite remarkable how much she managed to observe of the Meeting, and comment on afterwards, without once moving her head. She knew exactly who and how many had attended and how they had looked.

"Whoso hearkeneth unto me shall be quiet and fear no evil," Hester repeated to herself determinedly, her eyes fixed on her gloved hands in her lap as she sought solace and inspiration. It would have been easier to concentrate her thoughts if she had not been uneasily aware of William's eyes directed upon her from his seat on the Elders' bench.

There were some household purchases that Aunt Kitty always insisted on making herself, saying that the servants could not be trusted to select the very best quality merchandise. The truth was that she loved shops anyway. She spent happy hours peering into this shop window and that—the grocer, the apothecary, the confectioner, the haberdasher—and her small, plump figure was a familiar sight to the proprietors of all high-class establishments as she rootled and poked among the wares—rejecting, considering and spending a great deal of time over the choice of the most trifling item.

One afternoon Hester accompanied her aunt to Mr. Todd, the tea dealer in Goodramgate, with the object of purchasing a particular blend of Ceylon tea. This accomplished, they made their way to Mr. Terry's confectionery shop, where Aunt Kitty, after much deliberation, bought some mint lozenges and some damson drops. By the time they left the shop it had begun to snow and soft white flakes drifted down across the cobblestones.

Aunt Kitty clicked her tongue in annoyance. "What a nuisance, my dear. I had several other items on my list. However, I suppose we should return home before the weather worsens. Buttons I *must* find before we do, though, and some plain ribbon for my bonnet. Thy guardian's drapery shop is not far from here and it is quite the best in York. If thou dost not object to a little snow, Hester my love, I know I shall quickly find what I want there."

They hurried along to the corner of College Street, where the bow-fronted shop, lit by gas lamps within, beckoned alluringly like some enchanter's cave. Aunt Kitty pressed her nose to the glass panes and exclaimed with pleasure at the rich selection of goods so temptingly arranged in the window: lengths of silk, satin and velvet, cobwebby lace, ribbons of every color in the rainbow, pincushions, wools, umbrellas, shawls, ladies' feather-trimmed bonnets, gloves, stockings, buttons, scarves, trimmings, fans of mother-of-pearl, carved ivory, pierced horn . . .

"I told thee that it was the very best draper's in York," Aunt Kitty said with a satisfied sigh.

They went inside, and the jangling doorbell brought forth an attentive and courteous assistant. Hester found herself examining the place with some curiosity. Originally quite small, the shop had been extended to include the next-door premises and was large and well lit. The merchandise was clearly of the finest quality and was carefully and cleverly displayed. A long wooden counter separated customer from assistant, and Hester, staring at this, found it impossible to imagine Kirby England standing behind that barrier of highly polished mahogany as a boy of fifteen or so. This then was the counter that he had succeeded in "jumping over" to such riches and notoriety.

Aunt Kitty, buttons and ribbon quite forgotten, had been diverted by some rolls of pretty material at the back of the shop, and Hester, seeing that she would have some time to wait, settled herself patiently on a chair beside the counter. She listened to her aunt discussing the relative merits of Canterbury and

India muslin with the assistant and was idly fingering through some patterns left on the counter when the doorbell jangled loudly again and Kirby England walked in.

Hester, who had glanced up at the sound, turned scarlet and dropped the patterns on the floor. She had understood him to be still away in London, and it was the greatest mischance to have been found here by him: somehow to have been discovered in *his* shop made it all the more vexing.

He had stopped dead at the sight of her sitting there in her gray mantle and bonnet, but he recovered himself quickly and moved forward to retrieve the patterns for her.

"Miss Gurney! I'd no notion you were in York!"

She dropped the patterns quickly back on the counter. Aunt Kitty, abandoning her muslins, greeted the shop's proprietor with far more enthusiasm than her niece would have wished.

"My dear madam," Kirby responded, bowing low to her, "I am honored to have you as a customer. Had I known you were coming I should have been behind the counter to serve you myself."

Aunt Kitty giggled appreciatively. "Thy days behind the counter are long since past," she said, wagging a finger at him. "More's the pity, I say. Thou must have been an excellent draper."

He smiled. "I hope I still am. I keep a close watch on all my businesses, which is why I am here now. I reckon to know nearly every item on sale in this shop."

"*Amazing!*" cried Aunt Kitty, much impressed. "When thou art such a *busy* gentleman and hast so much else on thy mind!"

Kirby glanced at Hester, who was glowering at a selection of fans displayed nearby. "I had no idea that my ward was in York, or I would've called on you. I've been away in London several weeks."

"So we understood."

"But now that I'm back," he continued firmly, "I insist that you both come to dinner at my house. Will Friday next suit you?"

To Hester's dismay, Aunt Kitty accepted with alacrity, and worse was to come. The snow, by this time, had settled quite thickly and Aunt Kitty, peering out of the window, gave a cry of alarm.

"I don't know how we shall manage to walk home in this!"

"There's no need for you to do so," Kirby told her. "My carriage is just outside. You shall make use of it."

Hester would have preferred to walk ten miles in a blizzard than make use of anything belonging to him, but since she could not expect Aunt Kitty to agree, she remained silent.

The smart four-wheeled britska was standing outside the shop door, its glossy black and brown paintwork mirroring the gaslight. A coating of snow lay like a veil across the folding hood and encrusted the small square panes of glass in the windscreen. Aunt Kitty was thrilled by its racy style and extravagance.

"Does it go very *fast?*"

"Not today—not on this slippery surface," Kirby said with a grin as he handed her up. "Another time I'll take you out myself and we'll break the record to Tadcaster and back!"

He took Hester's arm and helped her up too. "Don't fret, lass. I'm not coming with you. I've business to see to here yet. But make sure you come to dinner on Friday with your aunt or I'll be out to fetch you myself."

He shut the door after her and the carriage moved off down Goodramgate.

"I must tell thee, Hester," Aunt Kitty said quickly, before her niece could speak, "that I have every intention of accepting thy guardian's invitation. Nothing would prevent me from seeing inside that house, and I hear the dinners he gives are wonderfully lavish. Only the thought of that mother of his as hostess spoils my anticipation of the evening, but I shall support her in order to satisfy my curiosity."

It was useless to argue: Aunt Kitty could be very determined when she wished. Besides, Hester could not be certain that Kirby England would not carry out his threat if she failed to appear.

On the following day Henry Latham called at No. 1 Precentor's Court. Aunt Kitty was lying down with a headache, and so Hester received him alone in the parlor. She thought he looked drawn and tired; long absences away from the fresh, open air of

Yorkshire and long hours spent in the stuffy confines of Westminster did not seem to agree with him, and he had a dispirited air. After a while she remarked on this.

"The truth is," he told her with a wry smile, "I have fallen in love."

"In love? But that should make thee happy, not miserable!"

"Not in this case."

"Is there anything I can do to help?"

He looked at her consideringly. "Now that I come to think of it, Hester, I think perhaps you can . . ."

"Well, who is she?"

"Adelaide England."

The very name was enough to make her blench. She could vaguely remember the girl at the Assembly Rooms, but Adelaide had spent so much time hiding behind her mother that her recollection of her guardian's sister was poor.

"She is very pretty, Henry. I do remember that. But isn't she very young?"

"She is the same age as yourself, but seems younger perhaps because she is so shy. That's why I think you might be able to help me, Hester. You and she could become friends. She is a delightfully charming girl. I know you will love her when you come to know her better."

"Know her better?" Hester said uneasily. "That is very unlikely—"

"With her brother as your guardian, you are surely bound to meet—especially while you are staying in York. You must call on her and her mother."

"As a matter of fact, we are asked for dinner there this Sixth Day."

"Well then . . ."

"Thou dost not understand, Henry. I want as little to do with my guardian as possible."

"Surely you are not still so prejudiced against him! Believe me, Hester, you could not have a better man to look after you."

"I do not share thy opinion, but don't let's argue about it. How would my becoming a friend of Adelaide England help thy suit in any case?"

"Adelaide is completely dominated by her mother. I believe Mrs. England is determined to keep her under her thumb forever. Whenever I call she guards Adelaide as fiercely as a dragon and I scarcely manage to speak with her at all. Every question I address to Adelaide her mother answers. So long as Mrs. England is there I have no hope."

"Poor Henry! But I still don't see—"

"If you became sufficiently well acquainted with Miss England, you could invite her to stay at Benbow Hall—*without* her mother."

"I'm beginning to understand. Then thou couldst, I suppose, by a curious coincidence, also call at Benbow?"

Henry smiled at her. "Exactly!"

"What about her brother?"

"Oh, Kirby would approve the match—he's already said as much. I should never address her without his permission."

No wonder he approves, thought Hester. As one of the county's most eligible bachelors, Henry would be a fine catch for a draper's sister.

"Then let him *order* his sister to marry thee. I am sure he is quite capable of it."

"Oh, Hester, be serious and forget how much you dislike Kirby for a moment. I don't want her to be influenced by *anyone*. I want her to accept me by herself. She is a very timid creature and has been bullied all her life, so far as I can see. I want this to be of her own will and wish."

Hester was touched. She thought Adelaide England a very lucky girl and hoped she would have the good sense to appreciate Henry's fine qualities and stand up to her mother. With luck, Henry's plan might succeed. She was as fond of him as if he had been her own brother and wished very much for his happiness.

"I'll do as you ask, Henry. I have no idea if Adelaide and I will deal well together, but if it is possible I shall invite her to Benbow."

The snow still lay deep over the streets of York when Aunt Kitty and Hester set out in the carriage for Monkgate. Christmas was just passed and the year 1836 about to begin.

Monkgate was deserted that evening except for the solitary

hunched figure of a fiddler who stood on the pavement outside No. 44. His melancholy playing carried far on the night air, filling the stillness of the snowy street with a sad lament. As their carriage drew up he ceased his bowing and shuffled forward hopefully. Hester searched her reticule for some coins. The man's face was long and thin and his hands, in ragged mittens, looked blue with cold. He took the money with pathetic gratitude, blessing her several times before recommencing his mournful tune.

As they passed into the bright, warm interior of the house the image of the poor wretch left behind in the bitter cold stayed in Hester's mind. She looked about her with scorn at the overdecorated hall, the grand staircase and the enormous pink and crystal gasolier overhead.

"Quite wonderfully vulgar, isn't it, my dear?" Aunt Kitty whispered in her ear as they progressed up the stairs. "It must have all cost a fortune."

There were a dozen or so other guests already assembled in the long drawing room on the first floor. Kirby England was not present, but his mother advanced towards them, gowned in violet satin and bedecked with a great quantity of amethysts. She greeted them with stiff condescension, her sharp eyes lingering critically over their plain Quaker dresses, as once before at the Assembly Rooms.

The other guests were all well-to-do citizens, sleek, prosperous people, and just the kind Hester had expected to find at her guardian's house, where invitations would be extended only to those who might be of some service to him.

Aunt Kitty, in her affable, good-natured way, soon engaged herself in conversation with a group of guests. Hester remained a little apart, feeling alien to the whole affair. She was surprised when her hostess came up to her again, plucked at her arm and drew her out of earshot of the rest.

"I am glad of this opportunity of speaking to you, Miss Gurney," she said in her oddly pronounced way. "We are not well acquainted, and I must tell you bluntly that I have always thought it an imposition by your late father to have burdened my son with the responsibility for a ward he had scarcely even set eyes on."

Hester was too taken aback by this to reply.

Mrs. England continued, glaring at her fiercely: "I hope you will not be misled into thinking that the situation gives you a prior claim on my son. It would be kindest to tell you now that he has no intention of wedding anyone but the highest born."

Hester stared at her incredulously and found her voice at last. "I too welcome this opportunity to speak frankly," she said in shaking tones. "Since thou hast raised the subject, I will tell thee that the burden of thy son's guardianship is no less for me than for him since I should have preferred it were almost anyone else on earth! And pray rest assured that nothing would prevail on me to marry thy son—if that is what thou implied—whom I consider to be one of the most unpleasant men I have ever had the misfortune to meet!"

Thoroughly upset both by her hostess's attack and her own failure to keep her temper under control, Hester moved away quickly before more could be said on either side. She came face to face with Adelaide England, who looked at her anxiously.

"Miss Gurney . . . I am so very sorry. I could see that Mama said something to offend you just now."

With an effort, Hester remembered her promise to Henry and said with a friendly smile: "No. But I may have offended *her*, and I am sorry for that."

"Mama can be *very* outspoken," Adelaide said in distress. "I'm sure she must have provoked you unforgivably. It's usually her way with people, but truly she doesn't mean it; she is always afraid they are looking down on *her*. I hope you will not think the worse of us."

Hester was contrite. She had been half ready to include Adelaide with the rest of her objectionable family, but studying her guardian's sister again, she saw how wrong this would be; she could detect no resemblance whatever to *his* dark and coarse looks and behavior, or to their termagant mother. The object of Henry's love was clearly a gentle, sweet-natured creature, as well as very pretty. She looked well bred, her manners were refined and her voice bore no trace of the Yorkshire accent so aggressively marked in her brother and ill concealed in her mother. Presumably, thought Hester, the exclusive school she had been dispatched to in York had pummeled all trace of her origins out of her. She had no difficulty in understanding Henry's attraction, and thought that he and Adelaide would suit each other perfectly.

The two girls talked together for a while, and Hester steadfastly ignored the malevolent glances darted across at her from time to time by Mrs. England. Adelaide gradually lost her shyness and began to chatter freely. She was soon telling Hester of her unhappy school days where the other pupils had never ceased to torment and tease her about her lack of breeding and her poor background.

"I often wish that we had never left our village. I was happy there and have never been so since we have come to York. Our past must always count against us here; we shall never really be accepted."

"Nonsense! People will like thee for thyself. Besides, what does it matter what they think, anyway? Those that turn from thee for such a reason are not worth knowing."

Adelaide sighed unhappily. "You sound like my brother speaking. I wish I could believe you were both right."

Their host had still not arrived when they sat down to dine. Mrs. England excused her son's absence, saying that he had been delayed at an important meeting and had sent a message that they should continue without him.

Hester found herself seated between two unsavory neighbors: on her left a gross and greedy gentleman whose stomach protruded so far forward that he was unable to draw near enough to the table; he had little time to spare for conversation between stuffing his mouth with whatever was set before him and gulping his wine, and a great deal of both food and drink fell into the yawning space between mouth and plate; on her right sat a much thinner and more talkative citizen, but one who found great amusement in her Quaker speech and dress and whose hand repeatedly wandered beneath the table to fumble and grope, as if by accident, at her knee. The first gentleman sickened her, the second enraged her.

The dining table was very long and brilliantly set with silver and glass. There were at least two candles to each guest, and these cast a rich glow over the scene. Footmen in powdered wigs and livery passed round the dishes, for the service was *à la française*, in the new fashion.

Four different soups and four fish, with lobster patties on the side, began the meal. These preceded the *hors-d'oeuvres* and eight *entrées* which, in their turn, were followed by several roasts, including a haunch of venison, with six *relevés*, four *flancs* and eight *entremets*. Without pause, the guests went on to attack a variety of game birds and fowls, and after, a selection of sweet foods. In all, more than forty dishes were served before the table was finally cleared for the dessert and ices and the diners were able to help themselves from the spreading branches of a magnificent gilded epergne festooned with hanging glass trays piled high with nuts, fresh and dried fruits, sweet biscuits and cakes.

Hester picked at her food and thought of the cold and hungry fiddler outside in the snow. Once or twice she thought she heard his playing above the noisy talk and laughter.

At last the ladies withdrew from the room and Hester seated herself in a quiet corner and wondered how soon they might decently leave.

"Miss Gurney will play for us now!" Mrs. England called challengingly across the drawing room. "Miss Gurney must entertain us until the gentlemen rejoin us."

"I'm afraid I don't play."

"Not play! Not *at all?* But I thought all young ladies learned to play the pianoforte."

Aunt Kitty came spiritedly to her defense. "Thou must excuse my niece. Our faith does not advocate musical entertainment; that is why she has not learned to play."

Mrs. England opened her mouth to express her views on the matter, but before she could speak her son's voice came loudly from the doorway.

"If you want someone to play, Mother, then Adelaide will do so. Fetch your music, Adelaide."

While his sister hurried to do as he bid, Kirby England came forward into the room, apologizing easily for his lateness. He went from one guest to another, exchanging a few words with each, and Hester had the opportunity to see at work something of the charm of which Aunt Kitty had spoken. She was amazed at his effect on the ladies present, who all smiled and simpered as though he were no less than a royal prince. Before he could reach her the doors were flung open and the gentlemen entered —in varying stages of inebriation—to rejoin their ladies. Adelaide, seated at the piano, began to play.

The evening wore slowly on. Several other ladies took turns at the pianoforte and two of the gentlemen stood up to sing. Hester, listening to them, began to feel that perhaps she had not missed a great deal by having no musical education.

To her surprise, Kirby England made no attempt to speak to her, and watching him talking and laughing with the other guests, Hester felt a little peeved. It was not that she *wished* him to come near her at all, but that, having insisted in so bullying a fashion that she attend, it seemed to her ill mannered of him not then to trouble to address a single word to her. It was near the end of the evening before he came over to her and sat down in an empty chair beside her.

"I apologize for my mother's tactlessness, Miss Gurney," he said. "She has no understanding of Quakers."

"It was of no consequence," she replied shortly. "It's not the first time that we have been thought odd!"

He glanced sideways at her with a smile, taking in the small straight-backed figure in its plain gray dress with white lawn collar and cuffs and the hair neatly plaited in coils.

"Nor, I reckon, will it be the last. As I understand your people, Miss Gurney, one of your beliefs is that no distinction should be made between one person and another, which is why you all dress so plainly and alike. And yet everything about you— clothes, speech, self-denial—sets you *apart* from other men. The Quakers are a contradiction in themselves: they talk of there being no necessity for any *outward* form of religion, but their very peculiar behavior is just as outwardly demonstrative as any hymn singing or creed chanting or incense throwing."

"That may be thy view," she said coolly. "But our peculiarity is thought to help keep our identity; we are taught to beware of conforming to the world and its many temptations."

"If a hedge keeps in those that are on one side it will just as well keep out those who are on the other. A peculiar people must also be a very inward-looking people."

"Not necessarily. Thou must agree that Quakers are justly noted for their philanthropy."

"Oh, aye. I can't deny that."

"And that people who concern themselves so much, for example, with the fate of slaves in foreign lands can hardly be accused of being *inward*-looking!"

"Trouble is though that those same men sometimes seem more sensitive to the sufferings of distant Negroes than to the slaves under their noses at home. I know one or two Quaker abolitionists whose concern for slaves contrasts oddly, to my mind, with the wretched beings in their employ toiling away from morning to night among the wheels of their own machinery."

"I was not aware that thou concerned thyself so much with the working conditions in mills and factories."

"I don't. Neither do I set myself up as a moral man. Tell me, did you go to one of those Quaker boarding schools? Is that where you learned to be so *peculiar* and to sit so straight?"

In spite of herself, the corners of her mouth moved in a smile. "I was sent to Tower Street School in York. We had our hair cropped very short and we were taught to keep ourselves upright when sitting or standing. Our teachers prayed very hard that we might become as cornerstones polished after the similitude of a palace."

"And did you?"

"I'm afraid not. But we did learn reading, writing, spelling, English grammar and mathematics, as well as some Latin and French. Quakers believe that girls should receive an equal education to boys."

"Then they've more sense than I thought."

"I'm surprised thou agrees. I should have thought thee the kind of man who would expect a woman to be only decorative and dutiful, a pretty possession with no mind or opinion of her own."

"Yet again you misjudge me, Miss Gurney. I admit that the prospect of a woman spouting Latin and French at me doesn't thrill me very much, but that's probably because I wouldn't understand a word of it. But I see no reason why women shouldn't be as well educated as men; in my experience, they are often far more intelligent. I'm all in favor of it. I sent my sister to an academy in York in the hope that she'd learn something; unfortunately, she didn't."

Remembering Henry, Hester said: "I liked thy sister and hope to meet her again. Wouldst thou object if I invited her to stay with me at Benbow?"

He looked very surprised indeed. "Not at all. But I can't imagine what you and Adelaide could find in common; she's something of a ninny."

"Thou art too severe with her."

He shrugged his shoulders. "I get impatient. She's too timid by far; it brings out the worst in me. If she does come to visit you, try to teach her some spirit, will you? Tell me, by the way, are you satisfied with the new manager at the colliery?"

"Perfectly."

"And you've enough orders?"

"Yes. And I'm grateful for thy help."

"The York and North Midland line'll be open within the year," he said. "We shall cross the Leeds to Selby line at South Milford, so transport'll be even easier for you then."

"Oh, the Leeds to Selby railway company are proposing to build a branch line out to Garford. Hast thou not heard?" she told him triumphantly. "We'll have no need of thy line, as and when it is completed."

"It'll be nowt but a little branch railway south of Garford that'll never pay its way," he said. "I've heard all about it. You'll have no direct line to York—or any other city. Don't set any store by it."

"I should set more store by thy railway then—even though it is not completed?" she said tartly.

"Certainly. You'll find mine the best. Listen, I wanted to talk to you about the colliery. While I was away in London, I met a mining engineer, a Mr. Scott, who's well known for his investi-

148

gations into underground explosions. He told me that the gas causing these explosions forms easily in old mine workings that are not properly ventilated—"

"My father was aware of the danger of bad ventilation. And the miners all carry Mr. Stephenson's safety lamp."

"That may be. But I went down that mine of yours myself and the air's so bad in parts of it that I could hardly breathe. I walked all over it, and there's old workings where gas could accumulate, given half a chance. From what I saw, there's a good case for sinking a third ventilation shaft. Mr. Scott will be coming north in a week or two. I think he should look at the mine and give his opinion."

"If Papa had seen any reason for sinking another ventilation shaft, I'm sure he would have done it."

"Knowledge marches on with time, lass. Much more is known about mining explosions now. Do you want one on that Quaker conscience of yours?"

"No," she replied seriously. "Of course not. If Mr. Scott will be good enough to come to Benbow, I will listen to what he advises."

They discussed the matter for a few more minutes before he changed the subject, asking if she had enjoyed the dinner.

"Dost thou wish me to answer that honestly—or politely, as a guest should?"

He smiled. "I'm told honesty is the best policy."

"Well then, to be absolutely truthful I found the sight of so many already overweight ladies and gentlemen filling themselves with so much food, which they could all have foregone to great advantage to their health and looks, quite revolting! I cannot see the necessity for so many dishes."

"My guests expect to be entertained on the grand scale," he said dryly. "If I provided them with less than forty dishes they'd either be insulted or think me on the verge of bankruptcy!"

"Why dost thou have such people to thy house?"

"They're useful, that's why." He nodded towards them. "Every one of those overfed gentlemen over there could be of some service to me."

"And thou of service to them, I suppose."

"Well . . . they think so."

"Are they friends of thine?"

He laughed, very amused. "*Friends!* Nay, lass, they're not friends. If I were in trouble, not one would raise a little finger to help me."

"I don't understand thee," Hester said, shaking her head.

"Of course you don't. How could you? We're chalk from cheese, you and I."

She said, suddenly remembering: "There was a fiddler playing outside thy house when we arrived, a poor, starving man. I was thinking of him when I watched all those plates of unfinished food being carried away—"

"He was there when I came in," he interrupted her. "I sent him to eat in the kitchens. The servants will see he's well fed before he goes on his way." He saw her surprised expression and added dryly: "Quakers don't have the monopoly on philanthropy, Miss Gurney. And I can remember too well myself what it was like to be cold and hungry. It's something you never forget."

He stood up and, with a nod, left her. Beyond a few words of farewell as they left, Hester did not speak with her guardian again.

Mrs. England was upset; she had imagined herself slighted several times during the evening, not to say *insulted* by her son's ward. When the last guest had left she complained at length.

"And as for your Miss Gurney, what an insolent creature she is—so rude and offensive."

"Is that so? And just how did she offend you, Mother?"

"I took the trouble to give her a simple warning, which I thought necessary, and she was not at all grateful for it."

"And what was this warning you felt she should have?"

"You're a rich man, son, and successful . . . There's a lot of women in York after you as a husband."

"But what has that to do with my ward?"

Mrs. England said huffily: "She'll be no different from the rest,

I daresay. I told her that just because she was your ward she needn't think it gave her any special claim on you . . ."

Kirby roared with laughter. "No wonder she answered you bluntly! Mother, my ward has a large fortune of her own; she's no need to hunt for it in a husband. But even if she were penniless and starving in the gutter, I'm the last man on earth she'd want to wed!"

"That's just what she said."

His laughter died and he turned away. "If you will attack people like that, Mother, you must expect them to resent it. Miss Gurney is not the kind of lass to accept what you said all meek and mild."

"Last time you hadn't a good word to say for her."

"What I think of her is my own affair, Mother. But just remember not to insult her again with accusations of fortune hunting or wanting to marry me—especially not under my roof."

Mrs. England left the room. She lacked the grace and dignity to sweep from it in style: instead she marched out of the door with an ungainly, angry stride.

Her son, left to himself, poured a glass of brandy and lit a cigar. He wandered over to the fireplace and sat beside the dying coals. He thought in a detached way of his ward. He had noticed this evening that she was far better-looking than he had realized: it was not only her gray eyes that were rather striking, but the rest of her features were not as bad as he had first considered, and her hair, though so plainly dressed, was very thick and shining. He was surprised how much he had enjoyed talking with her. He had invited her to the house by way of revenge, revenge for the dislike and dismay she had shown so openly on her face when he had come into the shop that day. She could not have looked more shocked or appalled if he had been the devil himself sprung up through a trapdoor like they had on the stage at the Theatre Royal. There had been another reason: it had been at the back of his mind also that she would be impressed by the grandeur of 44 Monkgate and by the lavish hospitality. He should have known better. To a Quaker miss the place would be nothing more than a vulgar extravagance; and as for the food and the guests, she had made her views plain enough on both.

Kirby kicked at the dwindling fire with the toe of his shoe; the coals flared up and then died away again. He smoked his cigar thoughtfully for a while and then hurled the butt into the ashes and went, disgruntled, to bed.

CHAPTER VII

The ostlers and innkeepers and such riff raff,
The rail road will blow them away, just like chaff;
They may 'list for Her Highness, the great Queen of Spain,
And curse the inventors of rail roads and steam.

Broadside ballad

Adelaide's visit to Benbow Hall took place finally in the following spring. Before it there had been an exchange of letters and a
great deal of disagreeable opposition on the part of Mrs. England. It had required Kirby's intervention before she would
agree to let Adelaide go.

Aunt Kitty traveled with Adelaide from York and stayed on at
Benbow. As Henry had foretold, Adelaide lost much of her
shyness once she was away from her mother's side, and she
proved herself to be a delightful companion.

The weather was kind and they passed pleasant days together,
Hester and Adelaide taking long walks in the afternoons while
Aunt Kitty dozed peacefully indoors by the fireside. They talked
of many things on those walks, and Hester heard about the tiny
stone cottage in the Wolds where the England family had once
lived, and about the progression from there to the rooms above
the draper shop and, finally, to the big house in Monkgate.

"I was only five years old when my brother went away to
York," Adelaide told her. "I saw so little of him in the years after
that when Mama and I went to live with him he seemed like a
stranger to me. And, to be truthful, he still does. I find it hard to
believe that he is my brother . . . he is so clever at everything

. . . so rich and successful. He's no part of the cottage we lived in and the life I remember. And he gets impatient with me sometimes; he says I mind too much about what other people think. He thinks me very feeble."

"He is very unfeeling, then."

"Oh, he's not unkind; don't think that of him. But I can't help being rather frightened of him. Do you mind having him for a guardian?"

"I'm not frightened of him—if that's what thou means."

Adelaide shook her head. "No—I didn't think that. I can see that you're not. But I don't think you like him very much."

Hester did not know how to reply. "I daresay thy brother finds me as tedious a ward as I find him overbearing a guardian," she said at last.

"I don't think he does find you tedious at all," Adelaide said. "I was watching you both the other evening when he was talking to you. He never troubles to talk a long time with anyone unless he finds them either interesting or useful to him. I'm sure you cannot be of any *use*, so he must find you interesting."

Hester smiled at her friend's naïve conclusion. She was thankful that they had somehow circumvented the thorny question of her feelings towards Adelaide's brother; she would not have wished it to spoil their friendship.

Henry Latham came to Benbow Hall and stayed for three days—the most he could spare from his parliamentary duties. Hester, who had been feeling something of a conspirator, was relieved to see the pleasure which his sudden arrival aroused in her visitor. Adelaide was very nervous at first with him, but freed from the domination and sharp tongue of her mother, she blossomed like a flower, and Henry, deeper in love than ever, was triumphant at the success of his scheme.

The afternoon walks from the Hall now included Henry, and Hester tactfully lagged a little way behind the other two, stopping on the pretext of tying her shoelace or to pick some flowers. She had been in no doubt of Henry's feelings, and by the end of the three days she was in little doubt as to Adelaide's towards him. The most gratifying adoration that a man could wish shone from her eyes whenever they were turned on Henry. And seeing this, Hester was content. She knew she need have no worries about Adelaide's happiness with Henry; he would be the kindest, most considerate husband imaginable. All in all, it would be a perfect match.

"I shall ask Kirby's permission to propose to her as soon as I return to York," Henry told Hester as he left Benbow. "Do you think she will accept me?"

Hester smiled. "Of course she will. She loves thee already. I wish thee good fortune and joy, Henry—though I do not envy thee one thing."

"What is that?"

"Thy future mother-in-law!"

William Gurney stood in the center of the drawing room at 44 Monkgate and looked about him; the Palace of Satan, he described it to himself, digging his heel into the deep pile of the carpet beneath his feet. It was no more than he had expected and only served to confirm his view of the owner.

"*Lay not up for yourselves treasure upon the earth; where the rust and moth doth corrupt, and where thieves break through and steal: but lay up for yourselves treasures in heaven . . .*" he intoned under his breath, pacing about the room. He fingered the heavy richness of the curtains. "*The pomps and vanity of this wicked world.*"

There was a long glass on the wall oposite him and he noticed, with gratification, how strikingly his plain and somber figure contrasted with the prodigal opulence around him.

He was still engaged in studying this reflected contrast when the door opened and Kirby England walked into the room. The jumped-up draper was a big enough man to dominate his surroundings, even in that large room.

"What can I do for you, Mr. Gurney?"

"It is a matter of some sensitivity . . ."

Kirby drew out a gold watch from his waistcoat pocket, glanced at it and replaced it. "Sensitive or not, I must ask you to be quick and come to the point of this visit. I've a meeting in twenty minutes that won't wait."

"Very well. My cousin, Hester Gurney, is thy ward."

"Aye, we both know that, Mr. Gurney."

"I will not pretend that I understood, or agreed with, my late cousin appointing thee as his daughter's guardian."

"No need for pretense," Kirby said easily. "We both know that as well."

"Thou art possibly unaware of the understanding that existed between my late cousin and myself regarding his daughter's future . . ."

"That depends which understanding you're referring to."

"I am referring to the fact that it has always been understood that Hester and I should be married," William said. "I have held a deep and sincere affection for my cousin since her childhood and only her extreme youth has prevented me from speaking to her earlier. Her father wished the match."

"That's odd. It's not the impression I got."

"What dost thou mean?"

"I mean nowt but what I said. Amos Gurney told me in very clear words that he didn't want you to marry his daughter."

William went pale, but he kept his temper carefully under control; this devil's spawn should not confound him. "My cousin's mind was deranged by his illness. He suffered from delusions."

"On the contrary, he seemed as sharp as a needle to me."

"I repeat, he had lost his reasoning."

"His reasoning was very sound: he didn't think you'd make his daughter happy."

"That's nonsensical! Hester and I are ideally matched. She knows that."

"She's willing to wed you then?"

"Naturally, I have not asked her that—yet. She is still in mourning for her father . . ."

"And still under age."

William frowned. "When she has fully recovered from her grief, there is no doubt that she will consent to marry me."

"Then you've nothing to worry about, Mr. Gurney. And I don't see how I can do anything for you."

"I have thy assurance then that thou wouldst not stand in my way?"

"Stand in your way, Mr. Gurney? I don't follow you. As soon

as my ward is of age she may marry whom she pleases. It will no longer be my concern."

"I am speaking, of course, of while she is still under age. I had proposed waiting until her twenty-first birthday, but there is still more than a year before then and my affection for my cousin is so deep that I am reluctant to delay our marriage so long."

"Is that so?"

William Gurney said stiffly: "Thy consent will be required as a formality . . ."

Kirby was gazing absently out of the window, down into the street.

"Very right and proper of you to come to me, Mr. Gurney. And since you've been good enough to put the question so straight, I'll return the compliment and tell you here and now that so long as Miss Gurney's under my guardianship—until the twenty-ninth of June next year, to be exact—there's not a chance in hell that I'll ever give my consent to your marrying her."

William took one step forward and then, with an effort, restrained himself.

"Thou speaks of Hell. Thy sins on earth will assure thee a long acquaintance of that place."

"Aye . . . I'll take that chance."

"A sinner such as thyself has no right to come between a man and woman whose union would be blessed in the sight of God."

"I have if it isn't blessed in the sight of her father," Kirby said pleasantly. He took out his watch again and flicked the case open with a broad thumbnail. "It's time for this conversation to end."

"One moment. I have not finished speaking yet. Thou refuses thy consent, but I warn thee that I intend to take steps to prove thy unworthiness to have any say whatever in the matter."

Kirby paused, his hand already on the doorknob. "Just what steps had you in mind, Mr. Gurney?"

"I know a great deal of thy affairs, far more than thou imagines. I have made it my business to do so as a man of public conscience and as legal adviser to my cousin."

"Oh, aye."

"I have heard interesting rumors concerning thee," William continued. "Most particularly to do with thy management of the York and North Midland Railway Company."

"Exactly what sort of rumors, Mr. Gurney?"

"Unwarranted delays in completing the railway line, mistakes and misjudgments, shares offered and taken as bribes, figures falsified in accounts, no auditors appointed, profits made for thyself by speculation in iron and in iron contracts with the company of which thou art chairman . . . There is no end to it. The Society of Friends are not the only people in York to believe thee dishonest. There are many others. I am not without influence in this city, as thou must be aware. Thy prospects of election as the next Lord Mayor will be small."

"I see. But if I agree to your marrying my ward before she's of age you'll somehow manage to stifle that public conscience of yours?"

"I would be reluctant to incriminate my wife's guardian."

Kirby opened the door. He said over his shoulder with a smile as he went: "Spread all the rumors you like, Mr. Gurney. You may do your damnedest. You'll find it makes no odds. I'll be the next Lord Mayor of York and you'll never have my consent to marry my ward."

William was left alone again in the big drawing room; he found he was shaking from head to foot. He clasped his hands tightly together and, closing his eyes, prayed hard for strength and calmness to reenter his soul. When he opened his eyes again he saw a manservant waiting patiently and discreetly to show him out. He reached the street in time to see the tail end of Kirby England's carriage disappearing down Monkgate in the direction of the city walls. William stood on the pavement and stared after it. His face, beneath his broad-brimmed black hat, had lost its drained pallor and shone with a newfound zeal. He had just seen the Light more clearly than ever. It was God's will that he should be the instrument of this sinner's downfall and destruction on earth. As for Hester, he would marry his cousin in the end, he had no doubt of that. The Lord had spoken to him of it and he had faith in Him.

Kirby England traveled to Benbow Hall to bring his sister and Aunt Kitty back to York at the end of their stay. This was much to Hester's annoyance—even more so when she discovered that, as her two guests were busy preparing for the journey in their rooms when he arrived, she was obliged to entertain her guardian alone in the library. Looking at him, she decided that he appeared even more plutocratic than ever. His black hair was longer and his side-whiskers curlier, while his clothes were more obviously expensive in both cut and material; he wore more ostentatious jewelry than she remembered—a new and elaborate gold watch chain adorned his waistcoat and there was a heavy gold and ruby ring on the little finger of his right hand and a big diamond ring securing his cravat. He took a chair, very much at his ease, which vexed her even more.

"I'm grateful to you for having my sister here," he told her. "She has too little company of her own age in York."

"That's a pity."

"We are not accepted yet by the best society in York, as you may have noticed," he said with grim irony. "I won't have her associating with anything else."

"That must make thy sister lonely."

"You think I'm wrong to want nothing but the best for her, Miss Gurney?"

"I think that the best, as thou terms it, does not necessarily bring the most happiness."

He smiled. "Once again we disagree. To my way of thinking, there's no point in settling for anything less."

Hester did not answer him. There seemed little advantage in arguing over something that would so soon be resolved in any case. If Adelaide married Henry Latham, she would be accepted in the first circles and would no longer lack for company.

Kirby also let the matter drop. He changed the subject by saying that he had heard from Mr. Scott, the mining engineer, that he would be coming north within the month and that he had agreed to visit Benbow Colliery to give his opinion on the ventilation system.

"I've another thing to tell you," he added. "Your cousin, William, came to see me a few days ago at my house."

"William went there!"

"Aye. I thought you'd be surprised to hear it."

Hester said nothing.

"Don't you want to know what it was?" he teased her.

"I imagine it is not my concern."

"Oh, it concerns you very much. He wants to wed you, and he came to see if I'd give my consent to it while you're still under age. He's decided he can't wait until you're twenty-one. I gather from him there's been a sort of understanding between the two of you for years."

He was watching her face, half turned from him as he spoke, but she showed no reaction.

"And what answer did thou give him?"

"In a word—no. Your father didn't want you to marry Cousin William. Did you know that?"

"We never spoke of it."

"Then you'll have to take my word for it. He spoke of it to me clear enough. Your cousin seems very sure of you. Do *you* want to marry him? Are you in love with him?"

"What is the point of my answering such a question? Thou hast refused thy consent, so there's an end to the matter . . . at least until I'm twenty-one," she said composedly.

"But I'm curious. Do you, or don't you, love William Gurney? Or don't Quakers have ordinary human feelings like other men and women?"

He had deliberately provoked her, and this time she responded angrily.

"My *feelings*, at least, are not in thy charge. And Quakers, whom thou so despises, love and hate like anyone else!"

"I don't despise 'em," he answered mildly. "In fact, there's a lot of things I respect about your Friends. I've seen, though, that they can hate; I wondered if they could also love." He paused. "I hope you've more sense than to consider your cousin for a husband. Don't ever be foolish enough to marry him, lass."

The trill of Aunt Kitty's voice could be heard from the hall. Kirby stood up. He looked down at his ward.

"I give good advice on most things, you know. You should be grateful. Those railway shares I bought for you are going up fast in value, just as I told you they would. They'll make you a tidy sum in the end."

"I wish I shared thy faith in that railway."

"You would if you weren't so prejudiced against me. The York and North Midland will only be the first of hundreds I'm going to see built. Ten years from now I'll own railways reaching right across the whole length and breadth of this kingdom."

"Then I suppose we must all bow to thy steam majesty, the railway king?"

He laughed. "A railway king? King of my Railway Kingdom? I like the sound of that! Aye, lass, that's exactly what I'm going to be."

"Kirby, this is the most wonderfully exciting thing that has ever happened to me!"

"More exciting than me?" he said in mock reproach.

"I'm afraid so."

"Impossible!"

Rosa smiled up at Kirby as she sat beside him and he took her gloved hand in his and raised it to his lips.

It was a fine summer day with blue skies and a brilliant sun above them. The open carriage in which they were riding swung out through the city gates, and the crowded streets of York were left behind.

Enchanting and beautiful Rosa, thought Kirby, watching the actress's face in the shadow of the absurdly overdecorated hat she wore. She had been away in London—and away from him—too long, he decided, and he had missed her. Compelled to spend most of his time in York in order to gain support for the coming mayoral election, he had not seen her for months. Meanwhile, news had reached him occasionally from London of Rosa's triumphs at Drury Lane and Covent Garden. The capital's audiences had lost no time in taking her to their hearts, and her performances had been nothing less than a sensation. He looked at her carefully. Her face had a new glow; the inner strain that had lain beneath the bright gaiety had gone. Success had not spoiled or tarnished her, as it did some, but had only added to her radiance. He was glad.

She pulled at his coat sleeve. "Come now, be serious and tell me what to expect or I may be most dreadfully frightened! Are you quite sure this steam engine won't explode and blow us to pieces?"

She was not, in fact, in the least nervous, as he very well knew, or he would not have arranged this ride for her.

"I promise you it won't do anything of the kind," he said gravely. "It's quite safe. Mr. Stephenson wants to run this new locomotive on the completed stretch of our railway south of York. You'll be our very first passenger."

"He must be such a clever man. Will he mind my being there? Shall I be in the way?"

Kirby smiled. "You in the way! George will be as charmed by you as any other man. He'll love you."

Their carriage turned into a large courtyard on the outskirts of the city and drew to a stop. Rosa gave a small squeak and pressed her hand to her mouth.

Mr. Stephenson's jaunty little locomotive steam engine stood waiting for her on its iron rails. To Rosa it appeared a fire horse, consisting, so far as she could tell, of a boiler, a stove, a platform, a bench and, behind the bench, a barrel containing water. Small curls of white vapor rose from its funnel with a gentle hissing noise. Rosa gazed at the strange creature with deep admiration; she was conscious of the pent-up power that must lie within its round iron body and in the bright steel pistons that were poised, immobile but ready, like strong hip joints, over the wheels. Behind the engine was attached an open carriage with bench seats.

Kirby handed the actress down and she walked across to meet the fire horse's master, who stood beside it like any groom. Quite unafraid, Rosa advanced to pat the locomotive's shiny flanks, and when it was suggested that she take her seat in the carriage, she instantly asked to ride on the engine's bench.

Mr. Stephenson looked doubtfully at her exquisite lilac silk dress and at the ridiculous hat with its glorious multitude of flowers and feathers. He pointed out the thick layers of coal dust and warned of flying sparks. But Rosa was not to be put off.

"I don't care a straw for my dress or hat. They can both be blackened and burnt to cinders and I shall think them well lost for the experience. Please let me ride beside you, Mr. Stephenson."

The engineer melted beneath her imploring blue eyes and helped her up onto the bench. Kirby climbed up behind them and Mr. Stephenson turned his attention to the controls. To Rosa's breathless excitement the wooden planks beneath her feet began to creak and move and their iron steed rolled forward along the rails that stretched far away before them into the distance. The little fire horse's lazy breathing had become an urgent snorting, and rapid puffs of steam escaped from the funnel into the air as though the creature fretted to bolt away with them and was kept in check only by the strong hands of its master and inventor.

With the empty wagon rattling along behind them, they went at a steadily increasing pace. Mr. Stephenson shouted above the clank and clatter of metal upon metal and the hissing of steam that they were moving at fifteen miles per hour and that he would very soon increase their speed to twenty-five miles an hour or more.

With kindly courtesy he explained carefully to Rosa some of the engine's mysteries. He opened the firebox door so that she could see the roaring furnace within and feel the great heat of it scorch her face. She bent down to watch the leaping flames and to see the hot shimmer of gases rising from the burning coals to be drawn along a battery of hollow copper tubes. Water surrounded these tubes and was heated by the gases passing through them before they finally escaped through the blast pipe in the smokebox and up the chimney. The heated water turned to steam and entered the cylinders, mounted horizontally and in line with the driving wheels, to drive the pistons, which turned the wheels. Rosa had no difficulty in grasping the essential principles of the steam horse's digestive system.

Mr. Stephenson showed her the steel handle used to apply or withdraw steam from the pistons, the lever to make the wheels turn forwards or backwards, the dampers to let air in under the fire, the glass water gauge and the steam safety valves. She blew the warning whistle and even shoveled a load of coal onto the fire, spreading it so evenly and so well that Mr. Stephenson told her that he'd make a fireman of her yet.

They rattled on, gathering speed and leaving a trail of live coals that fell from the bottom of the firebox onto the track behind them as they went. Rosa asked if they could go still faster, and the engineer was delighted to oblige and to show off a little to the pretty young woman beside him. Soon they were racing along at over thirty miles an hour. A long white plume of smoke streamed out behind them like a banner carried in a battle charge. The flat green fields flashed past and sheep and cows stampeded from them in terror.

Rosa took off her singed and sooty hat and drank in the air which rushed towards her. She closed her eyes, and the sensation of flying like a bird was quite delightful. She had no feeling of fear: the smell of hot steam and oil, the rhythmic clankety-clank of the wheels and the chuff-chuffing of the brave little fire horse that bore her was nothing but exhilarating.

They entered a green and gloomy cutting, deep in shadow. Its sides rose steeply above them, sixty feet or more, and the moss and ferns growing there had already covered the scars of the navvies' work. It was cold out of the sun, and the noise of the engine echoed eerily against rock walls.

Suddenly they plunged into the black mouth of a tunnel at the end of the cutting and Rosa, for all her fearlessness, could not help screaming. It was as though the earth had swallowed them in one ravenous gulp. Blackness closed about her and the sound of the engine became a deafening roar in her ears. Sparks and burning cinders flared about her like meteors and smoke choked her lungs. Their friendly steam horse had turned into an alien monster, breathing destruction and doom, and was bearing them remorselessly down into the dark depths of the underworld. She shut her eyes in terror, and when she opened them they had left the tunnel behind and were out in the sunlight once more. The iron horse had reverted to the delightful, innocent little puffing creature she had thought it before.

A mile or two further along the line they came across a wagon heavily loaded with spoil. Mr. Stephenson slowed the locomotive to a stop and the wagon was hitched to the front of the engine, which he then reversed back along the track the way they had come, pulling the load after them without the slightest difficulty. Rosa was intrigued by the way the engine could be made to run forwards or backwards without having to turn round. It was most obligingly adaptable.

The return journey was further enlivened for her by a handsome gentleman riding a large and powerful gray horse. Seeing the engine go by and Rosa waving at him, he at once gave chase, galloping recklessly along beside the line with all the speed he could muster from his mount. He pursued them for half a mile before his horse stumbled and pitched its rider from the saddle. Unhurt and undismayed, the gentleman got to his feet and, raising his hat with ironic and exaggerated gallantry, bowed low. Rosa waved her own bedraggled hat and laughed. The distance between them lengthened rapidly, and soon the defeated rider was no more than a small, indistinct figure standing in the Yorkshire landscape, the gray horse drooping exhausted beside him.

Rosa returned to York with her lilac dress ruined beyond repair by burns and tears. Her face was streaked with coal and her hat a disaster.

"I have fallen in love both with your steam engine and with Mr. Stephenson."

"In love with George?" Kirby said, pretending dismay. "Am I going to lose you to him?"

"Very probably. Now I am a famous actress I can pick and choose, you know," she told him pertly.

"Then choose the richest man you can find," he answered. "And marry him. You must have had plenty of offers in London."

She looked down at her hands. "Yes, I've had offers all right. Princes, dukes, counts, millionaires have all offered to make me their mistress. One or two have even wanted me to be their wife." There was bitterness in her voice. "Do you know that last week an English marquis proposed to me? Imagine that! Rosa Love from Scarborough could become a marchioness—if she wanted."

She laughed and fiddled aimlessly with her ruined hat.

"Will you accept him?"

"I might, or I might not. I don't love him. He's over sixty and talks as though his mouth was full of hot potatoes. I could scream with boredom in his company."

"Think hard before you turn down an offer like that, Rosa. Since when has love had owt to do with a sensible marriage? You'd make a beautiful marchioness."

She grimaced. "All very well for you to talk, Kirby. It's different for a man. I'm not so sure I'd enjoy being a marchioness; I love my singing. If I married him I'd have to give it up."

"For a realist you can sometimes be very romantic," he said. "You know as well as I do that the theatre is nothing but a sham life. Behind all those pretty lights and music and color is a gray world of disillusion and disappointment. One day you'll grow too old to sing, and no one will want to pay good money to listen to you anymore. What will you do then? Take my advice and marry your marquis. A coronet and security for life are worth a yawn or two, and if he's an old man you may not have to put up with the boredom for very long."

Rosa frowned and picked at a burned feather in her hat. "You can be very cold-blooded, Kirby."

"I know . . . So can you."

"Would you miss me?"

He bent and kissed her lips. "You know very well that I would. But I'd be the last man to blame you for going. You and I are alike, Rosa. I knew that from the first moment I saw you. We're both after the best we can get out of life, and no one's going to stand in our way. We've lasted this long together because we both understand that, and each other."

She raised her hand to his cheek and looked into his face solemnly for a moment. Then she smiled brightly.

"Don't let's talk about it now, Kirby. You'll come and hear me sing tonight at the theatre?"

"Aye. I wouldn't miss it. They're damn lucky to have got you there again."

"It's only one performance. I owe the Theatre Royal a lot— and you most of all, Kirby. It's thanks to you that I'm not in the gutter, starving."

He shook his head. "Nowt to do with me, lass. It's yourself

that's taken you where you are now. Just see you make the most of it and never forget what it's like to be poor."

A Council meeting kept Kirby late that evening, and when he took his seat in a box the curtain had risen on Act Two of *Fra Diavolo*. The scene was impressive: a distant view of Naples by moonlight, seen through an immense Gothic window. It was a great improvement on the dismal decor that had disgraced the Theatre Royal in past years. In the darkness below him he could see the faint glimmer of the glass chandeliers hung in front of the boxes.

He sat back and waited for Rosa's entrance. He could have shut his eyes and still known the exact moment when she came onto the stage. As always, she caused a sudden stillness in her audience so intense it could almost be heard and felt. Kirby listened to her singing "O Joy of Hour" and thought that her voice was more beautiful than ever. He watched her with pleasure and thought what a pity it was, in many ways, that they would never marry each other. He liked her very much but he did not love her—any more than she loved him. Not that love had anything to do with it: he had no intention of marrying for anything but the most practical reasons. And marriage with Rosa would be impractical—for both of them. Rosa needed her marquis, or his equivalent, to raise her forever beyond the reach of the past. And he himself needed what? Some blue-blooded, horse-faced daughter of the aristocracy to bear him blue-blooded, horse-faced children and so infuse into his family the one thing it lacked—breeding.

Kirby smiled in the darkness; it was a hard, cynical smile. Rosa's song was ending. He leaned forward, his elbows resting on the ledge before him, and clapped loudly with the rest. Rosa came to his side of the stage and, looking up, curtsied to him alone.

CHAPTER VIII

Come all you young fellows and let us be free,
Again fill the glasses, now merry we'll be
Success to all trades in the reign of our Queen,
And the boiling hot water that travels by steam.

A railway song

The accession of the young Queen Victoria touched Aunt Kitty's romantic soul deeply. As she said more than once to Hester, who was staying with her aunt in York, the thought of an innocent girl ascending the throne of England (after all those appallingly wicked old uncles), and taking on her slender shoulders such a dreadful burden of responsibility, was enough to make her weep.

"Such tender years! Think of it, my dear. She is only eighteen years old, a mere infant!" Aunt Kitty dabbed at her eyes. "But thank heavens there is not yet another unsavory or unsatisfactory uncle instead. I feel in my bones that she is destined to lead us into happier times. She will be one of our great queens."

"I feel sorry for her," Hester said. "It must be a frightening task."

"Indeed, indeed! But we must hope it was a comfort and strength to her to see how loyally and with what enthusiasm the whole country has received her. I am thankful to say that our city has played its part well in the celebrations. It was a great pity thou wast not here last week, my love. Thy guardian had the whole front of the Mansion House illuminated with gas flares, and the most splendid banquet was held there for eight

169

hundred guests, with no fewer than seventy dishes! The streets were completely blocked by the crowds who came to look at it all."

"I can believe it. It sounds very much in his style."

"He is a very popular Lord Mayor, my dear," Aunt Kitty said, looking reproachful at her niece's disparaging tone. "He is considered to be a great benefactor, and his hospitality at the Mansion House is proverbial; even the Whigs have to admit that."

"Oh, yes. I read about his inaugural Civic Banquet in the newspaper. It was celebrated with a limitless flow of wines, an unnecessarily large number of dishes, interminable speeches, the passing of the city's gold loving cup, and at the end of it all Henry presented him with a pair of very large gold-plated wine coolers."

"Just so! And why not? The wine coolers are the talk of York. They must have cost Henry a fortune, although he can well afford it. I still cannot quite accustom myself to the fact that he is Kirby England's brother-in-law now. He and Adelaide make a most charming couple and there is no doubt that they are exceedingly happy together. A few of the nastier tongues have been wagging, of course, that she is not good enough for him, but in *my* opinion, it is Henry who is the fortunate one to have found such a sweet and gentle bride."

"I agree."

"And her brother being Lord Mayor of York must overcome any prejudice against her lack of pedigree."

"I doubt if having Kirby England for a brother would constitute any recommendation."

"Oh, Hester, I could shake thee sometimes! Thou art so blind to his good qualities. Thou misjudges him sadly."

"Whatever thou thinks of him, Aunt Kitty, *I* can only be thankful that there are only twenty-eight more days left of being his ward."

"I am astonished thou hast not also counted it in hours and minutes, if not seconds!"

Before they could argue further, a maidservant knocked at the parlor door to announce that Mrs. Henry Latham had called.

"Show Mrs. Latham in by all means," Aunt Kitty cried, pleased by the unexpected visit.

Adelaide had altered greatly since her marriage to Henry. Where she had been youthfully pretty before she had now become serenely beautiful, and much of her nervous shyness had vanished, to be replaced by a quiet air of contentment. She was wearing a day dress of blue muslin with wide skirts, and over this she wore a pelerine mantlet of matching blue, trimmed with a band of lace. Her bonnet, with brim and crown in one, was of blue and cream silk, tied beneath her chin with wide satin ribbons.

Aunt Kitty and Hester greeted her warmly.

"How well marriage becomes thee!" Aunt Kitty told her. "Tell us, is dear Henry in good health? Will he soon return from London?"

"He is to come back this week," Adelaide replied. "And he has written that he has fixed on a house for us in London, in a street called Cheyne Walk. He says I shall love it; there is a view from the drawing room right across the River Thames. I'm sure he is right, but nothing could be more perfect than living at Murton Hall."

"Henry's family seat is acknowledged to be one of the finest in Yorkshire," Aunt Kitty agreed. "But thou wilt certainly find London a most exciting place."

"To be honest, I rather dread the thought of it! We shall have to entertain important people—all strangers to me—and I must be so careful always to do and say the correct thing . . ."

"My dear, just be yourself and they will all love thee."

"I hope you are right."

"I am seldom wrong," said Aunt Kitty unblushingly. "I have seen too much of human behavior. It is so good of thee to call on us, my dear. Hester is staying with me for a week or two—keeping me company in my old age."

"Then I hope you will both be able to accept the invitation that my brother asked me to deliver to you."

"Invitation?" Aunt Kitty pricked up her ears. "How very nice! Do let me see."

She whisked the envelope away as soon as Adelaide took

it from her reticule. Extracting a stiff, black-engraved card embossed with a great deal of gold decoration, she settled her spectacles more firmly on her nose to read it.

"A Coronation Ball to be held at the Mansion House! My child, how thrilling!" She lowered the card and looked at Adelaide over the rim of the spectacles. "Of course, thou must understand, my dear, that we Quakers do not customarily attend such affairs. But since it is a special occasion to celebrate the Coronation of our dear new Queen, I feel it would show great disrespect were we to refuse to be present. We shall most certainly come."

"I'm so glad. Hester, you will come too, won't you?"

"Of course she will," Aunt Kitty said quickly. "It is the day before her twenty-first birthday. We shall be able to celebrate both the Coronation and Hester's coming of age at the same time."

Adelaide stayed with them for a while before leaving to pay duty calls. Aunt Kitty's spirits were high. The prospect of the ball delighted her. Adelaide had told them that there were to be a thousand guests and that the Mansion House was to be sumptuously decorated and dazzlingly lit for the occasion. On Coronation Day itself, a huge civic procession was to take place in the streets of York, and on the Lord Mayor's orders, a feast had been planned at which fourteen thousand children and adults would be admitted free.

"I told thee thy guardian was a generous man," Aunt Kitty said to Hester.

But the munificence of the new Lord Mayor's regime did not impress Hester. She saw it all as nothing more than an attempt on his part to feast his way into the hearts of citizens and electors, to drown all discord and opposition in an endless flow of champagne and sherry and to curry favor and popularity with the city's poor by outward lavish displays of charity.

On June 28, in the year 1838, the people of York fêted Queen Victoria's Coronation Day with all the patriotic fervor of loyal subjects. The narrow streets were crowded with jubilant citizens and every inn was full to overflowing.

The long civic procession took place with triumphant pomp,

winding slowly through the city to the sound of the Minster bells pealing loudly in salute. Hester opened the windows to hear the bells better; she loved the noise of them ringing out over the old city, reaching far beyond the walls and across the distant fields, as they had done for centuries.

That evening the Mansion House was brilliantly illuminated. The arms of the City of York stood out proudly in their pediment above four pilasters. At the top of the building, beneath the roof, was a glittering imperial crown of lights and the letters V R in characters about four feet high.

The crowds in St. Helen's Square were so great that Aunt Kitty and Hester's carriage had some difficulty in reaching the door. The revelers pressed about them, peering in the windows, shouting and singing. Aunt Kitty reached for her smelling salts.

"Drunkenness and dancing in the streets! I am thankful our Queen cannot see such disrespect."

They gained the steps and entered the Mansion House by the front door. The staterooms were on the first floor, reached by a grand staircase. Double doors with painted panels opened into a long room that occupied the entire width of the house. It was high-ceilinged, with pale green walls, and supporting columns decorated with green and gold leaves. There was a large marble fireplace at each end of the room, and overhead glass chandeliers lent their sparkle to an already glittering scene.

The heat was oppressive. Banks of flowers and foliage and verdant screens of hothouse plants lined the walls, and their heavy scent cloyed the air.

As for the clothes of the assembled guests, Aunt Kitty and Hester, plainly dressed in gray and black, according to their belief, stood dumbfounded at the spectacle of extravagant evening finery. What gowns! What jewels! What furs and feathers! Aunt Kitty raised her lorgnette fan with a trembling hand and scanned the room.

"Hast thou ever seen anything to equal this? I know I have not!"

So preoccupied were they that they did not notice the Lord Mayor's approach, whereas he had observed their arrival the instant they had set foot in the ballroom. It had not been difficult:

the Quakeresses stood out from the rest of the guests more clearly than if they had been dressed in the most vulgarly ostentatious or outrageous fashion. It was fortunate for them that they were unaware of this.

Hester could not help noticing the apparent ease with which her guardian had assumed his high office. The gold mayoral chain hung about his neck as though it naturally belonged there. He might have been born to power and riches instead of acquiring both.

He had no time to say more than a few formal words of welcome to them before the next arrivals clamored for his attention. Aunt Kitty and Hester moved on to the sanctuary of a quiet corner from where they could observe the assembly and from where Aunt Kitty's eye could hunt the ballroom with the thoroughness of a bird of prey. Within a short while she had located a great many people that she knew and quite a number she did not, which vexed her.

The two women received many curious stares, especially from the more fashionably dressed. Aunt Kitty was far too busy to notice the whispered remarks and the condescending smiles in their direction, but Hester gradually became uncomfortably conscious of how different they looked from all the other ladies present. Their high-necked gray gowns, untrimmed and severe, must look quite absurd in the eyes of those who wore such low décolletage and such bright colors. She felt herself begin to grow hot with embarrassment. They were sadly out of place in this brilliant gathering.

An orchestra took their places in the gallery above the doorway and dancing began. A quadrille was followed by the Lancers and Sir Roger de Coverley and a gallop. Hester watched, fascinated. She had never seen any of these danced, and before long her feet were tapping away in time beneath her skirts. The urge to join in was almost irresistible, if unthinkable. It all looked so carefree and gay. The swirling skirts of the ladies made shifting patterns of color down the length of the room; jewels sparkled as their wearers turned this way and that, bare shoulders gleamed, ringlets and curls bobbed and quivered.

At last the musicians struck up a lilting waltz melody, one of the new, graceful tunes that Johann Strauss had brought with him to England from Vienna. Aunt Kitty was dismayed to see couples dancing in each other's arms; to Hester's ears the music was so hauntingly beautiful that she scarcely heard her aunt's shocked twitterings beside her. She began to sway imperceptibly in time to the waltz on her chair.

Aunt Kitty, recovering a little, raised her spyglass. "Do look over there, my dear, beyond that third pillar on the left. Thy guardian is dancing with Rosa Love, the singer. Isn't she exquisite? Oh dear, I cannot approve at all of this modern-style dancing, but it is undeniable that they make a very handsome couple. She has had the most wonderful success in London—everyone is talking about her. And Francis Grant has painted her portrait." She nudged her niece. "It is said, my love, that there is a *marquis* so besotted with her that he is only waiting to make her his wife. My dear, just look at that sapphire necklace she is wearing . . . *and* that bracelet . . . *and* that brooch. Can those be diamonds, I wonder? This lorgnette is useless. I wish I had brought my spectacles with me."

Hester followed Aunt Kitty's rapt gaze and saw that she had not exaggerated. The singer *was* exquisite. Knowing her guardian's reputation, it would have been surprising if she had not been. Kirby England and she danced well together, he with surprising ease for a heavy-built man.

It had become suffocatingly hot in the room. Hester, excusing herself, escaped for a while to find fresher air in the corridors outside. She wandered on until she discovered a long double window opening onto a balcony at the back of the house. She stepped out into the cool darkness of the evening. The balcony overlooked an empty courtyard where a fountain splashed, and it was very peaceful there after the ballroom. The sound of the orchestra playing another waltz reached her faintly and she began to move a little, in time to the music, taking a few tentative steps to and fro until she was twirling awkwardly round the balcony . . .

"You need a partner, lass."

She stopped dead. Kirby England watched her from the doorway. He was smoking a cigar.

He went on: "It's an easy dance if you can count to three. I should know. I learned it quick enough." He did not add that Rosa Love had taught him. "Why not try again?"

She was angry and embarrassed that he had spied on her clumsy attempt. "Thou knowest very well that I cannot dance."

He looked downwards. "Is there summat wrong with your feet then?"

"I meant, of course, that I am not allowed to."

"I know of Quakers who do. And you were dancing just now."

"That's different. I was just wondering how the steps went . . ."

He tossed the end of the cigar down into the courtyard and held out both hands towards her. "I'll show you."

She drew back. "That's impossible!"

"Impossible? I'm not such a bad teacher as all that!"

She began to feel muddled as well as cross. "I didn't mean impossible in that way. I daresay I could learn the step quite well but—"

"You're afraid to try?"

"Certainly not!"

"Then there's no excuse left."

Before she could protest he had moved forward and put his right arm about her waist and taken hold of her left hand. "Now, put this hand on my shoulder . . . so." He lifted her hand to his right shoulder, which was on a level with her head. "I take your other hand in mine and we're ready to begin."

She tried to pull away but he held her too firmly. "Pay attention to me for once. I step forward with my right foot and *you* step back at the same time with your left."

He did so, and Hester was forced to step back quickly to avoid him treading on her toe.

"Now, we both step to the side . . ."

Since she found herself balanced unsteadily on her left foot it was both natural and logical to move her weight to her right and to bring her left to join it.

"So far, so good," he told her approvingly. "This time step back with the *right* foot and to the side with your left—the other way round. And so on, over and over again. One, two, three, one, two, three, one, two, three . . . In a moment we'll be turning round, and you'll see how simple it is."

It was extraordinary to be revolving round and round the balcony in this fashion. She could, of course, have flatly refused to go on, but the fact was that she wanted to know whether she could master the dance as well as any of the elegant ladies she had watched in the ballroom. She forgot her dislike of her guardian and, with her eyes fixed firmly on her feet and his, she counted the beat beneath her breath.

"Don't look at the floor anymore," he said. "Your feet know what to do now without you staring at 'em. Look up at me—or if that's too painful, over my shoulder."

They circled the balcony slowly several more times, and Hester discovered that she could manage the steps with little difficulty. Because he was so much taller she danced on tiptoe, and when she stumbled or faltered he simply lifted her into the next part of the step.

Reaching the doorway, he stopped and led her from the balcony. "Come on, lass, let's see if you can waltz with an audience."

She tugged at his arm as he marched her down the corridor towards the ballroom. "I can't dance in there—"

"Why not? There's nowt to stop you that I can see. You've learned the step, you've got a partner and the orchestra's playing a waltz. What more do you want? Besides, you can't refuse your guardian, *and* host, a dance."

"At midnight I shall be of age."

"I know that as well as you. So, consider this a farewell dance, if you like. Let's celebrate the end of our association . . . as guardian and ward."

It was no use arguing; he was too accustomed to having his own way. She followed him meekly onto the huge ballroom floor.

He took her in his arms again and they moved off, slowly at first, beneath the sparkle of the chandeliers. As they turned, her gray dress billowed out above her ankles like a cloud and her black-slippered feet could be seen stepping neatly in time with his. She found, surprised, that after a time she no longer needed to count. It was rather like floating across the floor; he held her firmly round her waist and the glorious music of the waltz filled her ears. It was the most recklessly enjoyable thing she had ever done in her life and the sheer fun of it made her smile up at him with spontaneous happiness. He smiled in response, and as they danced together Hester forgot that this was the guardian that she professed to dislike and distrust so much. She fixed her eyes naturally upon his face as the one strong and steady rock in a whirlpool of spinning color about her. She was aware only of him. Faster and faster they whirled round and round the room—the Lord Mayor of York and his Quakeress ward—and every single eye was upon them.

Rosa Love, too, was watching them. She caught sight of Kirby's face as he looked down at his ward and knew at once, with shock, that he was head over ears in love with her. Impossible as it might seem, it was so. She knew him too well to doubt it. Kirby, the connoisseur of beautiful women, had lost his heart to the prim little Quakeress with the quick tongue. Rosa followed them with her eyes, and knew jealousy for the first time in her life. She wondered how long it would be before Hester Gurney learned that her despised guardian loved her.

"I blame myself entirely," Aunt Kitty said with anguished conscience as they returned home. "If thy dear papa were still alive it would certainly be the death of him to learn of thee waltzing in public—and with such *abandon!*"

"I was not abandoned, Aunt Kitty. No harm was done by it."

"No harm!" her aunt said faintly. "With all of York watching thee and making comments! Thou should have refused thy guardian. Did he not understand that Quakers do not dance—and certainly do not waltz?"

"It would have been ill mannered and difficult to refuse. Besides, dancing is not such a dreadful sin."

"It is to Edith Frohawk. And thou may be sure that it will come to her ears. When we go to Meeting for Worship next First Day we shall receive some very cold looks."

"Then I shall return them. I do not see that it has anything to do with Edith Frohawk whether I stand on my head in public. And I am of age now, Aunt Kitty, so thou cannot be held to blame in any way for my behavior."

Aunt Kitty, admitting the truth of this, felt reassured and began to talk instead of all she had observed—apart from her niece waltzing—during the evening. Soon she was prattling on cheerfully, and Hester leaned her head back against the carriage cushions, only half listening to the stream of gossip. The clip-clop of the horses' hooves struck out a rhythmic beat—one, two, three, one, two, three . . . She could hear again the lovely Viennese music and smiled to herself. She wondered if the Queen was celebrating her own Coronation in London by dancing and whether she, too, loved to waltz. . . .

The following morning Kirby England called at the house in Precentor's Court. Aunt Kitty had gone out to make a special purchase of tea from Mr. Todd, the tea dealer in Goodramgate, and he found Hester alone in the parlor. She was sitting in a brown velvet chair, working at some embroidery, which she put aside as he entered the room.

He came in with his usual confident stride and, refusing to sit, stood himself in front of the fireplace.

"I've brought you a birthday present," he told her without preamble.

"There was no need—"

"I'd be a miserly guardian if I didn't, wouldn't I?"

He produced a small box from his waistcoat pocket and handed it to her. "Open it up and tell me if you like it."

She took it from him reluctantly and lifted the lid. Inside an emerald and diamond ring lay in a nest of red velvet. She blinked at it, dazzled, and then snapped the lid quickly shut. She held out the box to him.

"I couldn't accept such a valuable gift."

"Whyever not? I can afford it."

"I'm sure thou canst, but it must be worth a great deal of money."

"Are you saying then that I should have offered you some rubbishy trinket?"

"I don't know what to say." She still held out the box, looking distressed. "But I can't take it."

He made no attempt to touch the box, and when she tried to

return it to him, he pressed it firmly back into her hands. A ridiculous struggle ensued between the two of them, each attempting to give the ring to the other, and in the end the little box dropped onto the carpet and rolled away beneath the brown chair.

She was angry now and thoroughly alarmed. "Thou may be accustomed to other women of thy acquaintance accepting such gifts from thee, but please believe me when I say that *I* cannot and will not."

He had reddened. "No offense was meant, Miss Gurney, just the reverse. I'm not so stupid as to think for one minute that you'd count the price of a present like other women. But I didn't choose the ring lightly. I bought the best I could find in York because I planned you should wear it on your left hand . . . as my future wife."

His words so startled her that she stared at him in silence.

He added with grim humor: "I see you're shocked—and disgusted. The idea of me as a husband is so appalling to you that for once you've nothing to say to me! How can you be so surprised that I want you to wed me? I thought it was plain for all to see, the last times we've met. Didn't you guess when we waltzed last night? I would've spoken sooner but I couldn't while I was still your guardian. Now I can speak to you as any other man and tell you that I love you very deeply and want you for my wife."

Hester found her voice. "Is this some joke? Thou canst not be serious?"

"A joke? Why should I joke about such a thing? Don't you believe me? I tell you I love you and I'm asking you to marry me."

She saw, in dismay, that he was deadly serious, and for a moment she did not know how to reply. However much she might dislike him, if what he had said was true then she could not ignore the compliment he was paying her. But it seemed impossible to believe. She swallowed.

"Thou hast said many times that we are as different as chalk from cheese."

"What's that to do with loving someone?" He took a step towards her but stopped as she retreated behind the brown chair. "Hester, please listen to me. Hear me out. I've known many women—some beautiful, some worthless, some worth while—but I've never loved any of 'em. I've never loved any woman until I met you. When I first met you I thought you were the last woman on earth I'd ever love—"

"Indeed. I'm flattered to hear it. I assure thee that the feeling was mutual."

He moved forward quickly and this time managed to catch her hands in his. "Rough speech and unpolished phrases may not make much of a proposal, Hester, but if you marry me I promise you'd never regret it. Life with me would be good and I could take care of you as you should be taken care of. I'm rich and I'll soon be a millionaire. I'm going to buy a big estate outside York. We could live there and in London—or anywhere you wanted. You could have anything you wanted—"

"Is that supposed to make me throw myself at thy feet?" she interrupted indignantly. "Dost thou imagine that thy wealth alone could persuade me to accept thee when I do not, and never could, love thee?"

"How do you know that? How can you be so sure you could never love me? I could teach you, if you'd only let yourself forget some of your silly, stubborn prejudices."

She glared up at him. "Is it stubborn and silly then to prefer honesty to dishonesty and truth to lies? I could never love a dishonorable man."

There was silence. He dropped her hands.

"Then you refuse me."

"I do."

"Had I been born a gentleman I wonder if you'd've turned me down so readily," he said with rare bitterness.

"Thy birth has nothing to do with it. I shall always be grateful for all thou hast done for me as guardian. The colliery—"

"Gratitude! I don't want your gratitude." He moved away from her. "I suppose there's nowt more to be said between us. You'll have to excuse me for having inflicted such an unwelcome proposal on you. So, what will you do now?"

"I return to Benbow soon."

"Back to your schoolteaching? Safe from all dishonorable men? Are you going to stay a schoolmarm for the rest of your life

—or will it be Cousin William after all, or perhaps some other pure-white Quaker? Good-bye, Hester."

"The ring," she said, retrieving it hurriedly from beneath the chair. "Thou hast forgotten it."

He glanced back from the doorway and shrugged his shoulders. "Keep it. Give it to some charity of yours. It's of no use to me."

The door banged shut behind him. Hester sank down into the brown velvet chair and covered her face with her hands.

Aunt Kitty, returning later to the house, laden with impulsive purchases she had made at the shops en route to and from the tea dealers, found her niece in a state of agitation.

"My dear child, what has happened? Hast thou seen a ghost? What is that in thy hand?"

Hester held out the little box without a word and her aunt, prising the lid open, gave a gasp of appreciation at the ring's magnificence.

"Where did this come from?"

Her niece told her.

"Thy guardian gave this to thee?"

"He tried to. Naturally, I refused it."

"Naturally? I call it most *unnatural!* It is quite the most exquisite ring I have ever seen."

"It was intended as a pledge of marriage."

Aunt Kitty's mouth fell open. "Marriage? Thou means thy guardian *proposed* to thee?"

"That's just what I mean."

"And thou refused?"

"Of course."

Several of Aunt Kitty's purchases slid to the floor as she sat down to recover herself from the shock.

"My dear, I would never have guessed it. How could I have been so blind! But, now I consider it, I do remember noticing the way he was always watching thee . . . How extraordinary! It must have been a great surprise for thee, my dear, but I must confess I cannot think of a better husband for thee. He would look after thee so well, and thy fortune would continue to increase most satisfactorily with his management."

"Thou hast forgotten two things, Aunt Kitty. First, I do not love him—"

"To be sure, that is a drawback, but not necessarily a bar. One can learn to love, I'm reliably informed, and he is one of the richest and most important men in the county. I have always thought him very charming."

"Thou hast also forgotten that in marrying a non-Quaker, I should be disowned."

Another package fell to the carpet as Aunt Kitty pressed her hand to her mouth. "Very true, child. I had quite forgotten that for the moment. Perhaps thou wast right to refuse him, after all." She looked regretfully at the open box in her other hand and at its winking treasure. "But what a pity . . . what a pity!"

By the end of the autumn Tom Bartlett could read the most difficult passages from the Bible. Hester and Miss Fowler had recruited a Miss Whittaker to help them at the Garford school, where they now had more than fifty pupils, and the three women worked with dedication. At least six of the children were proving exceptionally clever, and most of the remainder were eager to learn. Occasionally a child failed to appear, and Hester discovered that the reason was invariably the parents' suspicion and jealousy of that child's new learning. There was seldom any hope of persuading them to allow a son to return, and none at all if it was a daughter. Few miners could see the need for girls to have any schooling, and many refused to allow their daughters to attend the school at all. In their view it was a waste of time, and the girls were needed to help with the washing and cooking at home, and to look after younger brothers and sisters.

If Hester thought of Kirby England during those busy autumn months, it was very rarely. Once or twice, in the middle of a reading lesson, she would suddenly be reminded of him by listening to some child talk in the broad Yorkshire accents of her former guardian. It made her wonder what he had been like as a boy in his village in the Wolds. Had he looked like poor little Tom Bartlett with his anxious-to-please air, his thin, under-

nourished limbs and his patched clothes; or, much more probably, had he been like her brightest pupil, a tall, dark-haired lad
with bold eyes and aggressive strength in every movement? She
refused to think of their last meeting: the memory of it was still
painful and embarrassing. She had returned the ring by messen-
ger to his house in Monkgate, and so far as she was concerned,
the matter was closed—if not completely forgotten.

When she could spare time from the school, Hester went up to
the colliery, riding in the horse-drawn wagon up through the
wintry beech woods onto the moor, where the mine's dark chimneys rose up against the sky. The viewer had long ago justified
Kirby England's judgment in recommending him, and the colliery was producing well. More than a hundred men were in her
employ. The best men earned up to twenty-eight shillings a
week now, and they were provided with four-room cottages at a
rent of one shilling and eightpence a week, with enough potato
ground to grow from six to nine loads. Hester, determined to
carry on her father's charitable care of his employees and their
families, saw that free blankets and coal were distributed where
needed and financed a soup kitchen at Garford depot for the
benefit of the poorer tenants.

Mr. Scott, the mining engineer from London, had inspected
the pit and warned her of the necessity of improving the ventilation to new standards of safety. Inadequate ventilation, particularly in the old workings of the mine, could lead to a firedamp
explosion. Work had begun immediately on sinking a third shaft,
as well as installing a new ventilation fan.

But within weeks of the new shaft being started, a sudden
breach in the tubbing of Elizabeth Pit main shaft stopped everything. A whole section of the tubbing was blown out, and water
poured down the shaft with cataract force at the rate of four
thousand gallons a minute, far more than the pumps could control. It was discovered that the tubbing was so badly corroded
that every attempt to seal the gap only resulted in its breaking
up further. Within a few days the water had flooded the mine, rising above the engine and pouring over into Hester Pit. The
Hester pumps worked night and day, helped by the Elizabeth
winding engine fitted with lifting tanks, but it was four months

before the pits were finally free of water. Hester, in her dismay at the disaster, could only thank God that, by a miracle, not a single life had been lost in the flooding. But the effect on production was catastrophic: machinery had been damaged, orders were lost, men had to be laid off . . . and where everything had gone well, nothing could now go right. Timber on the estate was found to be diseased, sheep to have foot rot, cattle to be infected with a mysterious sickness; and the following spring was so cold and wet that the crops would certainly suffer for it. Finally, her steward, a man she had known and trusted since childhood, became ill and died.

It was then that William came to Benbow. And Hester, beset with troubles, was glad to see him. Never had he appeared to better advantage in her eyes: he was sympathetic, punctilious, solicitous, ready with advice . . . To see him sitting in her father's old chair beside the library fireplace, in the familiar dark Quaker clothes, speaking the soothing Quaker speech, reminded her poignantly of her loss and of how much she missed a source of wise counsel.

A hailstorm and flooding prevented William from returning the same day to York, and the bad condition of the roads afterwards prolonged his stay for two more days.

On the morning of his departure he proposed marriage to his cousin, pointing out with judicious care all the obvious advantages in gaining a husband so well equipped as himself to help shoulder her burdens. He was eloquent and earnest; she was lonely and, at that moment, in desperate need of support. William could not have timed his proposal better. When his carriage finally drew away from Benbow Hall she had accepted him.

CHAPTER IX

See from his den the monster roll.
Now quick, now slow, without control
He seems to move, bent upon evil,
A docile fiend, or half-tamed devil.

Lines by a schoolboy on the opening
of the York and North Midland Railway

"This is just the first of many openings, Mr. Caley. By next year
we'll have extended our line south to Normanton to link up with
the Midland Counties Railway. York to Normanton, Normanton
to Derby, Derby to Rugby and Rugby . . . to London! An uninterrupted railway line two hundred and seventeen miles long
which will convey a passenger from York to London in ten
hours, and according to Mr. Stephenson, it'll soon be a damn
sight quicker than that. What d'you think of that?"

The engineer grinned. "I say good fortune to you, Mr. England, and hope to share in the building of those future railways."

Kirby clapped him on the shoulder. "Aye—you'll be doing that
all right, Mr. Caley. You've done a grand job for us so far. It's
taken us close on six years to get this far and it's been a bloody-
hard sweat. None of it your fault, and you've never faltered. I'm
obliged to you for your loyalty."

The two men were talking together at a gargantuan breakfast
which had been arranged at the Mansion House by the directors
of the York and North Midland Railway Company. It was a pre-
liminary to the official opening of the line and a trial trip to be
taken to Milford and back by a party of distinguished guests.

Until the chairman had come across to speak with him, John Caley had been feeling uncomfortably out of place in such elegant surroundings. He was more at ease with the mud and dust and discomfort of his daily life—more familiar with viaducts, bridges, cuttings, inclinations and drains than with the cushioned ease he saw about him. The polite murmurings of the assembled guests, the chandeliers and soft carpets were moon miles from the roar of gunpowder explosions, the rolling thunder of falling rocks, the sweating, grunting curses of the navvies, the broken limbs, the blood, the toil, the danger . . .

He watched Kirby England speaking with an important-looking arrival and found it hard to equate the urbane Lord Mayor and prosperous railway company chairman with the man he remembered throwing off his coat that day to make a running with a loaded barrow up the perilous cutting slope. He considered Mr. England detachedly and decided that he was two men: the one he observed now and the other a man who still, in his heart, reveled in and relished his past, who was proud of his strength and proud of his roots in Yorkshire soil.

Kirby England made a short but powerful speech, and the whole party moved off from the Mansion House in a procession of carriages, driving through the streets towards the newly built station. It was a cloudless May day, with blue skies, bright sunshine and a gentle, refreshing breeze. The Minster bells rang out loud over the city, flags had been hoisted and flew from almost every building and a cannon boomed in salute down beside the river.

The procession reached the station near Thief Lane. It was a spacious erection, standing on high iron pillars, and the train that awaited them there consisted of two engines and nineteen carriages. The railway company staff, who had previously carefully swept the whole length of the line to remove all possible impediments, stood by dressed in smart green uniform. And, to add to the atmosphere of anticipation and excitement, a brass band was playing vigorously.

The distinguished guests packed themselves into the carriages, as did the brass band, and when all was ready a bell was rung loudly. The driver of the front engine blew upon his whistle and with a mighty snort of steam the engine began to move, its big wheels turning slowly along the iron rails. At seven minutes past one, precisely according to plan, the long snakelike body slid smoothly away from York station under the broad arch of Hold-gate Lane bridge and was soon lost to sight of the crowds who thronged the station and the adjacent walls and ramparts. The hundred or so passengers experienced the thrilling sensation of being borne along with increasing swiftness until they flew with the speed of a racehorse past the admiring spectators, who still for many a mile stood at both sides of the line, cheering wildly. The very first train of the York and North Midland Railway Company carried its passengers triumphantly across the country-side on that May afternoon and the brass band played away in an open carriage, music and steam in melodious harmony as they sped through fields, and Johnny Raws watched openmouthed to see the iron horse go thundering by.

At Milford the train stopped and passengers descended to in-spect the line. They climbed back aboard again and were whirled back to York at the dizzy speed of some twenty miles per hour. Then the real work of the day over, they all fell to eat-ing a second time. Two huge dinners had been arranged by the company: one at the George Inn for the less distinguished guests —clerks, engineers, inspectors and so on; the other at the Guild-hall beside the Mansion House. Two hundred (and John Caley was gratified to find himself among them) sat down to dine in that splendid and ancient hall at half-past four and did not rise from the table until ten. The chairman presided, with Mr. George Stephenson on his right hand as guest of honor. An end-less round of speeches and toasts took place amid emotion and exhilaration. Kirby England rose at last to speak.

"My lords, ladies and gentlemen. Our fair City of York has now, today, entered the Railway Age. From this day on the sight and sound and smell of locomotive steam engines will become increasingly familiar to us all. But the small line we've opened is nothing compared with what we're going to build in the future, and the journey you made today is nothing compared with jour-neys you'll be making in the future. I predict that within a dec-ade you will be able to travel by railway from York to any part of the land. And where man may travel, so may goods of all kinds, with equal speed and regularity. Industry and trade will flourish with the coming of the railways; this country of ours will become the greatest in the world, her prosperity nourished by iron arteries and iron veins reaching to every part of her body. London will be her head, Edinburgh her feet—but York, I prophesy, will be her heart!"

He was interrupted by a tumult of applause and the drumming of fists on tables. When silence fell again, he continued in quiet and level tones that nonetheless reached the very furthest corner of the Guildhall.

"In our midst, ladies and gentlemen, we are honored to have the one to whom we owe an inestimable debt for today's opening. If ever a man deserved to be held up to the public approbation of the whole world, that man is Mr. George Stephenson. His is the genius that gave us the engines you saw today and that took you all to Milford and back in safety and comfort; his is the courage and foresight that fought on when many were against him, many thought him mad and many refused to believe in the reality of steam locomotive engines at all. So far as this company is concerned, Mr. Stephenson helped to bring us through our difficulties when doubts were entertained as to this railway being a profitable venture. He invested considerable sums of his own money in our company, demonstrating to those doubters his confidence in us—and in railways. My lords, ladies and gentlemen, I give you a toast . . . Mr. George Stephenson!"

Mr. Stephenson replied in the modest manner that was characteristic of him, reminiscing on his career, which had begun at the age of eight when an old widow gave him twopence a day to keep her cows off the wooden colliery tramway by her land. From there he had progressed to various jobs at the pits where his father worked. He drove horses for twopence a day, became a picker at sixpence a day—picking stones and dross out of the coal—and, at the age of fourteen, became assistant fireman to his father on one shilling a day. He had set his heart on working on the pumping engine at the pits, and when this ambition was finally achieved, it was the beginning of a lifelong preoccupation with steam engines and their development. His achievements were all the more remarkable to his audience when he revealed that he had never been to school, his family being too poor, and had not learned to read and write until the age of eighteen. The famous engineer sat down to applause that raised the rafters of the Guildhall.

The Mayor of Hull then rose to propose the health of the chairman of the York and North Midland Railway Company, reminding all present of the debt the City of York also owed to him, a debt which he suggested would increase significantly with the coming years. Finally, the guests streamed across from the Guildhall to the Mansion House, where a large party of fashionables danced until four o'clock in the morning.

Henry Latham, who had been among the company throughout the day's celebrations, drew Kirby to one side and the two men repaired to a quiet anteroom. Kirby poured them glasses of brandy from a decanter on a side table. They lit cigars and sat talking over the success of the opening.

"I'm flattered you should have called the engine The Latham," Henry said. "It's good to think one's name may go down in history books—if only on the side of a locomotive steam engine!"

"I like to acknowledge my debts," Kirby replied. "Thanks to you, our Bill went through Parliament."

"I wouldn't say that *you* were exactly idle in the matter of canvasing support at Westminster."

"I did what I could, but you're the Member of Parliament, not me—that's the difference. By the way, how's that son of yours?"

"Thriving. You must come and visit us soon at Murton Hall and meet your new nephew; he's dark-haired, and we both think he has a look of you."

"Poor lad, I hope not! You want a son with an air of his father's breeding, not the looks of a peasant."

Henry smiled. "If he has half your energy and ambition I shall be content."

"I'm not so sure *he* will be . . . Come to think of it, some of my happiest hours were spent behind the counter in my draper's shop."

"Nonsense, Kirby, you know very well that it would never have satisfied you for long." Henry set his glass down on the table beside him. "Have you heard anything of Hester Gurney?"

Kirby looked at the end of his cigar. "Nay. But there's no reason why I should. Our connection ended the minute she came of age, and that wasn't too soon for her."

"There was a time," Henry said thoughtfully, "when Adelaide was quite convinced that you and Hester might marry. At the time I thought it nonsense, but I've sometimes wondered—"

"Stop wondering then. You were right in the first place—it was nonsense." Kirby rose to replenish his glass. With his back turned, he asked: "How is she, do you know?"

Henry shrugged. "Since her marriage we've seen little of her; they spend all their time at Benbow Hall. Hester writes to Adelaide from time to time but says very little about herself. She is expecting a child, you know, and hasn't been well." He looked across at Kirby. "Speaking of marriage, I heard rumors today about you and a certain duke's daughter. From all accounts, she's besotted with you."

"Aye, the silly lass thinks I'm an amusing change from the refined young scions of the aristocracy that she's used to. She'll learn."

"Even so, a duke's daughter isn't to be sneezed at, and a pretty one too! I'm surprised you're not more enthusiastic about it. I always thought that was precisely the sort of wife you had in mind."

"Mixing my common yokel's blood with the blue blood of the nobility, you mean? Aye, not so long ago it would've given me a lot of satisfaction. Now I'm not so sure that I care. I don't need them. Besides, the daughter's much too compliant for my liking—she'd bore me to death in six months, and her father's riddled with debts—which is the only reason he'd be able to overcome his aversion to having me as a son-in-law!"

Henry refilled his glass and resettled himself comfortably.

"So Rosa Love married her marquis in the end."

"Aye, she'd the good sense to do that."

Henry sighed and drew on his cigar, watching the smoke rise above him. "She's one of the most beautiful women I've ever seen and she sang like an angel. Do you remember when I took you to the Theatre Royal to hear her? It seems a long time ago."

"It's six bloody years! That's the time it's taken us to build the railway we've opened today, and that's a deal too long in my book. Mind you, from now on it's going to be easier all the way. Up till now we've had to fight for every inch of line, but now we've public opinion on our side. People've begun to see the light. They *want* the railways to come. I'm going to see that they get 'em."

"You're going on then?"

"Going on? What else should I do? Sit back and admire the little line we've just opened and keep patting myself on the back? Not bloody likely! Like I've told them umpteen times—this is just the beginning of it all. I'm going to build railways all over the country. Give me another six years, Henry lad, and you'll see what I'm talking about!"

"Will you stand again for Lord Mayor?"

Kirby shook his head. "I won't have the time to spare. I've served two terms and that's enough. I want something different now."

"And I suppose you always get what you want."

"Usually, lad . . . but not always."

They returned to the guests and the dancing. Kirby was soon to be seen dancing with the fat wife of the Mayor of Hull, and then with a string of dignitaries' wives. He waltzed with the duke's daughter, who gazed up at him with an innocent and undisguised admiration. As he whirled her round the floor to the Strauss music, he remembered his waltz with Hester Gurney. She was the only thing in his life that had eluded him. Even when she had turned down his proposal so vehemently, he had been convinced that he would win her in the end. Nothing had so far defeated him, once he had put his mind to achieving it, and he had wanted Hester Gurney as his wife. The news of her marriage to her cousin had put him into a black rage and a despair such as he had never known. She was beyond his reach and now she was to have another man's child . . . The duke's daughter was startled, but delighted, to be seized in a still closer grip and swung savagely round and round the ballroom.

Hester's daughter was born late that summer. But the child, a tiny waxen creature, lived only a few hours before quietly expiring. The birth had been difficult and Hester herself had been very close to death. She lay in her bed for weeks afterwards, too weak and ill to care much whether she lived or died. She grieved deeply for the child she had lost, who would have been her one consolation in what had become a joyless existence. And there were long hours spent alone to reflect on the terrible mistake she had made in marrying William. The wise-counseling, considerate cousin had become a cold and autocratic husband, intent on subduing her mind and will to his.

There was no doubt that in his way he loved her—if such behavior could go by the name of love. On the first night of their marriage William had insisted that they pray together at the bedside; he had knelt beside her, entreating at great length God's blessing on their union. But what had followed had been a chill and inhuman conjoining, without tenderness or consideration. As the months passed she felt increasing despair and disgust. The flesh and the devil were one in William's mind, and his resentment of his need of her demonstrated itself in callous and even cruel treatment, as though he sought to prove in himself an inner purity that was above carnal lust. It seemed to Hester, in those dark days after the child's death, that God had in no way blessed their union, despite all William's prayers.

When at last she had recovered her lost health and strength, Hester began to come downstairs for a while each day. She discovered that, in her absence, William had taken over her father's old desk as his own and that all old papers and possessions had been removed. She concealed her indignation. William was, after all, now master of the house. He had taken over complete control of the Benbow estate since their marriage, and in his opinion, there was nothing wrong with the estate that a little pruning here and there wouldn't cure. He had engaged a new bailiff—a dour, cold man whom Hester did not like. While she had been ill, he told her, they had dismissed some idle and incompetent men and evicted a tenant from one of the cottages since the man had not worked for eight weeks or more . . .

"Not Jeremiah Barwick?"

"I believe that was his name."

"But thou shouldst not have done that!"

William frowned. "Why not? The man was always drunk. I

saw him staggering and incapable myself several times, and thou knows my views on intemperance. I shall not tolerate it—any more than thy father did."

"Papa disapproved, certainly, but Jeremiah has not been able to work because his arm was so badly broken in a tree-felling accident. It did not mend well, and if he drinks now it is probably to dull the pain he still suffers."

"His arm seemed sufficiently well mended to raise a bottle constantly to his lips. I suggest thou leaves such matters to me. Thou hast no need to worry thyself about them any longer."

"The estate will always concern me," she told him. "The tenants are like friends to me."

"They are in my charge now," William replied. "I have spoken on the affair and that is an end to it."

Hester saw by his face that it would be useless to argue further.

"Very well. But perhaps we may speak of the colliery at least. Hast thou good news of that? Canst thou tell me at least how work is progressing on the new shaft and ventilation fan?"

"It is not."

"Not progressing at all?" She stared at him. "But the shaft was well advanced—"

"I have stopped it."

"Stopped it! But, William, the new shaft is badly needed to protect the men from a firedamp explosion. The mining engineer from London recommended—"

"I know precisely what Mr. Scott recommended, my dear. I have read his report with great attention. But I have learned in life to use my own judgment. I have ordered the work to stop because there was no doubt in my mind that the shaft was a wasteful and unnecessary extravagance." William made an arch with his fingers on the desk before him. "I was not surprised, by the way, to learn that it was Kirby England who first suggested the whole idea. It is typical of his high-handed meddling and his readiness to squander other people's money."

"But the recommendation was the engineer's, not Kirby England's. Surely the viewer explained to thee that the ventilation is bad. The old workings—"

William held up his hand. "That is enough, Hester. There is no need to repeat the tale to me. The viewer did indeed outline an unproven theory at some length and with, I might add, no little impudence on his part."

"Didst thou not understand?"

"I understood very well the danger of having such a subversive manager in charge of the colliery. I dismissed him at once and replaced him last week with an altogether more satisfactory man."

"But he was quite excellent! All the men respected him."

"He was also yet another of Kirby England's suggestions, I believe. I was astonished to find so much of thy former guardian's influence still prevalent at Benbow. Thou shouldst be thankful to be rid of anything to do with him. I feel bound to add, Hester, that I find thy interest in all such matters very unwomanly. I discovered recently, to my surprise, that thou wast in the habit of visiting the mine, before our marriage, and of hobnobbing with the colliers—going amongst them as if thou were no better than a common servant girl."

"But surely I *am* no better than any servant girl, William," she answered him. "Are we not taught to believe that we are all God's children and equal in His sight?"

"Thou hast a position to uphold, Hester, and it is thy duty to do so. It is a question of authority. To fraternize with the workers is to court trouble. They will only take advantage of it and we shall have a strike on our hands."

"It has never led to that so far. And Papa was not above fraternizing with them, as thou calls it."

"Permit me to know best, Hester. Times have changed. There is a great deal of unrest in the country. I forbid thee to go near the colliery again. Thou must leave all business matters to me. Concern thyself with thy school—if thou must. Although I should have thought it best left to others, considering thy poor state of health now. In fact, I should very much prefer that thou didst not continue thy work there."

"I'm sorry, William, but whatever thou says, I shall never give up the school. I am quite well enough to carry on there."

He tapped his fingers together thoughtfully. "We shall see about that, my dear."

There was nothing more she could do, either for Jeremiah Barwick or for the colliers. Jeremiah and his family had already packed up and left the district, and no one could tell her where they had gone. She could not imagine how they would survive: their only hope would probably be the workhouse. As for the viewer, such a good man would have little difficulty finding new work, but how would Benbow Colliery fare without him? She worried about the mine and, most of all, she worried about the safety of the men. Who would be proved right about the ventilation shaft—William or Mr. Scott? William was no fool and had excellent judgment, she knew, in legal affairs, but if he were wrong this time the colliers might pay for it with their lives.

Mrs. England sat in the drawing room at 44 Monkgate watching her son. He was pacing to and fro before the hearth in the way he always did when thinking something out. Presently, he stopped.

"Do you remember me promising you that one day I'd buy a big country estate, Mother—a proper gentleman's seat?"

"I do, son."

"I've found the one I want. I'm going to buy Dewsborough Park, castle and all. It'll cost me half a million pounds, but that includes the village of Dewsborough and—even more useful to me—a big slice of flat land north of Market Weighton. Any new railway line projected between York and Hull would have to pass through there and I can put a stop to it. I'll build my own railway . . . *and* my own station at Dewsborough."

Mrs. England looked bewildered. "Dewsborough! But that belongs to the Duke of—"

"Aye. I've decided I fancy buying his estate more than I fancy marrying his daughter."

Mrs. England was far from displeased to hear this news. She had not cared for that simpering lady any more than she had cared for Hester Gurney. However, she was a little daunted by the thought of living at Dewsborough Castle.

"It's a mighty big place," she said doubtfully. "I've seen pictures of it—all those towers and turrets—and there must be hundreds of rooms."

"Fit for a king, you might say," her son said. "Never fear, Mother. We've as much right to live at Dewsborough as any blue-blooded idler. We'll keep this house on in York, and before long I'll buy another one in London as well."

"Everything is going well for us, isn't it, Kirby?"

"Aye, it is that. I always told you the railways would make me my real fortune, didn't I? Now that the York and North Midland has opened its extension to Altofts junction and joined up with the North Midland and Midland Counties railways we've at last got a direct route to London. Which means it's important we let no rival lines operate near York: there's no sense in having two lines where one will serve an area. So, I've arranged to lease the Leeds to Selby line with an option to purchase anytime and a guarantee of a five-percent dividend on the company's capital so long as the lease lasts." He grinned to himself. "The directors had no choice but to agree—they're in bad straits from overspending and their shareholders are grumbling. It'll be worth every penny to put paid to the competition I saw threatening us. A new line's been opened between Manchester and Leeds, and together with the Leeds and Selby, they'd've taken all east–west traffic away from the York and North Midland. As it is, I'll close down the Leeds to Selby line to passengers and reroute all traffic through the North Midland and ourselves."

"Close it down! I don't understand. I thought you wanted railways *built!*"

"So I do. But too much competition, too many lines serving the same area, will kill the railways before they've half begun. The weakest must go to the wall for the strong to survive. The Leeds and Selby Company were fool enough to let themselves become vulnerable, and we'll take their passengers and goods. The Hull to Selby line will still be operating, for a while, because the directors of that company were able to stand out against us with their monopoly of Hull traffic. But they'll soon find they've lost that. I've bought the steam-tug service between

Hull and Selby, so they'll not find it so easy to survive as they thought."

He stopped pacing and sat down, adding with a faint smile, "If I didn't know you better, Mother, I'd say you were almost shocked by what I've just said. You should know me by now. I didn't get us out of that stinking little hovel on the Wolds to this house and a place like Dewsborough by playing the perfect gentleman."

"Oh, I know. But when I listen to you talk like that it all seems such a gamble . . . such a risk."

"That's the fun of it. And there's more. I've just been proposed as chairman of a company that's to build a railway from Darlington to Newcastle. By God, it's going to be a challenge but it's going to be an important line. It'll carry the Durham coal and it'll be the first step towards a line right up the east coast to Edinburgh. We'll be building across hilly country, with a network of old colliery lines leading from the pits down to the sea. There'll be vested interests at every yard, as well as construction problems, and we'll have the Great North of England Company —run by a pack of Quakers—at our heels. They're building a line from York north as far as Darlington, so it stands to reason they'll be after control of the line from there to Newcastle. There'll be a fight between us, but we'll win in the end. They've had too much trouble so far and they've run out of capital. Whereas the York and North Midland declared a dividend of six percent at our half-yearly meeting and George Stephenson's been elected to our board of directors. We've the shareholders' confidence now and nothing will stop us!"

He had been speaking almost to himself, and now he stood up again and paced about restlessly. Mrs. England followed him with her eyes; beneath her pride in him lay a faint unease, a presentiment of trouble ahead. The old specter of poverty raised its head.

"There's another scheme I've in mind that'll please you," her son was saying. "At the York and North Midland annual meeting there was unanimous acceptance of my proposal that five hundred pounds be granted out of profits to survey two new branch lines—one from York to Pickering to connect with Whitby and the other to Scarborough. I had a look over my property at Whitby the other day; it's only a little fishing village, but I reckon a railway could make it the Brighton of the North. As for the Scarborough line, it'll pass right by our old village, Mother. There's a coincidence for you! You'll be able to look out of the carriage window and see your old home as you go by, but that's as close as you'll ever have to go to it again."

As usual, his brimming confidence quelled her inner fears. She smiled at him. "I'll like that, son—I'll really like that."

"Public confidence in him has never been higher," William Gurney said.

"Unfortunately, that is true," Elias Snell acknowledged. He flicked some mud from the side of his left boot with a small exclamation of annoyance.

William looked at him across the desk in his chambers and suppressed his irritation. He would have preferred a better ally in his hounding of Kirby England; he considered Elias too small-minded and concerned only with revenging the many humiliations he had suffered at the draper's hands. A similar vengeance was also in William's thoughts, but there was a larger aim for which he knew he had been destined—to rid the world of an evil man who was a threat and an affront to every decent Christian.

"I attended the half-annual meeting of the York and North Midland Railway Company," Elias continued, satisfied at last with the appearance of the boot. "It was most revealing."

"I hear a six-percent dividend was declared."

"It was indeed, and the inestimable Mr. George Stephenson was duly elected to the board. There were, however, one or two awkward questions asked by the shareholders . . ."

"Oh?" William's head lifted like a pointer scenting quarry.

"Yes. Some of us found it hard to make sense of the *very* odd accounts presented to us in the secretary's report. Mr. England has a strange way of charging to capital account items that one would have expected to see paid out of current revenue."

"Such as?"

"Such as clothing for railway police, iron rails, wood sleepers, insurance, coke . . . even interest on debentures! I put the suggestion myself to the meeting that it would be wise to appoint professional auditors, as is commonly the case with banks and insurance companies."

"And what was the chairman's reaction to that?"

Elias Snell smiled. "Mr. England was more than a little put out. In fact, he was very angry. He said it was the first time that he had ever heard of such a suggestion, that the accounts were always audited by the directors themselves and surely no one doubted those worthy gentlemen?"

"And no one does . . . yet?"

"No. The board has the shareholders' confidence—for the time being at least. As Mr. England so cleverly pointed out, the books are always open for every shareholder to inspect for himself."

"There was no other dissent?"

"None. If one does not count Mr. Rowntree, who stood up to warn his fellow shareholders against losing their privileges. 'Every shareholder an auditor,' he kept saying, but his warning fell on deaf ears—not surprisingly since the shares of the York and North Midland Railway Company now stand at a premium of twenty-four pounds, a capital appreciation of fourteen percent in less than a month! Who is going to be dissatisfied with that?"

"So we must wait."

"We must wait," agreed Elias Snell. "But never fear, the time will come for us to strike."

"And meantime?"

"Meantime, I and some other citizens who are of like mind to ourselves have in mind a campaign of invective against Mr. England in the press."

"He is part proprietor of the *Yorkshire Gazette*," William reminded him.

"There are other newspapers we shall use. A Captain Wyatt of my acquaintance is proposing to address a series of 'open letters' accusing Mr. England of unscrupulous dealings. You are no doubt also aware of the unease of the Darlington Quakers over Mr. England's proposed line from there to Newcastle? They offered him a lease of part of their line in the hope of keeping a finger in the pie, but he turned them down flat. He has, of course, no intention of losing control. I have already seen the text of one of Captain Wyatt's letters on the subject: he calls Mr. England's Darlington to Newcastle line 'an abortion with a crooked back and a crooked snout, conceived in cupidity and begotten in fraud.' Rather picturesquely phrased, I thought. It's bound to catch the public eye."

For the first time at that meeting William smiled. "The captain sounds a gentleman I should like to know better."

"I doubt if you would. He is a rather tiresome gentleman in fact. Unfortunately, we cannot afford to be too choosy about our supporters or we may soon find ourselves lone voices in the wilderness. A kind of railway fever seems to be taking hold of people. Everyone is talking of railway shares and speculating in projected railway companies. We are faced with a many-headed hydra to slay."

"I am only concerned with *one* head," William said softly. "And I shall not rest until it falls."

Elias Snell looked at his fingernails and polished them against his coat sleeve. "Quite so. Quite so. I share your feelings, my dear Mr. Gurney. In my view, the removal of Mr. England from power will render infinite service to this country in saving it from the ruination that threatens it. We are told that the railways will bring us peace and plenty, larders stocked full, factories, mills and pits working to capacity, fleets of ships loaded with corn . . . but in my opinion, there is another side to the coin. In exchange we shall be left with a land of endless iron ways, mountains of coal, belching chimneys, ugly excavations, bridges and viaducts and these dreadful steam monsters roaring and shrieking everywhere."

"I consider railways and everything connected with them to be nothing less than the work of the devil," William said. "And it is the subtle poison of avarice diffusing itself throughout the country that is promoting the devil's progress."

"Quite so," Elias repeated, averting his gaze from the Quaker's fanatical eyes. "We are united in a common purpose. There is also," he added thoughtfully, "the matter of the bridge."

"Bridge?"

"You have not heard about it? But then you come so seldom to York nowadays. The York and North Midland Railway Company are planning to improve the access to the station by building a new bridge across the Ouse into Lendal. The matter is shortly to be put before Parliament."

William frowned. "They might well find approval since Lendal leads to the Minster and the heart of the city."

"The owners of the existing ferry across that particular point of the river happen to be my clients," Elias said with a dry cough. "Naturally enough, they oppose the whole scheme, as do the shopkeepers and landlords of Micklegate and Ousegate by the old Ouse Bridge. Altogether an increasing number of traders in York have begun to realize that their interests and those of Mr. Kirby England may not always coincide so happily as hitherto."

"Thou wilt no doubt encourage them to continue so thinking?"

"You may rest assured that I will."

Elias Snell went away and William sat considering the situation. So far, so good. And yet the pace of the hunt was much too slow for his liking. He did not, however, underestimate the task he had set himself, nor the caliber of the quarry he pursued. Critical letters in the newspapers would do little more than cause passing comment, soon forgotten; and the caperings of a few small shopkeepers motivated only by personal gain or loss would cause Kirby England no more trouble than flies round a lion. What was needed was proof: positive proof of fraud or negligence or dishonesty—of whatever kind. Nothing less would bring Kirby England down. And for that, he could only wait.

CHAPTER X

Railway Shares! Railway Shares!
Hunted by Stags and Bulls and Bears—
Hunted by women—hunted by men—
Speaking and writing—voice and pen—
Claiming and coaxing—prayers and snares—
All the world mad about Railway Shares!

Verses in the *Illustrated London News*

"Fancy, my dear, my railway shares have trebled in value since I bought them," Aunt Kitty said. "To think that I ever doubted the good sense—the absolute necessity—of locomotive steam engines."

Hester turned from the parlor window; she had been listening to the Minster bells and watching a long-haired ginger cat washing itself meticulously in the summer sunshine on a wall across the street.

"I'm glad for thee, Aunt."

"But didst thou not also have shares in the York and North Midland Railway Company that thy papa left thee?"

"William sold them some time ago."

"How shortsighted of him, my dear. But never mind. Thou canst always buy more. No doubt thy former guardian would be willing to advise thee in the matter."

"I doubt it. I haven't seen or spoken to him for several years."

"Well, he has become so important all over the country now that York can no longer claim him as her own," Aunt Kitty said.

"I hear that in London he is received by the most influential people—the Duke of Wellington, Mr. Gladstone . . . It is even rumored that the Queen herself expressed a wish to meet him and to travel on one of his railway lines."

"I have read something to that effect in the newspapers. In fact, it is hard to open a newspaper these days *without* reading something of him."

"Just so! And *everyone* subscribed to his testimonial. Of course, with a first dividend of twenty-one shillings being paid on each of the York and North Midland shares, shareholders were in a mood to be generous to their chairman. He was presented with a most magnificent silver centerpiece and candelabrum; I have not seen it myself but I am assured that it is of exceptionally fine craftsmanship."

"Really?" Hester said with an irony in her voice which Aunt Kitty either pretended not or failed to notice. "He may add it to all the other extravagances in his house in Monkgate then, I suppose."

"Oh, he's hardly to be found there these days, my dear. When he is not in London—and he has a *very* large house there near Albert Gate, I'm told—he is at Dewsborough Park. Hadst thou not heard that he bought the castle and the whole estate?"

"I believe I did read something about it."

"The trouble is, child, that thou art far too much at Benbow," Aunt Kitty said reprovingly. "Thou might as well be buried alive, the way thou lives there now—seeing no one, going nowhere. I have never seen thee so pale or in such poor health and spirits. If William had not finally agreed to let thee come on this visit to me, I think I should have gone to Benbow myself to fetch thee away, whether he liked it or not!"

Hester turned away. She would not admit, even to her beloved aunt, how unhappy her marriage was. Since the loss of her baby she had existed through long, dreary months at Benbow. No other child had been conceived, and her revulsion against William was now so strong that his touch sickened her. Mind and body had revolted against her husband. At their Quaker marriage she had promised to be, through divine assistance, a loving and faithful wife. Faithful she would be; loving she could not.

She had been surprised when William had agreed to her visiting Aunt Kitty in York. He disapproved of her aunt even more than her father had done. However, he had been alarmed by Hester's continued poor health and had weighed his disapproval of Aunt Kitty's frivolity against the possibility that a change of scene and air might result in restoring to him a better wife.

Aunt Kitty was as good as any apothecary's tonic. Within a few days Hester had begun to rediscover her former good spirits, and by the time Adelaide called on them after a fortnight she was already looking a great deal better.

Adelaide herself was blooming. With the birth of a second son she had acquired a fulfilled and matronly glow and her happiness was obvious to all around her. Hester herself talked so cheerfully and animatedly that Adelaide was convinced that her marriage must be a success, despite her previous fears to the contrary.

"You and William must promise to come and visit us at Murton Hall, now that you are feeling better," she said to Hester. "You would love little Harry—he is the most adorable baby. He looks just like Henry, whereas George has an England more than a Latham look and reminds us very much of Kirby."

"My dear, thou must tell us all about Dewsborough Park," Aunt Kitty said quickly, turning the subject away from babies. "How splendid it must be! I should so like to see it one day."

"Then I shall arrange it for you at once. Nothing could be simpler. Kirby will not have the least objection, I know, to my taking you there myself."

"Of course I shouldn't like to intrude—" Aunt Kitty demurred with a false show of reluctance.

"But you won't be intruding one bit. Mama is at Monkgate at present. I think she secretly prefers it to living in that enormous castle. And Kirby is away in London. No one is there except the servants. Let us go tomorrow."

Aunt Kitty still hesitated politely, but Hester knew quite well that she had no intention of turning down such an interesting invitation. She herself had no objection to the plan . . . so long as Kirby England was safely away in London. She was rather curious to see with what new magnificence he had surrounded himself.

"I have an even better idea," Adelaide went on enthusiastically. "Wouldn't it be the greatest fun to go by railway?"

"By *railway?*" Aunt Kitty's jaw dropped and she looked as though she had never heard of such a thing.

"It's very easy, and would be much quicker and much more comfortable than going by horse and carriage. When the branch line was made out to Market Weighton, Kirby built a private station of his own at Dewsborough, just where the tip of the park meets the line. We could take the train from York station tomorrow, and I shall arrange for a carriage to carry us the short distance from Dewsborough station up to the castle."

"I have never set foot near a railway carriage," Aunt Kitty confessed worriedly. "I'm not at all sure that I should enjoy the experience at my time of life."

But Hester was intrigued. "Neither have I, Aunt, but I think Adelaide's idea is a good one. I have only been in the colliery wagon, which, I believe, is not at all the same as traveling in a first-class railway coach. Now is thy chance to show that thou really meant what thou said earlier to me about the absolute *necessity* of the steam locomotive."

"I did not mean that it was necessary for *me* to be conveyed by them. I am perfectly content to leave that pleasure to others."

But in the end they persuaded her and plans were made for the three of them to journey to Dewsborough Park the following day.

The morning was fine and sunny. Aunt Kitty spent a great deal of time preparing herself for the ordeal she anticipated. Her traveling clothes were carefully selected. "Not that I have any precedent to look to," she told Hester. "What *do* ladies wear when they travel by railway?"

"The same, no doubt, as when traveling by coach. Come, Aunt Kitty," Hester teased her. "We are not journeying to Russia, remember. Dewsborough is only fifteen miles or so distant and there is no need to take a valise."

"How do I know I shall not be stranded for the night? I am sure those steam engines are unreliable."

"If thy railway shares are so reliable, then it follows that the steam engines must be too. Besides, we can always return by horse and carriage."

Adelaide called for them and they set off for York station. Aunt Kitty was fluttering with nervousness, and her fears were in no way allayed by the sight of the hissing iron monster that waited to convey them eastwards out of York. She eyed it with alarm and doubt. "It looks as though it may blow up at any minute. All that steam must be dangerous! And look at those heavy wheels on that narrow rail! How do the wheels stay on and how can the rails bear the weight?"

Adelaide had to admit that she did not know the answer. However, she was able to assure Aunt Kitty that she had traveled by railway to London and back many times without the train ever once falling off the line. She found it delightful, she said, and far less tiring than going by coach.

They walked along the line of carriages drawn up behind the steam engine, and Aunt Kitty was horrified to see the third-class wagons—roofless and without even a bench to sit on and crowded with standing passengers crammed together like sheep in a pen.

"Don't worry, you are not traveling in one of those," Adelaide reassured her. "Or those," she added as they passed the second-class carriages, whose occupants fared a little better since they at least had a roof over their heads and wooden benches to sit on.

They came to a first-class carriage, and Aunt Kitty, still beset by doubts and fears, was pleasantly surprised to see how comfortable and well appointed the interior was. The carriage was elegantly fitted with blue upholstery. On each side of the compartment were three seats piped in needlecord, and separated from each other by armrests. The insides of the doors were thickly padded with buttoned leather and the windows, with quarter lights on each side, resembled exactly those found in any horse-drawn coach, and were therefore comfortingly familiar. Maroon damask curtains hung on a wooden rail and were caught back with silk cords at the sides of the windows to give maximum light. There was a thick blue carpet on the floor, and the wooden ceiling overhead was painted prettily with blue and gold scrolls; a glass-shaded oil lamp hung from a hole in the center of the ceiling, and Adelaide explained that this was lit and lowered from above by the guard who traveled on the roof.

Much reassured, Aunt Kitty settled herself in a corner seat, arranging her gray skirts carefully. She beamed up at Adelaide.

"This is very comfortable, my dear. It is really no different from being in a coach. I had no idea that it would be so *civilized*."

"In winter we would be supplied with footwarmers," Adelaide told her. "But of course there is no need for that today."

"Just as well for the second- and third-class passengers," Hester remarked. "I take it that they do not get such benefits, although they must be in need of warming far more than the first-class! The poor things looked very uncomfortable."

There was a loud crash on the roof above them that shook the carriage. Aunt Kitty started violently.

"It's only the guard stowing some luggage on the roof," Adelaide said quickly.

Aunt Kitty, who had quite thought the engine had exploded, shut her eyes in relief. Scarcely had she done so than the station bell rang loudly, a whistle blew and the carriage gave a small jerk beneath their feet and began to roll forward. With a faint gasp Aunt Kitty clutched at the armrest beside her.

"It's moving very fast!"

"Not yet, Aunt Kitty. We haven't even left the station!"

They drew out of York with a rhythmic clanking of wheels, the carriage rocking and swaying gently. Once they had left the city behind, the speed increased noticeably and the scenery began to flash past the windows. Aunt Kitty had kept her eyes tight shut since leaving the station, but when, after some time had passed and she found engine, carriages and rails still in partnership, she reopened her eyes and relaxed her grip on the armrest a little. The movement of the train was very soothing, and so long as one did not look out of the window at the dizzy rush of fields and trees going by, there was really no way of knowing that they were racing along at thirty miles an hour. It was also a comfort to reflect that there were no poor horses being ill-treated in the cause of this journey.

Hester had no fears. She sat quietly enjoying the novelty and excitement of the ride. The crude old horse-drawn wagon at Benbow Colliery had not prepared her for this smooth and luxurious form of traveling. It was so fast and so infinitely superior to any other way. She gazed out of the window and wished that her father had lived long enough to see the railways he had always believed in progress so far.

It seemed that the journey was over almost as soon as it had begun. The train slowed down and drew to a gentle halt.

They descended onto the platform at Dewsborough and Hester looked about her. Kirby England's private station was small but exceedingly well kept. The red brick station house, with its three curious chimneys shaped like railway arches, was immaculate. The picket fencing was freshly painted white, the platform carefully swept, and a neat line of marigolds, antirrhinums and hollyhocks stirred in the wind. All around lay flat, open fields where black and white bullocks grazed peacefully in the sunlight.

The guard's whistle blew and the train drew away from them to continue its journey to Market Weighton; steam engine and carriages rattled noisily away into the distance. The silence that had been disturbed returned again to the station.

An open carriage and coachman waited for them beyond the white gate. It carried them up a wide avenue of elm trees that began just beyond the station and continued, straight as a die, for more than a mile. As they neared its end they saw Dewsborough Castle lying before them. Hester held her breath. She had not expected anything quite so magnificent.

The castle was spectacularly beautiful. The immense E-shaped building of honey-colored stone shone like a jewel in its emerald-green setting. Row upon row of windows glittered like diamonds set in gold, and a huge and graceful dome rose like an imperial crown above the long central block. Swans sailed majestically on a nearby lake and fallow deer stood in the shade of ancient oaks. It had a fairy-tale quality, but this was no Prince Charming's palace, Hester reminded herself. This was the Railway King's

Castle—the property of a ruthless schemer who aspired to greatness.

Aunt Kitty had been rendered almost speechless, and did not really recover her tongue until they had left the carriage and mounted the long flight of steps to the front doors. They entered a great hall, a sumptuous chamber of marble, whose black and white floor stretched away in the distance towards a grand staircase which rose to divide itself into two flights that curved away into the shadows of the upper stories. Richly carved pillars lined the walls, rising seventy feet high to meet the dome's curved ceiling, where painted horses of the Sun plunged and cavorted among golden chariots, winged angels, cherubs and all kinds of mythological creatures. The four elements—earth, air, fire and water—were all represented, as well as Apollo and the nine Muses, the Continents, the Rivers and the twelve signs of the Zodiac.

They craned their necks painfully, and Adelaide told them that it was the work of a Venetian painter, while the house had been designed by Sir John Vanbrugh.

"*Most* impressive, my dear," Aunt Kitty said in a whisper to Hester that echoed clearly round the marble hall. "But I don't think I should care to *live* here one bit. It must be very cold in winter."

Refreshments of cordials and ratafia biscuits were served to them in a large and airy room overlooking a terrace at the back of the castle. From the windows they admired a vista of close-cut lawns, clipped yew hedges, circular flower beds, fountains playing and, in the distance, a small temple built of the same pale golden stone as the house.

Hester could detect none of Martha England's influence in the restrained furnishing of the room. It was decorated in the classical style, with pale blue silk curtains and exquisitely beautiful furniture. The overpowering splendor of the great hall was missing. She asked Adelaide who had been responsible for the furnishing and was told that the castle had been bought with all its contents complete, excepting some family portraits, which the duke had taken with him. This struck Hester as a strange and unsatisfactory way of acquiring a home—if "home" was a word that could ever apply to such a place.

After they had rested a little, Adelaide took them on a grand tour of the castle. They began in the hall, where, apart from the painted domed ceiling, there were a number of fine Greek and Roman statues to be seen. Aunt Kitty averted her eyes from such an abundant display of nudity and expressed her disapproval.

"But they are all works of art and extremely old," Hester pointed out.

"If they were twice as old I should still be of the same opinion, my dear. Whoever was responsible for them in the first place should have seen to it that they were decently clothed!"

The remainder of the castle, however, met with her unqualified approval. Its rich, unashamed magnificence was after her own heart and every room impressed, from the saloon with its enormous glass chandelier, ormolu mirrors and William and Mary gilt chairs, to the Music Room with its Broadwood pianoforte, Meissen china, Adam inlaid satinwood and hardwood tables and Dutch marquetry, and to the Tapestry Room with walls hung with woven pictures of the Four Seasons. They walked on down the Long Gallery to the chapel, which seemed shockingly overdecorated to Aunt Kitty and Hester, accustomed to the stark simplicity of the Meeting House.

Adelaide led them up the grand staircase, Aunt Kitty puffing and panting a little by this time and supporting herself on Hester's arm. They passed blank spaces left by the removal of the duke's family portraits. As they reached the top, however, one large painting confronted them—a portrait of the present owner of Dewsborough Castle, who stared down at them. The artist had caught his subject well and the picture was plain and without embellishment, which suited the sitter perfectly. The direct gaze and the blunt features were unmistakable, as well as remarkable. The portrait could not be passed by without comment. This came, naturally enough, from Aunt Kitty, who adjusted her spectacles to inspect it more closely.

"What a handsome likeness of thy brother, Adelaide," she said admiringly. "I have always considered him such a fine-looking man, haven't I, Hester? No wonder they call him the Railway

King. He quite puts me in mind of that William Cowper verse, *I am monarch of all I survey, my right there is none to dispute.*"

"Unfortunately, that is not true; there are some who do dispute it," Adelaide said, looking up at the portrait. "Henry says there are many who would like to topple Kirby from his throne."

"I doubt if they would succeed. Don't worry, my dear, all successful men have their enemies. There are always those who like nothing better than to see the mighty fall. But thy brother is a strong and clever man. I should have no fears on his behalf."

They had reached a wide landing which led into a further gallery, a narrow room with high windows overlooking the deer park and full of sunlight. After that they followed Adelaide through an astonishing number of bedrooms while Aunt Kitty rhapsodized over the bed hangings, the delightful little items of furniture, the ornaments, the chairs, the yellow silk Chinese wall covering, the *verre églomisé* looking glass . . .

"The sheer *quality* of everything takes my breath away," she said, stroking a walnut *secrétaire* with appreciative fingers. "How I should love to own any one of these fine pieces!"

They returned to the top of the grand staircase and began to descend slowly to the hall below, talking amongst themselves. It was not until they came to the half-landing, where the two upper flights converged into one, that Hester, lifting her head, noticed the man standing in the hall below them. Her shock at recognizing it to be Kirby England was so great that she missed a step and had to grab quickly at the handrail to save herself from falling. The awkwardness of his finding her poking and prying round his property in his absence seemed so acute that she felt herself blush to the brim of her gray bonnet.

Kirby England, for his part, had been almost unable to believe his eyes. To watch her coming down the staircase towards him was to see a dream become reality. Many times he had imagined her here at Dewsborough . . . as she might have been had she become his wife. He had seen the start she had given at the sight of him with a grim satisfaction. At least she was not indifferent to him, whatever else she felt towards him. His own feelings were unchanged. He was as much in love with her as ever. He loved this little Quakeress with her gray eyes, her gray dress and bonnet . . . but she was not, and never could be, his. He had got everything else he had ever wanted—except her. The three women had reached the bottom of the staircase, and Kirby stepped forward to greet them without any outward sign of his inward thoughts.

Adelaide spoke first. "Kirby! I thought you were in London—"

"Aye—so I was." He bent to kiss his sister's cheek. "But I came back sooner than apparently expected. I arrived a few minutes ago."

Aunt Kitty, all pink confusion, hurried forward. "I do hope that thou dost not mind us visiting Dewsborough in thy absence like this. We were so interested to see the castle and Adelaide was quite sure thou wouldst not object."

He bowed to her with gentle courtesy. "Dear madam, far from it. It gives me great pleasure to see you. I only wish that I had been here earlier to show you round myself."

He moved to Hester, who had remained at the foot of the staircase. He took her hand in his.

"Mrs. Gurney . . . it's a surprise to find you here. I would not have expected *you* to be interested in any property of mine."

She had recovered some, if not all, of her composure and said frankly: "Dewsborough could not fail to interest anyone. It's beautiful."

He smiled down at her. "Aye . . . It is that. Are you impressed?"

"How could I not be?"

"Easily—knowing you. I'm glad you're here."

He thought she was looking too thin, and there were dark shadows beneath her eyes. *She* saw how time had taken its toll of him; he looked very tired, and his face bore lines that had not been there when they last met.

He let go of her hand abruptly and turned to his sister. "Did you include the gardens in your tour, Adelaide? They shouldn't be missed."

Aunt Kitty said that much as she *longed* to see the gardens she was too exhausted to walk another step. The train journey had been more tiring than she had realized, and she thought they must have walked several miles round the castle. Kirby immediately suggested that she rest for a while and insisted that they stay for luncheon—two proposals which were promptly and gratefully accepted by Aunt Kitty.

Adelaide took Aunt Kitty's arm and Kirby turned back to Hester.

"Since your aunt is too tired, can I show you the gardens? I promise you they are worth the effort."

She hesitated. The glimpses she had caught of them from the windows had been tantalizing and the sun was still shining brightly, but she was nervous of his company and uneasy with the situation. Aunt Kitty decided the matter in the end by calling over her shoulder as she departed with Adelaide:

"Oh, do go on, my dear! Then thou canst tell me all about them. If I were younger and stronger *I* should not miss the chance."

To refuse seemed ungracious and ill mannered and to add to the mistake she had made in coming here at all in the first place. Kirby led the way out of a side door onto the terrace. They walked along its length and she thought how beautifully the castle was situated. The green of the Yorkshire countryside extended as far as they could see; there was nothing to mar the view, nothing to spoil the perfection of the setting.

A wide flight of stone steps led down from the terrace to a parterre of lawns, hedges and flower beds, all set out in faultless symmetry. In the middle lay a large circular pool, and a fountain in its center spouted jets of clear water high into the air. Hester stopped to admire this, watching the way the sunlight made the falling drops glitter against the blue sky.

They went on.

"Well, are you still impressed?" he asked her after a while.

"Exceedingly. It's all very magnificent. But—"

"But? But what?"

"It must feel a little like living in a museum. It's too perfect to be a home."

He laughed. "A home! I don't know the meaning of that word. I don't have such a thing . . . just properties where I happen to stay."

"Why didst thou buy Dewsborough?"

"Several good reasons. As a good investment, to impress particular people like yourself . . . Oh, and to put a stop to any rival railway being built between York and Hull."

"How so?"

"I own Dewsborough village and a great deal of land besides what you see before you. Any rival railway would have to cross that land."

"Then thou art as obsessed by railways as ever."

"As ever," he agreed. "But you must admit that my obsession, as you call it, has borne plenty of fruit."

They strolled on towards the little domed temple that Hester had noticed earlier from the windows. As they drew nearer she saw that its columns were of white marble and that niches above the doors contained four small statues.

"The Temple of the Four Winds," her guide told her. "The statues are of Vespasian, Faustina, Trajan and Sabina. You see how hard I have tried to make up for my lack of schooling."

Inside it was cool and dark after the bright day. The floor of polished stone shone like glass. The walls were of black and gold marble and the ceiling of white and gold plaster.

"The marble is artificial—clever, don't you think? The temple was built by one of the duchesses who used to meet her lovers here in secret, about a hundred years ago."

His voice echoed round the walls. Hester touched the false marble curiously and examined a little stone figure of the god Pan in a niche. She turned to see Kirby lounging against the wall, arms folded, watching her.

"You've been ill, I heard."

"It was nothing."

"Is there owt I can do for you? You've only to ask."

She surprised him by nodding and saying immediately: "As a matter of fact, there is one thing."

"Tell me. If it's in my power, it'll be done."

"Very well. Wilt thou reopen the Garford branch line that thou closed soon after thy company leased the Leeds to Selby railway? Without the line both the colliery and local trade have suffered."

He stared at her. He had expected some trifling favor. He had

217

not bargained for this. "Nay, lass, I'm sorry, but that's impossible. You've asked me something I can't do. There was no choice but to close it down."

"Hast thou any idea of the consequences of thy action? Now that thy company controls the Leeds to Selby line there is no service other than a twice-weekly market train. Tradesmen in Garford can now only have their goods delivered as far as Micklefield station, and sometimes they are not notified of the goods' arrival for several days. As for our colliery, we can no longer compete with others for the York market since our coal has to be carried the long way round by *thy* railway and there is often two or more days' delay. Our agent in York has to send customers away with empty carts. And now the Great North of England Railway has reduced coal dues to allow the Durham pits to undercut us."

She did not add, as she might have done, that William's mismanagement had made matters infinitely worse than they need have been. He might forbid her to go to the colliery, but he could not keep the truth about it from her. His mishandling of the miners, as well as the estate tenants and workers, had caused discontent and near-rebellion. The new viewer he had appointed was a brutal man and hated by all. Conditions at the mine had deteriorated, risks were taken, safety precautions ignored. Output had fallen so seriously that the colliery was in danger of having to close down, and William was blaming it all on Kirby England's ruthless decision to shut the Garford branch line. It had certainly added to their problems, but she knew in her heart that it was by no means the whole cause of them.

Kirby England shook his head. "I'm sorry," he repeated. "I'd give a lot to be able to do as you ask, but I can't reopen that line. It was making the company less than two pounds a week. I've a responsibility to my shareholders, and they don't expect me to subsidize unprofitable branch lines with their money. They want profits and dividends—that's all they're concerned with!"

"And what of thy responsibility to ordinary people? I have heard thee speak of the great benefit the railways would bring to every man, woman and child in this country, or is the benefit only to disappear into the pockets of a few, after all?"

"You misjudge me, as always. Thousands have already profited by the railways I've built, and millions more will do so before I've finished. But there's no room for sentiment in railway business—or in any other business, come to that. Would *you* keep open a coal mine just for charity's sake? Could *you* afford to do that? I couldn't."

"Thou hast well earned thy reputation for ruthlessness."

"I daresay. But I've also earned my shareholders' confidence."

She turned from him towards the door, but he called after her.

"Just a minute! I haven't finished. There's two things I *can* do to help. First, I'll see that there are no more delays in your coal reaching York by way of the York and North Midland Railway. Second, if the Great North of England has lowered its coal dues, then we can do the same and Benbow will be able to compete fairly with the Durham pits."

She turned back slowly. "Thou wouldst do that?"

"Wouldst and couldst," he mocked her. "There'll be no objection to lowering dues if it'll encourage and increase the volume of goods carried by the company. I never do owt for nowt. We'll be helping each other."

She began to thank him but he stopped her.

"Enough said—it's only good business. I'd do much more for your good opinion of me, but I've told you before—I don't want your polite gratitude. I'd sooner you didn't pretend with me."

They left the temple and began to walk back through the gardens towards the castle. She was silent, thinking of what he had just said and wondering how much she had misjudged him. Presently he asked her how she had found the railway journey to Dewsborough.

"We enjoyed it very much. It was the most comfortable journey I have ever made, and Aunt Kitty thought so too. But then I can only compare it with the colliery wagon."

He grinned. "Then you must have found *our* railway carriages something of an improvement in the way of comfort."

"The first-class ones—yes. I thought them very fine. But as for the second- and third-class, I was thankful we were not traveling in *those*. Is it right that the poor should have to journey in such dreadful discomfort? In the open third-class wagons the passengers must be choked by all the steam and smoke, as well as blistered by sparks. And in winter they must freeze in the wind."

"You bring me severely to task, as usual," he said with equanimity. "And you're right to do so. The second- and third-class conditions *are* bad—there's no denying it. But I'm proposing to improve matters considerably, to provide roofing for the third class and seats for the passengers, and to make the second class generally better. But it'll all take time. And don't forget that first-class passengers don't pay extra brass to see others with cheaper tickets enjoying the same standard of comfort as themselves."

"Thou art a hard man."

"A practical man," he corrected her. He glanced at her sideways and saw that she was half smiling. "You're looking better already. Happen the air of Dewsborough suits you."

They reached the terrace and went indoors to rejoin Aunt Kitty and Adelaide. Aunt Kitty was already much revived and was anticipating luncheon with high expectations. She was not disappointed. The dining room itself was enormous and the table a long stretch of richly polished mahogany. The silver and napery were of the very best and the china service exquisitely patterned in green and gold, while the servants who waited on them moved about with the soft-footed, unobtrusive skill of the highly trained. As for the menu—the broth, fish, saddle of mutton and apple pie were all superb English fare and could only have been cooked by a master chef.

Their host, at the end of the table, seemed perfectly at home and looked as though he had spent all his life in such surroundings of wealth and splendor. Aunt Kitty, seated at his right hand, lost no time in seeking his advice as to her railway investments.

"Some shares I bought recently have dropped alarmingly," she told him, mentioning a recent new railway venture that was not one of Kirby England's.

"I know of it. Don't worry. I'll buy a few shares in it myself. When news gets about that I've shown some interest the shares'll rise. As soon as they do, sell yours at once—they're bound to fall again."

Aunt Kitty was both pleased and grateful, but her niece took a different view and said so.

"Is it right to make use of people's trust in thee in such a way?"

He looked across at Hester. "If people choose to be greedy fools of their own free will it's not my fault, Mrs. Gurney."

"And how is Mrs. England?" Aunt Kitty inquired quickly, seeing Hester's mouth open again.

"Well enough, thank you. She's at the house in Monkgate at the moment. It suits her better than Dewsborough; she doesn't care for this place much."

"What a pity. Does she prefer thy London home, perhaps?"

"Aye. She likes everything about London. At first she hated the place—you know how society folks can be. They made a good deal of fun of her. A great many jokes circulated at her expense."

"I'm sorry to hear that," Aunt Kitty said, her kind heart upset at the thought. She could imagine the sniggering and jibes that Martha England would have endured from smart London society.

"Oh, they don't do it anymore. Not now. Not since the Duke of Wellington called on her and came to dinner."

"The Duke of *Wellington!*"

"Aye. I did him a favor over some shares; he was good enough to return the compliment and do us a favor when he heard some of the stories. It was quite an entertainment to see them all change their tune. Society folk amuse me. They're like sheep and just as stupid."

Luncheon finished, they soon had to leave for the return journey to York. But before they did so, Kirby, cunningly addressing himself to Aunt Kitty, had invited them to attend a ball he was giving at Dewsborough the following week.

Hester said at once that she would be returning to Benbow before then, but Aunt Kitty drew her firmly aside.

"Thou art not to leave me so soon or I shall be most upset. And after thy host's kindness today we should not risk offending him by refusing this invitation. He might easily interpret it as a slight on our part."

"If William should learn of it—"

"Bother William! He is safely at Benbow anyway. I shan't tell him of it and nor wilt thou—or anyone else, I'm sure."

Hester gave in, seeing how much Aunt Kitty longed to accept.

They returned to York by an afternoon train and Kirby himself accompanied them to the private station. He handed them into the railway carriage and stood watching from the platform until the train was out of sight.

The Dewsborough ball had created a great stir in York. It was the first to be held there since Kirby England had acquired the property. Everyone of importance in the city had been invited and those without invitations pretended they could not attend.

Aunt Kitty had spent agonizing hours deciding between a brown silk and a black bombazine; in the end she elected to wear the black, thinking it more dignified and fitting to a grand occasion.

Hester had nothing suitable with her; she had brought only the plainest day dresses from Benbow. Aunt Kitty bore her off to her dressmaker.

"I really cannot allow thee to go to Dewsborough in gray calico. Let us by all means dress plainly, as we believe right, but I see no reason why thou shouldst not at least wear the best-quality silk."

She would listen to no argument, and within four days the dress was ready. Edith Frohawk, the vigilante of the York Meeting House, could not have quarreled with its simplicity, but she would certainly have sniffed loudly at the heaviness and lustre of the silk that was much more blue than gray. Still less would she have approved the way in which Aunt Kitty persuaded Hester to wear her hair instead of her plaited ear-coils.

With customary panache Kirby had arranged for a special train to take York guests to Dewsborough. This time there were no second- or third-class carriages to be seen. The passengers traveled in smut-free comfort, and Aunt Kitty, who had completely conquered her fears, took to railway travel as a duck to water. She announced (unblushingly) to their fellow passengers that she had always considered it the *only* way to travel nowadays.

The evening was warm and still as they drove in carriages from the station up the wide avenue. Dewsborough Castle was lit by the last rays of a dying summer sun. Hester thought it one of the most beautiful places she had ever seen. The somberness of Benbow had not been apparent to her until she had seen Dewsborough. Despite its enormous size, the castle was full of a lightness and grace that Benbow lacked.

The great hall was full of guests who had already arrived from all over the county. Nearly a thousand notables had converged on the castle to form one of the most glittering assemblies in living memory. Nothing to equal it had been seen at the Mansion House in York, even in Kirby's reign as Lord Mayor.

It was impossible in the crush to speak to their host. He was constantly surrounded by a dense ring of courtiers, all eager to talk with him.

"He might be royalty," Aunt Kitty said, fascinated. "Our dear Queen herself could not attract more attention. Now I see why they call him the Railway King!"

A large orchestra began to play in the saloon and music filled the air.

"No expense spared of any kind," Aunt Kitty said delightedly, counting the musicians. Nothing had escaped her all-seeing eye. She had noted everyone and everything, and Hester knew that she would be able to describe it all in the fullest detail months, or even years, later. She wondered what William would have said if he could have seen such extravagance. The ball must be costing Kirby England thousands of pounds. She remembered something he had once said to her and wondered also if this evening's guest list had been compiled of people "useful" to him. Did he have true friends amongst these predatory-looking people of consequence? Would any of them lift a finger to help him if he were in need? He had once told her they would not, and watching the hard, arrogant faces, and listening to the barbed conversations and braying laughter, Hester believed him.

It was much later that Kirby England found them sitting in a corner of the saloon.

"I have been looking everywhere for two ladies in gray," he told them. "You have both misled me this evening."

"We are in finer feathers than usual—in thy honor," Aunt Kitty said, pleased by his obvious approval and by the way he kept staring at Hester.

"Last time you berated me for waltzing with your niece. Will it upset you if I ask her to dance again?"

"I have come to think of dancing as a lesser evil than I imagined," Aunt Kitty conceded, putting Edith Frohawk firmly from her mind. "I'm sure it would do no harm. But Hester must answer for herself."

"Can you remember how to waltz?" he asked Hester.

"How could I forget anything *thou* taught me?" she replied with exaggerated awe. "Thy steam majesty does me great honor. I'm sure I should curtsy first."

He smiled at her, amused by her teasing. "No need for that; I'm a very benevolent monarch. But mind you, don't tread on my foot—as once you did."

It was her turn to be teased and she reddened, reminded of the first time they had met. Aunt Kitty watched as he led her away and gave a deep, sad sigh.

Hester found that she had not forgotten the steps. The mirrors on the saloon walls reflected innumerable images of the big, burly black-haired man as he waltzed with the small, dark-haired girl in her silk gown that was more blue than gray. Heads turned, mouths moved behind hands, necks craned. Who was she? They saw how his eyes never left her face, how he talked and laughed with her as they danced, and with what seeming reluctance he let her go as the music came to an end. Then they dismissed her as of no possible significance, after all. She was neither beautiful nor aristocratic and, despite the expensive gown and prettily dressed hair, she had none of the glittering style that he was known to demand in women.

Hester returned to Benbow two weeks later. For the first time in her life she dreaded the homecoming. The parkland looked bleaker and the house darker than she could ever remember.

William was away overnight on business in Leeds and for that she was thankful. In the morning she went to the schoolhouse at Garford to see how Miss Fowler and Miss Whittaker had been faring in her absence. She was anxious to resume her work there, and the children she had grown to love had never been far from her thoughts.

Morning school should have been in progress, but she found the small building deserted except for Miss Fowler, who was in the process of clearing out a cupboard. The elderly spinster had dust on her hands and cobwebs in her hair, and when she saw Hester at the door her mouth opened in surprise.

"Mrs. Gurney—I didn't expect to see you again here."

"Whyever not, Miss Fowler? Where's Miss Whittaker? And where are the children?"

Miss Fowler stared at her. "But I thought you knew . . . We—Miss Whittaker and I—understood that you had decided not to go on with the school."

Hester felt as though she must be dreaming. "How couldst thou imagine such a thing? I told thee that I would continue teaching the moment I returned from York. What has happened? Why aren't the children in class?"

Miss Fowler brushed the dust from her hands. She said slowly: "Those that were left were sent home. Mr. Gurney told us that your health was too poor to allow you to come anymore. He said it had been decided to close the school down. I should have known it could never have been of your choosing."

Hester sat down on one of the benches; a deep anger was beginning to grow within her.

"Tell me again, Miss Fowler. My husband told thee that this school was to be closed?"

"That is so."

"Because of my ill health?"

"In part."

"Thou spoke of 'those that were left being sent home.' Why did the others leave?"

Tears were filling Miss Fowler's eyes; she fumbled in her pocket for a handkerchief and dabbed at her cheeks. "It's too terrible to speak of, Mrs. Gurney. The poor children, the poor, poor children. I could do nothing to stop it. One day they were all here and the next only a few of the girls came to class."

225

"But why? What reason could there be? They were all doing so well and learning so much."

"They have gone to work at the colliery."

"*Down the mine!* Canst thou mean that?"

Miss Fowler nodded and wiped her cheeks again.

Hester said in disbelief: "It's not possible. Children have never worked at Benbow before. My father never allowed it."

Miss Fowler said nothing. She looked away and fiddled with her handkerchief.

"I see," Hester said at last. "My husband is responsible for this. I shall stop it at once. No child will be forced to work there."

The spinster put a gentle hand on her arm. "My dear, you may find it difficult to stop it. Incentives were offered to the miners if their children went down, and there were threats of dismissal if they did not."

Hester stood up. She walked down the classroom between the lines of empty desks. She touched Tom Bartlett's desk as she passed. Where was he now? Was he sitting in darkness four hundred feet underground—frightened and alone, with hopeless terror in his eyes instead of eager willingness? And what of her brightest pupil—the boy that reminded her of Kirby England? A tall, strong lad like him would have been set to a tough task—hurrying heavy corves of coal through the long black tunnels, slaving and sweating until his youthful brightness and energy had been exhausted and, finally, destroyed. And what of Daisy Kelly and Janet White? Were they amongst the little girls now condemned to endure long, sunless days?

She turned round to Miss Fowler. "The school will reopen, I promise. Leave everything just as it is. The children will come back."

When William returned to Benbow later that day, he found Hester sitting in the library. He was pleased to see that she looked improved in health after her visit to York; there was color in her cheeks and a new strength in her bearing. He bent and kissed her face.

"I am glad to have thee home again, my dear."

"Art thou, William? I am glad too that I did not stay away any longer. I have discovered how busy thou hast been in my absence."

"As always, my dear. Thou knowest how much there is to be done."

"I went to my school today."

"The school? Ah yes—that reminds me. So many of thy pupils left that it seemed hardly worth it being continued. I told that teacher so. It would seem, my dear, that for all thy worthy efforts, the miners' children are more interested in working for their living than in book learning. And who can blame them? Money in the pocket is bread in the mouth."

"Thou coerced them down the mine! It was *not* of their own free will! Thou threatened their fathers with dismissal if they refused!"

"I do not like thy tone, Hester. And little purpose will be served by abusing me for something that was necessary for the welfare of all. Thou hast always prided thyself on thy concern for the miners, hast thou not?"

"I care very much about them."

"Then thou canst not fail to appreciate the sense in employing their children. Production has been so low over past months that I have had half a mind to close down the colliery completely. However, the cheap labor these children can provide may enable us to keep it going for the time being. Wouldst thou perhaps prefer the men out of work and for them and their children to starve? They have made their own choice. It is not for thee to interfere."

"I shall reopen the school. Thou canst not stop me."

"Reopen it by all means, my dear, but thou wilt find thou hast no pupils. And there is nothing thou canst do to bring them back now."

She looked at him with loathing. "One day they will come back—despite thee. I swear it. But I shall never forget or forgive what thou hast done."

CHAPTER XI

O'er iron roads (o'er levell'd hills conveyed,
Through blasted rocks, or tunnell'd mountains made)
By Steam propelled, pursues his rapid way
And ends ere noon, what erst employ'd the day.

Railway verse

London in winter was a forbidding place in the eighteen-forties. It was a city of wet and slimy pavements, of dirty streets, dark and sinister alleys and cobbled courtyards where yellow gaslight burned feebly through wet fog. Down beside the river the mud lay deep and stinking, and ragged mudlarks scavenged the banks, squelching through rotting refuse and ordure to gather what the tide had brought—bits of coal, metal, bones, rags, wood —anything that might be sold for a few pence.

Kirby England stopped to watch the urchins for a while as he walked along the embankment on his way to Westminster. He leaned his arms on the wall and, looking across the gray river, reflected on the irony that here before him was the wealthiest city in the world and yet, here too, he had seen more dreadful poverty and misery than anywhere else. The city had two faces. On the one hand were the well-built houses of the rich, the fashionable squares and crescents, the smart shopping streets—the Strand, Piccadilly, Regent Street—the coffee shops, the cigar divans, the chop houses and the busy traffic of drays, carts, bright-lettered omnibuses, four-wheel and hansom cabs, saddle horses, broughams, chaises . . . And cheek by jowl with all this thriving prosperity lived destitution and despair. In those same smart streets he had watched small boys darting in among the fast-moving vehicles to turn cartwheels almost beneath the horses' hooves to earn a few coppers, and he had seen a pathetic variety of crossing-sweepers—scrawny, pale-faced children, sick old men, stick-legged Indians—who cleared the road of dung for the swells and their elegant ladies to pass by.

Kirby had witnessed plenty of poverty in the North, but not on such a huge scale as this. He had walked the streets of London and passed a hundred beggars—blind or crippled, and sometimes both. He had seen scrofulous, narrow-chested children working as bootblacks and sellers of lucifer matches, slum whores lurking in alleys, thieves and pickpockets, men and women reeling from the gin palaces, where they had sought a few hours of oblivion from a life that was unbearable . . . He had seen the hideous rat-ridden tenements where these people lived, dark and damp with sewage and overrun with a hopeless humanity so degraded that decaying, uncoffined bodies were left to lie for days among the living, and disease, depravity and crime flourished like vile, rank weeds alongside the smugly ordered gardens of the well-to-do.

Among the close-packed houses of the city he had come across an underground slaughterhouse where the noise and stench were unimaginable, its walls and floor thick with putrefying blood and fat and into which sheep were hurled so that they broke their legs before being knifed and flayed by the men working in foul and grisly conditions below. Nearby there were fat-boilers, glue-renderers, fell-mongers, tripe-scrapers, dog-skinners and the like, all exuding a terrible charnel stench.

Even less fortunate than the inhabitants of the verminous warrens were those with no home at all—of which there were many—who lived and slept where they could, in doorways, in alleys, in barges on the river and, now, beneath the new railway arches. . . .

That morning Kirby had been early to Camden Goods station to watch the arrival of the trains bearing goods for the London markets. He had stood in the gray dawn mist observing the night trains disgorge their loads of fish, meat and all kinds of produce —Aylesbury butter, dairy-fed pork, apples, cabbages, cucumbers, watercress . . . all for the daily consumption of the big metropolis. And no sooner did these trains depart than others arrived with Manchester packs and bales, Liverpool cotton, American provisions, Worcester gloves, Kidderminster carpets, Birmingham and Staffordshire hardware, crates of pottery from North Staffordshire and cloth from Huddersfield, Leeds, Bradford and other Yorkshire towns, all to be delivered in the City before the hour for the commencement of the day's business. Later there had been other trains arriving with the heaviest goods—stones, bricks, iron girders, iron pipes, ale (in great quantities from Allsopps' and Burton breweries), coal, hay, straw, flour, grain and salt. He had watched it all brought by railway into the capital city with a deep pride and satisfaction in the thought that much of it was due to *his* railways. And there was further relish in considering how, in the end, the locomotive steam engine had triumphed over all its detractors and enemies.

Kirby walked on along the embankment towards the Houses of Parliament, where he had arranged to meet Henry Latham. It was the latest in a great number of meetings they had had to discuss railway matters. On this occasion the subject was the proposal by a rival company for a London and York Railway to run directly south from York to Doncaster and thence to Lincoln, Peterborough, and so to London—some thirty miles shorter than the York and North Midland's circuitous route between London and York via Rugby, Derby and Normanton.

"Subscriptions for a capital of four and a half million pounds are already secured, I hear," Henry told Kirby. "And most of it is in London. The scheme is already before the Board of Trade Railway Committee, before it comes to Parliament. The Provisional Committee, by the way, includes ten peers and thirty-two Members of Parliament—many of them Whigs and no friends of yours, Kirby. I feel bound to say that the Board are likely to report favorably and that the Bill, in my opinion, stands every chance of going through."

"Then we must find a way to stop it."

"If the Board gives approval, that may prove to be beyond even you."

"The Bill will still have to be examined and passed by the two committees in the House of Commons."

"True. But the Committee on Petitions will merely see whether it complies with standing orders; after that it will be referred to a Select Committee after the second reading."

"Well then. You know as well as I do, Henry, that these parliamentary committees are antiquated war-horses. They're open to all kinds of manipulation and intrigue, a veritable paradise for obstructionists, as well as a rich harvest ground for counsel, solicitors and witnesses. And I know of MPs—and so do you—who go from one railway office to another to hawk their support as a peddler would his wares."

"Still, it may not be easy," Henry insisted cautiously.

"It won't be that difficult either. The London and York project is no more than a bubble. Just like hundreds of other silly railway schemes that clutter up the Board of Trade. I happen to know that their capital is totally insufficient for the line. It's three hundred and twenty-eight miles long—or would be if they ever built it—the gradients are terrible and their approach to London lies through thickly populated districts where the price of land will be enormous. I'd have no hesitation in giving them a challenge. If I left London by *our* Birmingham route line with twenty carriages, I'd still beat them to York. What's more, on a foggy day when the rails are greasy I doubt they'd get there at all!"

"But you can't afford to ignore the possibility of their Bill being passed."

"Who said I would? I told you, lad, I'm going to *stop* them. Has it occurred to you that, apart from my other lines, I now control the whole of the Midlands area since the amalgamation of the North Midland, the Midland Counties and the Birmingham and Derby Junction railways? With that lot alone I've four and a quarter million pounds of capital. We can afford to fight hard. I'll employ as many counsel as need be and we'll find out every flaw in their case—and there'll be plenty, mark my words. We'll go through their subscription list for fictitious names and paupers—just for a start. London and York would never have raised the capital to take their line as far as

Grantham if they'd done it honestly. And while counsel are busy, I'll call a shareholders' meeting of my own Midland companies and ask them to approve making an application to Parliament for three new branches from their main line—from Swinton to Lincoln, from Syston to Peterborough and from Nottingham through Newark to Lincoln." Kirby drew an imaginary map on the wall behind them with his forefinger. "If there's a need *we'll* be the ones to provide for it. I've worked it out. I'll ask that the directors be given power to raise two and a half million pounds of new capital."

"Isn't that something of a gamble?"

"It's *all* a bloody gamble, lad! It's been so from the very start. But I'm no petty promoter. I want to see railways constructed and administered throughout the country on a proper, regular plan—not left to haphazard speculation, harebrained schemes like the London and York, or shortsighted local enterprise. Duplicate lines shouldn't be permitted, and no railway should be sanctioned which can only pay a dividend at the expense of other lines."

They discussed the affair further, and Henry promised his brother-in-law his support at Westminster. He had never denied it; he had not forgotten the help Kirby had given him in the past.

Kirby's London house was a magnificent mansion in Albert Gate, said to be the largest private house in London. Outside the entrance stood a large bronze statue of a stag, and a broad flight of stone steps led up to the front door. He had paid fifteen thousand pounds for it and spent another fourteen thousand pounds on its furnishing and decoration. In spite of that, he felt little affection for the place—it was a necessary acquisition, a possession marking the progress of his ambition. The only property he had come to care for was Dewsborough, which he looked on as the true capital of his kingdom. He had grown as fond of the castle as if his own family had lived there for generations past; there he could breathe clean northern air, not the stifling air of London.

In the evening he was to entertain a group of titled and influential people to dinner at Albert Gate and his mother was to act as hostess. Since the Duke of Wellington had effectively abated much of the ridicule she had endured when first coming to the city, Mrs. England had begun to enjoy the role of grand hostess. Her unfortunate taste in dress and her attempts to copy the fashion for all things French, larding her conversation with inaccurate French words and phrases, still provoked a good deal of amusement—but it was concealed rather than openly contemptuous, as before.

That evening, Mrs. England followed her usual custom of telling her maid to dress her according to the number of guests invited: the more present, the more elaborate her tenue. "Dress me for twenty," she instructed on this occasion, which implied a moderate display of wealth. To see Mrs. England dressed for anything above fifty was an amazing sight.

Among the guests were Rosa and her husband. Rosa, as Kirby had predicted, made an exquisite marchioness. Her gown of blue watered taffeta matched her eyes and diamonds glittered round her throat and on her ears, wrists and fingers. Kirby watched her across the table, and it amused him to think that both of them had dragged themselves up from nothing to be able to sit in company with the smartest people in the land. It also pleased him to watch Rosa and think of their recent secret meetings at a high-class milliners in Bond Street, where a discreet proprietor had shown them to an upstairs room. . . . He turned his gaze from her and thought instead of Hester Gurney, far away in Yorkshire and miles from this scene of overdressed and overblown society. The viscountess on his left repeated her question for the third time, startled by his grim expression and wondering if her host were ill. With an apology, Kirby brought himself back to reality and answered the trivial query with as much patience as he could muster.

After dinner, when the gentlemen had rejoined the ladies, Rosa sang for them. She stood gracefully beside the pianoforte, her golden hair gleaming in the light from a candelabrum, and when she began to sing her voice was as pure and lovely as ever.

> "Drink to me only with thine eyes
> And I will pledge with mine.
> Or leave a kiss but in the cup
> And I'll not look for wine."

Across the room, her eyes met Kirby's as he stood listening behind the others.

> *"The thirst that from the soul doth rise*
> *Doth ask a drink divine.*
> *But might I of Jove's nectar sup,*
> *I would not change for thine."*

She sang on to a hushed and enchanted audience, and when she had finished, declined to go on despite their pleadings. A stout woman in bright pink satin volunteered to take her place, and after a few moments, Kirby and Rosa were able to slip quietly and unnoticed into the adjoining conservatory. They walked among the banks of luxuriant and exotic green plants, palms and trailing foliage. It was cool and dim and smelled of sweet-scented flowers and damp earth. An off-key rendition of "Where E'er You Walk" reached them from the drawing room. Rosa seated herself on a white iron bench while Kirby leaned against a post and folded his arms.

She looked up at him. "Shouldn't you be with your guests?"

He grimaced and cocked his head in the direction of the singing, wincing at a missed high note. "To listen to *that* . . . after you! Nay, that's above the call of duty!"

She laughed. "You still like my singing?"

"I still like *everything* about you, lass. You know that."

"Do you?" She looked down at her hands; a large diamond cluster ring shone on her finger, and she twisted it round and round.

Kirby watched her. "What's the matter, Rosa? Aren't you pleased with life? You should be."

"I know."

"I gave you good advice when I told you to marry your marquis. Look at you now compared with the obscure little actress you were when we met. You're famous in your own right and, on top of that, you're married to one of the richest peers in the country. Of course you should be pleased with life . . . Any woman would envy you. Look at those diamonds you're wearing. They must be worth a king's ransom."

"They are." She smiled and held up her hand so that the ring caught the shaft of light from the drawing room. "But I'm beginning to learn that jewels aren't much comfort when your husband is old and boring. In fact, life has become rather tedious—except when I see you. I miss the theatre, Kirby. I loved it, you know."

"Be honest with yourself, Rosa. You're looking back with rose-colored spectacles. You've already forgotten what a hard life it was. When I first met you, you'd have done anything for security—not to have to worry about the next meal. You'll never have to again now."

"I know. That's partly the trouble. I'm bored because everything is so easy. There's nothing to fight for, nothing left to achieve. You should understand that, Kirby."

"I do. And I understand also that failure can easily follow success. *He that climbs the highest has the greatest fall.* Don't forget that. You left the stage at the top of your career; you'll never have to fall."

"What about you, Kirby? I've met many people in London who talk as though they'd be glad if *you* fell. Be careful."

"Don't worry about me. I can look after myself. Just remember one thing, Rosa. If ever I should fall don't you be foolish enough to try and help me. It would do you no good."

"After everything you've done for me? If you ever needed help of course I'd give it—if I could."

He shook his head. "I'd never let you. I'm a proud man—remember. I fight my own battles. Always have and always will."

"Are you happy, Kirby?"

"Happy? What a question! I don't think about it. Does it matter?"

"It does to me. I don't think either of us is happy. Ironical, isn't it? For all our wealth and success, we've never found the happiness that the poorest people can enjoy."

The song had finally come to an end and a thin trickle of polite applause could be heard coming from the drawing room. Kirby pulled Rosa quickly to her feet.

"Stop talking nonsense. We're wasting time."

He began to kiss her and, as always, she responded willingly. The stout woman in bright pink satin, encouraged by the ap-

236

plause, began to sing "Cherry Ripe" before anyone moved quickly enough to stop her.

"You didn't tell me you'd met Prince Albert!"

Mrs. England held the morning newspaper in her hand and gaped at a cartoon on the front page, depicting her son and the prince shaking hands and captioned, "The meeting of two crowned heads."

"Didn't I? I must've forgotten."

"How could you forget meeting Prince Albert himself!"

"There's little to tell you, Mother," Kirby said. "I was invited to a reception given by the President of the Royal Society a few days ago; Prince Albert was there and I was introduced to him."

"What was he like? How did he look?" she asked, avid for details.

"Much as you'd imagine. He looks highbred and intellectual and speaks with a strong German accent."

"What did you talk about? What did he say to you?"

"He asked my opinion on the future of atmospheric railways."

"On *what?*"

"The atmospheric system of locomotion," Kirby explained. "It's a method of propelling trains along by air pressure through a pipe laid between the rails, using stationary steam engines."

Mrs. England did not understand a word, but did not let it detract her. "And what did you say to him?"

"I told him the idea was humbug."

"You said that to the prince!"

"Aye. Why should he object to an honest answer? He was rather amused by what I thought, as a matter of fact. He laughed when we were talking. I gather that's a rare event."

His mother was silent for a moment, digesting this. Then she said: "You may be invited to meet the Queen herself one day."

"More than likely," he agreed matter-of-factly. "The prince told me she's looking forward to making a journey on one of my railways—probably when she visits Cambridge soon."

Mrs. England's imagination ran riot: she saw herself curtsying to the Queen, being invited to Buckingham Palace, staying at Windsor Castle, dancing with Prince Albert . . . and she saw envious and respectful faces about her. Oh yes, she would have the last laugh on those who had laughed so much at her in the past!

Her son had no such visions. He was perfectly conscious of the privilege of associating with royalty, but he was not a man to be overawed by it.

News of Kirby England's triumphs in London had spread to York, together with numerous tales of the railway lines he was projecting and of companies he had bought—among these the Great North of England Railway. Rumors that he was thinking of buying this company had been circulating for some time, and Kirby made a sudden, dramatic move, very much in his style. He offered Great North of England shareholders terms which their chairman was forced to advise would be madness to resist. They were invited to lease their line to his group of companies for five years at a guaranteed ten-percent interest on all classes of their shares, and thereafter the Newcastle and Darlington Junction Company, controlled by Kirby, was to buy the whole line outright at the rate of two hundred and fifty pounds for every one-hundred-pound share.

Kirby plunged from one gamble to another. Investors had at first fought shy of a line he proposed building between Leeds and Bradford, but when it became known that the Railway King himself had put his name down for six hundred of the fifty-pound shares then there was a rush to follow suit. The new shares rose to a large premium immediately after issue, so that in a few weeks the premium alone on Kirby's own shares amounted to six thousand pounds.

The spate of critical letters and articles that had been appearing in Yorkshire and national newspapers began to increase. The *Railway Times* waxed sarcastic: *Mr. Kirby England, it is very evident, is not a Railway Reformer for nought. He does not make and unmake Boards of Directors for the mere excitement of the sport. Oh no! He is much too far north for that. He has the more sensible object in view of putting money into his purse. Who, after this, will venture to assert that railway tinkering is not a good trade—better, far, than toiling behind a counter, or sweating for the lieges beneath the capacious folds of an alder-manic gown?*

Elias Snell, reading this in York, was maliciously gratified. Kirby, seeing it himself, was merely amused. He was too occupied in floating another new company, the Newcastle and Berwick Railway, to be concerned with such things. And the shareholders of the York and North Midland had just agreed that the company should invest fifty thousand pounds in the North British Railway. Not only did Kirby now control the Midland railways, but he was also building up a second great system out of the railways north of York—conjuring into existence new companies to build fresh sections of the east coast route to Scotland.

Furthermore, he had just accepted chairmanship of the Eastern Counties Railway—a long, straggly line of one hundred and fifty miles from London to Norwich. Although nearly three million pounds of capital had been spent on it, it had been badly run, with notorious delays on trains and inexcusable inconvenience to passengers, and the last half year's dividend had been no more than a paltry one percent. Kirby took the chair for the first time at a special meeting in Shoreditch, and on this occasion the *Railway Times* was more polite.

The honorable gentleman was received with a loud and long-continued burst of cheering from one of the most densely crowded meetings we have ever attended they wrote. *The large room at the top of the tavern shook with the violence of the applause with which the honorable chairman was greeted.*

The Eastern Counties Railway was the lame duck among Kirby's flock of railways, but there was nothing he liked better than a challenge—the chance to work the magic transformation from loss to profit which his shareholders had come to take for granted. He promised them that the Eastern Counties Railway bid fair to become a sound property and a safe and sure medium for investment. It carried more goods traffic in proportion to its passenger traffic than any other line with a London terminus. He proposed to make the railway the basis of a complete new trunk line to the North through towns not touched by the London to York railway—towns such as Cambridge, Lincoln and Doncaster. Capital was to be raised for this project by the issue of millions of pounds' worth of "Eastern Counties Extension Shares." The promoters of the former Cambridge and Lincoln line had promised to come in and exchange their scrip for one and a half million pounds in the new shares. The old Northern and Eastern Railway would be bought in for another one million pounds, and the York and North Midland would subscribe two hundred thousand. Somewhat over one million pounds would be put up by the holders of the existing Eastern Counties Consolidated Stock, and, finally, the rest of the shares—bringing the total value to four and a half million pounds of capital—were to be offered to the London and York shareholders, who were to be invited to merge their own undertakings in the new scheme and exchange their fifty-pound shares for twenty-pound shares in the "Eastern Counties York Extension Stock."

Kirby England now controlled more than a thousand miles of railway line, and everything he touched turned to gold. No one could have foreseen that he had just made what would one day prove to be the major blunder of his career.

Henry and Adelaide's house in Cheyne Walk was both elegant and comfortable, with a pleasant view across the river. When in London, Kirby occasionally dined alone with them, and one evening, over port, he and Henry discussed the extraordinary railway fever that had spread across the country with such speed and effect that men now talked commonly of *getting up steam* and of *railway speed*, and measured distances in hours and minutes. The number of railway journals had increased from three to twenty and journalists everywhere wrote in lyrical terms of the merits of steam—of the romance, beauty and poetry to be found in steam engines, railway stations, viaducts, cuttings and tunnels . . .

"It's nothing less than a mania. The whole country's become railway-mad," Henry said. "Projects for new lines appear week after week. I doubt if there is a practicable line between two considerable places, however remote, that hasn't been earmarked by a railway company, and sometimes two or three rival lines have been started simultaneously. Prospectuses pour forth from Moorgate Street and Gresham Street, and the darkest cupboard under the stairs there seems to contain a railway secretary or clerk. There is dishonest subscription signing, and signatures are bought at ten shillings a head. Every morning omnibuses from the suburbs disgorge an absolute horde of stock jobbers at the Royal Exchange, and a colony of solicitors, engineers and seedy accountants has settled like vultures around Threadneedle Street. I'm sure there's been nothing like it since the South Sea Bubble. *The Times* has been warning against overspeculation for months, saying it will bankrupt the country, but with money so easy to borrow and a bank rate of only two and a half percent it's too simple to take up scrip and pay a small deposit with borrowed cash. And everything must pay a huge dividend . . . everything is expected to yield a fat profit!"

"Why should you worry if greedy people allow themselves to be led by the nose like asses and lose their money on schemes a babe in arms could see are hopeless?" Kirby said, lighting a large cigar.

"Because the country's resources are being drained away into all these railways while other industries are starved of capital. Last year one hundred and thirty-two million pounds was invested in railways, and that's equal to the total value of our annual exports and greater than the whole public revenue! *That's* what alarms me. And huge sums are being squandered on innumerable, unnecessary lines which would be far better spent on education, public health, housing and all the social reforms that are desperately needed. Look around the poor districts of London alone and you'll see what I mean."

"I already have. And I agree with you—at least so far as unnecessary railway projects are concerned. I myself won't be connected with any proposed line which would depend for survival on what it can abstract from a neighboring existing line. A public necessity should be shown and local traffic be sure before any new line is started. A railway must be remunerative like any other business. The madness lies with those who disregard that simple rule."

"Unfortunately, it's enough for it to be even *rumored* that you are interested in some useless new line for the Stock Exchange to be in ferment and prices to rise like a rocket!"

Kirby shrugged and poured himself more port from the decanter Henry had slid across to him. "Stories of me being interested in such projects are put about deliberately by their promoters. I told you, Henry, *I* never concern myself with the building of any railway line unless there's a need for it. There's nowt I can do to stop hundreds of false rumors circulating about me, or to prevent genteel provincial ladies or gullible old clergymen signing bubble subscription lists and losing their life savings. Time and time again I've warned against duplicate lines that can never pay their way, but people don't listen. They think their fortunes will be made by *any* railway. If there's a mania, as you say, it's a mania like the air we breathe, and nothing and nobody can stop it."

"Until it explodes in our faces?"

"Aye—until then. I think myself that there will be a violent reaction in the course of the next two or three years, when speculators' expectations will be badly disappointed. Many of the railways will turn out totally unproductive and all this indiscriminate building of new lines will do nothing but harm to the existing ones. If any means can be devised to protect established lines in their traffic, it will be a blessing to railway property."

"What about the Government?"

"The Government! Are you proposing the Government take over? I've great respect for Mr. Gladstone and his Select Committee on Railway Speculation, but I fancy the public would rather be in the hands of the railway companies than the Government. What has the Government ever done for railways? They've not contributed a single shilling towards them, and the whole burden and risk has been carried by gamblers like myself. No, Henry. The only ultimate solution is for all small, unprofitable lines to be absorbed into a few great ones. That would prevent waste, reduce costs and give the public a much better service. I control four large railways systems myself—the York, Newcastle and Berwick, the York and Midland, the Midland and the Eastern Counties. I know what I'm talking about."

Henry smiled dryly: "A point of view somewhat in your own

interests, Kirby. If we are not careful I can see you becoming a positive Railway Napoleon!"

"Aye. But it so happens that my interests and those of the traveling public coincide."

"I still say that the only answer may prove to be state intervention," Henry said, sipping at his port. "The state will have to purchase railways and so cut the Gordian knot of competing and monopolistic interests."

"God help us all if that comes about! And how would the state assess a fair price on the railways? And if they bought them they'd have to buy out the canals too."

Henry said: "Nevertheless, I think it may come to it one day. I'm sure you're right that there will be a strong reaction from the public against this railway mania in a year or two. There's a good deal of grumbling and discontent already. A Colonel Snape stood up in the House the other day and said he thought *all* railways were public frauds and private robberies!"

Kirby puffed at his cigar. "I'm very familiar with the likes of him! If he had his way this country would stand still and we'd all be going about on bloody horseback forever! They make me sick, those sort of people, with their narrow minds and their vision that sees no further than the end of their well-bred noses. But I've got their measure now. The days are long gone when I used to lose my temper when some crusty old gentleman told me that to travel at more than twenty miles an hour smacks of revolution!"

Henry laughed and their conversation turned to other topics. Even so the subject stayed in the MP's mind and caused small prickings of unease from time to time. Until a little while ago he had believed that nothing but good could come from widespread railway building; now he was beginning to have doubts. These doubts were increased by several critical articles he had noticed in the press lately about his brother-in-law.

The opening of the thirty-nine miles of line which formed the Newcastle and Darlington Junction Railway took place on the anniversary of the Battle of Waterloo. Kirby traveled up from London for the occasion, and a grand opening train made its way to Gateshead during the afternoon, preceded by a special "Flying Train" which had come from London bringing copies of a daily paper printed only that same morning—a record achievement of three hundred and three miles covered in little over nine hours, including stops.

At Gateshead a magnificent reception awaited Kirby and Mr. George Stephenson, who accompanied him. Every place that commanded a view of the line was crowded as they arrived. The spectators waved and cheered, ladies waved handkerchiefs, the Tyne shipping was decked in bright colors, and the rapid firing of a cannon, the loud pealing of church bells and the music from a brass band in front of the station all competed with each other.

A banquet followed the opening ceremony. Kirby, rising to speak to the assembled guests, outlined Mr. Stephenson's scheme for a great bridge to run at high level across the river from Gateshead into Newcastle—to be built, he informed them, by a company specially formed for the purpose, with himself as chairman, Mr. Stephenson on its board of directors and Mr. Robert Stephenson as its engineer.

"I am often charged," Kirby went on, standing as was his habit with his right thumb stuck through the buttonhole of his coat lapel, "with being a railway speculator. I plead guilty to the charge! But in mitigation I can say that I've found laborers standing to be hired when no other man hired them, and given them employment and good wages. It's all very well to *talk* about the poor, but I like to *act* for the poor. Politicians can preach about poverty all they like, but I give work to hundreds of folks who'd otherwise have starved to death while all the pretty speeches were being made about 'em. Is it a just charge against me that by these means I've also made a fortune? Is there any gentleman here present who would not like to make a fortune of his business?"

His audience responded with warm applause, and Kirby continued solemnly. "Citizens of Gateshead, you have now entered the glorious age of railway travel and you are rightly proud of your new line. And yet I must tell you that travel is only in its infancy. We've only just begun. In fifty years that which is now so

244

fast to us will seem very slow and that which is now so distant will seem very near. That is my prophecy for the future."

At the end of his speech they stood to clap and cheer him louder than ever before.

It was the first of an epidemic of banquets in the northeast as the opening of one new line followed another. At Whitby, Kirby was entertained royally by the directors of the little Whitby and Pickering Company, a hitherto isolated horse-drawn line that the York and North Midland had purchased and linked with York. He was popular with the fisherfolk of the Yorkshire coast, who liked him not only for the economic benefits he had brought them but also for his pride in his own humble Yorkshire origins. He was without arrogance or condescension, talking as readily to the ordinary fisherman as to any high-ranking dignitary.

In the same month, Kirby bought the Durham and Sutherland Railway in the teeth of fierce competition. He followed that by purchasing the Pontop and South Shields line, at whose terminus at Jarrow Slake in the Tyne he proposed building a new dock costing two hundred thousand pounds. He also leased the Hartlepool Dock and Railway to the Newcastle and Darlington Company, thus linking up that town with his main line. *The Times* newspaper commented:

By these arrangements Mr. England has secured almost an entire command of the railways in the northern division in the County of Durham, and it is calculated that he will be able to ship the coals of the great colliery owners at considerably less cost than they now incur by use of their own private lines.

It was no surprise to anyone when Kirby was appointed Deputy Lord Lieutenant of Durham and began to appear at a number of distinguished country house parties which included some of the most important people in the land. Wherever he went he was lionized and fêted.

The Scarborough line passed through the heart of Kirby's native countryside, and of all his railways, it was dearest to his heart. For its opening Kirby had returned to his own people, and they turned out to do him honor with flags and brass bands and church bells. In Scarborough itself every shop was closed and every workman took a holiday on the opening day, and the

Mayor and corporation, with followers, marched down to the station to receive him under a richly decorated triumphal arch.

Altogether Kirby England had spent thirty million pounds and had built or acquired one thousand, four hundred and fifty miles of railway across the country.

But if Scarborough was his favorite line, York remained his favorite city. His affection for it was unaltered and undiminished, and no honor could have given him greater satisfaction and pleasure than the freedom of the City of York, which was granted him, while one of the streets was named after him. After the ceremony he gave a huge banquet which was attended by the Archbishop of York, the Duke of Leeds, eight mayors and hundreds of other notables. The *Standard* newspaper observed that of all people, Mr. England was entitled to give a grand dinner since he had provided dinners for so many others:

Two hundred thousand well-paid laborers, representing as heads of families nearly one million men, women and children, all feast through the bold enterprise of one man, and not feasting for one day or one week but enjoying abundance from year's end to year's end. Let us hear what man or class of men ever before did so much for the population of the country?

CHAPTER XII

And the demon took in hand
Moleskin, leather, and clay,
Oaths embryonic and
A longing for Saturday,
Knee straps and blood and flesh,
A chest exceedingly stout,
A soul—(which is a question
Open to many a doubt),
And fashioned with pick and shovel,
And shaped in mire and mud,
With life of the road and the hovel,
And death of the line or hod,
With fury and frenzy and fear,
That his strength might endure for a span,
From birth, through beer to bier,
The link twixt the ape and the man.

Patrick MacGill—*The Navvy Chorus*

"I shall do everything in my power," William Gurney said, "to see that Kirby England's company do not succeed in building their line across Benbow. I have considerable influence in Garford and I intend to use it to encourage support instead for the Leeds and York Railway. *Their* proposed route is infinitely preferable and their prospectus far sounder."

"But the Leeds and York Railway would not serve us nearly so well," Hester protested. "I have seen their prospectus, and their line is to pass *north* of Garford, whereas the York and North Midland will go through Garford itself."

"They also propose to go through Benbow parkland on their way. I confess that I am astonished thou couldst even consider favoring any scheme of Kirby England's, Hester. To suggest that his railway would be preferable is absurd! And I can remember, if thou hast forgotten, how he once turned down the chance to build a railway through Garford and across Benbow land."

"I have not forgotten. The railway was Papa's greatest wish."

"And his greatest disappointment when it was never built. But that seems no good reason for giving Kirby England a second opportunity. I see no reason, myself, for *any* railway to be built in this vicinity, but if we must have one at all, then let it be the Leeds and York company as the lesser of two evils."

"Then Benbow Colliery will suffer for thy prejudice."

"Prejudice?" William stared at her. "I am not *prejudiced* against Kirby England. My opinion is not prejudged in the slightest degree. I am acting on the certain knowledge that he is a rogue."

"But the line his company proposes will give Garford and our colliery a direct link with York and Leeds at last. Garford people are bound to prefer it."

"No one who works for the Benbow estate will give it his support, I can assure thee, my dear Hester. And everything will be done to hinder that company that I can contrive. We shall not discuss this further," William added coldly as Hester began to speak again. "No survey party from the York and North Midland will be permitted to trespass on Benbow land. I shall see to it that no theodolites are set up on *my* estate."

John Caley lay flat on his stomach beneath some bushes. Above him, through the dark leaves, he could see the moon sailing high on night clouds. He held his breath, listening intently to the sounds about him. He could hear a faint rustle as one of the other men in the survey party shifted his position a little a few yards away. An owl hooted once, and somewhere in the wood an animal squealed suddenly.

The Benbow men had passed within six feet of his head a few moments ago. The twigs cracking beneath their heavy laborers' boots had sounded like small explosions in his ears. He had seen the men silhouetted against the moonlight and caught the glint of the guns they carried beneath their arms. He shivered slightly and wiped his damp forehead; he was not a cowardly man but he had no wish to be shot in the leg like a dog, and the view of the local inhabitants he had spoken to was that Mr. William Gurney was capable of going to any lengths to keep York and North Midland surveyors off his land.

He had also discovered that Mr. Gurney was unpopular in Garford and in the local people's view compared very unfavorably with the previous master of the Benbow estate. Amos Gurney was remembered with respect as a good man who had striven to improve the lot of everyone in Garford. His daughter was also spoken of with affection, but her marriage to her cousin was talked of with much shaking of heads and expressions of regret. Things had not been happy at Benbow, it was said, since Mr. William Gurney had taken charge. In the matter of the two rival proposed railways, he was considered to be acting high-handedly and without any thought for the benefit the York and North Midland scheme would bring to Garford. Mr. Amos Gurney had not objected to a plan to build a railway across the southern part of Benbow land years ago, so the refusal of William Gurney to allow the surveyors on the estate was bitterly resented. At last they had a chance of a main line being built direct through their town, but unless the survey could be accurately and properly conducted across Benbow land, the battle would go to the Leeds and York company, who would build their line several miles away to the north. Accordingly, John Caley had been given willing assistance by the men and women of Garford: the miners, the wheelwrights, the quarrymen, the saddler, the cobbler, the innkeeper, the tanner, the poachers . . . They had spied, reported and kept watch for him every yard of the way.

The survey had had to be carried out at night by the light of moon and shaded lantern. It was not the first time, by any means, that the engineer had done a survey by stealth to avoid an irate landowner. But he would be very thankful to get this particular one finished. The Benbow men had been heavily armed and had looked unpleasantly purposeful; he had no doubt that they would use their guns. He had always thought that Quakers were peaceful folk who abhorred the use of weapons or violence of any sort, but evidently William Gurney did not share that view—at least not where surveyors from the York and North Midland Railway Company were concerned.

John Caley lifted his head cautiously and listened hard: there was silence. The men had gone, he decided, and it was safe to continue. At the same time, he heard a softly whistled signal from one of the Garford poachers stationed deeper in the woods, telling him that the way ahead was clear. He called quietly to the men behind him and, getting to his feet, began to move noiselessly through the undergrowth.

Kirby England's brown and black britska bowled smartly up the drive to Benbow Hall. The grays drawing the carriage trotted fast, harness jingling, manes blowing and breath vaporous in the frosty winter air. Kirby looked out of the window at the distant walls of Benbow Hall. He thought of the first time he had come here—when Amos Gurney had been alive. It was still a gloomy-looking place, in his opinion, without any uniformity of architectural style and not a vestige of elegance. On that first day he had come, cap in hand so to speak, to persuade its owner to let him conduct a railway survey across his land. Today, sixteen years later, that railway was at last being built. The new survey had been accomplished despite William Gurney. The Bill had been passed in Parliament, the rival railway company, the London and York, had retreated, beaten, and the work was already in progress. Amos Gurney would have been pleased. If there was such a place as Heaven (which Kirby doubted), then the Quaker would surely be smiling down with approval.

It was late in the afternoon and already beginning to turn to dusk. In the distance, at the southern tip of the parkland, he could see men moving about among the heaps of spoil and felled trees—all familiar evidence of railway construction in progress.

Kirby turned his head back towards the house. He had not

seen Hester Gurney since the night of the ball at Dewsborough several years ago, and the little news he had learned of her had been through Adelaide, who still corresponded with her from time to time. He thought it very probable that William Gurney would refuse him admittance. The Quaker's almost maniacal opposition to the company's railway line had nearly cost him the Bill's safe passage through Parliament. Kirby had himself attended a meeting of local Garford landowners and gentry and had finally succeeded in convincing them that the projected line was fully calculated to meet all their needs and wishes. The ordinary town folk had needed no persuasion—they were on his side from the first—but William had done a great deal of damage among his own kind and Kirby had been faced with deep suspicion and hostility. It had required all his skill to carry the day.

The coachman swung the britska round and halted the grays precisely opposite the door. Kirby mounted the steps to lift the iron knocker. A manservant whom he recognized answered his ring.

"Mr. Gurney is away in York, sir."

"Is Mrs. Gurney at home?"

"I will inquire, sir, if you will come with me."

Kirby was shown into a room he had not seen before, a small parlor which was dark and rather cold. A fire had only recently been lit in the grate, and he warmed his hands at the fitful flames while he waited.

She came into the room so quietly that he did not realize she was there until a slight sound made him swing round to see her standing near the door. The sight of her made his breath stick in his throat; she still affected him as no other woman could. She looked unchanged since they had last met—perhaps a little paler and thinner, but otherwise the same. He saw at once that she was disconcerted by his call and uncertain how to receive him—but not, he thought, watching her carefully, necessarily displeased. She came towards him and, giving him her hand, invited him to sit down.

"Thou wished to see William, I believe. He is away in York just now."

"So I gather. But my business can be done with you just as well."

She looked away. "If it's about the railway—I'm afraid William has been against it from the first—"

"It had come to my notice."

"He did not want it built across our land, especially not *thy* railway. If he had been here today he would not have admitted thee to the house."

"Aye. I can well believe it. But as he's not here we don't need to worry about him." He stood up and went across to the window to look out across the parkland towards the site of the railway. "I was thinking as I came here what a pity it was that your father wasn't still alive to see this railway come."

"If thou hadst built the line thou originally proposed to him he might have been," she pointed out.

He turned with a smile. "True enough. But better late than never. One way and another, I think I've honored my obligations to your late father."

She changed the subject, offering him some refreshment, but he refused.

"I shan't be long. I'm to dine and spend the night at a house just beyond Garford. I only came to ask one thing concerning the railway. I've been looking at the construction work that's been done so far. As things stand at the moment, a small section of the line will be clearly visible from this house. I'm proposing, and Mr. Caley our engineer agrees with me, that a tunnel should be made at that point, just before Hollins Wood, where the line can be seen from here."

"But the extra expense—"

"Would add to the cost a mite certainly—but nothing we can't bear. And it can be done quite cheaply by cut and cover. The excavation would be very shallow and would leave a mound of earth across the deer park, but John Caley tells me that it would be possible to turn it to some good account as a feature and, of course, the railway would then be hidden from you completely. What do you say?"

"I can't speak for my husband," she replied. "But *I* am all in favor of thy suggestion. And since William loathes the very thought of thy railway coming anywhere near here, much less across Benbow land, he will surely welcome the prospect of it being put out of his sight."

"That's settled then. The work will be carried out as soon as possible."

"I'm surprised to find thee dealing with such a small matter," she said. "I am constantly reading in the newspapers about how important thou hast become—second only in the country to the Duke of Wellington himself!"

"You shouldn't believe everything you read in the newspapers."

"I don't," she assured him. "Even so, our view across the park must be a very small matter for thee."

"Not at all. I always make it my business to know every detail about my railways. From the first line I ever had constructed down to this one I've always walked every yard of the route. I like to see things for myself. I trust my own judgment most, and I learned early on that it's the best way to avoid costly mistakes."

She stood up and, going over to the fireplace, tried to coax some life into the coals. He sensed that she was nervous. After a moment's silence she said suddenly:

"I am thankful thou hast come here today."

"I never thought to hear you say that."

"We may need thy help . . ."

"You've only to ask. I've always said so." He waited.

"It's not the railway itself," she said, "but the men who are building it. There's been a lot of trouble since the navvies came. They moved into this district like an invading army and they terrorize Garford. Nothing is safe from them. They loot and steal and destroy everything they choose."

"The navvies are a law unto themselves," Kirby said. "They live and die violent lives, but without them the railways would never be built. The work is so hard and the way of life so rugged only a special breed of men could survive."

"Does that give them the right to terrify peaceful citizens—to break the laws? And they are always drunk. On Saturday nights the people in Garford lock themselves in their houses. Sometimes

253

there have been dreadful fights between Garford men and the navvies—sometimes they even fight among themselves."

"I'll do what I can," he promised her. "I'll speak to the contractor, but even he will have little control over them. It's only a temporary nuisance. In time they'll move on to the next part of the line and everything will return to normal again."

"That may be too late for us."

"What do you mean?"

"I told thee that there had been a lot of trouble. The navvies have been poaching on Benbow land. When William found that out he was very angry. Soon after that the navvies put up some huts near the railway—on our land. There's no more room for them to lodge in Garford and nowhere else for them to go. They live in these makeshift wooden shacks in the most dreadful conditions—like animals, or even worse. William ordered them to be taken down. He refused to have them on Benbow land; he said he would not have such evil places on the estate."

"What then?"

"He told our men to pull down the huts. There was a fight with the navvies and our men were forced to retreat. But William refused to give in. This morning the huts were burned to the ground —when the navvies were busy working on the line."

"That was stupid! They're bound to retaliate. Like for like is their motto."

"There's worse to come," she said. "There was a child—a baby girl—in one of the huts. She'd been left there by her mother, who'd walked to Garford. The Benbow men thought the huts were empty . . ."

"What happened to the child?"

"She was badly burned. The navvies rescued her, but she may die . . . I have done everything I can for her—sent for our own doctor to attend her." Hester put her hands over her face. "I should have guessed what William might do: it was typical of him. I might have been able to prevent such a dreadful tragedy."

"Don't blame yourself," he said gently. "It was nowt of your doing. And the child will probably be all right. I told you, they're a tough breed. But I'll go myself at once and see if anything more can be done."

"But if she dies—"

"*If* she dies there could be more trouble from the navvies. But don't worry about it. Let me go and sort it out with them. I'll talk to them . . . reason with them."

Kirby hid his concern behind matter-of-fact speech. In reality, he was seriously alarmed for Hester's safety, alone at Benbow with William away in York. The burning of the shanties was bad enough—the navvies would think nothing of setting fire to Benbow property in return: cottages, barns, stables, hayricks, even possibly the house itself—but the injury or death of a baby might provoke an even worse revenge. The child was probably the neglected bastard brat of one of the camp women. Kirby had seen the way the navvy children lived, sometimes sleeping in cages hung from the rafters like animals, frequently half starved when beer drained away most of their father's wages and, inevitably, the victims of drunken, brutal treatment. None of this would make any difference. If the child died the navvies would seek revenge. There was no time to be lost in going down to the encampment. He could arrange for new huts to be constructed, compensation to be paid, the best medical care for the child.

He took his leave quickly of Hester. She went with him to the door. Outside it was growing very dark and a cold wind blew across the park. Kirby walked down the steps towards his carriage, and then he stopped suddenly to listen.

The sound of tramping feet had reached his ears, carried towards him on the wind. He waited. Even before he saw the light of the flares they held and heard the angry voices, he knew what it was. A pack of navvies bent on destruction and revenge was marching up the long driveway towards the house. He could hear the steady pounding of their heavy boots, like the inexorable approach of an army.

Kirby waited no longer. He went back to Hester. "Go inside at once and see that every door is bolted. Stay there until I tell you it's safe to come out." He pushed her roughly backwards out of sight. "Go on! Hurry up and do as I say!"

But she resisted him. "No! If there's going to be trouble with the navvies I shall face it. *We* are to blame for what happened. Let me speak to them."

He was angry in his fear for her. He shook her hard. "Don't be such a little fool! Do you know what they'd do to you? I know what I'm doing and I know the navvies. I can handle them. But for God's sake, *you* keep out of sight!"

"I'm going to stay here—"

"You're not!"

He picked her up in his arms and carried her through the doorway, dumping her down in the hall before an astonished manservant.

"See that your mistress stays inside," he ordered the bewildered man. "And bar every window and door."

There was no time to delay longer; he could hear the navvies plainly now. The manservant slammed the big front door shut behind him and the bolts slid home. Kirby did not look back, nor did he hear Hester calling to him to take care.

The navvies were within fifty yards or so of the house, and he waited for them at the top of the stone steps. He saw that they had been drinking—enough to be in a vicious mood but not enough to dull their wits. They marched on towards him—a weird and motley collection of men, dressed in strange clothing. They wore velveteen, square-tailed coats, double-canvas shirts, bright-colored waistcoats, gaudy handkerchiefs knotted about their necks, moleskin trousers and hats of all shapes and kinds— some of white felt with the brim turned up, some caps of sealskin, some knitted, some of cloth. Few of the men were under six feet tall and all were as muscular as prizefighters.

At the foot of the steps they stopped. There was silence for a moment as they looked at Kirby and sized him up. Kirby waited. Presently the leader came forward and put one foot on the lowest step. He was a huge man. He wore a pea jacket well marked with dirt and grease, a rainbow waistcoat with a double row of big mother-of-pearl buttons, and a red-spotted handkerchief round his throat. A sealskin cap covered his head and his moleskin trousers were so stiffly encrusted with mud and clay that they rattled against the tops of his hobnail boots when he moved. He wore straps round his knees and a long skiver of tin was wedged between strap and trouser on his right leg.

He moved up another step and growled: "We want Mr. Gurney!"

"Mr. Gurney is not here."

The navvy leader bent and drew the skiver of tin from under the knee strap. "We know he's here and we've come to teach him a few lessons. He burned down our huts and murdered a babe. She died an hour ago. We'll see how he'd like his children burned to death in their home! We'll give him a taste of his own medicine!"

"Mr. Gurney has no children. There'll be no revenge for you that way. And the death of your child was an accident."

"Burning our huts wasn't no accident! Out of our way! We'll see how *his* house burns!"

"You'll see nothing but a prison's bars if you take one more step. I'm told a man may as easily die from jail fever as on the gallows."

There was a pause and some muttering among the navvies. One of them called out: "Where's Mr. Gurney? We want to see him."

"I told you, he's away—on business in York."

"Mrs. Gurney then—"

Kirby looked contemptuous. "What sort of men are you to think of revenging yourselves on an innocent woman? Mrs. Gurney had nothing to do with what happened—you have my word on that."

"And we don't believe you." The navvy leader held the sharp skiver out before him. "Out of my way or I'll use this on you."

Kirby stood his ground. He took off his coat with deliberate slowness and tossed it onto the step beside him. "You'll have to get past me to go any further. Let's see if you've the courage to fight this out between the two of us. Not thirty or more of you against myself, one woman and a few elderly servants, but one man against t'other. A fair fight. If I lose there'll be nobody to stop you . . . but if I win then you all go away. What do you say? Is it agreed—or are you afraid to fight on equal terms?"

There was a ripple of interest among the pack of men. There was nothing the navvies liked better than a good fight; it was as much a part of their lives as poaching, robbing and randying.

Bare-fisted fights were often arranged for the camp's entertainment, preferably between men with a grudge against each other, and the match was fought until one man could go on no longer.

The navvy leader hesitated. If he refused the challenge the men behind him might think he had lost his nerve. He was cock of the camp and his name was not Fighting Jack for nothing. And yet, things were not going the way he'd planned. They had come to burn and loot and avenge themselves for what had been done, and he was determined they would not be cheated of it. His fellows began to call out restlessly: "Come on, Fighting Jack! Give him what he asks! Show him what you're made of!" And one or two derisive, taunting murmurs reached him. With an oath he flung down the skiver so that it clattered noisily on the stone. He stepped back down the steps, dragged off his pea jacket, rainbow waistcoat and shirt, and stood flexing the muscles in his huge arms. Kirby had shed his own shirt and went down to meet him. In silence the navvies formed a ring round the two men, holding their flares aloft to light the contest.

It began slowly. The two men circled each other, arms lifted at the ready, like animals prepared to fight to the death and therefore unwilling to rush the engagement. Stripped to the waist, there was little to choose in physique between them and little to distinguish the rich man from the navvy. Kirby with his thick and curling black hair, big hands and heavy build looked as much a laborer as the navvy.

A hiss of excitement broke the silence as the two men suddenly came to grips with each other. Sweat trickled down skin and mingled soon with blood as they wrestled and fought with a savage ferocity. No quarter was either given or expected. There were no rules and no chivalry shown of any kind. The grunts and groans of the protagonists were accompanied by appreciative shouts and yells from the onlookers, who increased the size of their ring, falling back as the fight grew fiercer still. The two men rolled over and over on the ground, locked in combat like fighting grizzlies. Fighting Jack had Kirby by the throat, and when he failed to choke him to death kicked at his head with his hobnail boots. On their feet again, they fought with clenched fists, raining blows on each other wherever they could. It was twenty minutes or more before the contest came to a sudden end. Kirby tripped the navvy up with his foot, and as the man fell heavily he caught him a chopping blow across the neck. Fighting Jack crashed to the ground like a great boulder and lay spread-eagled and insensible. The circle of navvies stared curiously down at his bloodied face, and a rustling sigh spread round from one to the other like the sound of leaves stirred by the wind. Without a word the biggest amongst them stepped forward and, stooping, hoisted Fighting Jack to his feet, lifting him across his shoulder like a sack of grain. Another picked up the pea jacket and rainbow waistcoat; a third, the sealskin cap that had fallen early in the fight. The unconscious navvy was carted away, his head lolling against his carrier's velveteen coat. The rest of the navvies followed with shuffling feet. The flares bobbed away into the darkness and they were gone.

Kirby picked up his shirt and waistcoat and put them on gingerly. Every bone in his body was aching and every inch of him felt bruised from the attentions of Fighting Jack's hobnail boots. He could feel the blood running down his cheek from a cut on his head and wiped it away with his shirt sleeve. His lungs rasped and heaved as though he had run several miles. But with the pain and exhaustion there was also an exhilaration and satisfaction such as he had not known for years . . . not since he was a lad and had fought with other village lads up on the Wold, and not since he'd made that running up the railway embankment. With a grin he hooked his coat over his shoulder and started up the steps. As he did so the front door swung open and Hester flew out to stop dead at the sight of him.

He wiped the blood away again and gave her an ironical bow. "Your humble servant, ma'am. They've gone."

"Thou art badly hurt!"

He shook his head. "It's nothing."

She was badly shaken at his appearance and at the fight that she had witnessed from the window. The violence of it had appalled her, and throughout she had been certain that he would be killed. The servants were sent for water, and she insisted on washing and dressing the wound on his head. He protested mildly and told her that a glass of brandy was all that was

259

needed to set him to rights. She fetched him one, and when he had swallowed it at a gulp, refilled the glass, watching him drink. To tease her a little he shut his eyes and groaned loudly once or twice. The expression of horror and dismay he saw on her face, through his half-closed lashes, was profoundly gratifying. He leaned his head back against the chair.

"I don't think they'll come back, but I'll sleep here tonight—just to be sure. Have you a gun in the house?"

"A gun? We've never kept such a thing at Benbow."

"I forgot about your Quaker scruples for a moment," he said, and omitted to tell her, since he was sure she did not know, that William had armed his estate workers to the teeth against his survey party. "Never mind, we'll do without. My fists served me as well as any firearm and can do so again. I'll send a servant to round up some of your laborers to keep watch in the grounds tonight."

Later he settled down to a night's vigil in Amos Gurney's old chair beside the library fire, a candle burning on the table beside him. He dozed a little, and again he had the sensation that the dead Quaker's spirit was somehow present in the room.

Hester went to her bed, but could not sleep. It had begun to rain and the wind moaned about the house. Every strange sound brought her sitting bolt-upright, convinced that the navvies were outside. It required little imagination to picture them stealing back through the night to surround the house. She was ashamed of her fear, but the longer she lay in the dark the less she was able to suppress it. Her only comfort was the thought of Kirby England downstairs—and that was disturbing in itself. After meeting him at Dewsborough again she had found herself searching for news of him in the papers, and over the years she had followed everything he had done, gleaning every item of information she could. But she had never expected to see him again . . . certainly never dreamed that he would come to Benbow again, especially after the trouble that William had made for him over the railway. But he had come. And he had risked his life for her.

There was a faint clinking somewhere outside below her window. She listened hard and heard it again, as though a pebble had been shifted and rolled across the path. The tiny noise was more sinister than anything loud could have been. She slid from the bed and opened the shutter a crack. There was no moon to give shape or substance to the night, just rain and wind and darkness. She closed it again quietly, put on a robe and, pausing only to light a candle, hurried downstairs.

The library was in darkness and the fire had burned low. Her own candle showed her that his had gone out and that he had fallen sound asleep in the chair. He looked so tired and bruised and battered that she did not want to wake him. While she hesitated he suddenly opened his eyes.

"I heard a sound outside—"

He was on his feet at once. "Wait here. I'll take a look."

She heard him leave the house by the side door that led to the stables. After that there was no other sound for a long time. Minutes passed that seemed like hours while she waited and wondered. She moved towards the windows, and as she did so, a great gust of wind rattled the wooden shutters like a skeleton's bones, the candle she carried snuffed out in the draught and the library door slammed shut. She stood alone in the blackness, with only the faint red glow from the dying fire to guide her.

There was a soft click as the door opened again. Whoever it was had come into the room and was moving towards her and stumbling into the furniture, knocking over a small table. The colorful oath that this produced in the familiar Yorkshire tones brought a smile of relief to her.

"Are you all right, lass? Are you there?"

"I'm here. The candle went out."

He came closer, feeling his way through the darkness. "There's nowt out there. I had a good look round. It must've been some animal you heard—a fox, most likely."

Neither spoke for a moment. He was so near now that she could hear his breathing and feel the warmth from his body, although she could not see him. He put out his hand and his fingers touched her cheek. He said softly:

"You're shaking, love. Are you cold?"

"No."

"Frightened?"

"Not anymore."

He reached out with his other hand and drew her towards him until he held her close, stroking her loose hair as though he were comforting a child. His coat was damp from the rain and smelled of cigar smoke. She pressed her cheek against it and closed her eyes.

"I still love you; you know that, don't you?" he said. "I've never stopped loving you."

She said something, but the words were muffled by the thick cloth of his coat.

He began to kiss the crown of her head, so gently that she scarcely felt it. "Hester . . . you once told me that you could never love me. Do you still think that?"

He sensed, but could not see, that she lifted her head and smiled at him in the darkness. This time he heard her answer, but before she had gone halfway with all that she wanted to tell him, he interrupted her with a long kiss that left her breathless.

"Just tell me that again! Tell me a hundred times! It could never be enough!"

She did so willingly, but once was enough for him to begin to kiss her again. She could not have resisted him even if she had wanted to. Instead she clasped her hands about his neck and kissed him back. With a violent oath he lifted her off the ground and into his arms.

"How dare he come here in my absence! I leave my house for no more than twenty-four hours to find he has forced his way in here and spent the night under my roof!"

"He did *not* force his way in," Hester said with quiet coldness. "I agreed to see him, although he came to see thee. And he came only to propose a way of concealing the railway from us by Hollins Wood."

"Which thou agreed to, I have no doubt."

"It seemed an idea that could not fail to please thee."

"Please me! My dear Hester, thou shouldst know by now that nothing connected with Kirby England could *ever* please me! To have anything to do with him is to be tainted by the devil! What a coward he is! He bides his time until my back is turned and

262

then persuades my wife to agree to some trickery designed to put more money in his pocket."

"Was it cowardly to face that gang of navvies alone and stop them looting and burning Benbow?"

"They work for him, don't they, my dear? Of course they did as he told them. He had probably encouraged them in the first place just to try and frighten us. I, after all, dared to oppose him, and where opposition is concerned men like him are utterly ruthless."

"That's not true. The navvies did not even know who he was. I'm certain of that."

William looked at her sharply. He was pale with anger. "I don't wish to hear thee defend him. He is evil itself."

Hester turned away from the inquisition of his eyes. She was afraid of what he might read in her face . . . that he might read there that she loved Kirby England.

She said to William: "Hast thou forgotten about the child who died? Dost thou have no regret or guilt? She died because of thy orders."

"It was the Lord's will and His punishment for the depraved and sinful living of those men. It was better for the child to die and be received into God's Heavenly Kingdom than to live on earth in a place of such wickedness and vice. She will be saved from eternal damnation. Thou shouldst be glad for her sake—as I am."

"How canst thou really think that!"

"Because I know it to be so. And as for the burning of the huts, the fire cleansed Benbow of their filth. Why should I allow such people to pollute my land just to satisfy the everlasting greed of dishonest, grasping speculators? The responsibility is Kirby England's. I should like to know what retribution he intends to offer me for the aggression and violence shown by *his* railway workers."

"I only know that he went directly this morning to speak with the contractor and with the navvies themselves."

"And what will that achieve?" William cried contemptuously. "The railway is all that concerns him; he will ride roughshod over everything in its path, as he always has done. Well, I shall insist that the men who came here last night are severely punished by the law. And I shall require thee to identify them."

She looked at him in dismay. "That would only bring more trouble for us. Besides, I scarcely saw them. It was dark."

"It matters very little which of them thou chooses to identify, my dear, so long as an example is set for the rest. They must learn that their vileness will not go unpunished by man as well as by God. I shall make certain that no navvy ever dares set foot near this house again."

After luncheon William sent for his horse and told Hester that he intended riding over immediately to see the contractor at the railway line. Nothing she could say would dissuade him: he was inflexible.

The rain had not ceased since the previous night, and an hour after William's departure it began to pour down in torrents and lash against the windows with storm force. Hester stared out at the dismal scene and wondered whether Kirby was already on his way back to York. She pictured the britska traveling fast, its wheels churning through the mud and wet as they carried him ever further and further away from her. She stood there alone for a long while in the growing gloom of the afternoon and had just turned away, at last, from the window when a dull, rumbling roar suddenly filled her ears and the floor shook and shivered beneath her feet. Objects clattered and danced in the room with a frightening symbolism, and Amos Gurney's old Bible fell from its shelf with a mighty thud.

Hester knew instantly what had happened: there had been an underground explosion up at the mine. Nothing else could have accounted for that earth-shaking boom. The terrible price had finally been paid for William's refusal to sink another ventilation shaft and for all the neglect that had followed.

Hester paused only long enough to snatch up her cloak before running from the house to the stables. The lad who saddled one of the horses for her was jittering with fright, convinced that the world was coming to an end. His fear had communicated itself to the horse, who plunged about nervously as Hester left the stable yard. She steadied the animal as best she could and set off across the park on the long route across country up towards Benbow Moor. It was tortuous and difficult even in the most favorable weather, and by now the heavy rain had turned the track to deep mud. Kippax Beck was in flood, the waters racing down the hillside in a froth of white foam, and at the ford the water was deep and treacherous. The horse slipped and stumbled over the crossing before they reached the other side.

The mine's tall chimneys appeared through the squalling rain, and she saw that the great black wheels stood motionless. As she drew near, she saw men running about near the pithead and she could hear shouting.

No one paid any heed to her. She reined in the horse and slid from its back. Her legs were shaking. She tethered the horse and ran towards the pithead. Thornton, the brakesman she had known since a child, was there talking to another man whose back was turned and half hidden by machinery. Catching sight of her, the brakesman said something to his companion, who turned. It was Kirby England.

He moved quickly towards her and caught hold of her shoulders. "Hester, love, you shouldn't be here. This is no place for you."

"My place is here—with the miners," she answered. "I heard the explosion from the house."

"It's bad, lass. No point in pretending otherwise. I was down at the railway with the contractor when I heard it too. I came up on the wagon to see what could be done."

"How many men are down?"

"Fifty-six, by the last count. Thornton here tells me it could've been much worse. The hewers had just finished their shift and come up—else there'd've been many more. It's the putters and hurriers mostly . . . and some of the trappers."

"Dear God . . ." Hester thought of Tom Bartlett and the other children. Her mind seemed frozen with horror. She could not speak.

Thornton, the brakesman, came forward. His face looked gray and old. "I was just about to send down an empty corf," he said, "when there was an almighty gust of wind from below that blew the corf clean up and out of the shaft again. My hat was blown off high over the headstock gear. And when I looked down all I could see was smoke . . . nothing but smoke and fumes. There wasn't a sound to be heard."

Kirby said: "Two of the men are willing to come down with me to see if anybody's left alive. We're going to try."

Thornton shook his head. "It'd be madness to go, sir. We'll have to wait a day or so to be safe."

"By that time any left alive will be dead. Wind us down, man, and we may save some souls at least."

The brakeman did all he could to dissuade him, but Kirby had made up his mind and the outcome was therefore in no doubt. Hester knew better than even to attempt to stop him. She waited in silence while Kirby and the two volunteers made ready for the descent. He came across to where she stood.

"We'll be needing your prayers," he said with a smile.

She tried to smile back but her face was too stiff. It was hard to speak. "Thou shalt have them. I shall pray every minute until thou returns safely."

He looked down at her for a moment, understanding her. "Courage, lass. Now's not the time to let go."

She watched as the three men were lowered by rope and empty corf down into the smoking blackness of the shaft. They disappeared from sight, and after that there was nothing to be done but to wait. By now some of the miners' womenfolk had gathered to wait with her. A few were weeping openly, but most were silent and patient. This was the limbo, the purgatory common to all mining disasters, when nothing was yet known for sure and waiting was all women could do. Hester began to pray.

The descent had been a grueling ordeal. By the time the three reached the foot of the shaft they were gasping for breath. Foul air, dust and smoke tortured their lungs and the heat was like a furnace. Impenetrable blackness surrounded them; their lamps worked feebly and they had to grope their way along the main tunnel—inch by inch. Progress was hopelessly slow and time too short. Kirby knew from his aching lungs and bursting head that they would not last long in such conditions. They stumbled over two men who lay in their path, and Kirby swung his lamp low to shine briefly on faces disfigured and distorted by a violent death.

Nothing could be done for them; it was the living they had come to find. They crawled on, stopping every so often to listen. The dripping of water that Kirby remembered had ceased and there was a terrifying silence about them; there was no sound of life, and yet somewhere in the darkness of this underworld were fifty-six men and boys.

They had come no more than a matter of yards from the shaft when they found three men still alive. Two were unconscious, but faint moans from the third had alerted them. The injured men were lying against the wall, and Kirby, bending low to examine them, thought they looked done for. They decided to go on and see if there were others, marking the place where the three lay. There were fallen rocks half blocking their passage, and somewhere, from the deepest depths of the mine, they heard a loud rumbling. The ground began to shudder beneath their feet. The wooden pit props creaked like ship's timbers in a storm, and dust and small stones showered down upon them. Kirby wiped the sweat of heat and fear from his forehead and licked the salt from his lips; to die down here like a rat in a trap was not a death he relished one bit. His foot caught against something and he held out the lamp. At first he could see nothing before him but what looked like a few rags. He prodded it with his boot and saw that it was a child. He knelt and turned the small body over to see better, and as he did so the child's eyes opened, shining with silent tears in the lamplight. One tear overspilled to run down a coal-black cheek. As Kirby held him, the boy tried to speak, then sighed quietly and closed his eyes. His head lolled sideways.

"He's dead," one of Kirby's companions said over his shoulder. "Nowt to be done for him."

Kirby laid the dark-haired boy back on the ground and he stared down at him. There wasn't a single mark of injury on the child: he looked no more than peacefully asleep. The boy reminded him somehow of himself when young. He looked round. There was nothing to cover the lad with . . . no way of giving him a decent burial. He bent down again and folded the child's arms across his chest.

They went on a short way and the air grew fouler every moment. The leader of the two miners stopped suddenly.

"We can't go no further. There's a bad fall . . ." His lamp showed that a solid wall of rock barred their way. There was no hope of shifting it; each rock was bigger than a man could handle. As they examined it they heard the rumble of another fall close by.

"Best get back quick," one of the miners told Kirby, "if we want to get out alive."

"Wait a moment—I swear I heard shouting just then."

The miner caught his arm. "Nay. They're all dead. And even if they're not there's nowt more we can do about it. Best not listen too hard . . ."

They retraced their steps to the three survivors and half dragged, half carried one each over the remaining yards to the foot of the shaft. As they cleared the end of the tunnel the roof collapsed in behind them with a deafening roar, and suddenly a mighty rushing torrent of water exploded all around them as though a dam had burst. It poured down on them from every side, so that they floundered and gasped frantically at the shaft bottom like men drowning in a well. The empty corf swung above them. One miner was hoisted aloft with one of the unconscious men. Kirby and the second miner struggled to keep a foothold and to hold the injured men's heads above the rising black water. Rats in a barrel, Kirby thought, his fingers scrabbling desperately for something to grip in the rock wall beside him . . . just like bloody rats in a barrel.

He signaled to the other man to go next, and was left alone with the third injured miner slung roughly across his shoulder. But for his enormous physical strength, neither would have survived. The icy water rose above waist level, and Kirby felt his fingers go numb from the effort of holding onto the wall. If he had let go they would both have been swept away into the mine. The water in the shaft pulled at his legs like a whirlpool, buckling his knees with its strength and rising higher and higher, minute by minute.

The empty corf was lowered just out of his reach. To gain it he would have to release his hold on the wall. At that moment a wave of water knocked the lamp from his other hand and he was in complete darkness. Anger filled him that he should die like this. He let go of the wall and plunged across the foot of the shaft to where the corf had been. His hand groped the blackness, felt the side of the corf. It swung away from him. Again he touched it, and this time gripped the edge, and then above it, the rope. With his last remaining strength he hauled himself and the miner across the wooden basket and felt the jerk of the rope beneath his hand as they were hauled upwards to the living world and safety.

They had rescued two furnacemen and one putter. Fifty-three souls remained below—dead or dying. The miners' women, shawls over their heads, children clinging to their skirts, wept quietly in the rain. Hester stood apart from them—waiting. Kirby went to her.

William had not returned to Benbow Hall by nightfall. Later a search party was sent out to look for him, but returned without success.

It was not until the following day that his body was discovered. He had been hacked to death with a sharp weapon—possibly, but not positively, a pickax, in the opinion of the police—and his corpse had been hidden in the colliery railway tunnel. Apart from his terrible bodily wounds, his face bore the marks of severe bruising, as though it had been kicked again and again by heavy-booted feet.

There was no proof that the navvies had been responsible for the murder, but about that time Fighting Jack and three other navvies who went by the names of Cat's Meat, Contrary York and Frying Pan had disappeared from the navvy encampment. They had moved on, in the rootless, wandering way of their kind, to change their names and find work elsewhere.

CHAPTER XIII

There's a bad time going, boys,
A bad time going!
Railway shares have seemed to be
A sink for all men's property
In the bad time going.
Lines which used to quarrel then,
To prove whose purse was stronger,
Shall be controlled by honest men—
Wait a little longer!

Punch, 1848

"As chairman and representative of the board of directors of the Eastern Counties Railway Company, Mr. England, you are required to provide an answer to my question to this court."

Elias Snell's high-pitched voice carried clearly across the crowded courtroom. His lawyer's wig made his face look thinner and more saturnine than ever.

"I'd be glad to answer you, Mr. Snell," Kirby England said unhurriedly. "But I need more notice of the question. I haven't the relevant facts before me."

The lawyer stroked his chin with his long fingers. "I find that remiss—not to say negligent of you, Mr. England. However, I am able to supply those facts myself and will shortly call witnesses to substantiate what I have to tell the court." He turned towards the jury. "You will hear evidence that will tell you that the driver of the luggage train—running *four hours* behind schedule

—on that snowy, foggy night of January eleventh, had only *three weeks'* experience in driving a locomotive engine! Imagine that, gentlemen! After just three weeks he is permitted to take control of a lethal machine, which subsequently crashed into the rear of a stationary passenger train, killing twelve people."

Elias Snell paused dramatically and then continued in quieter but equally carrying tones: "There can be no doubt in your minds that the driver of the goods train was directly to blame for the accident. But who, I ask, is *indirectly* responsible? We have been told of *economy* measures taken, of the sudden reduction in wages and salaries to employees of the Eastern Counties Company, of the employment of boys instead of men to work the points at junctions on the line, of the recruitment, at low wages, of drivers discharged from their previous posts for drunkenness and carelessness . . . of continual breakdowns and engine troubles and of the growing hostility of the railway servants, whether dismissed or retained, towards a board of directors who had shown themselves increasingly callous about property and life— an attitude which has ultimately, and inevitably, resulted in this tragic accident. The blame, gentlemen, lies with those whose grasping cupidity allowed their own aggrandizement to supersede the necessity of carefully watching and directing their servants, or of studying the comfort and protection of the public. Woe to the unfortunate passengers when a board of directors begins to calculate how many policemen they can save on their line, or how much they can put into their pockets by contracting for second-rate, instead of first-rate, materials for carriages, rails and engines—and, be it added, men!"

Murmurs of agreement spread throughout the courtroom. Elias Snell had not finished yet.

"Furthermore, gentlemen, Mr. England maintains that these economy measures were taken as a result of the depressed state of trade in this country. I say that is *humbug!* I suggest that the truth is that they had to be taken in consequence of the chairman's mismanagement of his company. I have examined the accounts of the Eastern Counties Railway Company myself very closely and I ask this court to consider, among other irregularities I discovered, whether a board of directors that pays dividend out of *capital* is likely to be fit to administer a company's funds—let alone be responsible for innocent lives!"

The murmurs had swelled to an indignant rumble. Order had to be called in the courtroom. Elias Snell sat down with a faint smile on his lips.

"The driver of the goods train was acquitted, Mother."

"I can't think why they charged him in the first place," Mrs. England said. "It was an accident."

"As you say—it was an accident. But unfortunately twelve people are dead because of it. The driver was acquitted but myself and the board were publicly censured by the court. The man was too inexperienced for the job."

Mrs. England was outraged. "What do *they* know about running a railway company, I'd like to know! Let them try and see if they can do better!"

Kirby said nothing. He poured himself a glass of brandy and sat down in a chair beside the fire. Despite the blazing coals, the drawing room at 44 Monkgate was cold. He twirled the glass round between his hands.

"Shall I tell you something interesting, Mother? At the last count it was estimated that so far seventy railways have conveyed twenty-five million passengers for more than three hundred million miles in this country with only three fatal accidents. Now, that's an achievement to be proud of. But I'm afraid it doesn't alter the fact that *this* accident should never have happened. I should have taken my own advice and closed down the Eastern Counties Railway long ago. I was a fool ever to take it on. It's too long and carries far too little passenger traffic. Never keep a line open that doesn't pay its way . . . God knows how many times I've told that to others! We've cut costs to keep it going and I've paid dear for it."

He stared down at the half-empty glass. "It's going to mean a lot more trouble for me."

She looked at him in alarm. "I don't understand you, Kirby. What do you mean, more trouble? Surely it's finished and done with?"

He said slowly: "It's just begun, Mother. Eastern Counties is

273

in a bad way, and an inspection of accounts brought certain things to light at the court hearing . . ."

"What things?"

"Irregularities . . . mismanagement—for which I, as chairman, am responsible. But that's only part of it. The whole railway boom is almost over. The country's going through a depression and money's neither cheap to borrow nor plentiful to invest. The Bank of England can't support the credit system any longer on which our trade is founded. So . . . soon the panic will start. Share values will fall. Shareholders will demand explanations for declining dividends . . ."

"What will you do?"

He shrugged. "Fight. I've pulled plenty of rabbits out of hats in my time. Trouble is I've too many new railway lines begun and not completed. And within two months I've to repay nearly four hundred thousand pounds borrowed from banks on behalf of various companies of mine."

Mrs. England sat very still. She watched as her son poured himself another brandy but said nothing. She was afraid to speak . . . afraid to ask him questions to which she did not want to hear the answers. Her gaunt fingers began to pluck at the jet beads she wore round her neck.

"Resign! Resign!"

The half-yearly shareholders' meeting of the York, Newcastle and Berwick Railway Company, held at the De Grey Rooms in York, had begun quietly and in orthodox fashion. It had descended into uproar, disorder and angry confusion. The mood, at first, had been gloomy and forbearing as Kirby England moved the adoption of the report and announced to shareholders the lowering of the rate of dividend to six percent. The atmosphere had been changed by the putting of one question to the chairman by a shareholder who was a member of the London Stock Exchange. This question had been put with deceptive nonchalance and concerned the purchase of the Great North of England Railway Company by the shareholders by means of subscriptions to a new capital stock, at guaranteed interest.

"I have looked up old lists at the Stock Exchange," the questioner said casually. "And I should like to ask the chairman why the company paid twenty-three pounds, ten shillings for fifteen-pound Great North of England shares when at no time, over the period in question, have these stood higher than twenty-one pounds or so in value. The total number of shares stated to have been bought by this company is three thousand, seven hundred and ninety. I am sure that no more than odd hundreds were bought by the public . . . so that *someone* has received great benefits by selling them at this extravagant price to the company."

All eyes turned at once to the chairman, and there followed a barrage of questions which he was unable to answer satisfactorily. Yes, he had had three thousand odd of those shares, but if he had disposed of them to the company for a higher price than was justified, then he was prepared to do whatever the shareholders thought most just and fair. He would take back the shares and refund the purchase price with interest—although the valuation had been made independent of himself.

Henry Latham listened in horror from the back of the room and watched his brother-in-law under attack.

The London Stock Exchange member had risen again to declare that unfortunately, it was a question not of mere money but of their chairman's reputation. He insisted on the appointment of a Committee of Investigation. A short debate followed and this was agreed.

The meeting broke up in turmoil and Henry left quickly, without speaking to Kirby. As he walked away he was remembering the critical articles he had read in the press . . . the small, scurrilous rumors circulating at Parliament about Kirby since the train accident inquest. The stories of irregularities and juggled accounts that he had so far managed to ignore or discount . . . He had never been blind to Kirby's rough-and-ready business methods, but he had never believed him to be an outrightly dishonest man. He was a speculator, a gambler who was prepared to take risks where other men would not, and a completely scrupulous man could never have achieved all that he had done. And the ends had justified the means. Whatever his methods, Kirby had been responsible for building a railway system for his country quickly and efficiently. But for him there might have been no system but railway anarchy.

Henry kept a close watch on the *Yorkshire Gazette*, but the newspaper printed only a bare summary of the proceedings of the shareholders' meeting. There was hope perhaps then that the London newspapers would not pick up the story. His relief was short-lived. Barely four weeks later the half-yearly meeting of another of Kirby's companies, the Eastern Counties Railway, fell due, and this time Henry was dismayed to read a full account of the angry reception Kirby had received there. There had been prolonged boos and hissings, and the chairman's announcement of a paltry dividend of five shillings and sixpence had caused angry uproar. Before the end of the meeting the shareholders of that company, too, had demanded a Committee of Inquiry into the accounts.

And not even the shareholders of the York and North Midland, who had less to grumble about, were in any mood to be charitable. At the end of their meeting, amid scenes of dissatisfaction and suspicion, Elias Snell had come forward to assume the role of legal adviser to his fellow shareholders.

Nothing, Henry now realized, could now stem the tide that was flowing against Kirby. The Railway King's back was to the wall, and although people still believed in him in his own city, every passing day brought fresh accusations.

The findings of the two Committees of Inquiry were as damning as Henry had feared. He read in despair of board minutes lost, of entries in the journal of the purchase of shares being made without dates, of accounts imperfectly kept and, in the case of the fated Eastern Counties Company, of shareholders being served up dividends paid out of their own capital. Thirteen millions of capital (wrote the *Observer*) had been at the mercy of Mr. England to do with it as he chose, making and unmaking dividends, traffic, capital and revenue, just as he pleased, and disbursing sums of which he refused to render any account.

Worse still, so far as Henry was concerned, was the revelation that one of the committees had uncovered evidence of nine thousand pounds being spent on "Secret Service" under the heading of "Parliamentary Expenses," of which no details were given.

The money, Henry knew, must have been used to bribe Members of Parliament for their support in railway matters. The fact that he himself had had nothing to do with its dispensation in no way lessened the threat to his own reputation. Kirby was his brother-in-law and friend. But how could he continue to support him now? How could he publicly, as a Member of Parliament, condone dishonesty, bribery and corruption?

Aunt Kitty had been ill with pleurisy. The illness had kept her to her bed for several weeks and her recovery had been irritatingly slow. Added to her impatience at the boredom of being ill for so long was the frustration of being out of touch with things. She kept herself *au fait* with main events by reading the local newspapers from the first page to the last.

When she was well enough to come down to sit in the parlor she was very surprised, one morning, to receive a certain visitor—one of the last people she might now have expected to have time, or inclination, to spare for social calls.

He came striding into the room in his usual bold way, but Aunt Kitty was shocked to see how drawn and ill he looked. His face had become quite lined and his black hair had far more gray in it than she could remember when they last met. She invited him to sit down but he remained standing, hands clasped behind his back.

"I'll not stay long."

"I wish thou wouldst," she told him. "I am very glad of thy company."

Kirby England smiled at her. "Then you must be the only one in York to welcome it."

"Naturally I do. Thou art, and hast been, a good friend to us. I shall *always* welcome thee to my house. Sit down . . . please."

He did so reluctantly. She met his gaze.

"I am truly sorry for the misfortunes that have befallen thee. It gives me great pain to think of what thou must be suffering."

"Aye . . . well, thank you for those kind words. It seems the whole country is baying for my blood."

"I have been quite disgusted by what I have read in the newspapers."

"No doubt."

"Oh no—not by what has been said of thee," she went on quickly, "but by the unseemly haste with which thou hast been deserted by fellow directors and others who should surely have taken some share of responsibility. *They* owed thee loyalty and yet have been the very first to betray thee."

He shrugged. "I don't blame them for wanting to save their own skins. I daresay I'd do the same in their shoes."

"I don't think so."

"Someone has to be the scapegoat. The ramifications of railway finance run very deep and there are powerful interests, besides mine, at stake. Besides, I know too many secrets that could implicate too many respectable citizens. It's natural that they should do their best to finish me."

"I'm very sorry."

"Don't be. I neither need nor deserve your sympathy, and I didn't come to seek it, I assure you. I came about something else."

"Is it something I can do to help thee?"

"It is." He stood up and went a little away from her, pausing to choose his next words carefully. "It concerns Hester."

She waited.

"I have loved your niece for a long time now—ever since she was my ward," he said at last. "I asked her to marry me the day she came of age, but she refused me."

"I know. Hester told me. I thought at the time that it was a great pity she did not accept thee."

He gave a rueful smile. "At *that* time—yes, I thought so too myself. In fact, I was devastated by her refusal. I remember I was very angry. I had a high opinion of myself in those days . . . I don't think any woman had ever said no to me before . . . It never entered my head that she'd refuse me."

"And dost thou still love her?"

"More than ever," he said quietly. "But there can be no question of marrying her now. When William Gurney died I thought that at last it would be possible. If I'd asked her a while ago, before all this happened, she would have accepted."

"She loves thee?"

"Aye—she does."

"Oh dear . . . Oh dear."

"So you see," he continued grimly, "I need your help to convince her what folly it would be to have anything to do with me. I'd never ask her to share my life now. I've nothing but disgrace and ruin to offer her."

"Hester has a mind of her own. Knowing her as I do, I doubt very much if she would care. If she loves thee, then she would marry thee tomorrow—never mind the consequences."

"And knowing her as I do, I agree with you. But *you* could make her see sense—persuade her to forget me."

Aunt Kitty shook her head. "I couldn't convince her of the good sense of marrying thee before, so I'm sure I should not be able to convince her of the foolishness of doing so now. But I will try—if thou art sure that that is what thou really wants."

"Tell her that you have seen me and that I no longer love her. Say you have heard rumors about another woman."

"That will hurt her very much."

"Better that than a lifetime of pain and regret," he said harshly.

"I will try," she repeated.

He said good-bye and she laid her hand on his arm for a moment. "Thou art a good man, Kirby England. Whatever others say of thee, I want thee to know that I believe that to be so. And I think thou art right to give up Hester. I don't think thou couldst bring her happiness anymore."

He left her then, and she stood at the parlor window and watched sadly as he walked away down the street. A passerby, recognizing him, caught hold of his coat sleeve and began to shout abuse. Kirby England shook himself free and walked on out of sight.

Aunt Kitty let the lace curtain drop back into place. She lifted her handkerchief to dab at her cheek.

The young man was well born, handsome and rich. Without appearing to do so, Rosa had watched him throughout the evening, and so far she liked what she saw. She knew perfectly well that he had also been watching her and was therefore not a bit surprised when he followed her out onto the terrace, where she had wandered in search of fresh air after dinner. London could be stifling in summer. She turned from leaning on the stone balustrade to find him standing a little way away from her in the semidarkness. She liked the way he made no attempt to disguise his interest . . . the way he looked her over with open admiration. It reminded her of the time when she had met Kirby England years ago in that poky little dressing room at the Theatre Royal in York. She looked at the young man consideringly. Her husband had been dead for ten months, and Rosa was already tired of playing the bereaved widow. This man was a mere baronet, but a young and good-looking baronet as opposed to an old and doddering marquis. She liked his smile and the way his hair curled on the nape of his neck. And he was tall . . . She had always liked tall men. Rosa made up her mind and favored him with an encouraging smile.

They walked up and down the terrace together in the cool of the evening, the sounds of London faint in the distance beyond the garden. They talked idly of this and that—of horse racing, which Rosa had grown to love, of the theatre, which she had never ceased to love, and of society gossip and current scandals. Somehow Kirby England's name was brought up, and Rosa stiffened.

"I know him well. He is an old friend. I shouldn't advise you to speak ill of him in my hearing."

Her companion apologized at once. But being a young man of decided views, he risked continuing the subject after a while.

"I've heard it said that he's a broken man."

"Kirby—*broken!* Never!"

"The other day he was thrown out of Lord Stanley's house when he tried to attend some gathering there. It seems the whole of London society has turned against him."

Rosa looked distressed. "Poor Kirby—how dreadful!"

"Very humiliating it must have been," the baronet drawled. "It's remarkable how savagely the pack will turn against a stricken member. Not very edifying, I think. But what can one do? I'm told he's had to resign all his directorships and his London house is up for sale."

"I didn't know it was as bad as that."

"I'm afraid so. Strange, isn't it? The great Railway King whom everybody lionized such a short time ago toppled from his iron throne with a devastating finality. Nobody would invest so much as a five-pound note on his advice now, and yet once they hung on his every word . . ." The baronet sighed. "The human race can be sickening sometimes. In my opinion, the king and his subjects are much of a piece. The shareholders were ready enough to shut their eyes to everything but a fat dividend. So long as he gave them what they wanted, they would have forgiven him everything . . . everything but his failure to go on lining their greedy pockets. Then they turned on him with the rage of fellow gamblers when the game has been lost for them. There is a rumor that he's likely to be arrested any moment now and sent for trial."

"That can't be true! On what charge?"

"Fraud and embezzlement, I believe."

She turned away, shaken, and he followed and put a hand on her shoulder. He said quietly: "He may be an old friend, but there's nothing you can do to help him. And even if you could he wouldn't accept it—from what I hear of him."

"He helped me once. I wouldn't be here but for him."

"That's all in the past now, isn't it? It's your future you must think of."

It might have been Kirby himself speaking. She thought of how he had told her never to try and help him. *You and I are alike,* he'd once said. *We're both after the best we can get out of life and no one's going to stand in our way. . . . We both understand each other.*

The baronet said persuasively: "Come inside and sing to us. You promised you would and they're waiting for you."

He took her arm and she let him lead her indoors. She chose a song she had not sung for years—one that she had almost forgotten, but remembered now as though it were yesterday.

"*'Mid pleasures and palaces though one may roam,*
Be it ever so humble there's no place like home!
A charm from the skies seems to hallow us there,
Which seek through the world, is ne'er met with elsewhere.

Home Home, Sweet, Sweet Home!
There's no place like Home! There's no place like Home!"

Her voice was as clear and beautiful as when she had sung it on the delapidated stage of the Theatre Royal and Kirby England had first seen her.

The young baronet's gaze never left her. And he noticed, as no one else did, the unshed tears that were glistening in her eyes.

"I have been hearing such terrible tales about Kirby England," Aunt Kitty said in determined tones. Hester had come from Benbow unexpectedly to visit her and she had lost no time in trying to keep her promise.

She fretted nervously with her shawl, tugging it closer about her shoulders. "He is quite ruined, of course, and completely ostracized in York. No one of any consequence will speak to him. And not only that, Edith Frohawk told me the other day that he has been seen lately in company with yet *another* actress from the Theatre Royal—not so pretty as the one I can remember from years ago, but I suppose beggars can't be choosers. He must have lost nearly all his money. Dewsborough is up for sale, as well as his London house, and heaven knows what will happen to the one in Monkgate. . . . No *sensible* woman would look at him now."

"*Dewsborough*—up for sale? I can't believe it. How that must hurt him!"

"I told thee, my dear, he is disgraced and ruined."

"Don't keep saying that! I am ashamed to hear thee talk like this, Aunt Kitty! How couldst thou turn against him so easily? Thou art no better than Edith Frohawk!"

Aunt Kitty turned pink and squirmed a little in her chair. "My dear, I admit I used to think well of him. But I am grown older and wiser since then. I was a foolish old woman to trust him. We have been very fortunate that he has not cheated *us* out of our money and that thy fortune is still intact."

"My fortune is twice what it was—thanks to him—as thou knows. Aunt Kitty, I won't listen anymore to thee speaking like this of him."

"Why, my love, whatever is the matter? Thou hast always disliked him so and said that he was a rogue. Now thou hast been proved right. What is it to thee how I speak of him?"

"I love him, Aunt Kitty—*that* is what it is to me."

"But not so long ago thou hated him!"

"I thought I did. I was wrong."

There was silence in the parlor while Aunt Kitty clasped and unclasped her mittened hands in agitation and tried to think what to say next. "I am distressed to hear thee say so, child, for it can bring thee nothing but unhappiness. He will very likely go to prison and can never marry thee. I know he proposed to thee once, long ago, but he has certainly changed his mind since. He has never been noted for constancy, has he?"

"I know he loves me still."

"That is not what he told me a few days ago."

"He came to see thee?" Hester had gone very white.

"Indeed he did. And I remember our conversation very well. He stood exactly where thou art standing now and told me he hoped he had not caused thee any hurt. He had thought he loved thee but had lately lost his heart to another woman. This actress—"

"I am to have his child."

Aunt Kitty gaped at Hester in dismay. Her niece had spoken too clearly for her to be in any doubt of her words. "*His child! Kirby England's* child! Art thou sure? It can't be so! Hester, my love, tell me this isn't true. It is the most dreadful shock for me!"

Poor Aunt Kitty, seeing by Hester's face that it was true, sunk back in her chair and fanned herself weakly with her hand. It was several minutes before she could speak again, and Hester, contrite at having so upset her, had fetched her smelling salts and knelt beside the chair, holding them under Aunt Kitty's nose.

"Don't worry, Aunt. There will be no scandal, I promise. The child can be born as William's and no one need ever know. It could have been his, and I am the only person in the world, except thee, who *knows* that it is not. If Kirby England does not love me any longer, as thou says, then he shall never know it either. I should have more pride than that. But I am going to see him to find out for myself. I shall only believe it when I hear him tell me himself."

Aunt Kitty, eyes tight shut, gave a faint moan. She sniffed hard at the smelling bottle and decided that they might as well pack up and leave York now forever. Edith Frohawk would scent out the truth in a moment. Where scandalmongering was concerned, she was like a bloodhound. And how could any child of Kirby England's look anything like William's? The only hope was that it would take after Hester. . . .

"Hester, my love?"

There was no answer, and Aunt Kitty's eyes flew open. The parlor was empty, and just then she heard the front door shut. She hurried to the window and, lifting the corner of the lace curtain, was in time to see her niece, in bonnet and shawl, disappearing down the street.

The front door of 44 Monkgate stood slightly ajar. Hester, receiving no answer to her knock, pushed it further open and went inside. The hall was deserted: there were no servants to be seen and no sound of life to be heard. She stood and looked about her. The huge pink glass gasolier had gone; so had the magnificent turkish carpet that had covered the floor. The hallway was cold and bare.

She made her way slowly up the wide staircase onto the first landing. The drawing room door was shut, and after a moment's hesitation she turned the handle and looked into the room.

At first she thought it was deserted too. The curtains had been drawn and the room was in darkness. She was about to close the door again when a voice spoke.

"Who's there? Who's that creeping about? Don't think you can steal anything. I'll set the police on you!"

"It's Hester Gurney. And I haven't come to steal anything."

Silence. The voice spoke again, just as sharply.

"You may as well come in, now you're here. Though I don't welcome you. Draw back the curtains so I can see you."

Hester felt her way across the room towards the windows. She dragged back one of the heavy curtains and stared, shocked, at what daylight had revealed.

"*That's* how we've been treated by this city—after all my son has done for it!"

Every window had been broken—not one pane was left whole. Splinters of glass covered the carpet beneath, and bricks and stones lay about the room.

"And that's not all the damage that's been done."

Hester turned to where Mrs. England was sitting bolt-upright in a chair beside the empty fireplace. Her face looked gray and was as drained of expression as a waxwork. Her only movement was to pluck ceaselessly with her fingers at the jet beads around her neck.

"You're too late." There was a flat triumph in her voice. "They've been and taken him away."

Hester came towards her; the old woman's eyes shone with spite.

"I always knew you wanted him. But you'll never have him now."

"Didst thou say . . . that they had taken him away?"

"*Didst thou say!*" Mrs. England mocked her savagely. "Why don't you talk like everybody else? All that thee-ing and thou-ing! Just to be different, I suppose—to set yourself apart and make out that you're something special."

"Who came and where have they taken him?"

"The police, of course. They arrested him and took him away . . . took Kirby away to prison."

Her voice cracked and her hands twisted and turned the jet beads. Hester put out a hand but Mrs. England thrust it away.

"Don't touch me! Leave me alone! I want to be left alone!"

"But thou shouldst not stay here. Let me arrange for Adelaide to come and take thee to Murton Hall—"

"I told you—I shall stay here." Mrs. England nodded towards the windows. "*They* will never drive me away. This is my home."

Hester understood; she would have felt the same herself about Benbow.

"Is there anything I can do for thee? Let me help thee—"

"*You*—help me!" The words were spat out. "I'd sooner die. You turned my son down once, didn't you? Turned *Kirby* down!

285

He loved you then, and you thought you were too good for him. It's the only time I've known him to be a fool. Now you've changed your mind. I can see that by your face. But you'll never have another chance!"

The necklace broke beneath her fingers and the black beads bounced and rolled across the floor. Hester bent down.

"Leave them! Leave *me!* Don't ever come here again!"

Without another word Hester went to the door. She had half opened it when Mrs. England spoke suddenly again.

"Draw the curtains before you go."

She did as Kirby's mother asked, pulling the heavy velvet across the windows to shut out the daylight. The room sunk back into darkness and the old woman faded to a shadowy, still figure sitting beside the empty grate. Hester went out and shut the door quietly behind her.

The trial of Kirby England at York created a sensation. It lasted for several days, during which time the mountain of evidence that had been accumulated by the prosecution was examined. An unending stream of witnesses passed through the witness box and realms of facts and figures, too complex for the restless crowd in the public gallery to understand, were investigated. However, the general gist of it all was plain enough to the avid spectators who reveled in the Railway King's disgrace and downfall with all the satisfaction that another's misfortune can bring to the meanhearted. And the newspapers were merciless in their condemnation of the city's former hero. Even the *Yorkshire Gazette* had not a good word to say of its former proprietor.

Hester's child had been born the month before at the little house in Precentor's Court, and to Aunt Kitty's dismay and Hester's delight, the boy was the image of his father—black-haired and dark-browed. Kirby, as he stood in the dock, was in ignorance of his son's existence. He had refused to see Hester whilst awaiting trial and she, as the weeks had passed with no word from him, had come at last to believe Aunt Kitty. During the dark days of the trial she sat in silence in the parlor and suffered the torment of knowing *his* suffering. On the final day she could bear it no longer. The need to see him was too great, even if she could not speak with him. There was no room in the packed gallery, and so she found herself in a bleak corridor outside the courtroom. The jury had retired to consider their verdict and she waited, standing there alone in her gray mantle and bonnet, the object of many curious glances from passersby.

An hour or more passed before she was suddenly aware of the sound of doors opening, of the buzz and chatter from the courtroom. People were coming out, and she tried to hear what they were saying as they went past her. A dark-complexioned man, wearing a lawyer's wig and gown, stopped and bowed. She recognized him as one of William's acquaintances.

"My dear Mrs. Gurney, what a pleasure—and surprise—to see you here," Elias Snell said. "Can I be of some assistance to you?"

She had never liked him and she did not like him any better now. His eyes looked cold, and behind their false solicitude she saw the glint of some secret triumph.

"Canst thou tell me the verdict?"

His thick black brows rose almost to his wig. "I am astonished that you should find it of any interest, my dear lady. It has been the most sordid affair and one that I am sure you would not really wish to know about. I myself have found it very unpleasant to be involved in such a case. I wish I could wash my hands of all dealings with such infamy here and now, but unfortunately, I have still the matter of Dewsborough to attend to."

"Dewsborough?" she said indignantly. "What has that to do with thee?"

He frowned. "I have undertaken the purchase of the estate on behalf of some clients, a Scottish peer who wishes to acquire the land for the shooting. I believe he plans to demolish the castle itself. A fitting end, I should say, considering its previous owner."

Poor Dewsborough, with its golden walls and shining battlements, thought Hester sadly. The king had fallen, and now his castle was to fall too.

Elias Snell had bowed again and begun to move away. She called after him:

"The verdict—thou didst not tell me . . ."

"*Guilty*, my dear Mrs. Gurney. Surely there was no need for me to say. What other one could there possibly have been?"

He walked away with exultation in his step.

The corridor was now crowded with people. They streamed past, bumping and buffeting Hester heedlessly as she stood by the bench. She overheard their remarks. *"Good riddance to him, I say. Pity they're not going to hang him. That'd be too good for him! Swindler! Blackguard! Cheat!"*

A hand took her arm. "Hester! What are you doing here?"

Henry Latham's kind face looked into hers. He led her away to a quiet space beyond the corridor and made her sit down on a bench there.

"You don't look at all well. Surely you should not be out yet. Let me take you home."

"Is Kirby England there? I wanted to see him."

He stared at her. "He's not in court now. They've taken him away already. Did you hear the verdict?"

"Elias Snell told me."

Henry grimaced. "And took great pleasure in it, I've no doubt. He was the prosecution and an archenemy of Kirby's. He was responsible for starting the whole investigation. I don't think he ever forgave Kirby for taking his seat on the Council from him when he was just an upstart draper."

"A man like that would have a long memory."

"Well, he's certainly got his revenge now. Kirby is going to prison in disgrace while Elias Snell is now rumored to be the next Lord Mayor of York."

Henry was looking very distressed. He went on, half to himself: "I wish I could have done something to help him. The evidence I gave did more damage than good . . . I wish I could have helped."

Hester said: "It must have been hard for thee. Thou hast thine own career to consider. I can understand."

Henry sighed. "Adelaide has taken it well. Friends have been very thoughtless and unkind. Some of them have seemed to delight in the whole affair."

"Then they are not friends."

"Her mother is brokenhearted. She has become quite deranged, you know. She refused to leave Monkgate until yesterday, and had been living there alone with one old servant. Adelaide at last managed to persuade her to come to Murton Hall. She will live with us there now."

"At least she will not know poverty ever again."

"Nor happiness either, I think."

He took Hester's arm again. "Come, there's nothing more to be done here today. My carriage is outside. I'll take you home."

CHAPTER XIV

Rotten now is his credit, as the fabric that fed it;
Out at elbows in character, credit and cash,
Like a GUY he is fleered at, and scouted and jeered at,
And all that he's good for's squib-firing and smash.

Punch—The Great Railway Guy

The prison lay behind the old curtain wall of York Castle. It was dark, damp and unsanitary, and law-abiding citizens hurried past it—much as Londoners scuttled past Newgate.

The turnkey was drunk, but not so far gone that he had lost his natural inquisitiveness and sharp instinct for a likely penny. He jingled the keys and leered at Hester.

"'Tain't no use your coming here, missus. He won't see nobody—nobody at all. You might jest as well turn right round and take yourself home again!" He shuffled a little closer and Hester recoiled from the stench of cheap gin. "This ain't no place for a lady like yourself." He grinned stupidly at her, showing toothless gums, save for three black stumps. "And now that he's ill there's no sense in going near him. You don't want to catch the fever, do you?"

"He has a fever? Is he very ill?"

The turnkey shrugged his shoulders. "Couldn't say, could I? Sometimes they get better . . . sometimes they don't. I've seen it all the time in this prison. They die like flies."

Hester fumbled quickly in her reticule. She held out a large number of coins, so that the man could see them clearly.

"If he is ill he will be too weak to refuse to see me. Wilt thou take me to him at once, please."

The turnkey squinted down at the contents of her palm with rheumy eyes. He licked his lips and rubbed them doubtfully with the back of his palm. Hester added several more coins and the man, stirring them round with a dirty finger, counted them. He pocketed the money with the lightning skill of a magician and beckoned to her.

"Come with me then, lady. But mind the way."

He unlocked the massive oak door fitted with huge iron bolts and padlocks, and strengthened still further with iron bars. A regiment of soldiers would have had difficulty in breaking it down. Hester stepped inside after the turnkey and the foul and putrid smell of the prison half choked her. Despite the warm day outside, it was cold—so cold that she began to shiver. Around her the dark stone walls ran with moisture and the flags beneath her feet were slimy with dirt.

She followed the man's stumbling, weaving progress down a long and dismal passageway. They passed a number of doors, all banded with iron and with small barred peepholes at eye height.

The turnkey stopped at last at a door at the far end and applied one eye to the grille, shutting the other so that his face distorted in a grotesque wink. Then selecting a key from among the rest, he fitted it into the lock and turned it with both hands. He beckoned to Hester again.

"Him's asleep, by the looks of him. In you go, missus. I'll wait here. When you're ready to leave, knock on the door and I'll let you out."

He pushed it open and she edged past him into the cell. The key turned in the lock behind her and the turnkey's eye watched through the peephole.

It was a stone dungeon, no more than eight feet in length, with bare walls and a bare flagged floor. There was one small window, placed high up and out of reach and fortified by a double row of heavy crossed bars. The thickness of the prison wall beyond was such that no glimpse of the outside world could be seen beyond the faint glimmer of daylight that struggled through the bars. An iron candlestick was fixed to the wall on one side. There was no other item of furniture—no table, no chair and no bed. The air was stale and bad.

Kirby England lay on a thin mat in the far corner of the room. There was no pillow for his head and only one ragged blanket covered him. This was drawn up close about his neck, and as Hester moved nearer she saw that he was shivering violently. His eyes were shut, his face emaciated, unshaven and pale as death. She knelt down on the cold floor beside him, and he turned his head and opened his eyes. She took his hand in hers without speaking. His skin was dry and hot, and there were small purple spots on his arm. He moved his lips slowly, and she bent her head to hear the words.

"I didn't want you to come, lass. You shouldn't have come."

"Why not, when I love thee?"

He touched her cheek. "Nay, lass. That's impossible."

"How so? Thou art still the same man that I loved before. Dost thou not love me then?"

"Too much to hold onto you."

"Why wouldst thou not see me? I tried to visit thee so many times."

"Talk sense, love. I've told you why. What've I got to offer you now?"

"Thou knowest very well that I would never desert thee. I don't care what thou hast done. I believe thou art a great man who has done much good for his country. Even if I did not love thee so much I would still think that."

He began to shiver again and dragged the filthy blanket higher under his chin. She felt his forehead and it was burning-hot.

"This rathole's full of sickness," he said through chattering teeth. "A dog wouldn't survive in it. You should never have come here. Go quickly now before you catch this fever of mine."

"Not yet. Let me stay a little longer. There's something I must tell thee."

The turnkey's eye glinted at the peephole; she knew he was listening to every word and bent lower to whisper in Kirby's ear. He smiled at what he heard, but his cracked lips made it more like a grimace.

293

"I can't believe it. It's something I've always dreamed of."

"It's true. And he looks just like thee."

"Poor little beggar! I'm sorry for him in that case! He'd've done better to look like his mother." He gripped her arm. "Promise me one thing, lass. Don't ever tell him the truth. Let him be known as William's son. It'll do him no good to have it known who his real father was."

"I could never promise thee that. But I do promise that he shall never be hurt by it."

He seemed satisfied by this and drifted away into semiconsciousness. Some time passed before he reopened his eyes and said suddenly:

"What about the colliery?"

"I closed it down—after the disaster."

"Closed it down! What for? What's the matter with you, lass? There's work there for starving men and you know it. You must open it up again at once! Sink another shaft! Sink *two* new shafts, if necessary, but get the miners back to work! And that school . . . You can start that up again. Make the boy go every day and learn his letters properly. I don't want him to be half educated like his father . . ."

He muttered on feverishly and then asked for some water. She found a tin mug and pitcher in the corner. The water was scummy with dust, and as she poured it out a scuffling in the shadows caught her eye; the fleshy pink tail of a fat rat vanished down a crack between floor and wall.

She knelt down beside Kirby and held the cup to his mouth. When he had finished drinking and lain back again she took a newspaper cutting from her reticule.

"I've brought thee something from Aunt Kitty. She read it yesterday in *The Times* and wanted thee to hear it. Listen. *Mr. England was no mere speculator but a projector of great discernment, courage and rich enterprise.* Dost thou know who said that of thee?"

"Nay—I can't imagine. But they must be the only kind words spoken of late."

"Mr. Gladstone himself said that."

She put the piece of newspaper into his hand and folded his fingers over it. "Didst thou hear?"

He smiled at her, and for a moment she saw the faint shadow of his former self behind the fever-racked man.

"Aye . . . I heard all right. And it's bloody rubbish! But thank Aunt Kitty for me, all the same."

His voice had grown weaker. "Tell me, my love, what will you remember when you think of me?"

"I shall remember many things," she told him clearly. "The first time we met at the Assembly Rooms when I trod on thy foot; the time when thou taught me to waltz; the day we spent at Dewsborough . . . I shall remember when thou fought the navvies for me, when thou rescued those men from the mine, and most of all the time we were together at Benbow . . . And whenever I see a railway or a steam engine I shall think of thee because thou art, and always will be, the Railway King."

He had slid away from her in his sickness. She spoke his name several times, but there was no response. She waited a long while, listening sadly to the harsh and rapid breathing. Then she drew the ragged blanket more closely about him and kissed him gently.

The turnkey answered her knock. He unlocked the door and swung it open, nodding and beckoning. She looked back over her shoulder. Kirby had not opened his eyes, and the scrap of newspaper had fluttered to the floor.

The turnkey watched her face as he slammed the door shut and relocked it. "Should never've come, missus. I told you so. 'Tain't good for ladies. 'Tain't good for anyone. And ladies—they always cry."

"I want thee to see that a nurse attends him," Hester said. "And that he has a proper bed with clean sheets and more blankets."

"A nurse costs threepence a week," was the reply. "And a bed would be two shillings and sixpence, with an extra sixpence for the clean sheets." The man jerked his verminous head in the direction of the cell. "He's no money."

Hester thrust more coins into his hand. "This will easily pay for it. See that it's done at once." She added yet more silver. "And fetch him clean water. The water in there is filthy." With an effort she forced herself to smile at the ugly little man. "If thou takest good care of him I shall see that thou art well rewarded."

She followed him up the long, cold passage back to the entrance. He pulled back the heavy bars of the prison door and watched her go, jingling all the coins in his pocket and shaking his head.

Hester walked out into the light of day. She stood for a moment beyond the prison gate and the tears ran down her face. The sights and sounds of the city were all about her but she neither heard nor saw them. Carriages rattled past, children shouted and laughed below the castle walls and a boat hooted on the river. The clock of the great Minster struck the hour and, away in the distance, a railway engine whistled shrilly as it steamed out of York station on its way south to London.

CHAPTER XV

Toll for a knave
A knave whose day is o'er!
All sunk—with those who gave
Their cash, till they'd no more.

Punch—adaptation of a poem by William Cowper

The procession was a simple one. It wound slowly through the streets of York, and there were no flags flying, no guns saluting, no crowds cheering. But as it passed over Lendal Bridge to cross the river, the bells of the great Minster, and of other churches in the city, could be heard tolling. Tradesmen along the route had closed their shutters and pulled down their blinds, and small groups of silent citizens had assembled to watch the black hearse go by and to doff their hats.

The procession went through Micklegate and out into the country beyond the city walls. When York was far behind, the carriages left the high road, entered the valley of the Derwent and climbed up into the Wolds.

In the churchyard today tangled grass half hides the grave, and wind and rain have eaten away the name carved in the headstone. There is nothing left to tell the passerby that here lies the Railway King—the great speculator and builder of railways—returned to the countryside from which he came.